D0837599

TOUCH THE FACE
OF GOD

TOUCH THE FACE OF GOD

A WWII NOVEL

Robert Vaughan

THOMAS NELSON PUBLISHERS®
Nashville

A Division of Thomas Nelson, Inc.
www.ThomasNelson.com

Copyright © 2002 by Robert Vaughan

All rights reserved. No portion of this book may be reproduced, stored in a retrieval system, or transmitted in any form or by any means—electronic, mechanical, photocopy, recording, or any other—except for brief quotations in printed reviews, without the prior permission of the publisher.

Published in Nashville, Tennessee, by Thomas Nelson, Inc.

Library of Congress Cataloging-in-Publication Data

Vaughan, Robert.
    Touch the face of God : a World War II novel / Robert Vaughan.
      p. cm.
    ISBN 0-7852-6627-5 (pbk.)
    1. World War, 1939–1945—Fiction. 2. Bomber pilots—Fiction. I. Title.
PS3622.A94 T68 2002
813'.6—dc21
                                                      2001054373

Printed in the United States of America

02 03 04 05 06 PHX 5 4 3 2 1

F
VAU
03·21·62 lug 14.99 C.1

This book is dedicated to the memory of
Robert Richard Vaughan,
Faye Helgen Barr,
and all the other men and women
on both the home front and war front.

Prologue

London, England
Today

T he reception was held in the parish hall of St. James of Clerkenwell. The brochure proclaimed proudly that worship had been conducted in this same church for more than nine hundred years. Of course, nine hundred years predated its Anglican affiliation, but the retired Episcopal bishop from the Dioceses of Missouri wasn't a nitpicker. If people had been worshiping in this same location for nine hundred years, then their denomination was considerably less important than their purpose.

The bishop and his wife, their trip a Christmas present from their grandchildren, were part of an English Heritage tour package. It had been a particularly enjoyable week, and this, a reception being held at the historical St. James of Clerkenwell Church, was the last official event. After this reception the twenty-four members of the tour group would be on their own until they gathered for dinner at the Fox and Hound Restaurant the next night. From there, a bus would take them directly to Heathrow Airport for their flight back to the States.

The reception was a gala event, crowded with little knots of people who congregated around the hors d'oeuvres table, at the coffee and tea service area, or over by the windows. Each of these assemblies was possessed of a constantly changing dynamic, altering in scope and substance as men and women joined in or withdrew from the gathering. The bishop stood alone near the back wall, watching the proceedings over the rim of a cup of coffee.

"Your Worship, you don't need to be standing. Won't you let me get a chair for you?" one of the English guides asked.

The bishop chuckled. "Richard, I don't know whether I should be flattered by the title or insulted by the insinuation that I'm so old and decrepit that I'm incapable of standing for any length of time."

"I assure you, sir, I meant no disrespect," the young man sputtered, embarrassed by the thought that he may have committed some sort of faux pas.

"I'm just teasing," the bishop said easily. "I'm fine standing."

"Of course you are, a fine, strong man like you," Richard said.

"Now, who is teasing whom?" Both men chuckled. "About tomorrow," the bishop continued. "Were you able to make arrangements?"

"Indeed I was, sir. The car will collect you at the hotel at six and drive you out to Davencourt."

"Thank you."

"You do realize, don't you, that the chapel you want to visit at Davencourt is no longer in use?"

"Yes."

"The building is still there, right where it has been for nearly three hundred years, watched over by a sexton, I understand, but there are no services. I'm sure, however, that if you would like to conduct a service, the diocesan bishop would have no objection. Indeed, he might even be able to gather a congregation for you. There are those in the area who remember the chapel with fondness."

"Thank you, Richard, but that won't be necessary. I just want to visit."

"I hope you won't be disappointed. There really isn't much to see."

"I'm sure I won't be disappointed."

At 5:45 the next morning, the bishop stepped out of the hotel bathroom, showered, shaved, and fully dressed. He was wearing his clerics, a purple shirt front, complete with collar, and the gold cross given to him by the diocese upon his retirement. Walking across the room, he sat on the edge of the bed and looked down at his wife. When he did so, she opened her eyes.

"Good morning, sleepyhead," he said.

"Umm. What is that aftershave you're wearing? It smells good."

"I don't know what it is. I bought it in a little shop a few days ago. This is the first time I've used it."

"It's nice. I'll see what it is and get another bottle for you before we go home. So, you are about to leave?"

"Yes. You're sure you'll be all right without me today?"

"Of course I'm sure. I've already arranged to have lunch with some of the others, and I'll meet you at the Fox and Hound for dinner."

"I feel bad about leaving you."

She reached up to put her hand on his. "You go," she said. "This is something you have to do. I understand that."

"Love?"

"Yes, Dear?" She changed positions in the bed, pushing her head more comfortably into the pillow.

"Have I ever thanked you for sharing your life with me?" He leaned down to kiss her, and she smiled.

"Umm, that's sweet. Do have a nice day, Darling," she said in a voice that indicated she would soon be asleep again.

"Wait," the bishop told the driver. "Stop here."

When the driver stopped, the bishop got out of the car and looked out across the fence toward the field. From the road he could see nothing but high grass and the tops of wildflowers, waving rhythmically in the gentle breeze. For a moment, he wondered whether he was in the right spot. He walked out to the fence, then started to climb over it.

"'Ere, guv'nor," the driver called out in alarm. "You shouldn't be doing that. There's no telling what you might run into. If there's something you want, I'll be glad to get it for you."

"No, thank you," the bishop said, holding up his finger. "This will only take a minute." He walked about a hundred yards out into the field, then felt something hard under his feet. Looking down, he saw grease and oil smudges, and a huge grin spread across his face.

There wasn't much to it. All it was, was an irregularly shaped piece of concrete with not more than ten feet by ten feet of the original pad remaining. But in his mind's eye this broken piece of concrete was once more a great hardstand, one of the many that stood evenly spaced around the entire circumference of the U.S. Army Air Force Base at Davencourt. It took very little imagination for him to see, squatting on the hardstand, the battle-weary B-17 bombers of the 605th Heavy Bombardment Group.

He walked a few more yards, hoping to find a ribbon of concrete, two miles long and 150 feet wide. He remembered the runway, gently undulating as it stretched out into the distance, scarred by long, black marks made by the chirping tires of the heavy bombers as they touched down. He strained to hear the roar of engines and overrevved propellers, the tolling of the ground crews as they counted the returning bombers, the wail of sirens as ambulances and fire trucks and crash crews rushed to the aid of broken bodies and damaged airplanes.

But neither the runway nor the sounds were there. Now, sixty years after the fact, what had been an airfield was quiet pastureland, occupied not by the buildings, planes, officers, and men of the 605th, but by several dozen Hereford cows.

He stood there for a long moment cloaked in silence. Then, swallowing the lump in his throat, he turned and walked back to the car.

The driver didn't ask what he had been doing in the field, and the bishop didn't volunteer. Instead, he stared out the window at countryside that was once his entire life, but now wasn't even remotely familiar to him.

When the car stopped in front of a small brick chapel, a tall, thin man with sparse ash-blond hair was standing in front, waiting to greet them. He stepped forward to open the car door for the bishop, then made a slight bow with his head.

"Good morning, Your Worship."

"Good morning," the bishop answered, climbing out of the car.

"I'm Edgar Whitecorn, sexton of Davencourt Chapel," the man said. "I was told an American bishop would be paying a visit."

"I hope I'm not intruding."

"No, sir, on the contrary, I'm honored by your visit. We don't get many people around these days. And it's a shame to let a wonderful old church like this go unappreciated. It was designed by Christopher Wren himself, it was."

"Yes, I know. How long since it was last used?"

"It's been more than forty years since we had a vicar, and at least fifteen since our last service."

"May I go in?"

"Yes, sir, I'll unlock the door for you."

Hurrying ahead, the sexton unlocked the red-painted, iron-banded double doors, then pulled one of them open. The bishop was greeted with a distinctive but not unpleasant smell, the timeless aroma of leather-bound books, wood polish, and candles no longer used.

"It looks very nice, Mr. Whitecorn," the bishop said, a little surprised by the fact. He had expected to see the dust, mold, and mildew of a building standing fifteen years empty.

"Yes, sir," Whitecorn replied proudly. "I keep it as if we would be celebrating the Holy Eucharist next Sunday."

"And well you could hold a service here," the bishop replied. Looking toward the altar, he saw that the triptych was still there.

"You're looking at the triptych. Over two hundred years old, it is," Whitecorn said.

"It's as beautiful as it ever was," the bishop said.

"You've seen it before, then, sir?"

"Yes, during the war."

"Yes, it was here during the war. The Yanks had an airfield here then if memory is correct."

"Your memory is correct," the bishop said. For a moment he admired the three-panel piece of artwork that depicted the Transfiguration, then he walked forward, pausing to genuflect before going up to the triptych itself. Reaching into his pocket, he pulled out a knife, then opened it.

"'Ere, sir, what are you doing?" the sexton asked in alarm.

"Don't worry," the bishop replied. "I promise you, I'll do no harm."

The sexton watched anxiously as the bishop stuck the blade of the knife into a quarter-inch opening between the bottom of the triptych and the old base on which it sat. At first he was disappointed because the blade, going easily into the opening, made no contact. Then he felt it, and his pulse surged. He began working the blade around, trying to get purchase on the object. Finally he smiled when he realized it was beginning to move.

He worked the object all the way up to the edge of the opening, pulled it out just a little farther, and was rewarded by seeing enough of it protruding from the hole to allow him to grab it with his fingers. He pulled it all the way out, then opened his hand and looked down at it.

The object was badly tarnished, but there was no mistaking what it was. With a little polish it would be as bright and shiny as it had been the day it was put there, fifty-nine years ago.

"Blimey now, what is that?" the sexton asked in surprise.

"This is a set of U.S. Army Air Force wings," the bishop replied without further explanation.

St. Louis, Missouri
October 10, 1942

L ieutenant Mark W. White, U.S. Army Air Force, readjusted the
wings over the left breast pocket of his tunic. The action was necessary because one of the retaining clips had fallen off, and the wings,
only recently won, were hanging loose.

He was standing in the Grand Hall of St. Louis's Union Station. The
depot was teeming with humanity as men in uniform, most of them carrying duffel bags, hurried to or from trains, while harried women looked
after children, and redcaps scurried about weighed down with passengers' luggage. The vaulted ceiling, which towered sixty-five feet above
the marble floor, was an echo chamber for voices, the rumble of arriving and departing trains, and loudspeaker announcements.

"Your attention, please. Because of wartime travel conditions, priority must be given to our men in uniform. We ask that all other passengers have patience."

"But, please, I must have a ticket. I've been waiting for hours," he
overheard a woman's voice saying.

Glancing toward the ticket counter, Mark saw a very attractive young woman pleading her case to an unreceptive ticket agent.

"I'm sorry, miss. Military men and their families have priority over all tickets. Maybe the next train."

"But that's what I have been told for three trains now. My mother is ill. I must get to Newport News."

"Your attention, please. Because of wartime travel conditions, priority must be given to our men in uniform. We ask that all other passengers have patience."

The ticket agent pointed up. "Did you hear that announcement? I told you, there's nothing I can do. Now, please, step aside."

Almost without thinking, Mark started toward the ticket counter. "Lucy, darling, I was afraid I had missed you," he said. He took the startled young woman in his arms and embraced her. "Have you bought our tickets to Newport News yet?"

"What? I don't know . . . ," she started to say, but Mark interrupted her in midsentence.

"I don't know how we missed connections either. Everything is sort of crazy right now." Mark looked at the ticket agent. "I'm Lieutenant White. This is my wife, Lucy. We'd like two tickets to Newport News, Virginia, please."

"Yes, Lieutenant, of course," the ticket agent replied. "If the young lady had told me she was traveling with a member of the military, I would have given her a ticket right away."

As if too startled to speak, the woman stood by silently as Mark paid for the two tickets. Then, tickets in hand, he put his hand on her elbow and guided her away from the counter toward the middle of the marble floor.

"Come, Dear, tickets are so hard to get, we certainly don't want to be late, do we?"

She finally found her voice. "I don't know who you are or what you are trying to do, but . . ."

"I'm trying to get you to Newport News," Mark said quietly. "That is where you wanted to go, isn't it?"

"Yes, but not as your wife."

"Your attention, please. Because of wartime travel conditions, priority must be given to our men in uniform. We ask that all other passengers have patience."

"From the looks of things, being my wife, at least temporarily, is the only way you are going to get a ticket." Mark flashed a broad smile and extended his hand. "My name is Mark White."

"Well, you can just take that ticket back, Mr. Mark White, because I'm not going to play your game, whatever it is."

"I assure you, Lucy, it's not what you are thinking."

"How do you know what I'm thinking? And my name isn't Lucy," she said in exasperation.

"I'm sorry. Lucy is the best I could come up with on short notice. And so far you haven't told me your real name."

They were approaching a gate marked To Trains. There, a uniformed agent was checking everyone's ticket. Mark stopped.

"Look, miss," he said gently. "I'm just trying to be helpful. You looked tired and rather frantic back there, so I thought making you my wife would at least get you a ticket. Once we are on board, you can go your way and I'll go mine. If you wish, I'll spend the entire trip in the club car."

Slowly the anger passed from the young woman's face, and she actually found herself smiling. "Emily," she said.

"I beg your pardon?"

"My name is Emily Hagan." She stuck out her hand. "I'm sorry for the way I was acting. It's just that . . ."

"No need to apologize," Mark said. "You were right to be suspicious. I certainly wouldn't want my sister to be caught up by some smooth-talking guy in pinks and greens."

"Pinks and greens?"

Mark smiled. "The officer's uniform. The jacket is sort of green, and the trousers have a pinkish tinge to them."

"Your attention, please. Train for Nashville, Knoxville, Richmond, and Newport News is now boarding on track number seven."

"What do you say?" Mark asked. "Are we going to Newport News?"

"Is that where you were heading?"

"Sort of. I'm going to Langley Field in Hampton. I hear that's very near Newport News."

"Yes, it's quite close."

"Last call for all passengers for Nashville, Knoxville, Richmond, and Newport News. All aboard, please."

Mark started toward the gate. "Look, I can't afford to miss this train," he said. "Are you coming?"

Emily hesitated a second longer, then sighing, hurried after him. "This is positively the most outlandish thing I have ever done."

They drew the fourth seating in the dining car, so it was nine o'clock before they were served. After dinner they lingered at the table, engrossed in conversation. The window beside them, backed by the blackness of night, glistened with the reflected images of a handsome young officer and a very pretty young woman.

The only other people still in the dining car were a mother, her two small children, and a couple of white-jacketed porters who were busy busing the empty tables and cleaning the floor.

"Folks, we'll be closin' the diner in about fifteen more minutes," one of the porters said. "If you want another cup of coffee, this'll be the last call."

"Thanks, I'm good," Mark said, putting his hand over his cup.

"Miss?"

"I'm fine, thank you."

All during dinner Mark had regaled Emily with humorous anecdotes about incidents that had occurred during flight training. Emily listened attentively. Mark was sure that Emily was one of the prettiest women he had ever seen. She had eyes that were more amber than brown, high cheekbones, a narrow nose, full lips, and smooth, almost olive-complexioned skin.

"Is your mother really ill?"

The question seemed to come from nowhere.

"What?"

"Back in St. Louis, you told the ticket agent that your mother was ill."

Laughing self-consciously, Emily brushed a fall of dark brown hair from her forehead. "No, she isn't. But I had been in that depot for so long, and I was so tired, I was beginning to get a little desperate."

"Do you live in Newport News?"

"Yes. My father is one of the managers of the shipyard. In fact, I work there as well, in accounting."

"The shipyard? There's a shipyard in Newport News?"

"The shipyard is just about the only thing in Newport News. You don't know the town very well, do you?"

"No, this will be my first time there. If I get some time off, maybe you'll show me around sometime? Uh, I mean if you aren't married or anything."

"I'm not married or anything."

"Then it's a date?"

"Oh, I didn't say that."

"I'm rushing things, huh? Well, I suppose I could play on your sympathy, tell you that I may be going overseas at any moment, and suggest that a date with you would build a memory I could keep with me."

"I assure you, Lieutenant, I would let nothing happen on a date that would allow you to build memories."

"Oh, but you underestimate the effect a beautiful woman can have in even the most casual relationship."

Emily fished a pencil and piece of paper from her purse. "You are a smooth-talking so-and-so, I'll give you that." She wrote a number on the paper, then handed it to him. "Give me a call sometime, and we'll talk about it."

"Thanks!" Mark said, smiling appreciatively as he folded the little piece of paper and put it in his wallet.

The train passed over a crossing, and the warning bells sounded in the distance, built quickly to a crescendo, then faded off into the distance again.

"Folks, we're closing now," the porter said. "You'll have to return to your car."

"Very well, Mr. Porter," Mark said easily, handing him a dollar bill. "We thank you for your patience and hospitality."

"Glad to be of service to you and your lady, sir."

Mark stood, then pulled the chair back for Emily. "See, even the porter thinks you should be my lady," he whispered.

"Of course he does. You tipped him," Emily replied.

When they stepped through the door, they were greeted by a wall of noise: the roar of wind, steel wheels rolling on steel track, and the rattle and squeak of twisting vestibule plates. The noise quieted when they stepped into the next car, a Pullman. The porter was already making the beds.

"I'll turn down your berths next if you're ready," the porter called to them.

"Thank you," Emily replied.

"Well, I guess this is where I leave you," Mark said. "I'll, uh, be back in the club car if you need me."

Emily laughed. "Oh, don't be silly," she said. "If it wasn't you, it would be some other stranger in the other berth."

"You're sure you don't mind?"

"Well, I can't very well have you spend the night in the club car, can I? What would people think of me, treating my soldier husband so shabbily?" Emily teased. "Upper or lower?"

"Lower, if it's all the same to you," Mark said.

"Then lower it is," Emily agreed.

"Thanks." Mark reached down into a little canvas bag, called an AWOL bag by the GIs, pulled out a shaving kit, then walked to the end of the car to the men's room. He shaved, brushed his teeth, then returned to his seat. But by that time all the berths had been made, and all he could see was a long, narrow aisle between two walls of drawn green drapes.

"Oh, I should have paid attention to what number I was," Mark said. Though he was speaking to himself, he said the words aloud.

He heard Emily giggle, then she stuck her head out between the curtains. "You'd be in a fine fix now if it weren't for me, wouldn't you?" she asked. "You're down here." She slipped a bare arm out and pointed to the berth below her own.

"Thanks," Mark said, stepping into his berth. It took only a few minutes for him to get out of his uniform and slip under the sheet. Then, reaching over his head, he tapped on the bottom of Emily's bed.

"Emily?"

"Yes?" her voice was slightly muffled.

"Good night."

"Good night."

Langley Field, Virginia

Second Lieutenant Lee Arlington Grant stepped up to the bar of the Officers' Open Mess.

"Something to drink, sir?" the waiter asked.

"I'll have a Coke, please," Lee replied.

"A Coke and . . . ?"

"Just a Coke."

The bartender drew a fountain Coke and handed it across the bar.

"Thank you."

Picking up his drink, Lee walked out onto the patio. Looking east, he saw a B-17 just turning onto final, the pilot dissipating airspeed and altitude as he felt his way toward the ground. Lee watched the big bomber approach with flaps lowered and landing gear down and locked.

Lee was meeting his father here at the club. He was more than a little nervous about it because their last parting was on less-than-amicable terms. He had just been granted a West Point appointment, but gave it up when he received a letter of acceptance from Litchfield College. His choice of a Christian college over the U.S. Military Academy was not well received.

"A preacher?" his father had bellowed. "A namby-pamby preacher? Boy, your great-grandfather was with General William T. Sherman at Shiloh, your grandfather was with General Leonard Wood in Cuba, and I flew with Billy Mitchell during the Great War. You are named after the two greatest generals in American history, with all the heroes of Arlington Cemetery thrown in, and that means nothing to you? Does the family honor mean anything to you?"

"Must one fight a war to sustain family honor?" Lee asked.

"In the case of our family, yes."

That discussion had taken place four years ago, just before Lee's father left for an assignment in Hawaii. Although they hadn't seen each other since then, Lee did exchange letters with his parents during the four-year separation, and his mother, who was the correspondent, never failed to end her letters with, "Your father sends his love." Lee had no reason to doubt that.

Lee's parents were back from Hawaii now and were at Langley Field. Quite by coincidence, Lee had drawn the same assignment, though he hadn't seen either of them yet because today was his very first day at the new duty station.

"Good afternoon, Lieutenant," a voice said from behind him.

Turning, Lee saw a full colonel standing on the patio. He came to attention and saluted. "Sir," he said.

Colonel "Iron Mike" Grant stepped across the patio, extending his hand. "Hello, Son. It's good to see you. Your mother has asked about you already."

"I'll get out to see her as soon as I'm signed in," Lee promised.

"I believe your orders are for the Six-oh-fifth Heavy Bomb Group?"

"Yes, sir, I believe they are."

"You believe, or you know?"

"I know they are."

"Colonel Grant?" a waiter said, stepping out through the double doors that led back into the main dining room. "Your table is ready, sir."

"Thank you." Mike and his son followed the waiter inside. Other diners looked up at the two men, wondering who the second lieutenant was who would have the chutzpah to dine with a full bird colonel.

8

"I'm proud of you for joining the army," Mike said after the two were seated. "I would have chosen some other branch for you, perhaps the infantry, the artillery, combat engineers, anything other than the Chaplain Corps." He sighed. "But at least you are in uniform, and you are here."

"Yes, sir, but I don't plan to stay here long. I hope to get overseas as soon as I can," Lee said. "Maybe North Africa."

Mike buttered a roll. "Forget that. You're going to England."

"England?"

"So am I," Mike continued. "I'll be assuming command of the Six-oh-fifth as soon as the change of command ceremony can be arranged."

"Then I am to be under your command?"

"That is correct."

Lee was quiet for a long moment. "My coming here wasn't a coincidence, was it?"

"No."

"That's all the more reason I'm going to apply for a transfer."

"It won't do you any good."

"You mean you would stop it?"

"I would."

"Why? I don't understand you, Dad," Lee said. "On the one hand, you are upset with me because I haven't chosen a combat arm. Then you turn right around and get me assigned to your command so you can . . . what? Keep an eye on me? Protect me from all harm?"

"Something like that," Mike agreed. He stared across the table at his son. "Lee, you had an appointment to West Point. Do you know how many young men in this country would give their eyeteeth for an appointment to the military academy?"

"A lot, I'm sure."

"Probably nine out of ten would go if they could. Here, you have an appointment handed to you, and you happen to be the one out of ten who doesn't want to go."

"I'm sorry if I disappointed you."

"You not only disappointed me. You are now flaunting it by choosing to join the army as a chaplain. Is it your mission in life to embarrass me?"

"No, of course not. Dad, I'm as serious about my calling as you are yours."

"Uh-huh," Mike said. "Well, we'll see about that. In the meantime, I'm keeping you with me. I intend to keep my eye on you for the duration of the war. I will not let you do anything to disgrace your name or your heritage."

Langley Field, Virginia
December 4, 1942

As the B-17 turned from the base leg onto final, its greenhouse flashed once in the late afternoon sun. The dullness of the airplane's olive-drab paint job was somewhat ameliorated by orange wingtips, an orange diagonal stripe across the fuselage just forward of the dorsal fin, and an orange diamond on the tail. Those were the markings of the 605th Heavy Bomb Group.

Because he was pilot and plane captain, the name and nose art of the aircraft were the prerogatives of Mark White. He had named it *Gideon's Sword*, after the biblical warrior, and the artwork depicted a muscular arm, coming down from the clouds, clasping in its hand a short Roman broadsword.

"Gear down," Mark said.

The copilot, Lieutenant Paul Mobley, moved the gear lever down. "Three in the green," he reported a moment later.

"Left waist gunner to pilot. Confirm gear down and locked."

"Right waist gunner to pilot. Confirm gear down and locked."

"Flaps at sixty," Mark ordered.

"Flaps at sixty," Paul repeated. There was an audible whine as the electric motor activated the hydraulic pump. The flaps on the inboard trailing edge of the wing tilted down to sixty degrees.

"Over the fence at ninety," Paul said as they passed over the striping at the end of the runway.

Mark pulled back all four throttles, and the roar of the engines subsided.

Although they kissed down gently, one of the engines began popping, and a long streak of fire streamed out of the exhaust stack.

"Richardson, number two is acting up," Mark said.

Sergeant Stewart Richardson, who would man the top turret gun when they were in action, was also the flight engineer. "Sounds like a cracked distributor cap, Lieutenant. I'll get right on it," he said.

"You do that."

The B-17 finished its rollout, then turned off the active and onto one of the taxiways. Killing engines two and three, Mark used only the outboard engines to trundle back to the flight ramp where they were met by a yellow FOLLOW ME truck.

The truck led them to a parking spot where a parking guide stood, holding up two bright yellow batons. Using the batons to transmit his signals, the ground guide directed Gideon's Sword to its parking place. There, two flight line crewmen crawled under the wings to insert the wheel chocks. The guide made a cutting motion across his neck with his hand, and Mark pulled the fuel mixture levers all the way back to idle cutoff. With the engines quiet, the only sound remaining was the descending hum of the instrument gyros. He turned the fuel off.

"All switches off," Mark said.

Paul ran his hand over all the switches on the panel and overhead. The last switch he turned off was the master switch, then the airplane was completely dead.

"I hope we never have to drop bombs on Baltimore," Mark said as he filled out the flight log. "But if we do, we sure know how to get there. We must've flown a dozen bombing runs over Baltimore in the last two weeks."

"Only eleven," Paul said. "But who is counting?"

"I'm counting," Art Bollinger said. Art was the navigator. "Only twenty-one more days until Christmas. What do you think of that?"

"Are you expecting something from Santa Claus?" Mark teased.

Adrian Rogers came back from his bombardier's station in the nose. "I hope he gets a map," he said. "Did you fellas say we've been bombing Baltimore? Art told me we were in Cleveland."

"Cleveland?" Mark asked.

"Yeah, well, or maybe it was Omaha," Art said. "By the way, is there an ocean near Omaha?"

"Art and Adrian, my Double-A nose crew," Mark said, laughing. "I can't believe we're going to be counting on you two to get us there and bomb the place. Exactly where we get to and what we bomb will be anybody's guess," he teased.

The aircrew climbed down from the plane, and the ground crew took over. They started refueling and checking it out for the next flight. Parachutes and flight gear were pitched into the back of the alert vehicle, then the enlisted men of the crew climbed up for a ride back to the barracks, waving at their officers as they left.

Mark had managed to scrounge up a jeep for the officers of *Gideon's Sword*. Nobody knew how he did it; no one below squadron commander was authorized a jeep, but there it sat, a lock and chain passed through the steering wheel to keep it from being stolen.

Piling into the jeep, Mark, Paul, Art, and Adrian went to the BOQ for a quick shower and change of clothes, then to the Officers' Club for dinner. When they got there, the club was crowded, and the men had to look around for a table. As they were looking, a second lieutenant came over to them.

"If you gentlemen don't mind sharing a table, you can join me," he invited. "There are three empty chairs, and we can have the waiter bring one more."

"Thanks," Mark said. Then, noticing the lieutenant's collar insignia, he looked at the others. "That is, if you sinners don't mind sharing a table with a chaplain."

"Hey," Adrian said, holding up his hands. "My conscience is clean. *I'm* not the one who stole a jeep."

The others laughed as they followed the chaplain back to his table.

"I'm Lee Grant," the lieutenant said as they sat down. The others introduced themselves as well.

"Been here long, Lee?" Mark asked.

"I arrived this October," Lee answered. "Which you would know if you had been attending chapel. Not that I'm proselytizing or anything," he added with a smile.

"I had a professor who used to say that 'he who proselytizes is a Fuller Brush salesman for the Lord,'" Mark said.

Lee had just started to take a swallow of his tea, but Mark's comment startled him so much that he choked, and he quickly put his glass back down. "You wouldn't be talking about Professor Than Pyron, would you?"

"Yes, I am," Mark said. "If you know Pyron, then you went to Litchfield College."

"Yes, I did. I just graduated this spring. Class of forty-two."

"I'm class of thirty-seven," Mark said. To the surprise of everyone at the table, Mark began to sing:

> Fighting Bearcats, tear down the field
> Quick to conquer, never to yield.

Lee began singing along with him, and the two fell into a natural harmony. Others around them interrupted their own conversations to listen.

> Fighting Bearcats honor and true
> Courage is orange and blue
> Win for Litchfield,
> Strike up the band
> Hit 'em high, hit 'em low
> Stand up and show
> We're the pride of the great heartland.

When they finished, they were applauded, not only by the others around their table, but by several from adjacent tables.

"Did you play any sports?" Lee asked.

"Football," Mark said. "I played 'the rest of the team.'"

"I beg your pardon?"

"You know how the field announcer would introduce all the starters?" Mark asked. "Then, after all the starters took the field, he would always say, 'And now, the rest of the team,' and the benchwarmers would come running out. Well, that was me."

The others laughed.

"I ran cross-country," Lee said. "We didn't have announcers. They weren't needed. Nobody ever came to watch us except the other cross-country runners. What was your major?"

"Philosophy. Not exactly a discipline you can build a career around, but I got on as a reporter for the *St. Louis Globe* and I think it helped."

"So, you're a writer. That's . . . oh, my!" Lee said, gasping in recognition. "You are *that* Mark White, aren't you? Professor White's son?"

"Yes."

"You wrote *Man's Heavenly Quest.*"

"I'm flattered that you know that. Did you read it?"

"Of course, I read it. It was required reading for Professor Robison's class. But once I got into it, I would have read it anyway. It's positively brilliant."

What followed was a spirited discussion about the book, ranging from Mark's theory of the possible existence of a heretofore undiscovered manuscript as the source for the synoptic Gospels, to the Reformation.

By then the others at the table were looking at Mark and Lee in openmouthed astonishment.

"I never knew you wrote a book," Art said. "I'll have to read it sometime."

"What do you mean, you'll have to read it?" Paul asked. "You've been listening to them talk about it, haven't you? What makes you think you could read it? It has no pictures."

The others laughed.

"Wait a minute, listen," Adrian said.

"Listen to what?"

"Something's going on."

Looking around the room, they saw that something was, indeed, happening. The dining room was gradually becoming quieter as conversations would stop in midsyllable. News of some sort was spreading from one table to the other. Finally it reached the table nearest them.

"Operational . . . ," they heard someone say.

Mark leaned across to the next table to ask a captain what was going on.

"The Six-oh-fifth is operational," the captain replied.

"You think it's real?" Paul asked when Mark relayed the information. "I mean, we've been told this a dozen times already."

"Yeah, I think it is," Mark said.

"What makes you think that?"

"Well, let's face it, fellas. We haven't really been training to bomb Baltimore. One of these times the rumor has to be real, so why not now?"

2

Christmas Eve, 1942

Susan White was sitting on the right-hand side of the airplane. The DC-3 was arranged in rows of two seats on the left side of the aisle and one on the right for about three-quarters of the way back. At that point the cabin narrowed so that there was only one seat on either side.

The two seats just across the aisle from Susan were occupied by her parents, Harold and Edna White. Harold and Edna had been engaged in conversation almost from the moment the airplane took off from St. Louis. From time to time they had tried to include Susan, but the engine noise necessitated their yelling across the aisle so, for the most part, Susan was left to her own devices. She didn't mind it, though. It was her first time to fly, and she was enjoying the experience.

They were on their way to Norfolk, Virginia, in response to a written invitation to a Christmas Eve party being hosted by Lieutenant Colonel Vincent Todaro, air executive officer of the 605th Heavy Bomb Group.

"I cannot say when our group will deploy or where it will go," Colonel Todaro wrote. "However, it is only reasonable to assume that the time is drawing near, and this may well be your last and best opportunity to see your loved one."

Susan's father took that as a carefully worded hint that Mark would be deploying right away, so he managed to get them three airline tickets. Edna scolded him for his extravagance, but that very extravagance made airline reservations somewhat easier to come by than rail tickets. In addition, traveling by air would save them two days.

Susan was nineteen years old and a freshman at Litchfield College. She was also engaged to be married, though she was keeping that engagement a secret, even from her parents. Bob Gary, her fiancé, had just gone into the army, and they planned to be married as soon as he finished basic training. Thinking about him, she opened her purse, unzipped a little compartment, and took a peek at the small diamond ring Bob had given her. How she wished she could wear it on her finger as a public proclamation of their love. She couldn't, though, because her father was adamant that she must complete college before she even thought about marriage.

She was just closing her purse as the stewardess approached her seat. "Are you ready for lunch?" the stewardess asked with a practiced smile.

"Where do we go for lunch?" Susan asked. "Is there a place up front?"

"No, Honey, I'll serve it to you right here in your seat," the stewardess replied with a chuckle. Reaching up to the seat back in front of Susan, she turned a latch that lowered a tray.

"How clever!" Susan exclaimed. "What do we have for lunch?"

"Oh, it's quite nice today. We have chicken salad on a kaiser roll, a dill pickle, potato chips, and a lovely chocolate cake. Also, your choice of coffee, tea, or milk."

"I'll have coffee," Susan said. "Black."

Quickly and gracefully the stewardess laid the lunch out before her, finishing up by pouring a cup of coffee.

"Do you enjoy your job?" Susan asked.

"Oh, yes, Dear, I love it. But then, I love flying. Are you enjoying the flight?"

"This is my first time to fly," Susan admitted. "Although my brother is a flier," she added proudly. "He's a bomber pilot for the army, and we're going to visit him."

"I'm sure you are going to have a wonderful time."

With a friendly good-bye, the stewardess moved on down the aisle, tending to others, while Susan had her lunch. It seemed odd, eating a meal while moving at nearly two hundred miles per hour and flying thousands of feet above the ground. Looking down just forward of the wing, she saw a single house, sitting deep in the woods, and she wondered if the people who lived there were having their lunch as well. *What are they doing on this day before Christmas? Do they have a Christmas tree in their living room? Do they have children who are waiting eagerly for Santa Claus? Are they too poor for Christmas? Can they hear this airplane passing overhead, and if so, do they think about who might be in it?* She was certain that they did because she could almost feel a direct connection with them at this very moment.

It was dark by the time they reached Norfolk. As the airplane started its descent, Susan was startled when the propeller started glowing. Then she saw a long beam of light stabbing through the darkness, and she realized that the pilot had turned on his landing lights. She also saw glistening streaks of snow picked up by the white spear of light. That surprised her, for until that moment, she had had no idea that it was snowing.

Newport News

Stansfield "Bull" Hagan bowed his head to give the blessing. "Lord, bless this food to our use, and ourselves to Thy service. Bless all our servicemen, wherever in the world they might be during this Christmas season, and bless their families who wait and pray for them. In Christ's name we pray. Amen."

"Amen," the others repeated.

Emily had invited Mark to have Christmas Eve dinner with her, her mother and father, Carol, who was her sister-in-law, and Crystal, Carol's daughter. The only family member missing was her brother, George, who was a sergeant in North Africa.

Mark had met both Emily's parents before, but only briefly. This would be the first time they had ever had a conversation. Emily's father was a supervisor at the shipyard. George had worked there as well before he went into the army. Now, Emily was working there, one of many women who had moved into the workforce.

"So, Mark, how do you like flying the B-17?" Bull Hagan asked as he began carving the turkey.

"I love it," Mark answered. "I wouldn't want to do anything else."

"Oh? I thought most bomber pilots wanted to fly fighters."

"A lot of them do," Mark admitted. "But I'm perfectly content where I am."

"Oh, I just started carving on the breast without asking," Bull said. "Do you prefer white meat or dark? Or maybe you would prefer the drumstick?"

"Whatever you serve is what I want more than anything else," Mark quipped, and the others laughed.

"We invited Carol so we could add her sugar ration points to ours," Bull said.

"Oh, don't be silly, Bull," Sara said. "We invited Carol because she is part of our family and we love her."

"Well, yes, that too," Bull said. "But this way you were able to make a few pies, a cake, and some cookies. I just don't know what Christmas would be without sweets."

"I'm putting together a box of cookies to send to George. They ask that we not clog up the mail with frivolous packages, but they are loosening up somewhat for Christmas mailing," Sara said.

Bull chuckled. "Of course, they didn't loosen up until this very week, which means George's cookies may be there in time for Valentine's Day."

"Speaking as a soldier, I can tell you that he will enjoy them, no matter when they arrive," Mark said.

"Thank goodness the turkey isn't rationed," Sara said. "So everyone eat heartily."

The family kept up a running conversation during dinner. Watching Sara and Carol, Mark had the feeling that they were putting on a brave front, laughing over stories about George. His theory was substantiated a little later when one story caused Sara to cry. Seeing her cry was all it took to get Carol started, and for a moment, both women sat at the table and sobbed quietly. Respecting their feelings, no one else said anything for a long moment.

Finally Sara wiped her eyes, then apologized.

"Don't apologize," Mark said. "You have every right to miss him. I'm sure my family misses me, even though I'm not overseas yet."

"Mark, Emily tells me that you have written a book, and it has been published," Bull said.

"How did you know that?" Mark asked Emily.

"Paul told me."

"Paul?" Sara asked.

"My copilot. And, yes, sir, I did write a book, but it sounds more impressive than it is. It was actually written as a thesis for a religious studies class, and my instructor, Professor Robison, submitted it to a publisher. I didn't even know he had done that, and I was very surprised when the publisher contacted me with an offer."

"A religious studies class?" Sara asked.

"Yes, ma'am. I attended Litchfield College, which is a church-affiliated school. The course in religious studies was mandatory."

"Oh, that's nice. What denomination are you?"

"Sara! That's nobody's business but his," Bull said.

"If he is serious about our daughter, it is our business," Sara said.

"Mom!" Emily gasped.

Mark chuckled, then reached over to touch Emily. "I am serious about your daughter, Mrs. Hagan," he said. "That is, as serious as I have any right to be, given the war and the role I have chosen to play in this war. But to answer your question, I don't subscribe to any particular denomination. I consider myself more of a religious scholar than a religious man."

"A religious scholar, but not a religious man," Bull said. "That says nothing. Unless it's a fancy way of saying you don't believe in anything."

"Well, I can accept the concept of God, and I won't argue against the divinity of Jesus," Mark replied. "But I am absolutely convinced God does not takes a personal interest in individual lives."

"Well, you have to believe in that. Otherwise, you wouldn't believe in prayer," Sara said.

"As it affects human events? No, I don't believe in it," Mark said. "Understand, I don't detract from the value of prayer as a means of providing some psychological comfort or as a way of centering one's thoughts in order to live a moral and charitable life. But to ask God's help in getting an A on an exam?" Mark chuckled and shook his head. "If that was all it took, every student at Litchfield would graduate with honors."

"Sara, for heaven's sake, let the man off the hot seat, will you?" Bull said. "But I really must read your book sometime, Mark."

"I'll be happy to get you a copy, sir," Mark replied. "Now I wonder if I could ask you a question. Why are you called Bull?"

Everyone around the table laughed. "Brilliant ploy, Mark. Now you've got me under the gun," Bull replied. "I'm called Bull because I did a dumb thing once."

"Tell him, Dad," Emily said.

"Yes, tell him," Carol said. "You told me right after my first date with George."

"I didn't tell you. George told you," Bull said. "I just confirmed it."

"Well, you have to tell him now," Sara teased. "You can't just leave him hanging."

"I . . . uh . . . bet some friends I could put my head down and butt my way through a French door," Bull said. "And I did, so that's it."

"Tell him where the French door was, Dear," Sara ordered.

Bull sighed. "It was during the last war," he said. "I was a naval ensign over at Norfolk. I was attending a lawn party given by the admiral. The party was at his quarters, and the French door . . . uh . . . " He paused.

"Go on, Dear."

"Well, I didn't realize it, but the French door opened onto his daughter's bedroom. And when I bulled my way through it . . ."

"I was inside, changing clothes," Sara finished.

"You? You were the admiral's daughter?" Mark asked.

"In the flesh . . . in a manner of speaking," Sara said, laughing.

"Yet you two got married."

"We had to. Her father insisted on it," Bull said. "He said I had compromised her."

"That's not true and you know it!" Sara said. And though everyone but Mark had heard the story many times, they all laughed.

Carol had to leave after dinner in order to put young Crystal to bed, but the others gathered under the Christmas tree to sing carols. Mark had a good baritone voice and a natural ability to harmonize, and the songfest was very enjoyable for everyone. When the singing was over, they opened gifts. Because he was forewarned, Mark was prepared for it and participated in the gift exchange.

Before the evening got too late, Mark and Emily took their leave in order to attend the Christmas Eve party being given at the Officers' Club out at the base.

"I can't remember when I've had a more pleasant Christmas," Mark told Emily's parents. "And I'm sure it will be a long time before I have another one I enjoy as much. I want to thank you for making me feel so welcome."

"We enjoyed having you," Sara said. "And you are welcome in our home anytime."

"Thank you."

"Emily, you drive carefully now. The weather is quite nasty," Bull cautioned.

"I'll be very careful, Dad," Emily promised.

Although what was falling wasn't quite snow, it was a little more than rain. However, the heater in Emily's '40 Ford was a good one, and it poured out a steady flow of hot air, keeping Emily and Mark warm as they drove toward Langley Field. The windshield wipers slapped back and forth with a thumping sound as they pushed away the slush. They were listening to WGH on the radio, where at the moment, Bing Crosby was singing "White Christmas."

"Pretty song," Mark said, singing along with it.

"It's a sad song," Emily replied.

"Sad? How do you get that?"

"Think of all the men who are separated from their families now. They listen to this song, and they remember the white Christmases they used to know. Like George, somewhere in Africa. And you."

"No, you can't count me. I had a wonderful time with your family."

"I know, but what about your family? Don't you miss them?"

"I suppose," Mark said. "It's just not something I let myself dwell on."

"Tell me about your family."

"It's pretty typical, I suppose. My father is a history professor at the same college where I went to school. My mother is a housewife. My sister is a pest."

Emily laughed. "You don't mean that."

"No, not really. Susan is all right. Well, she's more than all right."

"Older or younger?"

"Younger. She's a freshman at Litchfield now."

As they approached the gate of the base, the song on the radio had changed to "Silent Night." Emily was driving, and she rolled the window down as the MP stepped out of his guard booth.

"ID?" the MP asked.

Mark reached across in front of Emily to show his ID card. The MP looked at it, then came to attention, saluted, and waved them through.

They drove past the chapel. The lights were on, and people were already beginning to go inside for the Christmas Eve service. Remembering that he had told Lee he might attend the service, Mark felt a twinge of guilt. "Oh, blast," he said quietly.

"What is it?"

"Lee Grant is the chaplain here," Mark said. "He's a friend, and I sort of told him I might drop by for the Christmas Eve service."

"Would you like to go to the service? I don't mind."

"No. I also told Colonel Todaro I would come to his party, and if I have to disappoint one of them, I'd rather disappoint a friend than the exec. Friends are more forgiving than air execs."

Emily chuckled. "Given your personal view on religion, that's an unlikely friendship, isn't it? I mean between you and a chaplain?"

"If I am interested in the concept of religion as a human endeavor, then it stands to reason I am going to have some religious friends. Besides, he also went to Litchfield. Not at the same time, but we have some mutual friends."

"Well, then maybe we should go to church. Really, I don't mind."

"No," Mark said. "I never attend chapel anyway. I don't know why tonight should be any different."

Emily turned into the O Club parking lot, found a spot, and killed the engine. She started to open the door, but before she did, Mark reached across the car to put his hand on her arm.

"Emily, wait," he said. "Before you get out, there's something I must tell you."

"Oh?" Emily replied, arching her eyebrows in curiosity.

Mark took a deep breath, then let out a long sigh. "The Six-oh-fifth is operational. We'll be leaving for England soon."

"How soon?"

"Sometime in January."

"That's less than a month."

"Yes."

Emily nodded, but said nothing for a long moment. Mark looked right at her and she tried to turn away to avoid his stare, but she couldn't hide from him. He saw a tear on her cheek, glistening in the ambient light.

"How long have you known?" she finally asked.

"A little over two weeks."

She gasped, then looked back at him sharply. "You've known for two weeks, and you're just now getting around to telling me?"

"I wanted to tell you earlier, Emily, but I couldn't. We were told we couldn't tell anyone. The married men couldn't even tell their wives until a few days ago."

"Oh," Emily said. "Oh, how hard that must have been for them. Here I am, feeling sorry for myself when so many wives and mothers are having to go through this. Oh, God bless them all."

"Are you all right?" Mark asked. "Would you like a few minutes?"

Emily wiped her eyes, then blew her nose. "No, I'm fine," she said. "Let's go on in to the party. I've already met some of your friends. I'm looking forward to meeting some of the others."

Lee would have preferred a little more ritual in his Christmas Eve service, but he was serving as chaplain to all the Protestant servicemen, and those who were members of some of the more fundamental denominations may have found the Episcopal service a bit too liturgical for their liking. Despite that, it was a very good service with the carols beautifully sung and the lessons movingly read.

Many of the young men in the congregation were aircrew, and once during one of the carols, Lee found himself looking out over their faces and wondering how many of them would be alive next Christmas. He got a lump in his throat and a stinging in his eyes, and he stared at his feet for two whole verses before regaining his composure. He said a quick, silent prayer for all the young men in the congregation, then expanded it to include all the servicemen serving everywhere in the world.

At the end of the service he stood at the door, shaking hands with everyone. Several of the young men had brought guests, wives in some cases, mothers in others. And because the 605th had been at Langley for three months, many of the men now had girlfriends from the Tidewater area, and they brought them. Lee greeted them all.

"Excellent service, Chaplain," a sergeant, who was an aerial gunner, said. "Only question I have is about Joseph. That man is a slow learner, don't you think? I mean, every year, it's the same thing. No room at the inn. You'd think he would call ahead for reservations, wouldn't you?"

When Lee registered the surprise the sergeant was looking for, the sergeant laughed out loud at his own joke. Lee laughed with him. "We'll just have to wait and see how he makes out next year," he said.

"Yeah, well, we'll be in England next year. Maybe he can find a place over there."

"Chaplain, you got someplace to go, you can go ahead," one of the enlisted men said. "I'll close up here."

"Thanks," Lee said. "Colonel Todaro is giving a party for the officers of the Six-oh-fifth, and I feel that I should at least make an appearance."

"Yeah, well, I wouldn't know anything about that, being as it's officers and all. But just don't do anything I wouldn't do, and you'll be all right."

"Count on it," Lee joked as he hurried toward the parking lot. Like Mark White, Lee had a jeep, but unlike Mark's, Lee's vehicle was authorized. It was cold and damp, and the windshield wiper was totally inadequate for the job, but it was a lot better than trying to walk over to the club.

The club had hired an orchestra for the party. It was a pretty good orchestra with a couple of better-than-average vocalists, male and female, and when Lee went inside, the woman was singing "When the Lights Go On Again." Lee stood just inside the door while he took off his raincoat. One of the club personnel hurried to take his coat and hat, then handed him a ticket stub. He saw Mark White coming toward him.

"Hi, Lee. Sorry I didn't make it to chapel, but come over to the table. I have someone I want you to meet."

"Ah, don't tell me. It's the young lady from town that you told me about."

"Yes, and someone else. Someone I think you know."

Curious as to what he was talking about, Lee followed Mark across the crowded room. By now, the orchestra had swung into "Deep in the Heart of Texas," and the entire audience was getting into it, complete with clapping and the responses of "Yeee ha!" when appropriate.

"Lee, this is my mother, Edna White, and my father . . ."

"Professor White," Lee interrupted, extending his hand and smiling broadly. "How wonderful it is to see you again, sir. I took your American history class, though I'm not sure you remember me."

"Now, tell me, Mr. Grant, how I could ever forget someone who thought Teapot Dome referred to a silver service set?" Professor White replied.

Lee blushed, and the others laughed. "Will I ever live that down?" Lee asked.

"I don't think so," Professor White replied.

"Isn't this a wonderful surprise?" Mark asked. "Until I arrived at the party tonight, I had no idea my family was here. Colonel Todaro arranged it. He contacted the families of everyone in the Six-oh-fifth and asked them to be here. He also asked them to keep it a surprise. I'll tell you, there have been some pretty grand reunions here tonight."

"I'm sure there have been."

In fact, Lee knew all about the surprise reunion because he had helped Todaro plan it, calling many of the family members, making travel arrangements, and locating hotel rooms.

"This is my sister, Susan," Mark said, introducing a young woman with the fresh-scrubbed look of a college coed. "And this," Mark added, putting his arm around Emily, "is the girl I told you about."

"The one you married in order to get her a ticket from St. Louis to Newport News?" Lee asked.

"What?" Mark's mother asked with a gasp. When Lee, Mark, and even Emily laughed, Edna knew it had to be some sort of joke, so she laughed, too, weakly at first, though with considerably more enthusiasm when Mark explained how he had managed to fool the ticket agent into giving Emily a ticket.

"It's too bad your family couldn't make it, Lee," Mark said. "I'd like to meet them sometime."

Suddenly the orchestra stopped right in the middle of "Blues in the Night" and rendered three riffs of "Ruffles and Flourishes."

"Officers and ladies!" someone shouted. "The group commander, Colonel and Mrs. Michael J. Grant!"

"My family just arrived," Lee said in an unassuming voice.

3

Langley Field
January 7, 1943

At five o'clock one Thursday morning in January, the residents of Hampton and Newport News, Virginia, heard a sound that was already commonplace for their cousins across the sea in England. One hundred ninety-two engines whined, coughed, then roared into life as the pilots of forty-eight B-17s prepared for takeoff. At exactly 0530, the *Truculent Turtle*, Colonel Grant's airplane, rotated, then climbed out at five hundred feet per minute. Thirty seconds behind him the second B-17 followed, its gear being sucked up into the wheel wells as it began its own ascent.

It took another half hour before all forty-eight bombers of the 605th Heavy Bomb Group were aloft and formed into four squadrons of twelve. Once formed, they started north along the coast. Their route would take them to Newfoundland, Greenland, Iceland, and then England. Their time en route, including an overnight stop at Iceland, would be forty-eight hours.

Most of the ground crew was already gone, having left by ship two weeks before, so they would be on the ground ready to receive the bombers when they arrived.

A few stayed behind as ground crew to help in launching the aircraft and to attend to final details. Then the same officers and men left the next day, crossing the Atlantic in one hop in two C-54 Skytrains. Lee Grant, who had been promoted to first lieutenant just before the group left Langley, was a member of that rear party, and he made the crossing in relative comfort. The plane was a four-engine Douglas transport that was faster than some of the fighter planes still in use.

Lee got his first glimpse of what was to be his new home from the air when the C-54 turned onto its downwind leg. Looking out through the window, he saw two long runways, already streaked with tire marks, a result of the fact that for more than a year the air base at Davencourt had been home to the RAF Stirling bombers. The runways made a large X in the middle of a huge concrete circle, so that it resembled two hands in a clock face.

Evenly spaced about one hundred feet apart, and stretching all the way around the circle like teeth on a gear, were smaller squares of concrete pads called hardstands. Nearly half of these hardstands were occupied by B-17 bombers. Many of the bombers had yellow maintenance stands pulled up to them as mechanics worked on their birds.

From the air, the geometric precision of the runways and bomber-filled hardstands made a very impressive show; thus, it was natural that this would draw his first attention. But after that, Lee surveyed the rest of the air base. He saw the aircraft hangars and the sandbagged areas where he knew bombs and ammunition must be stored. Then he saw the motor pool and finally the living quarters—row upon row of Nissen huts with nothing from his perspective to set the officers' quarters apart from those of the enlisted men.

He had no idea where the chapel might be. For all he knew, it could be in the back of an aircraft hangar somewhere. And if that was the case, then so be it.

The transport touched down on the runway, then began slowing as the pilot applied the brakes. Turning off the runway, Lee got a glance through the window of a jeep with a sign reading FOLLOW ME. The jeep pulled in front of the airplane and Lee lost sight of it, but he knew it was leading them to a parking place somewhere.

The passengers gathered their coats and baggage while at the same time stealing glances through the window to see what their new station was like. Lee knew that it was cold outside when he saw the ground guide. The guide, who was waiting with his batons to guide the plane in, was wearing a parka, a fur hat, and gloves. In addition, clouds of vapor were coming from his mouth and nose.

An aircrewman of the transport opened the door. "Gentlemen," he called. "Please be careful when you exit onto the stairway. It's cold, and there may be ice."

It was cold, but mercifully there was no ice. As Lee started down the stairs, he saw a jeep parked off to one side. A young enlisted man was standing in front of the jeep, holding up a sign. The sign read CHAPLAIN GRANT. Lee walked toward him.

"I'm Chaplain Grant," he said.

The soldier saluted.

"That's not necessary," Lee said quickly.

"For me it is, Chaplain, I work for you. I'm Corporal Gates, chaplain's assistant."

Smiling, Lee stuck out his hand. "It's good to meet you, Corporal. What's your first name?"

"Kenneth, sir. Uh, my friends call me Kenny."

"Do you mind if I call you Kenny?"

"No, sir, not at all. Oh, they're off-loading the duffel bags. If you'll show me which one is yours, I'll get it for you."

"All right. I have two bags actually, my duffel and a second bag with my vestments, chalice, and paten."

"Sort of a soul-salvation travel kit, huh, Chaplain?" Kenny asked.

Lee laughed. "You might say that."

Five minutes later, with the gear stashed in the back of the jeep, Kenny pulled away from the flight line. Already the two big transports were being serviced, readied for their return flight tomorrow.

"I was looking for the chapel from the air," Lee said. "But I didn't see anything that looks like it."

"Oh, wait till you see it, sir," Kenny said. "You are going to do a double-watusi back flip over it."

"A double-watusi back flip? Is that good or bad?"

"Oh, that's good. I mean this chapel is something else." Kenny turned between two hangars. "You see, here's the thing. This whole air base is laid out on a huge estate belonging to Lord Davencourt."

Lee looked around. "You mean, as small a country as England is, one man owns this much land?"

"That's somethin', ain't it? But for our purposes, it's good he does. He's leasing all this ground to the army for one dollar per year."

"Lord Davencourt must be quite a man."

"I reckon he is, but I don't know much about lords and ladies and such. There it is, Chaplain. Tah, dah!" he said musically. "Your chapel."

The chapel was relatively small, but exceptionally impressive. It was made of brick, surrounded by a beautifully sculptured garden, and flanked by a small but well-kept cemetery. The double doors were iron-banded and painted red.

"It's beautiful," Lee said. "And this is for our use?"

"Yes, sir. But if you think it looks good out here, wait until you see it inside," Kenny said, hopping from the jeep.

Stepping in through the doors, Lee saw stained glass windows flanking the narthex. One window was Jesus praying at the rock in Gethsemane; the other was Jesus being baptized. The nave and chancel were carpeted in red. The sanctuary was carpeted in gold, and behind the sanctuary was a three-piece panel of artwork, depicting the Transfiguration.

"That's called a triptych," Kenny said when he saw where Lee was looking.

"Yes, I know," Lee answered with smile.

"I didn't know it. Someone had to tell me what it was."

"It's beautiful," Lee said.

"It's over two hundred fifty years old. Same as this church."

"Where do the other chaplains keep their things?" Lee asked.

"There are no other chaplains stationed at Davencourt," Kenny responded.

"You can't mean I'm the only chaplain for the entire base?"

"Alconbury is only ten miles from here, and it has the Ninety-second Heavy Bomb Group, plus the One-eighteenth and Three-twenty-second Fighter Groups, so it's a lot bigger. There are six chaplains over there, three Protestant, two Roman Catholic, and one Jewish. One of the Catholic chaplains, Father Dilbert, spends his mornings at Alconbury, and his afternoons here. Same with Sunday Mass—mornings there, afternoons here. The Sixty-eighth Heavy Bomb Group is over at Molesworth. That's about five miles west of here. They have one Protestant and one Catholic chaplain, plus a Jewish chaplain. And Rabbi Golden spends his mornings over there and his afternoons here."

"What about me? Do I have a split assignment?"

"Not according to Celestial Command. According to him, you'll spend all your time here, since you are the only full-time chaplain assigned here."

"Celestial Command?"

"Well, that's what I call him," Kenny said with a laugh. "That would be Colonel Jim Henry. He's chief of chaplains for the First Combat Wing. That's who we belong to. According to him, when the boys of the Six-oh-fifth are told to go to the chaplain to get their cards punched, you're it."

"Do you know how many men are in the Six-oh-fifth, Kenny?"

"No, sir."

"There are two hundred and ninety-three officers, one warrant officer, one thousand four hundred and ninety-seven enlisted men," Lee replied.

Kenny gave a low whistle. "Wow, that's a lot of men. You can only get two hundred fifty in here, and that's if you crowd them a bit."

Lee looked around the beautiful little church. "Right. Well, if I started early enough, I think that before the Romans got here, I could squeeze in at least four services on Sunday. And if that's not enough, I'll start holding services in one of the aircraft hangars."

"You think you're going to have that many men coming to chapel?"

"Why not?" Lee replied.

"You're going to have to give brilliant homilies or be an awfully good salesman."

"Well, let's face it, Kenny, I'm selling the Word of the Lord. It's not hard to be a good salesman if you have a good product."

4

Tunisia
February 8, 1943

S taff Sergeant George Hagan made one more adjustment to the carburetor on the engine of the Sherman tank. "All right," he called. "Try it again."

PFC Don Roberts hit the starter, and the engine turned over, coughed a couple of times, nearly caught, then went back to a slow, nonproductive grinding.

"Hold it! Hold it!" George shouted.

Roberts stuck his head up through the driver's port. "What's the problem, Sarge? How come it won't start?"

"I think there is sand in the intakes," George said with a sigh. "I was hoping we wouldn't have to pull the manifold."

"Why don't we just get maintenance up here and let them handle it?" PFC Weiser asked. Mel Weiser, the tank gunner, was lying in the shade of the tank, reading a copy of *Stars and Stripes*. PFC Larry Wallace, the loader, was fiddling with the radio.

"Because if we let those guys have it, we'll probably never get it back," George said. "They can't put the top back on a bottle. What makes you think they can fix a tank?"

"The army thinks they can," Mel said. "That's the job they gave them."

"Yeah, well, they gave you the job of gunner, and you couldn't hit the broad side of a barn if you were leaning against it," George said, but he ameliorated his comment with a smile, showing that he was teasing.

"What about you, Sarge? What can you do?" Mel asked.

"Nothing," George replied. "Why do you think they made me a tank commander?"

"Hey, you guys, listen!" Larry shouted. "I've got the Armed Forces Radio Service. They're playing a show from Hollywood."

"And now, ladies and gentlemen here in America, and all you wonderful boys in uniform, fighting for our freedom and listening in on Armed Forces Overseas Radio Service, this is Hollywood calling!"

"It's Hollywood calling," Larry said.

"We heard that," Mel said.

Immediately on the heels of the announcer's lead-in, the band began playing "Hooray for Hollywood," while in the background could be heard the applause and cheers of the studio audience.

"Yes, ladies and gentlemen, for this special show tonight, nearly all of Hollywood is here. We've gathered every star in the constellation to bring a little touch of home into the lives of our brave boys overseas.

"So, here it is, boys, from the icy climes of Alaska to the tropic isles of the Pacific, from England to Australia, to the desert sands of North Africa . . ."

"That's us!" Larry said. "The desert sands of North Africa."

"Will you hush, so we can listen?"

". . . a great big Hollywood hello from all of us here in the good old United States. On the show tonight are Joan Crawford, Barbara Stanwyck, Rita Hayworth, Shirley Temple, Janet Gaynor, Olsen and Johnson, Abbott and Costello, Jack Benny, Mickey Rooney, Robert Taylor, Cary Grant, Frank Sinatra, and me. I'm Donnie 'I know where to scratch if you know where to itch' Fritz."

Donnie Fritz's introduction received laughter, then thunderous applause.

"Listen to that applause. Who all do you think is there to watch that show?" Mel asked.

"They're probably all 4-Fs and defense workers," Larry said. "They're making so much money off the war they're running out of places to spend it, so they take our girlfriends to shows like this."

"Who you kidding, Larry?" Don asked. "You don't have a girlfriend."

"Well, maybe I don't. But if I did, she'd probably leave me for a rich defense worker."

"If you had one, she would leave you for a seventy-year-old toothless retired street cleaner," Don said, and the others laughed.

"And now, here is a letter from the second platoon of Company B, the Seven-fifty-sixth Tank Destroyer Battalion," the announcer said.

"Hey, that's the Seven-fifty-sixth, you guys!" Mel said. "They're just over the hill a ways."

The announcer continued.

"The boys of the second platoon write, 'We'd like to hear the sound of Rita Hayworth frying a two-inch-thick porterhouse steak, smothered in onions. And let us hear that steak sizzle.' Okay, boys, here she is, Hollywood's own glamour girl, Rita Hayworth!"

The studio crowd applauded, cheered, and whistled.

"Hello, Donnie. Hello, boys," Rita said.

"Rita, you heard what the boys are asking for. Can you fry a two-inch-thick porterhouse steak, covered with onions?"

"Well, I don't know."

"You don't know what? You don't know if you can do it?"

"No, I mean, I don't know what a two-inch porterhouse steak looks like. We've had meat rationing for so long."

The crowd roared with laughter.

"Gee, they have it rough back there, don't they?" Don asked. "No steak?"

"Hush," George said. "I want to listen."

"You'll learn quick enough what a steak looks like when you see this baby. Bring it out, gents, but you guards better keep your pistols handy. When the crowd sees meat like this, they may attack."

"Oh, I don't know about that, Donnie," Rita said. "You're here, aren't you? That means the crowd has been seeing ham all night long, and they haven't attacked yet."

The audience laughed.

"Where does it say that?" Donnie asked. "Does it say that in your script? I don't see that anywhere."

More laughter.

"Okay, boys, we've got the burner hot, and there's Rita putting on the steak. My, oh my, oh my, what a big gorgeous hunk of red meat that is, just hanging over the skillet. Oops, pardon me, boys. That was my tongue. I'll just stick it back in here."

More laughter.

"Just so you boys won't think this is all going to waste, I'm pleased to tell you that I plan to eat every bite of it, right after the show tonight. Of course, Rita, you are welcome to join me. I mean, it's only fair, you cooking it and all.

"I'm afraid not, Donnie. The stagehands already have dibs on it. I'll be eating this steak tonight, all right, but I'll be eating it with them, not you."

"Just my luck. Okay, that meat is really cookin' now! Get that microphone down here by the skillet, men; you know what the boys of the Seven-fifty-sixth Tank Destroyer said. They want to hear it sizzle!"

Through the radio could be heard loud sizzling sounds.

"Man, oh, man, listen to that baby," Don said. "Right at this moment if I was given my choice between Rita Hayworth and that porterhouse steak, I don't know which one I would take."

"And now, here's a letter from a group of army nurses stationed in Hawaii. They want to hear a song by Frankie. Frankie? Frankie who?"

"Oh, that would be me, Mr. Fritz."

"'Oh, that would be me, Mr. Fritz,'" Donnie repeated, and the crowd laughed at his mimicry. "Listen to him call me Mr. Fritz, like I'm so much older than he is. Why, we're about the same age."

Laughter.

"Practically."

More laughter.

"Almost."

Louder laughter.

"Nearly."

Uproarious laughter.

"Okay, all you nurses out there, and you fellas, too, if you like a mellow sound, here's Frank Sinatra!"

This time the crowd's applause was intermingled with women's high-pitched screams.

"Don't know what all those dames see in that guy," Larry said, turning off the radio.

"Hey, here comes the mail," Don said.

When the others looked, they saw what he saw, a jeep leaving a rooster tail of dust behind it as it sped across the desert floor. George climbed down from the engine deck and wiped his hands with a shop rag as he stood with the others. The jeep slid to a stop, but the rooster tail didn't, and it rolled over them. They coughed and brushed at the dust. Their only consolation was that the mail clerk was sitting in about an inch of sand and was covered with it.

The mail clerk began going through his bag.

"Roberts," he called, tossing a little white envelope toward Don. "Roberts, Roberts. Weiser, Weiser, Weiser, Weiser. Roberts. Wallace, Wallace, Hagan, Hagan, Wallace, Hagan, Hagan. That's all," he said.

The men, with letters in hand, turned away from the jeep.

"Oh, except for this," the mail clerk added, pulling out a rather bedraggled-looking box. "Hagan, a package for you."

"A package?"

"Yeah. It says Merry Christmas."

"A little late, isn't it?"

"You got it as soon as I did, Sarge," the mail clerk said. He put the jeep in gear, then drove off, once more kicking up a rooster tail of dust.

"What you think it is, Sarge? Cookies?" Don asked.

"Nah, it's fudge," Larry suggested.

"You're both wrong. It's cake," Mel insisted.

"You're all three wrong. It's mine," George said.

"Oh, well, yeah, I mean we know that," Larry said, disappointment obvious in his voice. "We was just wonderin' what it was, is all."

"Relax, guys," George said with an easy smile. "Have I ever not shared with you?" He opened the box and looked in with a quiet groan.

"What is it?" Don asked.

"Better you should ask, what was it?" George replied. "It was cookies. Now it's crumbs."

"That's okay," Larry said easily. "Crumbs are good."

Reaching in to grab a handful of crumbs, George sat down in the shade, leaned back against the tank tread, and began to read his letters. He had one from his mother, one from his sister, Emily, and two from his wife, Carol. The others on his crew also began reading.

For the next several minutes all four men were busy with mail from home. Occasionally someone would dip a handful of crumbs from the cookie box, then pass the box over to someone else.

"Hey, how about this?" Mel asked, cookie crumbs dribbling down his chin. "My kid brother made twenty-seven points in a basketball game against Bishop Glen High. That beats me. My best game last year was twenty-two points."

"Last year?" Larry asked. "You mean to tell me that last year you were playing high school basketball, and this year you are in Algeria?"

"Yeah," Mel said. "I guess that's somethin', ain't it? I mean, last year, the most important thing in my life was whether or not we would have a winning basketball season. This year the most important thing in my life is . . . well, my life."

"Ahh, Dad bought a Packard," Larry said, grinning broadly. "A thirty-nine Packard. He says it's in real great shape."

"The thirty-nine Packard is a great-looking car," George said.

"Yeah, I won't have any trouble getting dates with that car when I get back," Larry said.

"Whoa, guys, listen to this," Don said. He began reading from the letter. "'Wolves have been working the north range, so last week your father and your sister went hunting. Julie used your thirty-thirty, and she got four of them. There's a bounty of twenty-five dollars each, so she made a hundred dollars. Dad told her she should pay you rent for using your rifle.'" Don looked up at the others. "How 'bout that? Julie got four of them."

"If she can shoot like that, she's not a girl some boy wants to make mad," Mel said.

"What about you, Sarge? What do you hear from home?" Don asked.

"My sister has a boyfriend," George answered.

"Don't tell me she's sold out and is dating one of those guys that work in the shipyard," Larry said. "I mean, I've seen your picture of her. She's one good-looking girl. I know I won't ever date her or anything, but I would hate to think of some rich civilian getting her."

George shook his head. "He's not a civilian. He's an officer in the army."

"I knew it!" Larry said, hitting himself in the forehead with the heel of his hand. "That's even worse! Officers always get the good-looking girls."

"Wait a minute," Don said. "My brother's an officer, remember? He's on a submarine in the Pacific."

"Yeah, well, that's different. Number one, he's in the navy, not the army, and number two, if he's on a submarine, he's got a real job. I'll bet this joker Sergeant Hagan's sister is seeing has some real cushy job, like defending the coast or something."

"No," George said. "He's a B-17 pilot, and he's headed for England."

"Oh," Larry said. He was quiet for a moment. "Sarge, you better write your sister. You better write her and tell her don't get too hooked on that guy. From what I hear, those bomber pilots don't live all that long."

"Maybe it's not all that serious," Mel suggested.

"It must be fairly serious," George replied. "My mother, my sister, and my wife all three told me about him."

"Did they tell you his name?"

"Yeah, it's White. Lieutenant Mark White."

5

Davencourt
February 10, 1943

T he Eighth Air Force was organized into bomber, fighter, compos-
ite, and service commands under the leadership of Major General
Carl A. Spaatz. General Spaatz's headquarters for the Eighth Air Force
was located in the suburbs of London at Bushy Park, Teddington, and
was known by the code name WIDEWING.

To Brigadier General Ira C. Eaker went the Eighth Bomber Command. His headquarters was in a former girls' school at High Wycombe
in Buckinghamshire, located about thirty miles west of London. The
Eighth Bomber Command's code name was PINETREE. The bomber
command was further organized into four bombardment wings. B-17
heavy bomber groups went into the First and Fourth Combat Wings;
while B-24 heavy bomber groups went into the Second Wing; and the
B-26 medium bombers went into the Third Wing. The 605th was one
of three heavy bomber groups assigned to the Second Air Division of
the First Combat Wing. The Ninety-second at Alconbury and the

Sixty-eighth at Molesworth were the other two groups assigned to the Second Air Division.

In addition to Davencourt, Alconbury, and Molesworth, there were Bassingbourne, Grafton Underwood, Polebrook, Thurleigh, Hardwick, Great Ashfield, Knettisham, Ridgewell, Thorpe Abbotts, Chelveston, Kimbolton, Bury St. Edmunds, Framlingham, Horan, and Horsham St. Faith.

Colonel Iron Mike Grant had not visited them all, but he had visited enough of them to notice the one thing that every base had in common. All were cold, wet, dank, and uncomfortable.

Colonel Grant was thinking about all this now because he was reviewing the table of organization of the Eighth Air Force and the 605th's place in it when his adjutant, Major John Ragsdale, stuck his head through the door.

"Colonel?"

Mike sighed and held his hand up. "Don't tell me, John, there are more forms for me to sign."

"No, sir," John said, smiling broadly. "General Westland's office just called. I think this is it. I think we finally have a mission, sir."

Grant broke into a huge smile and stood up so quickly that his chair turned over. "Is my driver out there?"

"Yes, sir."

"Call Colonel Todaro. Tell him to stand by. Sergeant Kelly!" he shouted, stepping into the main room. "Kelly, let's get a move on!"

When he looked around the anteroom, Kelly was nowhere to be seen. He turned back to Major Ragsdale. "I thought you told me Kelly was here."

"He was here just a moment ago, sir, I don't know . . ."

"I've got your jeep right out front, Colonel," Kelly said, stepping in through the door at that moment. "We're ready to go."

Grant smiled. "Good man," he said. "Now, let's see how fast you can get us over to Whitehall."

"Yes, sir!"

Kelly made the fifteen-mile drive in just under twenty minutes, which was very fast considering a speed limit of thirty-five miles per hour.

Whitehall Manor was a huge stone structure that rose like a castle from a sweeping lawn. In front of the driveway, linden trees guarded a pond. The trees' limbs had been stripped bare by the winter rains, and now they rattled dryly against the gray February sky. The pond was a permanent home for a half-dozen swans, kept there by constant feeding. At one time Whitehall was the summer home for the earl of Falmouth. Now, the towering edifice was headquarters for the Second Air Bombardment Division.

Mike was out of the jeep almost before it stopped. He bounded up the stairs, opened the great oaken door, pushed aside the blackout curtain, and found himself inside a high-ceilinged hall. He returned the sentry's salute, then walked through an anteroom marked COMMANDING GENERAL, where he was met by a major.

"You can go right in, Colonel Grant," the major said. "General Westland is expecting you."

"Thanks."

Mike knew that, like Whitehall, Davencourt was located on a large estate. The difference was that Lord Davencourt and his family still lived in their house on the estate. As a result all the buildings that had been put up to support the 605th—maintenance, billets, and administrative—were temporary huts made of corrugated tin. Mike's own office was located in such a hut, and he worked behind a standard military-issue gray metal desk.

On the other hand, General Westland's office was comparable to any bank president's office Mike had ever seen. Lined with book-filled shelves, the large room was equipped with polished oak furniture, including a large, ornately carved desk. An old, exquisite Persian carpet was on the floor.

Mike knew Westland and had served with him many times before. In fact, back at West Point, when Mike was a second classman and Westland a fourth classman, Mike knocked him out during an intramural boxing match. They weren't adversaries, but they had never been really close friends, and Mike often wondered if Westland still held that incident against him.

Westland was sitting behind his desk, holding a small swagger stick, the base of which was embellished by the polished brass shell casing of a fifty-caliber machine gun. Mike knew the story of the shell casing. It had been fired by one of the waist gunners in the B-17 in which General Westland had flown his one and only mission. Westland was tapping the swagger stick into the palm of his left hand.

"How are your boys, Mike? Do you think they're ready to go?"

"Yes, sir. Remember, we exchanged twenty percent of our personnel with other bomb groups the day after we arrived, so several of our crews already have experience. And the rest of them have had several practice missions. We're ready, Phil. We are as ready as we will ever be."

"Good, good. I'm going to send them out tomorrow. It shouldn't be that tough a mission, but it is more important than boring holes through the sky."

"What is it?"

"You're going down south to Eschwege. There's an airfield there that the Germans are using as a collection and clearing point for all fighter planes brought up to their forward bases. If we get a good strike, we might make a dent in the number of fighters they send up to meet us every time we cross the coastline. That's something that will certainly pay off in your future missions."

"I can see that it might."

"I'll have our intelligence people over for your briefing tomorrow."

"Thanks, Phil."

"You're going to have Todaro lead the flight, I suppose?"

"No. I'll lead it."

Westland nodded. "Yes, that's probably a good idea. You can get your mission in early and show leadership for your men while not taking too great a risk."

"Yes, sir," Mike answered.

Mike knew that Westland was not being facetious. Westland meant it when he said, "Get your mission," in the singular form. One mission was all Westland had flown, and he didn't expect Mike to fly any more. What Mike didn't tell him was that he intended to fly as many missions as his schedule would allow.

By midafternoon, word was all over Davencourt that the 605th would be flying their first mission the next morning. For supper that evening they had, according to the little felt-backed bulletin board that gave the menu in military terms: "Chops, pork; potatoes, mashed; peas, buttered; sauce, apple; bread, sliced; and cake, chocolate."

During supper Mark sat next to one of the pilots who had just come over from the Ninety-second. The pilot gave his name, then told Mark to call him Dusty, so within a short time, Dusty was the only name Mark could remember.

"So, you are about to join the elite group, are you?" Dusty asked.

"The elite group? What group is that?"

"The maligned minions of misguided souls searching ceaselessly for affirmation, appreciation, and approbation in a quixotic quest to negate Nazi nastiness by flying foolishly into flak while fleeing flaying fighter planes."

"Wow," Mark said, applauding quietly. "That's very good."

"Yeah, it is, isn't it?" Dusty replied. "It took me twelve missions to come up with that bit of alliterative doggerel."

"You've got twelve missions already?"

"Seventeen."

"You're one of the integrated crews, aren't you?"

Dusty laughed. "Integrated crews. That sounds like it should be a hyphenated word, like we're something not quite acceptable to polite society or the original members of the Six-oh-fifth."

"I didn't mean it like that," Mark apologized.

"I know. But that's the way it is."

"Whose squadron are you in?"

"I'm in Dixon's squadron."

Mark smiled. "Hey, that's great! So am I!"

"Listen, you want to celebrate a little ritual with me?" Dusty asked.

"What ritual is that?"

"On the night before every mission, I pay a visit to my airplane."

"What, you mean out on the hardstand?"

"Yep."

"That's a long way out. Our squadron is parked on the other side of the skeet range."

"There are a lot of bikes over by operations. We'll borrow a couple and ride over there," Dusty suggested.

"Okay," Mark agreed.

After supper, they rode, without talking, through the soft haze and purple twilight of early evening. They reached Dusty's airplane, *Lusty Gal*, first. The nose art was of a woman, filling out a sweater and a tight skirt. It was more a caricature than an attractive rendering. Her breasts were well out of proportion, and her face was slightly distorted, as if viewing her through flawed glass.

"If this is the girlfriend of the guy who had this plane first, then I feel sorry for him," Dusty said, noticing that Mark was studying the art. "I inherited this plane when I came over," he explained. "That makes tonight's ritual all the more important."

"What exactly is the ritual?"

"I'll show you."

Leaving the bicycle on its kickstand, Dusty walked over to the big wheel on the left main landing gear of his airplane. Then, standing on his hands, he raised and lowered himself until his forehead had touched the wheel three times.

"That's it? That's what you came out here for?"

"Yeah, what did you expect?"

"I don't know, maybe a pre-preflight."

"Nah, this is all I need. It's gotten me back seventeen times."

They rode over to *Gideon's Sword* and looked at it. By now Mark knew this airplane very well. He and his crew had picked it up back at Langley, and they put several hundred hours on it before they flew it across the Atlantic. Mark knew the Fortress's strengths and weaknesses as well as its idiosyncrasies. But tomorrow he would be asking it to do something it had never done before. He was going to have to fly to an area where there were people with the single and obsessively dedicated mission of shooting him down.

"You going to do anything?" Dusty asked.

"What, you mean like do push-ups over it?"

"Yeah, something like that."

"If it's all the same to you, I'll pass on that," Mark replied with a little laugh.

"Yeah, sure, whatever it takes," Dusty said. "Come on. Let's get back before it's totally dark and some trigger-happy guard thinks we're saboteurs."

"Chaplain, you want to come over to the chapel?" Kenny asked, catching Lee as he was leaving the officers' mess after supper.

"Something wrong?"

"No, sir, it's not that. It's just, well, maybe you had better come see for yourself."

When Lee got to the chapel a few minutes later, he was surprised to see nearly two hundred men there.

"It's the mission tomorrow," Kenny said. "They all want you to say a prayer for them."

"Open the chapel, Kenny," Lee said. "I'll say a prayer *with* them."

Kenny opened the chapel to let the men in. While they filed in and took their seats in the pews, Kenny lit the candles on the altar. Lee waited in the narthex and said a little prayer of his own: "Lord, give me the wisdom, the strength, and the faith to be able to serve these men."

When Lee walked up the aisle toward the front of the church, many of the men, familiar with the procession as a part of the liturgy, stood. When they stood, others joined them, so that by the time Lee reached the front of the church, everyone was standing.

"Please," he said. "Be seated."

There was a rustle of clothing as the men took their seats. Looking out over the assembly, Lee recognized several men that he knew were not aircrew members. That pleased him, for he knew they would be in no personal danger the next day, yet they, too, felt the need to ask God's blessing on tomorrow's mission.

"Well, I guess the day we have all been waiting for is finally at hand,"

Lee began. "Tomorrow, you are being asked to do something that no man should ever have to do. You are being asked to go out into a terrible arena where you must kill or be killed. How can any man of God find it within himself to do such a thing?

"And yet, consider the alternative. Hundreds of thousands, perhaps millions of men, women, and children have died at the hands of the evil that we fight. If we don't stop the Nazis, who will? And if they aren't stopped, then hundreds of thousands, perhaps millions more will die, not only in occupied Europe, but here, on this beautiful isle and eventually even in our beloved United States.

"When you shoot down airplanes, people will die. When you drop bombs, people will die, including innocent people. But you must not think of it in that way. You are fighting the immorality, not the people, and you are killing the evil, not the individuals."

"Chaplain, will you be out there tomorrow when we take off?" one young gunner asked.

"I'll be there when you take off, my prayers will be with you for the entire time you are gone, and I will be there when you return."

"Thanks."

"Remember, and take comfort from the Twenty-third Psalm: The Lord is my shepherd, I shall not want. He maketh me lie down in green pastures, He leadeth me beside still waters. He revives my soul, and guides me along right pathways for his Name's sake. Yea, though I walk through the valley of the shadow of death, I shall fear no evil for thou art with me; your rod and your staff comfort me. You spread a table before me in the presence of mine enemies. You have anointed my head with oil, and my cup is running over. Surely your goodness and mercy shall follow me all the days of my life, and I will dwell in the house of the Lord forever.

"Let us pray."

Some knelt, some stood, while the remainder bowed their heads where they sat.

"Almighty God, we entrust to Thy care and keeping the men of the Six-oh-fifth. Defend them with Your heavenly grace; strengthen them; give them courage to face the perils that will confront them tomorrow and on every day thereafter. Grant them, O Lord, a sense of Your abiding peace, through Jesus Christ our Lord. Amen."

"Amen," many said.

"I will leave the chapel open all night," Lee said. "Those of you who wish to do so may remain here in prayer and meditation. If anyone has need to speak to me personally, I will be available. God bless you, and God keep you in His heavenly embrace."

February 11, 1943

Finally after more than a month of getting organized and practicing formation flying, we flew our first real combat mission. Our target was a German airfield at Eschwege.

We were awakened at 0230, then hurried through the dark to have breakfast in the combat-crew mess. It was our first time in the combat-crew mess as you can only eat there on the day of a mission. The crews mess together, with the enlisted men eating on one side and officers on the other. We were served fresh eggs, as many as we wanted. I only had two, but some of the men had as many as four or five.

We received briefing on weather, flak, fighters, and target. Then we were told to leave all personal items behind in case we are shot down. It was a pretty sobering thought.

Takeoff and rendezvous for formation went smoothly. There was heavy flak over the target, and I saw one Fort go down. Several aircraft returned with wounded on board, but we came through without a scratch. Our Double-A nose crew did a good job today.

6

0230, February 11, 1943

L et's go," someone said, shaking Mark from a sound sleep. When he opened his eyes, he was staring into the glare of the CQ's flashlight. "Breakfast at oh-three-hundred, briefing at oh-four-hundred."

"Come on, are you kidding me?" Paul asked when the CQ shook him awake. "It's not morning. It's still last night."

"Come on, Paul, you're in the big leagues now," Mark teased. "If you can't cut it, we'll send you back to the minors for more seasoning."

As Mark walked over to breakfast a few minutes later, he thought of the significance of this moment. It was something he had waited on, not only since arriving in England, but virtually his entire life. He thought about all those hours he spent sitting in a booth at Waggies. Waggies was the soda shop where all the kids hung out, drinking malts and playing the jukebox. Sometimes the other kids teased him about reading flying magazines. He remembered seeing a picture on the back of one of the magazines of an army pilot standing alongside a blue-and-yellow biplane, his parachute hanging down to his knees, his leather helmet flopping open, grinning broadly as he talked to a beautiful girl in a convertible.

To everyone else, it was an ad for the car, the make of which Mark could no longer remember. But to Mark, there was nothing but the plane and pilot. At the time he had tried very hard to project himself into that picture. Now he *was* that picture, minus the convertible, the beautiful girl, the sunny skies, and the broad smile.

They had real eggs for breakfast, an unexpected treat until Dusty told him that they always got real eggs on the day of a mission. "That's so the guys who crash and burn won't have to do so with powdered eggs in their bellies," he added with a morbid laugh.

Mark laughed, also, but it was a forced laugh. He didn't think there was anything funny about someone crashing and burning, whether he had powdered eggs or real eggs in his stomach.

After breakfast they reported to the Nissen hut where they would get their briefing. They had been in it before, but all previous briefings were for practice missions. That was the first time they were there for the real thing. There was a huge map on the stage in front of them, but the map was covered with a black cloth, so they couldn't see what it said.

"Ten-hut!" someone shouted, and everyone stood as Colonel Grant strolled into the hut. He moved quickly down the center aisle, then putting his hand on the front edge of the raised platform, he vaulted up onto it.

"Gentlemen," he said, "I'll be brief. Do you remember, back in the States, all the times you bombed Baltimore? That is, those of you who could find Baltimore."

There was a ripple of laughter.

"Well, what you were doing then was getting ready for the real thing. Today is the real thing. Fly tight formations, maintain the box so the gunners will have good, clear fields of fire, and any German plane that comes within one thousand yards will have to face the best gunners in the Army Air Force, the gunners of the Six-oh-fifth!"

The last comment was greeted with a rousing cheer.

"All right, pay attention now. What you hear over the next several minutes could save your life."

The first briefer told them their target, Eschwege, and stressed how important it was to knock out as many German fighters as they could on the ground. He showed them where it was on the map, then indicated that a group of B-26s would be taking off at approximately the same time, heading north, in order to draw the fighters away from Eschwege.

The second briefer assured them that flak would be no more than moderate to light-heavy, and that if their plan of diversion worked, the fighter opposition would be minimal.

The final briefer was weather, who assured them that they would have no more than three-tenths cloud cover, so the bombardiers should be able to see their targets with no difficulty.

Colonel Todaro was last. He gave them engine-start time and formation. Mark wrote the numbers he would need on the back of his hand. He would be flying right wing off the lead ship. Major Dixon's squadron was the high squadron.

As the briefing broke up, Mark noticed that many of the men began congregating in three separate groups. For a moment he wondered what it was, then he realized that they were prayer groups, led by Protestant, Catholic, and Jewish chaplains. Lee was leading one of the groups, and for just a moment, Mark considered going over to him. He decided against it, however, feeling that to do so would be hypocritical. Instead, he went over to the equipment hut to suit up.

The equipment hut was jam-packed with hundreds of crewmen, all dressing at the same time. Mark chose an electric suit over flannel because he didn't like long johns. He put on a wool OD uniform over that, then a flight suit over that. Finally he pulled on fur-lined boots and a fur-lined leather jacket. Such protection was necessary because at twenty-five thousand feet, the temperature outside the airplane would be forty degrees below zero. The Flying Fortress was not pressurized, so there was nothing to keep the cold out. It did have heaters in the cockpit, but nowhere else. And even the cockpit heaters did little to push away the cold.

For now, though, the clothes were too warm, even in the cold English morning. Mark was sweating by the time he reached the ready truck, and he lay down on the parachutes and looked up at the stars in the still-dark sky.

Finally the others came out, and the ready truck started toward the flight line, each truck carrying a crew. Dusty's crew was already at its airplane when the truck carrying Mark's crew passed, and Mark saw Dusty standing by the wheel he had done handstands on the day before. He kicked the tire once with his right foot, then with his left, and Mark smiled, wondering if that, too, was part of his ritual.

As the crew boarded *Gideon's Sword*, Mark looked into the bomb bay and saw the racks were loaded with ten five-hundred-pound bombs, five on each side. They were big, fat, ugly things, and when he reached out to touch one, he jerked his hand back as if he had touched something dead.

Engine start was at 0600, and at exactly 6:00 A.M. a white flare went up from the control tower. Mark hit the switch for number one engine. The inertia wheel started low, then built up to a high-pitched whine. Mark hit the second switch to engage, and the engine coughed, then roared to life. Two, three, and four kicked off as easily. With all four engines turning, they sat in the slightly vibrating airplane, awaiting their departure time.

Because they were the high squadron, they didn't have to wait too long. Less than five minutes after engine start, *Gideon's Sword* was at the head of the runway, waiting for the airplane in front to clear. Somewhere out alongside the runway, a jeep was parked, and in that jeep, there was a traffic director with red and green lamps. As each plane passed a certain mark, the director would signal the next plane to begin its takeoff run.

When Mark's plane trundled into position, the lamp was red, but within seconds it turned green and Mark pushed throttles and prop levers full forward. The airplane started down the runway. Paul called off the speed. In no time, it seemed, they were at 90, then 100, 110. At 120 Paul called, "Rotate!" and Mark pulled back on the yoke. The plane lifted from the runway, and the vibration and bouncing ceased.

"Gear up."

The gear drew up into the wheel wells while, on the runway behind them, yet another B-17 was starting its takeoff run.

The group floundered around for a while, with Mark having to fight

58

the rough air caused by wing and propeller vortexes, until they were finally able to form up at about eighteen thousand feet. Mark wasn't exactly sure how it happened. One minute there were airplanes everywhere, just barely managing to avoid collision, and the next they were in a perfect box formation.

Art Bollinger, the navigator, had an easy ride of it because all they had to do was follow the leader. But down in Colonel Grant's plane, Mark knew, the navigator was having to sweat bullets, verifying his checkpoints and worrying about wind drift because he had the responsibility of navigating for the entire group.

Major Dixon and the other squadron commanders were also busy, keeping their element in the right formation, constantly checking on the other planes in their squadrons to keep them in tight.

All Mark had to do was hang on to Dixon's wing, but that wasn't as easy as it looked. He could feel sweat pooling in the chin cup of his oxygen mask, and the fur lining of the boots was making his right foot itch. The itch was maddening, all the more so because he knew there was absolutely no way he could scratch it.

When Mark looked up through the greenhouse window, he saw nothing but sun glare because the window was so dirty. He made a mental note to get on to the crew chief about that.

Mark kept jockeying the throttles, moving them too far, then too little, and as a result, the Fortress was wigwagging through the sky. He knew his tail gunner was having a rough ride, bouncing and sliding around back there, especially since he was riding backward, but Tim O'Leary had a stomach of cast iron. Once, back in the States, when they were caught in a violent thunderstorm, Tim was the only one who didn't get sick.

The group flew northeast across the Channel, then cut in at the Dutch coast. They were well out in the Zuider Zee before the flak started. It was the first time Mark or anyone else on his crew had ever seen flak, and they were almost mesmerized by it. It popped in front of them, silent puffs of black in a clear blue sky.

"Well, that's not very frightening," Mark said, but he didn't key his mike, so his words died, unheard, in his mask.

"Right waist gun to pilot, fighters, three o'clock high."

"Keep an eye on 'em," Mark said.

"Wait," Paul said. "They look like P-47s."

"They are P-47s," Sergeant Richardson said from the top turret.

The friendlies passed by overhead, perhaps headed for an as yet unseen squadron of German fighters.

They flew on for another hour without encountering any more flak or fighters. Then Adrian Rogers called out from his position in the nose. "Holy cow, look up there! There's flak all over the place."

"Yeah, I see it," Mark said. Unspoken was, what was he supposed to do about it?

"Navigator to pilot, we're at the IP."

IP, *the initial point, the place at which the bomb run begins,* Mark thought. Half his job was done, for his entire purpose, until this moment, was to get the airplane here, so the bombardier could take over and drop the bombs.

"Okay, Bombardier, let me know when you want it."

"Roger," Adrian answered. "Bomb bay doors open."

Mark followed the bomber stream, holding as steady as he could.

"Let me have it," Adrian said, and Mark took his hands off the controls.

Mark was nothing but a passenger. He had no flying to do; he had no gun to fire; he could do nothing but sit there with his hands in his lap while the bombardier flew the airplane with the bombsight. It was funny because a moment earlier he wasn't the least bit nervous. As only a passenger, however, he was very nervous, and he looked everywhere, watching for the flak that he was sure would be all around them.

He saw nothing.

"Bombs away," Adrian said.

"Radioman, see if they all left the racks," Mark called.

"All away," Bird replied.

"Bomb bay doors closed," Adrian said.

Mark put the airplane into a 180-degree turn. When he did so, they saw the flak they hadn't seen earlier.

"Sweet mama, will you look at that?" Paul said.

There was still nothing particularly frightening about it, though there was an awful lot of it, hundreds upon hundreds of little black puffs mixed in with the bombers.

"Oh oh, B-17 going down at nine o'clock," Eddie Gordon said.

Looking to his left, Mark saw the B-17 fall over onto its right wing, then start down.

"Come on, you guys, get out. Bail out," Richardson said.

"There's one. He came out of the bomb bay," the right waist gunner, Gilbert Crane, said.

"Crane, are you looking out the left side? Get back over to your station," Mark ordered.

"Yes, sir."

"There's two out through the nose. Must be the bombardier and navigator."

"Tail gunner is out."

By then the plane disappeared in a low-lying cloud bank.

"Anyone see any chutes open? Charley, Tim, you two guys had the best view."

"I didn't see any chutes," Tim replied.

"No chutes," Charley Phillips said. Charley was the ball turret.

"That don't mean anything," Richardson said. "If I had to jump from up here, I probably wouldn't pull my cord until I was through the clouds either."

Shortly after that the flak stopped, and once again, they became a group of airplanes flying as if in parade formation. But Mark saw another Fortress, trailing smoke, drop out of formation and start losing altitude.

From then on, it was just a long ride back to the Channel. No more flak, no more German fighters, no more crashing B-17s.

"Group commander to all squadron commanders. I authenticate Alley Cat. I say again, I authenticate Alley Cat. Queue your airplanes so that those with wounded go first, just as soon as we cross the Channel."

The authenticator was a means of prohibiting some excellent English-talking German radio operator into giving them false orders.

Authenticators, which changed every day, were used anytime a command was given.

"Roger," the squadron commanders answered.

"Plane commanders with wounded, call in now."

Mark was surprised that six aircraft in the group called in with wounded. One of them reported that the pilot was dead and the navigator, bombardier, and copilot were badly wounded.

"Who's flying the plane?" Dixon asked.

"The copilot is flying, sir. I'm helping him. This is Dobbins, flight engineer."

"Is the copilot going to be able to get the plane home?"

Another voice, racked with pain, came on the air then. "This is Lieutenant Kirby, and yes, sir, I intend to get this plane home if I have to get out and push!"

The thought of death and destruction within the group, within the squadron even, seemed somewhat remote to Mark. He was there, and he saw the flak, but nothing had come close to Gideon's Sword.

They started letting down when they crossed the Channel. At ten thousand feet, Mark gave the okay to take off oxygen masks. When he took off his mask, pooled sweat fell from the chin cup onto his jacket.

It seemed no time at all until they were over the field at Davencourt. They had to circle while the planes with wounded landed first, but because they were high squadron, they would have been last to land anyway.

Finally it was their turn, and Paul put the gear down when they entered the downwind leg. Mark turned base, then final. On final, as he was making his descent to the runway, a tiredness suddenly came over him, more profound than any tiredness he had ever felt before. He touched down about halfway down the runway, the wheels chirping when he did so. As he taxied to the hardstand, he saw the battle damage received by some of the other bombers. There were holes everywhere: in the wings, in the fuselage, and one of them had a hole in the vertical stabilizer that was big enough for a man to walk through. He felt almost guilty that Gideon's Sword had come through unscathed.

Lee was not prepared for how difficult the mission would be for him. He had been with them in the flesh at the morning's briefing, then in spirit for the entire mission. In the operations Nissen hut, the ground exec moved little magnetized bombers across a big metal sheet map, keeping the bombers on course according to time, speed, and flight plan. He had marked areas on the map where the group would encounter their first flak, where they would encounter the most flak, and where they were most likely to encounter enemy fighters.

Lee spent the whole day at operations, just watching those magnetized bombers move slowly, ever so slowly, across that big map. He didn't go to lunch, but at about two o'clock in the afternoon, he ate a peanut butter and jelly sandwich and drank a glass of milk, provided him by Kenny.

The phone rang, and Major Ragsdale grabbed it. He said a few words that Lee couldn't hear, then he hung up the phone and looked at the others with a big smile on his face.

"Strike report," he said. "We clobbered them!"

Everyone in the operations room cheered.

"What about our casualties?" Lee asked.

The others looked at Lee in a way that made him believe he had asked an improper question, and Major Ragsdale, speaking kindly, informed him that he had.

"Chaplain, we never give casualty reports over the radio," he said. "It gives the Germans too much information."

"Oh, yes, of course," Lee said. "I'm sorry. I should have realized that."

"That's all right. It's a natural enough concern. We're all worried about it."

Not until the map board showed the airplanes actually crossing the English coast did Lee abandon the operations Nissen and go down to the flight line. Here, dozens of crash trucks, fire trucks, and ambulances were waiting, the crash crews standing by patiently. A couple of men were tossing a ball back and forth, and they tried to interest a few others in a little game of pepper but no one was willing to join in.

"I hear them," one young man with particularly good hearing said.

"There they are!" another pointed out.

Looking east, Lee saw the formation coming back, mere specks in the sky now, but rapidly growing in size. Soon he could hear them as well, as the roar of nearly two hundred engines rolled down and ahead of the formation in one huge wave of sound.

Some of the bombers broke out of the formation and started heading straight in toward the field. Flares streamed out, indicating that there were wounded on board, and from behind him, Lee could hear the emergency vehicles starting their engines. A few of them pulled away from the line and, with sirens blaring, raced out to the runway to be in position should any of the aircraft crash on landing.

One by one they landed, then came trundling off the runway. Those with wounded on board were led straight to a staging area; the others taxied, almost wearily it seemed, to their respective hardstands.

Forty-eight bombers had gone out; forty-six returned. Lee's father's plane was one of the forty-six that returned, and Lee breathed a quick prayer of thankfulness for that. Almost immediately, however, he felt guilty about limiting the prayer of thanks for his father, and he quickly amended it to include every ship that returned. Then he prayed for the two that were lost, asking for God's protection for those who may have survived, and asking Him to receive into His glory those who did not.

He walked over to Interrogation, just to be there in case anyone needed him.

7

Tunisia
February 15, 1943

In deploying the U.S. Army's Second Corps, General Fredendall violated nearly every concept of tactics. He did not share the reconnaissance gathered by one element with the other elements in his command, he bypassed his immediate subordinates to issue orders that were best left to the battalion and company commanders, and he placed his own command headquarters several miles behind the front, tunneling underground, thus depriving him of even a long-distance observation of the battlefield.

As a result of these blunders, the American Army's Second Corps was in no position to defend against a well-led German attack that successfully punched through the middle of the American lines at the Eastern Dorsal Mountain Range's Faid Pass. The Germans managed to roll the main body of American troops back, cutting off what had been their flanks, leaving one battalion trapped on the slopes of Djebel Ksaira and another battalion stranded on Djebel Lessouda, a hill on the south side of the pass. General Fredendall completely abandoned the town of Sidi Bou Zid and the Eastern Dorsal and, in so doing, left behind more than twenty-five hundred American soldiers.

The Americans mounted a counterattack the next morning, spearheading the effort with tanks of the Third Armored Battalion. Shortly after receiving word to go, the Third Armored Battalion's M-4 Sherman tanks left the highway that led to Sidi Bou Zid, then started back across the plains approaching Faid Pass.

The Shermans moved across the desert floor in perfect parade-ground formation, raising a storm of dust as they rumbled forward with seemingly unstoppable power. As commander of one of those tanks, Sergeant George Hagan was riding in his seat, his head sticking up through the open turret hatch. The hot wind whipped up a fine, powdery dust that coated his sweat-covered face, clogged his nostrils, and ground between his teeth.

Despite the discomfort, however, George thought it was the most magnificent sight he had ever seen: an entire armored battalion of tanks moving en masse in a coordinated attack against the German positions.

In front of the line of attack was their objective, the town of Sidi Bou Zid. Nearby was Djebel Ksaira ridge. American troops occupied the high ground of the ridge, while the Germans controlled the approaches and slopes.

Noticing shadows racing across the ground in front of him, George looked up to see a flight of American P-40s passing overhead at less than five hundred feet. About a mile beyond the ravines they pulled up in a high, arcing climb, then rolled over and came screaming back down, firing their machine guns at the German positions. As they pulled away, they released bombs that plummeted earthward to explode in flame and smoke on the lower slopes of Djebel Ksaira. The lead plane was followed by a second and then a third, until all twelve planes had made a pass. After that, they came around for a second pass.

Rolling off the target, the P-40s headed back from where they came, flying over the tanks so low that George could see streams of oil coming from the engines, and he could clearly see the markings on the wings and fuselage.

It seemed that the P-40s were barely gone before the Germans responded with their own air attack, sending in a squadron of JU-87s. The Stukas were frightening with their "bird of prey" gull wings, fearsome with the wailing banshee screams of their dives, and terrifying with the deadly accuracy of their bombing. Like the P-40s before them, the Stukas came, attacked, and withdrew, all in less than a minute, leaving behind them three fiercely burning American tanks.

"Holy mackerel, Sarge, look!" Mel shouted.

Looking in the direction Mel had pointed, George saw nearly fifty German tanks attacking from the left. Then, glancing toward the right, he saw another fifty.

"Uh-oh, boys, this doesn't look good," George said, closing the hatch and dropping down to observe through the little slit in the armor. "Looks like they've got us outnumbered about two to one here."

The Germans had set a trap, and the American commander had taken the bait. Like a string of flashing lights, there was a ripple of fire from the muzzles of the panzers, and almost instantly a half-dozen American tanks were hit, including the Third Armored Battalion commander.

"Mel, take that one over there!" George shouted, pointing out a target of opportunity to his gunner.

"Up," Larry said, meaning the gun was loaded.

Mel sighted on the panzer, then fired. George watched the shell hurl across the desert sand, headed for the panzer. It scored a direct hit, but instead of penetrating the thick armor, the shell bounced off and, angling up, burst about ten yards above the tank.

Like some great beast shaking off a worrisome gnat, the panzer's turret swung toward George's tank, its gunner cranking quickly to bring the tube to bear. George waited until he thought the German gunner was about to fire.

"Don, hard left, now!"

The tank pivoted on its tracks, and the shell from the German tank whizzed by, barely missing them.

"Mel, shoot again, and this time, aim for the track!"

"Up!" Larry shouted.

Mel fired a second time, and George was rewarded by seeing the

German tank lurch hard to its right as its track was separated. It could still fire, but it could no longer maneuver.

For the next several minutes, George was unable to see anything but a cloud of dust as the American and German tanks scrambled through the desert trying to find some advantage. It quickly became evident that the Germans had the benefit of numbers and position. Added to that was the fact that the German shells were able to penetrate American armor with ease, while shell after shell fired from the American seventy-fives were bouncing off the German tanks or bursting against them with very little effect.

Through the smoke and dust of battle, George could see the fires of exploding and burning tanks. From the location of the fires, it was clear that the Americans were not only losing the battle, but were also in serious danger of being completely annihilated.

"What's going on up there?" Larry asked as he shoved another shell into the breech of the gun. As the loader, Larry was the only one in the tank who had no view of the outside world. "Will somebody please tell me something!"

"Does the name Custer mean anything to you?" George shouted back down to him.

"Withdraw! Withdraw!" The command came through George's earphones. George didn't recognize the voice, but he knew that the battalion commander's tank had been hit, so someone else had stepped up.

"Don, do a one-eighty!" George said. "We've been ordered out of here."

"It's about time," Mel said. "This situation was beginning to get downright serious."

The tank pivoted around, then Don poured on the gas. "Follow that wadi," George shouted, pointing to an old dry streambed. "It'll keep us in defilade."

When at last they broke out of the din, dust, and smoke of battle, George opened the hatch and crawled up to have a look around. He wanted to find the others so he could join up with them.

"This can't be right," he said.

"What can't be right?" Larry asked. "What is it? What's going on?"

"Wow!" Mel said.

"I can't believe this," Don added.

"What? What is it you can't believe?" Larry asked again. "Will someone kindly tell me what in the Sam Hill is going on?"

"Come up here and have a look for yourself," George invited, moving to one side to give Larry room.

Larry climbed up so he could stick his head out the top of the turret. "I see only three other tanks," he said. "Where are the rest of them?"

"That's the point," George said.

"What's the point?" Larry asked, still confused.

"They're back there," Mel said, making a motion with his head toward the desert.

Looking back, Larry saw more than a hundred fires from which ropes of thick, oily black smoke roiled into the bright blue sky.

"Are all those tanks ours?" Larry asked in awe.

"Nearly all of them," George replied. "I see a couple of German tanks, but only two."

"How many did we lose?"

"We went in with fifty-four. We came back with four," George replied. "The math isn't that hard to do."

George followed the other three tanks until they reached a road where a convoy of American trucks was making up. A lieutenant colonel was standing in the back of a jeep directing traffic. He held up his hand to stop the tanks, and George watched while the high-ranking traffic cop spoke to the tank commander in the first tank.

Now that he was close enough, George recognized the tank commander as Captain Pierce. It was Pierce's voice that had ordered the withdrawal from the battlefield. Pierce's voice came through George's earphones again as he passed on the lieutenant colonel's instructions.

"He wants us interspersed in the truck convoy," Pierce said. "I'll go in first. The rest of you slip in as he tells you."

"Captain, you think it's good to break up the battalion?" one of the other tank commanders asked. George didn't recognize his voice.

"What battalion?" Pierce replied dryly as his tank pulled into position.

When it was his turn, George's tank joined the truck convoy, then they started withdrawing.

"We're retreating, aren't we?" Mel asked.

"We're running away," Don added.

"Nah," George replied. "Now, if we were doing this, it would be retreating. But the brass is doing it, so it is a strategic repositioning."

The convoy ground on across the plains of Tunisia for the rest of the day and far into the tracer-illuminated and flare-lit night. Several times during the day and on into the night German planes attacked the convoy, and the ring-mounted machine guns on the trucks and the flexible machine guns on the tanks would open up, popping loudly and spitting a long string of tracer rounds into the sky. Most of the defensive fire of the Americans was ineffective, but once, while looking toward the back, George saw a German plane trailing a thin stream of smoke as it started back toward its own lines.

It soon became obvious, however, that the German planes were having a great deal of success because throughout the long day and into the night, George continued to see burned-out American trucks and, more disturbingly, blackened American corpses.

Finally they reached the range of mountains known as the Western Dorsal. There were five passes through the Western Dorsal, and the one the Americans chose to go through was Kasserine Pass. The Americans were tired, dispirited, weakened by the loss of three entire battalions, and disorganized. But at Kasserine Pass, the convoy stopped, and the men disembarked to form a defensive perimeter.

"Sergeant Hagan?" Captain Pierce's voice came through his earphones.

"Yes, sir?"

"They want all commanding officers and executive officers for a briefing. I'm the only officer left in the battalion, and you are the highest ranking noncom, which makes you executive officer of the Third Armored Battalion. I want you to come with me."

"Yes, sir," George said. He smiled at the others in his crew. "How about this, guys? I'm the XO of this outfit."

"We ain't goin' to have to salute you, are we?" Larry asked.

A few minutes later George and Captain Pierce approached a handful of officers gathered around a small field table. There was a map on the table and Lieutenant Colonel May, the same lieutenant colonel who had been directing the traffic, was leaning over the table, looking at the map.

"Sir, this is Sergeant Hagan," Pierce said. "Right now, he's my second in command."

"All right. Captain, Sergeant, you two have just joined the artillery."

"The artillery?"

"That's how I plan to use your tanks. There will be no maneuvering."

"Yes, sir."

Colonel May pointed to the map. "Gentlemen, we are at Kasserine Pass. We have to hold them because right over here"—he pointed to another spot—"is Tebessa, our most important communications and supply base. If the Germans get through us and take that, they will have effectively eliminated the Americans in this sector. Then they could attack the Brits from the rear. We'd have to abandon Tunisia and maybe all of North Africa. I hope I'm getting the point across, gentlemen," he said. "If we don't stop them here, we are going to have to pull way, way back."

"Back to where?" one of the officers asked.

"How does Cleveland sound?"

"Right now, Colonel, it sounds mighty good to me," one of the officers said.

Colonel May frowned at him.

"Do you have a plan, sir?" another officer asked.

"Yes. See how the pass narrows here? My plan is to let the Germans come pouring in like sand through an hourglass. In the meantime, we'll be waiting for them on the west side of this narrow stricture. And because of the restriction of the pass, they won't be able to amass any more troops against us than we can have waiting for them. Captain Pierce, I want you to put two of your tanks on this side, and the other two on this side. I'm sorry to split your command that way, but I believe it will be the best way to utilize your guns."

"Yes, sir."

"All right. Get back to your men and get them ready. And remember, whatever it takes, we are going to hold this pass."

As George and Captain Pierce returned to their tanks, Pierce said, "Sergeant Hagan, once we separate I'm going to give you autonomy.

You'll be in command of your two tanks . . . or I guess I should say guns since we won't be maneuvering . . . and I'll be in charge of my two."

"Yes, sir," George replied.

Though George told his men to choose a partner so that one could sleep while the other was awake, he found that he couldn't sleep that night. He tried to, but he was too excited, nervous, frightened, or all three. Therefore, when the German panzers began pouring through the pass the next morning, he was already wide awake.

He could feel them before he could hear them, a low shaking of the ground as though he were standing beside a railroad track while a train went by. Then he could hear them, a strange combination of low-pitched engine growl and high-pitched squeaking as the tanks' tracks clanked and clattered across all the sprockets and through all the gear wheels. Finally he could see them, huge black shapes materializing in the heavy fog that had rolled in with the break of dawn.

"Larry," he called. "Larry, wake everyone up! Here they come!"

"Ain't no need to do that. Ever'body's already awake," Larry replied.

"All right, Mel, you and Larry man the gun. Don, since the tank isn't going anywhere, you'll be down here on the ground with me. We're going to be infantrymen."

Mel and Larry climbed up into the tank. A moment later, George heard the turret move as Mel was bringing his gun to bear on the approaching target.

The target was German infantrymen, approaching by the tens, scores, and hundreds. They were faceless, phantomlike figures moving through the fog, holding their weapons at high port in front of them.

"Mel?" George called up to the tank.

"Yeah?"

"You don't have to wait for any command. When you've got a target, open up."

Almost before the words were out of George's mouth, Mel opened fire. And as if using his gun for a signal, all along the American line, firing began, from the heavy thump of the tank's seventy-fives to the whoosh of the bazookas to the staccato bark of machine guns to the scattered rattle of rifles.

The Germans returned fire, and the exchange was so intense that it was one sustained roar. There was a constant flash and gleam of muzzle blasts, puffs of smoke drifting up through the fog, and fire streaks of tracers as they struck the ground, then bounced away, tumbling along their crazed path. The firing continued for a half hour, an hour, still going long after the sun had burned away the fog. By then, visibility had improved somewhat, though smoke from the discharges continued to drift across the field.

George's eyes burned from the cordite, and his throat was so dry that he could scarcely breathe, though he wasn't actually aware of being thirsty. A German round exploded nearby, and in the blast effect of the shell he got a quick glimpse of a tumbling arm. With a sickened gasp he realized that the arm wasn't attached to a body, though a watch was still on the wrist, and it flashed gold in the morning sun.

The fighting continued unabated for another half hour. Then finally the German advance stuttered, halted, and the phantom creatures proved to be human after all as they turned and started running back.

"Cease fire!" someone shouted. "Cease fire! Cease fire!" and George realized that word was being passed down the line. He, too, took up the call, and a moment later, all the guns were stilled.

"We beat them back!" Don said. "They're gone! We whipped 'em!"

"Yeah, I guess so," George said quietly.

"Hey, come on! This calls for a celebration, doesn't it?"

"More than a thousand people lost their lives here today, Don. What's there to celebrate?"

"The fact that we aren't one of them?" Don replied.

February 23, 1943

Flew our second mission today, this one to Frankfurt. Moderate flak, few fighters. Tube to Bird's oxygen mask got twisted and he passed out for lack of oxygen. The situation was noticed by Stewart Richardson, who corrected the problem and revived Bird, which was lucky for Bird because had it gone unnoticed for much longer, he would have died for lack of oxygen. Flew number six in the lead squadron.

February 26, 1943

Third mission, to the sub pens at Wilhelmshaven. Flak was very heavy. Focke-Wulfs attacked us on the way in, Messerschmitts on the way back. Four Forts lost. We picked up several holes from machine-gun bullets, but nothing vital was hit. Eddie Gordon got a Messerschmitt, and his claim has been verified. That's our first enemy a/c, and Eddie had a little swastika painted at his gun station, the way fighter pilots paint them under their canopies.

March 4, 1943

On our fourth mission we bombed the Wilton shipyard. We were supposed to be escorted by British Spitfires, but there was a foul-up somewhere on timing or something, and they didn't show up. Three Forts turned back because of mechanical problems; remaining nine continued. We were hit by approximately twenty-five Messerschmitts and Focke-Wulfs. The air battle went on for twenty minutes. Stewart in the top turret, and Charley in the ball turret, each got a fighter.

One Fort fell behind and five FW-190s closed in for the kill, shooting steadily. A 20mm cannon shell exploded on the right side of the cockpit windscreen, killing the copilot and wounding the pilot. Top turret was shot out. Despite that, the Fort made it back. It makes everyone feel good when one of them that's shot up that badly returns safely because it gives us a little more confidence in the B-17. The B-17 is one strong airplane.

8

Litchfield, Illinois
March 6, 1943

Although Harold White had already finished breakfast, he remained at the table, reading the newspaper. Edna had finished breakfast, too, but was peeling apples for a pie she was making for lunch.

"Any coffee left?" Harold asked.

"Yes, I just made a fresh pot. You know how Susan is. She can barely get her eyes open until she's had her coffee." Edna brought the pot over and poured a cup for her husband.

"If you ask me, she can't get her eyes open this morning at all," Harold said. "Seems that she should have come down by now."

"Oh, Harold, it's Saturday morning. Let her sleep," Edna said.

"No wonder young people are always complaining about not having enough time to do anything . . . they sleep half their lives away." Harold went back to reading his paper.

"If she's not down here soon, I'll go wake her."

"Listen to this," Harold said, reading from the paper. "The U.S. Navy waited forty-one days before releasing the news that the carrier *Wasp* was sunk, sixty-five days to report the loss of the cruisers *Quincy*, *Vincennes*, and *Astoria*. And the army waited six months before admitting that the Japanese had captured some of General Doolittle's fliers. So much for freedom of the press."

"That's awful," Edna said. "It makes a person wonder at what we aren't being told. For example, what about the air war over Europe? I worry about Mark all the time. His letters never complain, but I just know it is awful for him."

"He's doing what he wants to do," Harold said. "You know how he is. From the time he was old enough to talk, he has talked about airplanes."

"I know. But that doesn't keep me from worrying about him every day."

"I don't worry about him," Harold insisted.

"Then you're like an ostrich, sticking your head in the sand. It's foolish to pretend that nothing is going to happen when we both know there is a very good chance that we will get bad news someday."

"If it happens, I'll face it then," Harold said. "But to worry about it every day . . . it would be the same as his dying every day."

"I wish I could put it out of my mind like you can," Edna said. She put the paring knife down and brushed her hands together. "What is keeping that girl this morning? Maybe I had better go upstairs and wake her."

"Tell her I'm going over to see her grandmother today, and if she wants to come along, she's going to have to get a move on," Harold said as he took another sip of coffee and went back to his paper.

The Whites lived in a large two-story brick colonial-style house that had been built just before the turn of the century. Edna loved the house, which was filled with oak: oaken floors, oaken woodwork, and a wide oaken staircase. It could be especially pretty at Christmas, and when the children were younger, Christmas was always a very special time. She didn't decorate this past season, in part because they went to Virginia to visit Mark. She missed not seeing the house decorated, though, and vowed that she would definitely decorate next year.

Edna climbed the staircase, glancing toward Mark's room when she reached the upstairs landing. His room was still pretty much as he left it, pictures of airplanes, a Litchfield College pennant, and a nearly deflated football that Mark had carried for a thirty-seven-yard touch-down run against Washington University of St. Louis.

Susan's room was across the landing from Mark's. Her door was closed, and Edna tapped on it.

"Susan? Susan, Honey, aren't you going to wake up this morning? Wake up, sleepyhead."

Not getting an answer, she pushed the door open.

When Harold heard Edna scream, he jumped up so fast that he knocked over the cup of coffee, sending out a wide brown stain across the white tablecloth. He paid no attention to that, but bounded up the stairs, taking them two at a time.

"Edna! What is it?" he shouted. Angling across the landing to Susan's room, he saw Edna standing by Susan's empty bed. She was holding a letter in her hand.

"What is it? What's happened?"

Unable to speak, Edna handed Harold the letter.

Dear Mom and Dad,

By the time you read this letter, I will be married. I'm sorry it had to be this way. Mom, so often as a young girl, I dreamed of the time I would get married, and I imagined you and I planning the wedding, picking out the wedding gown, planning the flowers, the food, going over the guest list, and meeting with the minister. And Dad, I pictured myself being escorted down the aisle on your arm. How I wish it could have been so.

But it could not be. Dad would not entertain the slightest suggestion that I be married now. And Mom, when I asked you to intercede for me, you said that it was too important to Dad that I finish school. Neither you nor Dad took into consideration the fact that Bob and I were in love and wanted to get married now.

We are not getting married because we have to. We are getting married because we are in love. Perhaps if there were no war, perhaps if Bob weren't in the army, we would have the luxury of waiting. But there is a war, Bob is in the army, and we know he will be going overseas soon. God forbid that he is killed while he is over there, but if it does happen, then we owe it to ourselves to find as much happiness as we can, while we can.

Please try to understand this. I'll write to you as soon as I can.

Love,
Susan

Fort Smith, Arkansas

Susan stayed in the car while Bob knocked on the door of a very large, old white-frame house that was in need of paint. According to the newspaper, which he had rolled up under his arm, there was an apartment for rent. It was the seventh place they had checked since arriving in town this morning. Three of the others had already been rented, one was taken off the market, and the two remaining apartments were much too expensive.

As she waited, she twisted the rings on her finger, the engagement ring she had kept secret for more than four months, and the wedding band Bob had put on her finger yesterday morning in the living room of a preacher's house in Paragould, Arkansas.

Arkansas required no waiting period. Anyone empowered to marry you could fill out the wedding license and perform the ceremony, all within a few minutes. The speed and simplicity of the marriage appealed to them under the circumstances.

They also married in Arkansas because Bob's first assignment, after basic training, was Camp Chaffee located just outside Fort Smith, Arkansas. Although Camp Chaffee would just be a continuation of his training, at least here he would have the weekends off from noon on Saturday until reveille Monday morning.

The weekends off meant that he and Susan would have a day and a half out of every week together. That didn't seem like much, but both knew that there were many soldiers and their wives who were separated by thousands of miles. Indeed, Bob and Susan realized that they, too, would soon be separated by thousands of miles. Therefore, they were willing to take whatever time they could have—provided they could find someplace to live.

The door to the house opened, and she watched as Bob stood on the porch talking to someone. Because of the darkness just inside the door, however, she couldn't see the person he was talking to. Susan sat in the car, saying a little prayer that the apartment would still be available and affordable, then she saw Bob smile broadly and turn toward her. He motioned for her to come on.

Feeling a little surge of excitement, Susan got out of the car and walked up the flagstone walkway to the front of the house.

"Mrs. Meyer, this is my wife, Susan. Susan, Mrs. Meyer."

"Joyce Meyer. How do you do, Honey?"

If Susan had to, she didn't think she would be able to guess within ten years of Mrs. Meyer's age. She could have been anywhere from thirty to fifty. She wore her ash-blonde hair tied back in a knot, and her rather stout frame was covered by a shapeless gray dress. She was wearing lace-up shoes and white socks.

"They have a place in the back," Bob said excitedly. "And get this. It's not an apartment. It's an entirely separate house."

"Well, it's more a cabin, really," Mrs. Meyer said. "Willie Mae used to live there. Willie Mae was our colored maid, but she doesn't work full-time anymore, so she's got her own house out in the bottoms. And what with the war and all, Amon figured why not rent the place out? I mean there's lots of nice young folks needin' a place to stay."

The front porch wrapped around to the right side of the house, then stretched all the way to the back. The porch was filled with wicker furniture, settees, chairs, ottomans, and tables. There was also a big swing at the corner of the porch, hung in a way to allow anyone sitting in it to look down both legs of the porch. Flowerless wisteria dangled from a trellis, while hydrangea bushes, not yet in bloom, billowed up from the ground around the porch. To one side was a garden filled with azaleas and crepe myrtles.

"Oh, I'll bet it is just lovely here when everything is in bloom," Susan said.

"It is," Mrs. Meyer said. "Amon's mama planted all the flowers."

"She has quite a green thumb."

"Yes, she did," Mrs. Meyer said. "Bless her soul, she went to be with the Lord two years ago. Ah, here's the cabin."

The smile left Susan's face, and she felt a sinking sensation in the pit of her stomach. The cabin was very small, built of unpainted, weathered wood. The front of it was so covered in morning glory vines that she could barely make out the door and the window. She had never seen anything so gloomy-looking in her life.

"It doesn't bother you that a colored woman once lived here, does it?"

"What?" Susan asked weakly. She was still trying to get used to the cabin. "Oh, uh, no."

"I didn't think it would, you bein' Yankee and all. You are a Yankee, aren't you?"

"A Yankee?"

"From up nawth."

"Oh, uh, yes. From Illinois."

"Uh-huh, I thought so, soon as I heard you talkin'. Like I said, our maid lived here, but black or white there's no sweeter person on the face of this earth than Willie Mae Jenkins. She has a grandson named Lorenzo, who's learning to fly airplanes at that colored college down in Tuskegee. I hope he does all right. He's such a nice boy."

"What's the house like inside?" Bob asked.

Mrs. Meyer snapped her fingers. "My goodness, what has happened to my mind? I came out here and plumb forgot the key. Y'all just wait here a moment an' I'll run back into the house an' get it."

"Oh, Bob," Susan said quietly. "This . . . this place." She shook her head.

"It might not be so bad," Bob said.

"Bad? It's awful."

Bob put his arms around her, pulled her to him, and sighed. "You're right," he said. "It's awful."

"There was nothing else in the paper, was there?"

Bob shook his head. "Nothing we can afford."

"Then we have no choice. We have to take it."

"No, we . . ."

"Here's the key," Mrs. Meyer said, returning at that moment. She walked ahead of them, then climbed up the two steps to the front porch, pushing morning glory vines aside as she did so. "Kind of walk up the steps where they're braced," she said. "The wood's so old, I wouldn't be surprised if it wouldn't break through on you."

When Mrs. Meyer pushed the door open, Susan expected to see a room full of dust, but to her pleasant surprise, there was none.

"Soon as we got it in our minds to rent this place, Amon and I came out here and cleaned it real good. I think it turned out just real cozy."

Though small, the inside was much nicer than the outside. Originally a one-room cabin, an L-shaped wall had been put up to divide it into two rooms. The front of the L formed an entry foyer, with a closet to one side. The inside of the L could be called a bedroom since it was filled, literally, with a bed. On the outside of the L was the rest of the house, a tiny living-dining area with a sofa and a dining table. There were no chairs; rather, there was a bench that could be pushed up under the table to make room when it wasn't being used. A narrow counter separated the living-dining room from a very tiny kitchen area. The kitchen was equipped with a very small sink and counter, a two-burner hot plate, and an icebox.

"The iceman runs regular," Mrs. Meyer said when she saw Susan looking at the icebox. "And it doesn't take much ice for that to keep things just real cool. There's no oven, but if you got a need to bake somethin', well, you're welcome to use ours from time to time."

"Is there a bathroom?" Bob asked.

"Oh, yes indeedy," Mrs. Meyer replied. "It's right there off the bedroom."

Mrs. Meyer pointed to what Susan had thought was a closet. The bathroom was little larger than a phone booth. The walls were completely covered with tin so that the entire room became the shower. The toilet bowl was inside the shower.

"The good thing about this is, you don't ever have to clean the toilet," Mrs. Meyer said with a little laugh. "'Cause ever' time you take a shower, why it just naturally cleans the toilet at the same time. Course, it doesn't have a lavatory basin, but there's no reason why you couldn't use the kitchen sink or a wash pan. Law, folks did that for years before there were bathrooms."

Bob turned the shower on, and after a few rattles in the pipe, the water started.

"There's no hot water," Mrs. Meyer said. "But if you're like most soldiers' families that come, why, you won't be here come next winter anyhow. And in the summertime down here in Fort Smith, you don't really need hot water."

"How much is it?" Bob asked.

"Twenty-five dollars a month," Mrs. Meyer said. "All our friends say we could get a lot more, but I say trying to gouge our soldier boys like that wouldn't be very patriotic. Not only that, it wouldn't be Christian."

There was a moment of silence, then Mrs. Meyer said, "Why don't I just step outside and let you two nice folks talk about it a bit?"

After she was gone, Bob looked at Susan. "Honey, we don't have to take this," he said.

"If we don't take it, what will we do?"

"If we can't find anything before I have to report to duty tomorrow morning, you can stay in a hotel for a week, then we'll look again next weekend."

"Oh, Bob, it would cost a fortune to stay in a hotel for a whole week."

"I don't care. If that's what it takes, we'll . . ."

Susan put her finger on his lips. "Hush," she said softly. "I think this place is sort of sweet. And you watch, I'll have it looking just real pretty in no time."

Bob grinned broadly. "Honey, just having you here is going to make it pretty enough for me. Call Mrs. Meyer in, and tell her we'll take it."

Near Tuskegee, Alabama

The Stearman trainer that Aviation Cadet Lorenzo Jenkins was flying coughed once, then the engine stopped turning. Now, with no place to go but down, Lorenzo had to look for someplace to put it. He was losing altitude rapidly and was barely lined up with a cotton field when he found himself slipping down into it.

The biplane's wheels snapped off the top strand of a barbed-wire fence, and the loud twang could be heard easily above the sound of the slipstream and the windmilling prop. The landing gear began to slap against the cotton plants, and the leaves and twigs thumped into the lower wing and fuselage. Finally the tires dug into the soft earth, and the aircraft tipped onto its nose, then rolled on over onto its back as gently as if being placed down by a giant hand.

Lorenzo unbuckled his seat belt and shoulder harness and fell to the ground, then rolled away quickly in case there was a fire. He stood there looking at the airplane for a few minutes then, convinced there was no immediate danger, crawled back into the cockpit to turn off all switches and shut off the fuel. That done, he picked up his parachute and walked back to the edge of the field. A young white woman was standing there, looking at him through eyes that were wide with awe.

"Why . . . you're a *colored* boy," the girl said.

The girl, who was pulling a long sack half full of cotton, looked to be eighteen or nineteen. She had red hair and green eyes and a spray of freckles across her nose.

"Yes, ma'am," Lorenzo said. "Would you happen to know where the nearest phone is?"

"I never knew colored boys could fly airplanes," she said.

"Yes, well, this colored boy doesn't seem to be doing all that well," Lorenzo said, looking back ruefully at the wrecked aircraft.

"Are you hurt?" the girl asked.

"I'm not hurt, but I do have to get to a phone. I need to call the base."

"My pa don't have a phone," the girl said. "There's one down at Dooley's Grocery Store. That's about seven miles from here."

Lorenzo looked around the field. He and the girl were the only ones there.

"You picking this field all by yourself?" he asked.

"Yes. Pa moved ever'one else over to the north field. He kept me here 'cause I'm the best there is at cleanin' out the culls."

"What's your pa paying?"

"Two cents a pound."

"You can't make much in this field, culling at two cents a pound."

The girl cocked her head and studied him. "You know cotton pickin'?"

"I've picked a few bales back in Arkansas," Lorenzo said.

"I thought maybe you had. You want some water? There's a couple of Mason jars over to the fence 'neath that tow sack. The empty one is the colored one, but I'll pour you some water into it outta mine if you want. The ice is all melted, but it's still cool enough to drink."

"Thanks," Lorenzo said, and they started toward the fence. When they got there, the girl got down on her knees and took her jar of water from under a small piece of burlap bag, poured a generous portion into the other jar, then handed it up to Lorenzo. He drank it, then wiped his mouth with the back of his hand and gave the empty jar back to her.

"Whatever are you doin' with that airplane?" the girl asked. "Did you steal it?"

"Steal it?" Lorenzo repeated, surprised by the question.

"I ain't never heard of no colored man flyin' an airplane before," the girl said.

"It would be kind of hard to steal a plane, don't you think?" Lorenzo asked. "I mean, you would have to learn to fly first. If you stole it without knowing how to fly it, you'd crash."

"Well?" the girl asked. "What do you think you just done?"

Lorenzo laughed. "Yes, I see what you mean," he said.

"Oh, here comes my pa," the girl said. "He musta seen you come down in our field."

Looking around, Lorenzo saw a pickup truck driving quickly up the dirt road that ran adjacent to the field. The truck was throwing up a billowing rooster tail of dust. Lorenzo climbed over the fence, then stood there until the truck stopped.

"What's your pa's name?" Lorenzo asked the girl as the driver got out.

"It's Mr. Montgomery," the girl replied.

Mr. Montgomery, who looked to be in his late forties or early fifties, had a red blotchy face and brown stringy hair.

"You the fella that crashed that airplane in my field?" he asked.

"Yes, sir. My name is Aviation Cadet Jenkins."

"Aviation Cadet, huh? Then you must be one of them colored boys they're tryin' to learn to fly over at Tuskegee."

"Yes, sir, I am."

"Well, I told 'em it wouldn't work," Montgomery said. He took a chew of tobacco. "You can train colored folks to do lots of things, but you can't train 'em to fly." He looked at the parachute. "Is that one of them parachutes you use to jump out of a plane?"

"Yes, sir."

Montgomery leaned over for a closer look. "I ain't never seen one before," he said.

Lorenzo showed him the D ring. "If you have to jump, you pull on this, and the chute will open."

"You ever had to do that?"

"No, sir."

Montgomery straightened up, then spit out a squirt of tobacco juice. "Well, even if I don't think colored boys can be learned to fly, I do give you credit for havin' the courage to try," he said. "I reckon you'll be wantin' to call up the army and tell 'em what happened."

"Yes, sir, if you could tell me which way to walk to find a phone."

"Ain't no need in you havin' to walk that far, especially carrying that parachute and all. Besides, you are one of our army boys, even if you are colored. Climb up into the back of the truck. I'll carry you down to Dooley's, then I'll see to it that he lets you use the phone."

"Thank you, sir, I appreciate that," Lorenzo said, throwing his chute into the back of the truck, then climbing up to sit beside it.

"Lou Ann, you ain't got this field near half culled out," Montgomery called back over his shoulder as he walked around to the cab of the truck. "Get back to work."

"I'm goin' to, Pa," Lou Ann replied.

Montgomery drove away. Lorenzo sat in the back, and through the billowing dust, he could see Lou Ann still standing there, just watching them until the truck was completely out of sight.

March 25, 1943

Fifth mission. Flew number two on the lead ship in a formation of thirty-six. Our target was oil refinery at Merseburg.

This was our most difficult mission to date. From the moment we crossed the French coast the enemy fighters were on us. We were without fighter escort, and FWs and MEs harassed us all the way to the target and all the way back to the French coast. Tail of Miller's ship shot off. Very sickening sight. Lost six Forts. When we returned, my crew chief told me Gideon's Sword had ninety-three bullet punctures. There was one in the window frame only three inches from my head, but I didn't know about it until we were safely on the ground. I'm glad I didn't know about it. Mission was seven hours and forty-five minutes.

March 27, 1943

Our sixth mission was supposed to be over Merseburg. When we took off, weather said there would be a break in the cloud cover by the time we got there, but shortly after crossing the Channel we were called back. The weather didn't break. The brass were disappointed that we couldn't complete the mission, but it adds to our count, so we weren't all that upset.

April 12, 1943

For our seventh mission we returned to Merseburg. German fighters attacked in strength. They came in so close together that by the time one fighter had completed its attack and pulled away, the second was there, then the third, etc. We sustained no damage, though the formation did lose four B-17s.

On the way back, oil pressure dropped to zero on number four engine, and I had to shut it down. We had no difficulty staying with the formation, though, and landed with number four feathered. Turns out it was a broken oil line. Sergeant McMurtry said it got too brittle in the forty below zero cold. It's a wonder that doesn't happen every flight.

April 15, 1943

Our eighth mission was a breeze. We bombed German troop concentrations at Le Trait. No enemy fighters, no flak. I wish all of them could have been like this. Crossing the Channel on the way back I heard the unexpected sound of machine-gun firing. When I inquired as to what the shooting was about, I was informed that Eddie Gordon, in the left waist, had bet Ross Bird, our radio operator, that he could shoot down a seagull. Eddie lost the bet.

April 25, 1943

Mission number nine. A Sunday mission. Somehow it doesn't seem right bombing on Sundays. This was a hard one. We bombed the locomotive and steel factories at Lille. Flak was heavy and accurate. Paul asked what I thought about dropping bombs on French civilians. The French are innocent victims of the war; they didn't start it. But their factories are being used to produce war matériel for Germany, and we have no choice. We're trying to concentrate on the military targets, and my hope is that casualties among the French are kept to a minimum.

Six Forts lost on this raid. Of the forty-eight original crews who made the flight over from Langley Field, sixteen have now gone down. I've lost some good friends: Dan Lamdin, Warren Branchfield, Ray Lumsden, Walt Morris, Bob Bostic, and Jimmy Winsome, among others. Bob and I used to play tennis back at Langley. Ray had been a cop in New York and was full of wonderful stories about life on the beat. Jimmy was an all-conference running back from the University of Illinois, and I could remember watching him play. All were decent, God-fearing, productive young men, and they are gone now. Gone, too, are the men and women who would have been their children; men and women who, no doubt, would have made valuable contributions to society in the next generation.

Have we denied ourselves a cure to cancer, a future Beethoven, Rembrandt, or Mark Twain because they were not even allowed to be born? When one figures the total cost of this war, it is staggering, with implications that could reach hundreds of years into the future.

Everyone is getting more and more scared before every mission now, and our chaplain, Lee Grant, is getting a lot of business, trying to soothe frazzled nerves. I wish I believed that Lee's kind of religious counseling would help me because if I thought it would, I would be first in line to see him.

9

Newport News, Virginia
April 30, 1943

E mily sat in the lunchroom of the shipbuilding company, reading her
latest letter from Mark. Like the other letters she had received from
him, this was what they called a V-mail letter, a small yellow page that
contained not his original writing, but a reproduced copy. Emily once read
an article explaining that by photographing the letters and putting them
on microfilm before shipping, two tons of mail could be reduced to just
forty-five pounds. Once the microfilm reached its destination, the microfilm was developed and printed on a small yellow page, then put in a little
yellow envelope. Because they sometimes came out of sequence, they had
started numbering their letters to each other. The one she was reading
now was number eleven, though she had not yet received nine and ten.

Dear Emily,
    I've flown (this part censored) missions now. By the time you receive
this, I expect it will be more. (this part censored) but I don't think (this
part censored).

I received a bit of unexpected news in the mail recently. You remember meeting my sister, Susan, at the Christmas party back at (this part censored). She wrote me that she and Bob Gary are to be married as soon as he completes basic. She asked me to say nothing about it to Mom and Dad, as they don't know about it, and she is certain they wouldn't approve. I imagine by now, or certainly by the time you receive this letter, Susan will already be married.

If I had been there, I would have tried to talk her out of it. It's not that I don't agree with her marrying Bob. Bob is a fine man, and I will be proud to have him for a brother-in-law. But I do wish he and Susan had been able to show a little more patience. I believe Mom and Dad could have been brought around. It's going to be tough enough for Susan with Bob away, and without Mom and Dad's support, it is going to be even tougher.

On the other hand, I have a certain degree of admiration for their spirit. I must confess that there have been times since I came over here that I have thought of our own situation and wondered what it would be like if we had married before I left. I know it would have been asking a great deal of you, and perhaps your parents would not have approved. I know I would not want to do anything to make the situation between you and your parents uncomfortable, so it is probably just as well that we didn't do anything foolish.

You remember meeting Lee Grant, the chaplain. I have to say that he has become a very close friend and I enjoy talking to him, but he is a very busy man. He is the (this part censored) and because (this part censored) monopolize his time. I feel like I'm robbing the men of their need for the spiritual comfort he can provide, so I ration the time I spend with him. However, I do visit with him as much as I feel is appropriate because unlike the other men, I'm not demanding anything from him. With me he doesn't have to be "on," and I think he not only appreciates that, but probably needs the respite.

Sometimes on the long flights, between checking cylinder head temperature, adjusting the propeller trim, watching manifold pressure and RPM, measuring fuel flow, keeping an eye on carb heat, maintaining altitude, heading, and airspeed, keeping the formation tight, monitoring the command radio frequency, and computing weight and balance, a person has time to think . . . to daydream actually. And one of my daydreams is of you and me coming through the chapel door at (this part censored), then passing under an arch of swords, having just been married by Lee.

Of course, I'm getting a little ahead of myself with such daydreams. So far I haven't even worked up the courage to ask you to marry me.

Love,

Mark

"Ah, there you are," one of the other girls who worked at the shipyard said, coming into the lunchroom.

"Hi, Midge," Emily said, folding the letter and putting it away. This wasn't the first time she had read it, and it wouldn't be the last, especially since this was the first letter in which he had actually mentioned marriage.

"A letter from your beau?" Midge asked.

"Yes."

"From the smile on your face, I'd say it was a good one."

"I'd say it was," Emily replied.

"Oh, I nearly forgot, Bull . . . uh . . . that is, your father . . . was looking for you a while ago. Have you seen him yet?"

"No, I haven't. I wonder what he wants."

"Oh, he probably just wants you to do double the work in half the time," Midge said, teasing about Bull's frequent exhortations to the work staff to do more to help the war effort.

"Oh, my!" Emily said. "I hope he hasn't gotten some bad news about George."

The smile left Midge's face. "Oh, dear, I hadn't thought of that," she said. "I hope everything is all right."

Feeling frightened now, Emily hurried toward her father's office.

Zelda MacIntyre, Bull Hagan's secretary, had been employed by the shipyard long before any of the other women. In fact, she had been there longer than just about any man, and the standing joke was that when the Confederate navy converted the *Merrimac* into the iron-clad *Virginia*, it was Zelda who handled the paperwork. She looked up from her desk as Emily arrived.

"You can go on in, Miss Hagan. Your father is expecting you," the secretary said.

Still worried, Emily started toward her father's office, but a sudden outbreak of laughter from just inside calmed her fears. She didn't know what it was about, but she knew that her father wouldn't be laughing if he had bad news to impart. On the other hand, if other people were in there, he surely didn't expect her. She looked back at Zelda.

"You're sure it's okay to go in now?"

"Oh, yes, he said to send you in as soon as I could find you."

Hesitantly Emily pushed open the door.

"Come on in, Emily," Bull Hagan called. "Here she is, boys," he said to his visitors. "One of the three most beautiful Rosie the Riveters in the entire war effort."

"What?" Emily asked. "Dad, what is this?"

"Do you remember when that photographer was here several weeks ago, getting pictures of our people at work?"

"Yes. I believe he said he was doing a story for a magazine."

"Indeed he *was* doing a story for a magazine, Miss Hagan. Our magazine," one of the men visitors said. Like the other two who were visiting her father, he was wearing a suit and tie. That made them stand out, for a suit and tie was unusual attire for the shipyard. "I'm Tucker O'Neal, publisher of *Home Front* magazine. You have seen our magazine, haven't you?"

"Yes, of course. It's a very nice magazine."

"We specialize in publishing articles, stories, and photographs that we feel our fighting men overseas will like," O'Neal said. "You know, to give them a feel of what it's like back home."

"And you're doing a story about our shipyard? That will be nice."

"Well, not exactly," O'Neal said. "What we are doing is a story about women in the factories, helping our war effort by producing our war matériel. 'A Date with Rosie the Riveter,' we're calling the story. And you are one of our featured Rosie the Riveters."

Emily held up her finger and shook her head. "I'm very flattered, but you understand I'm not really a riveter. I work in accounting."

O'Neal waved his hand. "That doesn't matter. It's all one and the same as far as our boys overseas are concerned."

"Here is the good part, Emily," Bull said. "Of all the girls they photographed, they selected the three most beautiful. And you are one of those three."

"You might be interested in knowing that we chose them in no specific order. We just said the most beautiful three," O'Neal said.

"Well, I don't know what to say. I'm flattered, of course."

"Say you will accept our offer," one of the other two said.

"Offer?"

"I'm Peter Varnum. This is Donnie Fritz."

"Donnie Fritz?" Donnie Fritz was star of stage, screen, and radio. He was a comedian who was best known for his ability to poke fun at the powerful. He was also a dancer with the unique ability to appear to be making awkward and ungainly moves that he could turn, on a dime, to a very graceful routine. "Oh, my!" Emily said, recognizing him now. "I thought you looked familiar. You are *the* Donnie Fritz, aren't you?"

"I won't lay claim to being the only man in the country named Donnie Fritz," Donnie said. He smiled broadly. "But right now, I'm the only Donnie Fritz in this room."

"He certainly is *the* Donnie Fritz," Varnum said. "And we are very pleased to have him with us."

"We?"

"I'm with the United Service Organizations. The USO."

"The USO. Yes, I know about the USO," Emily said. "You're the people who run the clubs by the bases so the soldiers and sailors will have someplace to go."

Varnum laughed. "Yes, that's true," he said. "And we are also the people who put together the USO shows that go around the bases here in America and to our bases overseas."

"You mean like Bob Hope?"

"Bob Hope?" Fritz quipped. "Bob Hope? Who is he? Is that someone I should know?"

"Don't you know who Bob Hope is? He's . . . ," Emily started, then seeing the big smile on Fritz's face, she realized he was teasing her. "You're pulling my leg, aren't you?"

"Yes, and what a lovely leg it is too," Fritz said.

"Bob Hope has done some wonderful things for us and for our servicemen with his shows," Varnum said. "At any given time we have several USO shows touring the world. When I said how pleased we were to have Donnie Fritz with us, I was talking about the fact that he is in the process of putting a new show together for us right now. He will be going to North Africa and England."

"Oh, how wonderful," Emily said. "I'm sure you'll be a big hit with the men."

"So will you," Fritz said.

"So will I? What do you mean?"

"I would like you to be a part of my show."

"Me? But what can I do? I have no talent. I can't act or sing."

"Don't worry about that. My writers will come up with something that will be a snap for you and the other two girls," Fritz assured her.

"The other two girls?"

"We found a young lady named Norma Jean Thompson working for Boeing in Seattle, and another named Betty Brubaker assembling antitank shells in New Jersey," Varnum said. "And like you, they were selected as one of the three most beautiful Rosie the Riveters."

"I want to use the three of you in a special skit," Fritz said.

"What sort of skit would that be?"

"I asked the same thing, Emily," Bull said. "Mr. Fritz has assured me it will be in very good taste."

"Dad, are you saying you want me to do this?"

"I want you to do what you want to do," Bull replied.

Emily looked at Fritz. "Mr. Varnum said the show is going to England. Will you be visiting the air bases?"

"Absolutely," Fritz said.

"Then I would like to go, but what about my work here?" Emily asked her father.

"We can cover for you while you're gone," Bull said. "And I've already talked to the people upstairs. They feel that it will be very good publicity for the company. They are all for it."

"You asked them before you even knew I would go?"

"Honey, as soon as I heard that they would be touring the air bases

94

in England, I knew there would be no holding you back," Bull said, laughing.

"When do we leave?" Emily asked Fritz.

"We plan to leave New York in about six weeks. But we want you in the city at least three weeks before we depart. If my writers are going to be able to come up with a skit, they are going to need you and the other two girls for rehearsals," Fritz said.

"Also, Miss Hagan, if you have no objections, and I'm sure you won't since the other two girls have already agreed, *Home Front* magazine will be doing a feature story about this whole experience," Tucker O'Neal said. "We'll start with pictures of you working here, then traveling to New York where you will join up with the USO show, then your rehearsals, and finally we're going to send our reporter and photographer overseas to get pictures of you three girls actually doing your act."

"Sure, that's fine with me," Emily said.

"Get with Allen," Bull said to his daughter. "Tell him what you are working on now, so he can reschedule it."

"Okay," Emily said. She started toward the door, then smiling broadly, she turned back to O'Neal, Varnum, and Fritz. "And thanks. Thank you very much."

"Emily?" Bull called.

"Yes?"

"I know you're excited about the chance to see your boyfriend in England. But you won't forget that you have a brother in North Africa, will you?"

"I won't forget," Emily promised.

10

Davencourt
May 5, 1943

Although chapel services were held in the Davencourt chapel, the Anglican diocese that was responsible for the little church had requested that no military operations of any kind be conducted from within the church. "No military operations of any kind" included the chaplain's administrative office. Because of that, Lee's office had to be located somewhere else, and the officer in charge of billeting and buildings chose the rear portion of the Nissen hut that belonged to the meteorology section.

There were some wags who insisted that the chaplain's office was there so meteorology could ask him to intercede with a higher power whenever better weather was needed. In truth, it was chosen because that was the only space available that was large enough for an office, a counseling room, and the chaplain's private quarters.

Corporal Kenny Gates did not bunk in the chaplain's office, but was quartered in the staff enlisted barracks about a quarter of a mile away. Kenny did have his desk here, though, as well as a telephone, a typewriter, and a mimeograph machine. The mimeograph machine was used to print the pew sheets for each Sunday service.

Lee made a point of letting it be known that his office did have a private counseling room, and he was always available to anyone who needed him, day or night. Since there were several officers and men at Davencourt who took advantage of that offer, Lee received a constant stream of visitors. Some came to share their latest letter from home—the joy of being a father, the heartache of receiving a Dear John letter, the pride of being the big brother or an uncle of a high school athlete. But Lee suspected that most of them came simply because they were afraid.

Fear was universal and palpable. It could be seen in the faces of the men as they queued up for chow. It could be felt in the earnestness of their Sunday morning prayers. It was an invisible presence at any gathering, from pre-mission briefings to suiting up to post-mission interrogations. It was even present at the intramural softball and basketball games.

"Daylight precision bombing," Major Dixon scoffed during a visit with Lee. "Ha, if that isn't the biggest hoax the U.S. military has ever tried to put over on the people of America. I remember reading that the high brass guaranteed the American people that we could drop a bomb in a pickle barrel from twenty-five thousand feet. Well, I can tell you with absolute certainty that the only thing we are guaranteed to hit from twenty-five thousand feet is the ground."

Mark White was also a frequent guest, but Mark's visits were different. There was no doubt in Lee's mind that Mark was also frightened, just as frightened as everyone else. But he didn't share his fears or even his observations about the nine missions he had already flown. Lee regretted that. Mark was probably his closest friend over here, and it was a great disappointment to him that he was unable to help Mark the way he was certain he had helped the others.

Ironically Mark helped Lee; like the aviators, Lee was under stress. Lee sweated every mission with the aircrews, standing on the apron watching as the bombers took off, keeping vigil over them while the mission was in progress, then praying the damaged airplanes, broken men, and wounded souls safely down as they returned. And though he was in no physical danger, he was under tremendous emotional strain. He needed some form of relaxation, and his theological discussions with Mark provided that release.

Mark fascinated Lee. He had never before encountered anyone who knew more about religion than Mark White, not any college professor or any member of the clergy. And yet, for all Mark's theological expertise, he was, to all appearances, a very unreligious man.

"I am not disdainful of Christianity or any other monotheistic religion," Mark said one day as he sat in Lee's office eating vanilla ice cream and chocolate sauce. "I think Christian churches of all denominations serve a useful purpose. It's just that I find them too simple."

"What do you mean by too simple?"

"They are basically models for moralistic behavior. And that's very good. I readily concede that mankind needs a model. But for the thinking man, religion does nothing to roll away the mystery. I mean, come on, heaven is paved with streets of gold? Heaven is much more complicated than that. It is the survival of the soul, embedded in God's memory. It is the shared experience of universal cognizance. It is . . ." Mark paused in midsentence and looked at the ice cream he was eating, then with an expression of surprise on his face he said, "Heaven is this ice cream and chocolate sauce. Lee, where on earth did you get this? We haven't had ice cream in the mess hall since we arrived."

"My chaplain's assistant came up with it yesterday," Lee replied. "He also came up with a freezer so I could keep it. He said he thought it might be appreciated by the aircrews."

"Appreciated by the aircrews? Once word of this gets out, you won't be able to keep them away. You say Corporal Gates came up with it?"

"Yes."

Mark shook his head. "You better hang on to that boy as long as you can. Though if he can come up with things like ice cream and freezers, he may wind up in the stockade."

"Don't think I haven't considered that possibility."

"Where is he now?"

"He's gone to High Wycombe to deliver some reports for me," Lee said.

When Corporal Kenny Gates left the PINETREE headquarters building at High Wycombe in Buckinghamshire, he saw a couple of military policemen standing near his jeep.

"Something I can do for you fellas?" Kenny asked as he began to unlock the chain he had passed through the steering wheel.

"You have a trip dispatch for this vehicle, Corporal?" one of the MPs, a sergeant, asked.

"I do," Kenny said, pulling a trip ticket from his jacket pocket. He showed the dispatch to the sergeant.

"Did you know this dispatch is nearly thirty days old?" the sergeant asked.

"Of course, I know. This is a staff vehicle. I only need to get it dispatched once a month."

"Staff?"

"The Six-oh-fifth Heavy Bombardment Group. We're at Davencourt."

"I know where you are," the MP sergeant said with a snarl. He looked at his clipboard, comparing the bumper number on the jeep with several numbers he had listed. "I don't see your bumper number here," he said, shaking his head.

"What do you mean here? What 'here' are you talking about?"

"Orders from PINETREE," the MP sergeant said. "Only those jeeps whose numbers are listed on this here report are authorized to be dispatched. All other jeeps will be confiscated for redistribution. Sorry, Mac, I'm going to have to take your quarter-ton."

"What? You're not serious! You're going to take my boss's jeep? He's not going to like that. And believe me, he isn't someone you want to make mad."

"Who do you work for?"

"You see the name there, don't you?" Kenny said. "It's Grant."

"Grant?"

"As in commanding officer of the Six-oh-fifth?"

"Colonel Grant?"

Kenny cleared his throat as he said, "Lieutenant," nearly covering up the word so it couldn't be understood.

"What? I didn't understand you," the MP sergeant said.

"Lieutenant," Kenny said again, not coughing this time, but saying the word very quietly.

The sergeant laughed out loud. "Your boss is a lieutenant? Ooh, and I don't want to get your . . . lieutenant . . . mad at me?"

"Hey, Bud, get this," the corporal said, looking at the dispatch. "Not only is his officer just a lieutenant, but he's a chaplain."

Both MPs laughed.

"Good try, Corporal Gates," the MP sergeant said. "But you don't win no cigar."

"If you take my jeep, how'm I supposed to get back to Davencourt?" Kenny asked.

"Ever heard of shank's mare?" the MP sergeant replied.

"Shank's mare? No, never heard of it."

"It means walk, Corporal."

"Are you kidding? It's thirty miles back to Davencourt."

"Better get started," the MP corporal said, laughing at Kenny's plight.

"Here's a receipt so you can show your . . . chaplain . . . what happened to his jeep," the sergeant said, filling out a form and handing it to Kenny. "Corporal Denton, take the jeep back to the headquarters motor pool. I'll follow you."

"Right," Corporal Denton said, climbing into the jeep. He started it, backed out, then waited while the sergeant returned to the MP jeep. Kenny just stood there, watching them both drive away, feeling a little sick inside.

What was he going to tell the lieutenant? And on a more immediate level, how would he get back?

The problem of getting back was solved right away, for even as his jeep was still in sight, he spotted a fuel truck with 605th bumper markings.

"Hey! Six-oh-fifth!" he shouted. The fuel truck driver put on his brakes, and Kenny hurried over to him. "I need a ride back to Davencourt."

"Sure, Mac," the driver replied. "Hop in."

Kenny told Lee about losing the jeep, then he dug through a pile of papers on his desk until he found what he was looking for.

"This will explain it," he said.

Lee looked at the paper quietly for a long moment, then he looked up at his corporal. "When did we get this?" he asked.

"A couple of weeks ago, sir," Kenny replied contritely.

Lee began to read aloud. "It says, and I quote, 'Due to Project Bolero, the rapid buildup of the Eighth Air Force, we have encountered an unexpected shortage of quarter-ton and three-quarter-ton vehicles. Effective immediately, only commanding officers and staff officers in the rank of lieutenant colonel or higher are authorized quarter-ton vehicles.'" Lee looked at Kenny. "Correct me if I'm wrong, but a quarter-ton vehicle is a jeep?"

"Yes, sir."

"Did you read this?"

"Yes, sir, I read it when we got it."

"But you didn't think it was important enough to show it to me?"

"To tell the truth, Lieutenant, I didn't really think it referred to us."

"You didn't think it referred to us? How could it not have referred to us? It may have escaped your notice, Corporal, but I am neither a commanding officer nor a lieutenant colonel," Lee said, trying not very successfully to be stern.

Kenny brushed a shock of hair back from his face. "I know that, sir, but me 'n' you, we're doin' the Lord's work, aren't we? Seems to me like that should exempt us from the order."

With a sigh, Lee laid the distribution form down. "As you can see, it didn't."

"It should have. How you goin' to do what needs to be done?"

"The Lord did all right, didn't He? And I don't think I've ever seen any mention in the Scripture of a jeep."

"Yeah, but think of how much more He could've done if He had had a jeep."

Lee laughed out loud. "That's outlandish. In fact, I don't know but what it isn't heresy."

"Heresy to an Episcopalian like you maybe, but to a good ol' Southern Baptist boy like me, why, it's just common sense."

May 8, 1943

    Mission number ten, a diversion mission to Cayeux. No flak, no fighters. I let Paul fly the entire mission. He has a really good touch on the controls, and by rights should have his own airplane, especially as we are now getting new, green crews to replace the crews we've lost.

11

Davencourt
May 8, 1943

I t had been a very easy mission in which only one squadron of the
605th had participated. They took off early in the morning to provide a diversion for a much larger formation that was striking deep into
Germany. Major Dixon's squadron flew north along the coast, then
crossed the Channel and flew into Holland in an attempt to draw
German fighters away from the main effort.

Mark didn't know how successful their mission was, but if success was
measured in the number of enemy airplanes they were able to entice up
to challenge them, the mission would have to go down as an utter failure. They did not see one fighter for the entire trip over and back, and
the only flak they encountered was very light and ineffective, thrown
up as they passed over the coast. It was almost as if the gunners had
known there was nothing to their formation and threw the shells up just
to remind the Americans they were still there.

The postflight debriefing was as easy as the mission had been. With no enemy fighters and very little flak, there was no new intelligence the interrogating officers could get from the aircrews. After only a summary interview, they were free to return to their quarters.

Quarters, for Mark, was a twenty-by-fourteen room that he shared with his friend and copilot, Paul Mobley. There were two beds in the room, or in GI parlance, "bunks, steel, with folding legs and wire springs." One of the beds was by the wall and the other by the window. Mark had the bunk by the window.

A small potbellied stove sat between the two beds, and though it would put out enough warmth to push the cold away, it had a prodigious appetite for coal. To stay warm all night, someone would have to get up in the middle of the night to restoke it. It wasn't a task either of them enjoyed, so more often than not, they woke up on cold mornings with a thin sheet of ice on the inside of the window.

There was a gray metal desk, which they shared, and an old Royal typewriter, which they did not. Because he had written the book *Man's Heavenly Quest*, everyone thought that he was an author. Technically he supposed that he was, since *Man's Heavenly Quest* had actually been published. The typewriter was Mark's attempt to live up to that image, and he started a novel, though he had written very little on it.

Providing light for the desk was a pole lamp with a bare bulb. He and Paul once discussed whether or not there was a shade on that lamp when they first arrived, and they came to the conclusion that there probably was, but someone had taken it. Against the wall at the foot of his bed, there was a trash can, which always needed emptying, and a big, ugly, window-sized wooden square. That was a blackout shutter, which was supposed to prevent light from escaping at night, but Mark had checked it and it didn't work. It let the light out while preventing air from coming in.

There was a shelf of photographs and personal items on the wall just over the head of his bed. One of the photographs was an eight-by-ten of Emily, taken at a professional studio. The picture was black and white, but it had been tinted to give it color. In the picture Emily was wearing a light pink sweater and a lavender silk scarf tied around her neck. Prominently displayed on her sweater was a little B-17 pin that Mark had given her not too long after they met.

The other photograph on the shelf was a picture of his family, also taken at a studio. In the picture his mom and dad were sitting on a bench, while Mark and Susan stood behind them. This picture had not been tinted.

Taped on the wall alongside the shelf was a poster of Betty Grable. The picture was of the back of Grable, and she was looking over her left shoulder, smiling at the camera. The picture was broken up into map grids, and on it the logo read, "Can you read this map?" It had been used as a training aid in a map reading class when Mark was in basic training. After he completed basic, he sneaked back to steal the picture.

Also on the shelf were three books that he intended to get around to reading someday, including one by Hemingway. There were four nails driven into the wall beside the shelf. Mark's leather flight jacket hung on the first nail. Nothing was on the second nail. A yellow towel was on the third, and a green washrag hung from the fourth.

Stacked up on top of his locker were a bunch of magazines and the sheet music to some popular songs. Inside the locker were all his uniforms, some hanging neatly, many more crumpled on the floor. When he wasn't on a mission, he also kept his forty-five pistol in the wall locker, stuck down in the shoulder holster that hung from a hook in the back. The loaded clip was always in the handle of the pistol, but he made certain that no round was in the chamber.

Paul's side of the room was pretty much like Mark's, though Paul had a portable record player and a stack of records. He had some Glenn Miller records, which Mark loved, and some Stan Kenton records, which he didn't care much for. He also had some Frank Sinatra and some Bing Crosby records, which he let Mark play, even when he wasn't in the room.

Mark had just about worn out Sinatra's "All or Nothing at All." He liked the song, but the main reason he played it so many times was that he could remember sitting in the front seat of Emily's Ford down at Buckroe Beach in Hampton, watching the moon reflect off the water while listening to WGH on the car radio. He knew he heard more songs than "All or Nothing at All," but for some reason his memory of that particular song was most vivid, and he couldn't hear it now without transporting himself back to that time and place. They had done some serious necking then, and now, when he heard the song, he could almost taste her lipstick on his lips.

When Mark returned to the room after the truncated interrogation, he saw three letters lying on his bunk. His spirits picked up considerably. There was something immensely satisfying about seeing new mail lying on the olive green of the blanket. Each unopened missive was a direct connection with home, and that was the next best thing to actually being there.

Mark had developed an art to reading them. He didn't just tear them open. He would hold them for a moment, as if in some way he could divine the contents. Only after he observed the prereading ritual would he open them, moving from those with the oldest postmarks to those most recently sent.

The letter from his mother was first. It was the second one he had received from her since Susan had eloped with Mark's boyhood friend, Bob Gary. Mark's mom explained how badly she and his father had been hurt by Susan. She accused Susan of betraying their trust.

I still love her and will love her always, and I know that your father does as well. But your father and Susan are so much alike, and now neither of them is willing to forgive the other, your father because she ran off to get married, and your sister because she believes he forced her to do that. In the meantime, until they can make peace with each other, I'm afraid she is lost to us. All I can do now is pray for her, as, every night, I pray for you.

There was also a letter from Susan, with the return address marked "Mrs. Susan Gary, Fort Smith, Arkansas."

You should see our little apartment. It's very small, but really quite lovely. It's a smaller house behind a big, old, southern home, so we are blessed with a beautiful lawn and garden. The big house has a porch that stretches all the way around the front and one side of the house, and sometimes in the evening, I sit in the porch swing and watch fireflies and listen to the night creatures. It's best on the weekends, of course, because Bob can spend the weekends with me.

I don't know where Bob will go from here. More than that, I don't know where I will go from here. I know that I can't go back to Illinois, not now, not with things the way they are. But I won't worry about that now. For now Bob and I are together, and we will enjoy these moments that we have, aware of the fact that there are so many loved ones who are apart.

The person who lived in this little house before we did was the maid for Mrs. Meyer. She is a Negro lady named Willie Mae Jenkins, and her grandson, Lorenzo, is at a place called Tuskegee, Alabama, learning to fly airplanes. I found that very interesting.

The last letter was from Emily. It was last by chronology, but Mark would probably have saved it for last anyway because he liked to savor her letters a bit more.

Dear Mark,

I have just read your letter in which you told me that your sister got married. I know you said that there may be some difficulty with your parents, but I say, good for her! The way things are in this world now, a person should reach out for whatever happiness she can find.

I must also tell you how thought provoking your letter was by your suggestion that perhaps you and I might have done the same thing. I think at the time, it would have been inappropriate for us, for, unlike Susan and Bob who have known each other since childhood, you and I had only recently met. I know that what I felt about you then is as real as what I feel about you now, but it would have been perceived as a "war wedding," and the stigma would have always hung over us.

How much better to think and plan a wedding in which your friend Lee would marry us. Yes, I think it will be wonderful to walk through the chapel door, arm in arm with you, while your fellow officers hold an arch of sabers over our heads.

But since your letter wasn't a proposal, then I will wait here like a good girl, patiently biding my time until you work up the "courage" to ask me to marry you. I must say, by the way, your suggestion that you needed courage to ask me to marry you, when you fly a B-17, gives one pause for thought. Now, really, Mark, am I more foreboding than a German fighter plane?

Love,
Your Emily

Finishing the mail, Mark wandered over to the Officers' Club. The club had a bar, a large collection of chairs and sofas, and a popcorn machine. Warm English ale, seltzer water, and Scotch were available for those who cared to drink them. But there were no soft drinks of any kind, which made it difficult for Mark because he liked to have a cola with his popcorn.

Someone had torn the back page from a *Life* magazine, showing a pretty girl in tennis whites, leaning against a yellow convertible, drinking a Coca-Cola.

Underneath that tear sheet, which was posted on the bulletin board, the person who had put it up wrote: "What are we fighting for?" He then listed three choices: "The girl, the convertible, the Coke." There were nearly as many names under the Coke as there were under the other two.

Another page on the bulletin board was an ad from an engine manufacturer. It was a stylized drawing of a German FW-190 being shot down by a smiling tail gunner. "Who's afraid of the big bad Wulf?" the ad read.

"We are!" someone wrote underneath, attaching a sheet of paper to that ad. Nearly everyone in the group, including Mark, had signed that paper.

Paul was sitting over by the radio, eating popcorn, and looking at a *National Geographic* magazine.

"You still getting your kicks by looking at naked pictures in *National Geographic*?" Mark teased.

"Come on," Paul said. "This is really educational. And those girls on Borneo aren't bad," he added.

Mark laughed.

"Hey, listen to this, everybody!" someone said. "Lord Haw Haw is talking about the Six-oh-fifth!"

". . . you know who you are," the oh, so English voice on the radio was saying. "You fly Fortresses out of Davencourt Air Base. The colonel they call Iron Mike Grant is your commanding officer. Colonel Vinnie Todaro, the bad boy from Chicago, is your air executive officer. Oh, I could go on, listing not only your commanders, but the plane crews as well. So far you boys of the Six-oh-fifth Heavy Bomber Group haven't suffered too badly. You're still new, and we do have a heart, after all. We wanted you to get broken in . . . before we break you. Ha, ha, ha. That's quite good, don't you think? Broken in before we break you?

"I feel sorry for you boys. Your idiot generals are trying to prove something called daylight precision bombing. Your bombs are really not being dropped with precision, you know. You are killing just as many women and children as the Brits are, and they are dropping their bombs at night when it is far, far safer for them.

"Have you thought about that, men? Have you thought about all the German civilians—old men, women, boys and girls, babies even—that you are killing with your bombs? I'm told that quite a significant number of Americans are of German ancestry. So, when you come down to it, all you are really doing is killing your own relatives—cousins, aunts . . . grandmothers. And for who? For the English?

"Do you know what the English really think about you? Have you heard their saying about Americans? They say that you are overpaid, oversexed, and over here. Now, do you really want to kill innocent people, as well as face the possibility of getting killed yourself, for a race of people who regard you as nothing more than buffoons?

"By the way, I thought you might be interested in knowing that we have singled your group out, Six-oh-fifth. We are going to give you our extra special attention. We are going to hurt you, and we are going to hurt you bad.

"This is Lord Haw Haw saying, 'Ta ta for now.'"

"You know, when this war is over, I plan to look up that august gentleman and kick his butt right up between his shoulder blades," someone said, and the others laughed.

"I saw you had mail on your bed," Paul said.

"Yeah."

"Anything from Emily?"

"Yes."

"What'd she have to say?"

"I'm not going to tell you that. Anyway, what's it to you?"

"Well, Emily is a very pretty woman. And you know me, I'm the con-summate copilot," Paul said with a broad smile. "If you get tired of her, I'm always ready to step in and take over."

"Are you now?"

"Well, I'm not going to grab the controls until it is absolutely neces-sary," Paul said. "But as a good copilot, I feel it is only my duty to be ready to react at a moment's notice."

"I'll let you know if I need you," Mark said, laughing at his friend.

12

New York, New York
May 12, 1943

he USO show was called Donnie Fritz's Home Front Review. The members of the troupe were staying in the Algonquin Hotel, in most cases two to a room, though in the case of "the three Rosies" as Emily, Norma Jean Thompson, and Betty Brubaker were being called, it was three to a room. Their room had two single beds and a canvas cot. The girls drew straws for the cot, and Norma Jean came up with the short straw.

Norma Jean was a buxom platinum blonde. Despite an appearance that suggested the contrary, she was a wide-eyed innocent. When Emily first met her, she thought Norma Jean might be putting on airs, but she wasn't. She really was a small-town girl who had never been more than fifty miles from home until she was selected by *Home Front* magazine as one of its Rosies.

Betty and Emily were concerned that Norma Jean was so naive that she would fall for any line a soldier gave her. Betty told Norma Jean to be sure to run it by either her or Emily if a soldier said something to her that sounded too good to be true. "Because it probably is too good to be true," Betty added.

It was like Betty Brubaker to be on the lookout for a soldier's line. She was, by far, the most cosmopolitan of the three. Living in New Jersey, she had visited New York numerous times and was able to walk down the street without looking up at the tall buildings, which, much to Betty's chagrin, was something both Emily and Norma Jean could not do. A saucy redhead, Betty had once considered show business as a career. In 1940, she had a few bit parts in some off-Broadway plays. But the parts had been too few and too small for her to make a living in the business, so she returned home to New Jersey.

The three girls had completely different backgrounds and personalities, but they brought an equal share of excitement to what they were doing now, and that commonality made them very comfortable with each other.

The star of Donnie Fritz's Home Front Review was, of course, Donnie Fritz himself. He was an immensely popular radio star, and a recent magazine article pointed out that only Jack Benny and Bob Hope had more lucrative radio contracts than did he.

Befitting his position, Donnie had a three-room suite at the Algonquin, and when someone teased him about it, he pointed out that he had made an offer, in good faith, to share his suite with any young woman in the troupe. It got the laugh he was looking for.

In addition to learning their skit, Emily, Norma Jean, and Betty were expected to be at the beck and call of the photographer and reporter Varnum had sent from Home Front magazine. They were keeping up a tiring schedule: they had read-throughs and skit rehearsals from eight until twelve every day, then a full cast rehearsal from two until three every afternoon. Often, after the other cast members were finished and released to go back to their rooms and relax, Emily, Norma Jean, and Betty were expected to tour the town for a photo layout that would, in the words of the reporter, ". . . enable Rosie the Riveter from Paducah to see New York through your eyes."

Tonight the three girls were to have dinner at Sardi's. A limousine would call for them at the Algonquin, and though they were tired, all three agreed that dining out at Sardi's would be a new and exciting experience. Their room resembled a girls' dorm in some university as they hurried about getting ready, borrowing a pair of hose, lending fingernail polish, combing each other's hair.

Betty had just finished putting "rats" in Norma Jean's hair when the phone rang. Emily, who was closest to it, picked it up.

"Three Rosies' room," she said. The other two girls laughed.

"I beg your pardon," a cultured voice said. "Would this be either Miss Brubaker, Miss Hagan, or Miss Thompson?"

"This is Miss Hagan."

"Miss Hagan, your limo is here."

"Thank you," Emily said. Hanging up the phone, then framing her face with her hands, she flashed a big, phony smile at the other two.

"What is it?" Norma Jean asked.

"Our pumpkin has arrived," she said.

Betty laughed.

"Pumpkin?" Norma Jean asked.

"Well, it's a chariot now," Emily said. "Rather, it's a limo. But I can't get over the feeling that all this is unreal, only there is no glass slipper waiting for us at the end of the trail. And there is no telling when the chariot is going to turn back into a pumpkin."

Flashbulbs lit up the night as Emily and the other two girls climbed out of their limo in front of Sardi's. Several passersby were drawn to the scene by the excitement, but the sidewalk directly in front of Sardi's was kept clear as police officers manned barricades to redirect pedestrian traffic.

The three Rosies were met in front of the restaurant not only by the photographers, but also by three young officers—an army major, a marine major, and a navy commander. Without any awkwardness as to who would be with whom, the army major offered his arm to Emily, and as the cameras continued to snap pictures, he escorted her inside. The navy officer was with Norma Jean, the marine officer with Betty.

Just inside the door they were greeted by the maître d', who led the six of them to a large table in a corner. It was the first time any of the girls had ever been to Sardi's, and as their escorts held their chairs out for them, Norma Jean happened to recognize one caricature among the many drawings of celebrities that decorated the restaurant wall.

"Oh, look!" she said excitedly. "There's Donnie's picture on the wall."

Betty chuckled. "So it is. I'm sure this table wasn't chosen by chance," she said.

As it turned out, nothing about the evening was chosen by chance. Their wine had already been ordered, as had the meal, and as each course was delivered to the table, the waiter had to run through a barrage of photographers. In a restaurant that was used to celebrities, the three beautiful women and their handsome military escorts quickly became the center of attention.

Emily's escort was Major Phil Mitchell.

"I drew this duty," Mitchell explained, "much the way one would draw the duty of division duty officer." He smiled. "But I must say that in all my army career, I've never drawn a duty that was more pleasant."

After dinner they went to the theater, then returned to the Algonquin for its famous after-theater chocolate cake.

"Oh, my," Norma Jean said. "If we keep eating like this, we won't be the three most beautiful Rosie the Riveters anymore."

"Emily," Major Mitchell said as he escorted her across the lobby to the elevator, "I don't know how much longer I'll be around, I don't even know how much longer you will be around, but I would love to take you out again sometime without the photographers and reporters."

Emily smiled at Major Mitchell. "I'm flattered by your offer," she said. "But I have someone."

"Military?"

"Yes. He's a bomber pilot in England."

Major Mitchell nodded. "I understand. And I admire you for being true to him. I wish you and your young man all the best."

Emily learned later that night that Betty and Norma Jean were also asked out. Norma Jean accepted her invitation, but Betty turned her escort down.

"Why didn't you go with him?" Norma Jean asked. "He was very good-looking."

"They were all good-looking," Betty replied.

"Yes, they were. But I know why Emily turned her young man down. She's in love with her flier. You don't have a boyfriend overseas."

"No, I don't," Betty said. "But that doesn't mean I don't have some-one I'm interested in," she added.

"You have a boyfriend?" Norma Jean asked. "Who? You've never mentioned him."

"It's still in the 'not quite' stage," Betty said.

Later that same evening, while Norma Jean was taking a shower, Emily looked over at Betty. "You know he's married, don't you?"

"Who?"

"Donnie."

"What makes you think . . . ?"

"Betty, give me credit for having eyes."

"All right, what if he is married? I happen to know that they aren't living together and they haven't lived together for more than a year now. They're going to get a divorce."

"Has he told you that?"

"No. Not in so many words." Betty sighed.

"You're sure you aren't just drawn to him because . . ."

"Because he's rich and famous?"

"Well, he is bigger than life."

Betty shook her head. "No. I've asked myself that. But I think I can see beyond that. Have you ever talked to him, Emily? I mean, really talked to him? He's gentle, and I know you may find this hard to believe, but he is also very shy."

"No, I don't find that hard to believe. I think a lot of shy people cover their shyness with an act. And who better to put on an act than a professional actor?"

"You won't say anything about this to anyone, will you?" Betty asked. "I mean, I didn't know I showed it so much."

"I won't say anything," Emily promised. "But what about Donnie? Does he know how you feel about him?"

117

"I don't think so," Betty said.

"Are you going to tell him?"

"I don't know if I have the nerve. Maybe he'll figure it out on his own. You did."

Davencourt

Kenny was still upset over the loss of the jeep. It just wasn't right. Chaplain Grant should have a jeep. Didn't they realize that he was the only chaplain at Davencourt? He needed the ability to go anywhere on the base at a moment's notice. After all, as Kenny liked to point out, the chaplain wasn't just any lieutenant. He was a lieutenant who was doing the Lord's work.

Besides, if the chaplain didn't get a vehicle soon, Kenny knew that his own "procurement opportunities" would be greatly curtailed. And in his own peculiar way Kenny justified his mastery of the extra-channel supply system as doing the Lord's work.

Kenny was pondering this problem when, glancing through the window, he happened to see a staff car passing by. Staff cars generally meant high-ranking brass visiting from PINETREE, or even WIDEWING. Visits from high-ranking brass didn't bode well. Anytime high-ranking brass came visiting, it generally meant that a very difficult mission was coming up, one that would tax the nerves and stretch the resolve of the aircrews.

The car stopped in front of group headquarters. Surprisingly though, it wasn't a soldier, but a young sailor who hopped out and hurried around to open the door. Three navy officers also exited the vehicle: a captain, a commander, and a lieutenant commander. After the three officers went inside, the young sailor lit a cigarette, folded his arms across his chest, and leaned back against the front fender of his car.

Kenny walked over to the small refrigerator. He had acquired the refrigerator from a merchant marine seaman in exchange for a twisted piece of gray-green metal that was clearly marked with a swastika. Although he didn't come right out and say the metal was part of an

FW-190, Kenny did talk about the aircrews' respect and fear of that particular German fighter. "They are gray-green in color," he said, "with a swastika painted on the vertical stabilizer, much like the one you see on this piece."

The reason Kenny didn't come right out and say it was from an FW-190 was that it wasn't. It was actually part of the wing-root fairing from a damaged Fortress. Under Kenny's directions, the metal had been converted into prime trading material by some enterprising young man in the sheet-metal section.

The German warplane souvenir might not have been real, but the refrigerator it purchased certainly was, and from it, Kenny extracted a Coke. Dropping the Coke bottle into his pocket, he went outside to talk to the sailor-driver.

"Hey, how's it goin'?" he asked.

"Fine."

"Would you like a Coke?"

"A Coke? Are you kidding? Where you going to get a Coke around here?"

Kenny pulled the bottle and an opener from his jacket pocket. He popped the top off, then handed it to the sailor, who looked at it with an expression of pure rapture.

"Do you know how long it's been since I had a Coke?" he asked. "Where'd you get this?"

"Sometimes when our guys come back from a really bad mission, a Coke does wonders for them," Kenny said without answering the sailor's question.

"Yeah, I can see how it might," the sailor replied, draining about one-fourth of the bottle in one long, Adam's apple–bobbing swallow.

Kenny ran his hand over the smooth paint job of the Ford. "Must be nice, driving around in a car all the time instead of a jeep or truck."

"I guess it is," the sailor said. "But this ain't my regular job. I just got assigned to drive Captain Murphy around while he's making his fact-finding tour. Soon as he's finished 'fact finding,'" the sailor added, twisting his mouth around the words, "he'll go back to Washington, and I'll go back to the *Gaffey*."

"The *Gaffey?*"

"It's a DMS, destroyer minesweeper," the sailor explained. "That's the armpit ship of the navy. We do nothing but escort convoys back and forth across the Atlantic. Then we finally put into England for a week, and do I get liberty? No, I haul brass around."

"Where'd you get the car?"

"The navy has a VIP motor pool in London. All I did was show up with a set of orders for Captain Murphy and they gave me the car."

"You don't say? Well, listen, it's been good talking to you, but I have to get back to work," Kenny said. "Take the last swallow so I can have the bottle back."

"Yeah, here it is, and thanks," the sailor said. "Thanks a lot."

"Don't mention it," Kenny said graciously.

It was another week before Kenny had the opportunity to get back to London. He arranged his own transportation, getting a ride into town with a supply truck after assuring Chaplain Grant that he would be able to find a way to return. Once in London, he took care of the business he was there to do, then he went to the navy VIP motor pool.

The motor pool was filled with jeeps, three-quarter-ton trucks, and sedans. Most of the sedans were Fords or Chevrolets, and they were painted battleship gray, or blue, and identified by navy markings. However, there were at least a half-dozen larger cars—Buicks, Chryslers, and Packards—that were black, with no indication of any kind that they were military. They were beautiful cars and would have been quite at home at any church, posh restaurant, or country club back in the States.

Kenny stepped into the office of the chief of the motor pool. An overweight, gray-haired chief petty officer looked up from his desk as Kenny came in. The chief was half-smoking and half-chewing a cigar, and he pulled it from his mouth and spit a few pieces of soggy cigar-leaf before he spoke.

"You're in the wrong place, aren't you, soldier? This is navy country."

"I might be in the wrong place," Kenny agreed. "But I was hoping you could help me."

"Help you how?"

"Well, first, let me ask you a question. A navy captain does outrank an army captain, doesn't he?"

The chief laughed out loud. "I should hope to smile he does. A navy captain is the same as an army colonel. A *full* colonel."

Kenny hit his fist in the palm of his hand. "I knew it," he said. "I knew I was right."

"So, you were right, huh? What did you do, just win a bet?"

"No, not exactly. Well, let me explain the situation to you. I've been told to provide vehicles for some high-ranking brass who are visiting from Washington. We've got an army colonel, a marine colonel, and a navy captain coming. But here's the thing. The army gave me a jeep for the army colonel, and they even gave me one for the marine colonel. But they said the navy captain isn't authorized anything better than a three-quarter-ton truck."

"What?" the chief bellowed, spraying loose bits of cigar as he did. "Why would they tell you that?"

"Because there's some dumb sergeant running the motor pool who doesn't know any better. He says that colonels outrank captains . . . even navy captains."

"Well, that sorry so-and-so. I tell you what, mate. I better never run into that sergeant in a pub downtown. Because if I do, and if I recognize him, I might just punch his lights out."

"That's what I told him," Kenny said. "I told him the navy wouldn't like the way he was treating their brass."

"What did he say?"

"He said he didn't care what the navy thought."

"What a bum."

"Yeah, that's what I thought too. Well, anyway, I've got this navy buddy who told me that you might be able to give me a vehicle for the captain."

The chief shook his head. "Sorry, friend, but all my jeeps are permanently assigned. About the only thing we've got on a temporary basis is—" Suddenly the chief stopped in midsentence. "Wait a minute. They were going to give the colonels jeeps and the navy captain a truck, you say?"

"That's what it all boils down to."

"We may just be able to go 'em one better then. Yeah." The chief laughed. "Yeah, and it would serve them right."

"I beg your pardon?"

"You got orders for this captain?"

"Yes, right here," Kenny said, showing him a set of orders he had manufactured by using the chapel's mimeograph machine.

The chief looked at the orders for a long moment, then he rubbed his chin.

"If I could find something for you, how long would you need it?"

Kenny sighed. "I don't know . . . how long can I have it?"

"You can have it indefinitely as long as you renew the dispatch every thirty days."

"Yeah, maybe I better do that," Kenny said. "What with the buildup of the Eighth Air Force and all, it seems like everyone and his dog is coming over here to have a look around."

"Ain't that the truth?" the chief replied as he began filling out the dispatch. "And the heck of it is, they come over here for no more than two weeks and are credited with time served in a theater of war. There's an awful lot of navy and army brass walking around back in Washington wearing a chest full of campaign ribbons when the most dangerous thing any of them ever did was take a wild ride in a London cab."

The chief tore the page from the dispatch book and handed it to Kenny. "See that 'forty Buick down there? Second from the other end?"

"That shiny black one? Yes, I see it."

The sergeant handed a set of keys to him. "Take good care of it. The last person to use that car was the undersecretary of the navy."

"I'll treat it like it's my own," Kenny promised.

May 14, 1943

Mission number eleven was deep into Germany. Flak was very heavy, and the German fighters swarmed around us like mosquitoes. Of all our missions, this was the worst. Fourteen Forts were knocked down, including Lusty Gal. There were no chutes seen coming from Dusty's plane. Eddie Gordon, our left waist gunner, was killed. He is the only member of our original crew that we have lost, and he was exceptionally well liked by everyone. I know that sometime in the future, if I actually do survive this war, I will want to come back and read more about this mission, so I should put more information in this entry, but I can't. I'm just not in the mood to make any further entries today. Mission was eight hours and five minutes long.

The more I think of the title of my book, Man's Heavenly Quest, the greater a mockery it becomes. How can man search for heaven when he lives in hell?

13

25,000 Feet Over Würzburg
May 14, 1943

W hat had been a quiet, almost pleasant flight in a clear blue sky changed sharply when Eddie Gordon's high-pitched, excited voice alerted everyone on board *Gideon's Sword*.

"German fighters, ten o'clock high!"

"I got 'em. They're comin' around," Richardson said in a low, calm voice, contrasting sharply with Gordon's excited outcry.

"Okay, boys, keep your eyes on them," Mark said.

The German fighters, ME-109s, flew ahead of the Fortress formation, then turned and came back toward them, attacking head-on.

Adrian Rogers on the nose guns and Richardson in the top turret opened up. The combined speed of the B-17 and the German fighters created a closing rate of more than six hundred miles per hour. Mark could see winks of light flashing on the leading edge of the fighter's wings.

"He's going to crash into us!" Paul shouted in alarm. "Do something, Mark!"

"Take it easy!" Mark said.

The fighter was coming straight toward them in a colossal game of chicken, but Mark knew there was nothing he could do to avoid collision. For the moment there was an unholy partnership between Mark and the German pilot. Both knew that only the German plane was quick enough to avoid impact. But to avoid disaster for both, the German pilot had to trust the American pilot to make no precipitous maneuvers.

The German flashed by, missing the bomber by inches.

"Wow!" Richardson said. "That guy was so close that if I knew German insignia, I could tell you what his rank was."

"There goes another Fort down!"

"Two more! That makes three! Three Forts going down at the same time!"

"Don't crowd the intercom!" Mark ordered. "For the moment we're more interested in German fighters than we are B-17s."

Suddenly, from beneath the airplane, a German fighter popped up in front of them, going away. The ball turret gunner, the nose gunner, and the top turret gunner were all able to track on him at the same time, and the sky in front was filled with glowing tracer rounds, streaming toward the fighter. Between every glowing round, Mark knew, were four rounds that couldn't be seen, which meant that a tremendously large number of shells were hosing into the German airplane. Smoke started streaming back from the fighter's engine cowl, and the blur of the propeller disk slowed to the point that Mark could nearly count the revolutions.

The German plane was fatally hit. It flipped over onto its back, and the pilot fell clear, rolling himself into a little ball for the long plunge down. Bailing out of the plane didn't mean that the German pilot was out of danger. He would have to pass through another bomber formation five thousand feet below this one, where more than one hundred spinning propellers waited for him.

Then, as suddenly as the German planes appeared, they left.

"They're gone!" Eddie Gordon said. He laughed. "We beat them off!"

"Not quite," Mark replied. "They left so they wouldn't get caught up in their own flak. Look ahead."

The sky in front of them was filled with hundreds of brilliant flashes of light and black puffs of smoke. It was the heaviest concentration of flak that Mark had ever seen.

"Those people are being downright unfriendly," Rogers said.

Mark was watching the *Battling Belle* when it exploded. One moment it was there, slightly below him at the ten o'clock position, riding serenely, all props turning, glass glistening in the sun. He had just seen the top turret twisting around as the gunner was searching the skies all around him. The next moment there was a huge flash of light. A great red wound opened up as pieces of plane and men tumbled from the sky, not one piece big enough to be able to differentiate between the two.

The entire event had occurred in absolute silence. Of course, it wasn't really silent. He knew the explosion had made noise, just as Mark was certain that the black puffs of flak all around them were making noise. It was just that the four roaring engines of his own aircraft created a wall of sound, thus giving the illusion of silence by drowning out everything else. He could see the violence taking place all around, but he could not hear it.

Then, all of a sudden he did hear something, a loud bang from back in the ship.

"Oww! I'm hit! I'm hit!"

"Who is it? Who's hit?" Mark asked.

"It's Eddie," Crane said.

"How bad?"

"I don't know yet. Uh, we got us a fire back here, Lieutenant. Looks like a pretty bad one."

"Paul, get back there and see what's going on," Mark ordered his copilot.

"Right," Paul answered, unbuckling himself from his seat.

Paul took a portable oxygen bottle with him, then started toward the rear of the bomber, stepping onto the narrow catwalk over the bomb bay and twisting sideways to be able to squeeze through the narrow constriction.

When Paul reached the waist gun area, he saw Eddie Gordon lying on the floor. Crane was using a fire bottle to fight a fire. For the moment, getting the fire under control was more critical than tending to Eddie, so Paul grabbed the other fire bottle and started to help. With two jets of CO_2 directed toward the fire, it went out. That taken care of, Paul knelt beside Eddie to take a look.

The left waist gunner was lying in a pool of blood, and his face was ashen colored.

"How you doin', Eddie?"

"I think he's hit in the leg, sir," Crane said.

Glancing toward Eddie's right leg, Paul saw a huge, ugly, gaping wound. "Yeah, I see it," he said.

Using a compress bandage, Paul patched the wound in Eddie's leg. "You'll be all right," he told the young gunner. "You've lost some blood, but you'll be all right soon as we get you back."

"I'm cold," Eddie said. They were the first words he had spoken.

"Well, no wonder you're cold. Look here. Your flight suit has come unzipped," Paul said. "How did that hap—" He stopped in midsentence as he reached to close Eddie's flight suit. He realized then that the suit hadn't come unzipped; it had been rent open. And the same shrapnel that created the tear had also opened up Eddie's stomach. A significant part of the young gunner's intestines were hanging out. Paul turned his head aside and closed his eyes.

"What is it, Lieutenant? Eddie's going to be all right, isn't he? He's going to be all right?"

Steeling himself, Paul looked back into Eddie's face. Eddie's eyes were still open, but it was now evident that they were unseeing. The young gunner was dead. Paul stood up then and patted Crane on the shoulder.

"I'm sorry, Gil," he said.

Paul plugged his intercom into Eddie's port. "Copilot to pilot," he said.

"Yeah, how is he?" Mark came back.

"Eddie's dead."

There was a beat of silence, then Mark asked, "How about the fire?"

"It's out."

"All right, nothing we can do for him now. You'd better get back up here. We're coming up to IP."

"Roger."

The Wing lost fourteen Forts on the Würzburg mission. Six of the fourteen were from the 605th, including *Lusty Gal,* Dusty's airplane. Mark hadn't seen *Lusty Gal* go down and didn't even know it was lost until he got back and Dusty didn't. Then he heard what happened from those who had been flying close to *Lusty Gal.*

"It caught an explosive round right in the cockpit. Dusty and his copilot must've been killed instantly because it nosed over and dived straight for the ground."

"See any chutes?"

"No, none."

Not just Mark, but the entire group took the loss of *Lusty Gal* hard because it was supposed to have been the last mission for Dusty and his crew. After this one, they would have gone home.

That night, after the post-mission interrogation of *"What kind of fighters did you encounter? How heavy was the flak? What sort of damage do you think your bombs did? How many aircraft are you claiming killed? How many aircraft are you claiming damaged?"* Mark borrowed a bicycle from the operations Nissen and rode out into the night. At first he had no particular place to go. He just felt the need to be alone in the open and the quiet under the brilliant spread of stars.

He lost a crewman today. He had known from the time he arrived that the odds were very strong he would lose one or more crewmen . . . maybe even the entire plane. But Eddie was the first crewman he had lost.

Eddie Gordon was from Memphis, Tennessee. Eddie loved barbecue and had promised to provide barbecue for the entire crew once they were back in the States. But he always insisted there was only one kind of barbecue, and that was Memphis barbecue.

"None of that stuff you get from Texas. I'm talking real, dry-rubbed, cooked-over-hickory pork shoulder barbecue."

Eddie had a dog named Suzie and a girlfriend named Jennie. On his wall locker in his billets, the picture of his dog, Suzie, got billing over the picture of his girlfriend, Jennie. Crane teased him by saying that it was because Suzie was prettier than Jennie.

"Of course she is," Eddie had replied, not realizing he was being teased. "All dogs is prettier than all women."

Although he hadn't consciously planned it, Mark realized that he had ridden out to the hardstand where, just last night, Dusty's airplane, *Lusty Gal*, had sat.

The hardstand was empty, but the ropes that had tied the bomber were neatly coiled, awaiting a return that wouldn't happen. The engine tarps and the pitot tube covers were still here. So, too, were the APU, or auxiliary power unit, the generator that supplied electrical power for starting, and the fire extinguisher. The wheel chocks were here as well, the ones that kept the wheels from rolling when the airplane was tied down.

The wheel chocks were actually nothing more than yellow pyramids of wood, held together by a little rope that was passed through drilled holes, then knotted on each end. Mark walked over to the chocks that would have blocked the right wheel, the wheel Dusty—whose real name Mark finally learned was Bogardous Carradine; no wonder he preferred Dusty—had "marked" in his night-before-mission ritual.

Mark looked around, then, seeing that he was alone, did a handstand over the chocks. He hoped that somewhere, somehow, Dusty was able to see that and got a laugh out of it. After that, Mark got back on his bike and rode all the way around the perimeter, feeling the tears stream down his face.

By the time Mark returned to the BOQ he was all cried out, but he wasn't over the pain. He felt very hollow inside, and for a moment he actually considered going to see Lee. He decided against it, however, thinking that to do so now would be the height of hypocrisy.

"Lieutenant White's hurting bad, Chaplain," Charley Phillips said. Charley was the ball turret gunner for *Gideon's Sword*. "We all are. I mean, Eddie was with us from the beginning, but Lieutenant White, well, he sort of feels responsible for all of us, you know? And besides that, Lieutenant Carradine's plane went down today, too, and him and Lieutenant White was good friends."

"Yes, I know," Lee said.

"You and Lieutenant White are friends, too, aren't you? I mean, I know you two talk a lot."

"Yes."

"You think you can do somethin' for him? Help him so's he's not hurtin' quite so much?"

"Charley, I would give anything in the world if I could," Lee said. "But you know how this works. The Lord's peace comes only to those who ask for it."

"Yes, sir, I know," Charley said. "It just seems like there ought to be somethin' we could do, though."

Charley Phillips wasn't the only one to come to Lee tonight. The day's mission had been a very difficult one, and many had come by to see him, to ask him to pray with them as they gave thanks for having survived the day, and to pray with them as they remembered friends who didn't.

Lee knew about Mark's day, and he knew the pain Mark must be going through. But he knew also that he couldn't push a rope. He couldn't help Mark if Mark wasn't ready to accept his help.

When the last man was gone, and Lee was in the chapel all alone, he went up to the sanctuary, then knelt at the altar rail, not as a pastor, but as a child of God, coming to the Lord in prayer.

"Oh, Lord," he prayed. "I have come to You so many times today, asking You to soothe the spirits and ease the pain of Your servants who are suffering so. And now I come one more time on a personal quest, asking that You breach the ramparts Mark has erected around his heart. Help him to understand that only through You will he find the peace that will restore his soul. In Christ's name I pray. Amen."

14

New York, New York
May 27, 1943

T he four-engine Boeing 314 glistened in the afternoon sun as it
rocked gently in the harbor. The passengers, with boarding passes
in hand, were queued up on a specially built pier that stretched out to
the open door at the rear of the giant flying boat. Looking at the airplane, Emily was amazed that anything so big could actually fly.

"Oh, isn't this just the most exciting thing?" Norma Jean asked.

"It certainly is," Emily replied. "Who would've thought a girl from
Newport News, Virginia, would ever be doing something like this?"

The huge Clipper was divided into compartments, each compartment containing ten seats, two sets of three facing three on the left side
of the aisle, and two sets of two facing two on the right side. In addition
to individual seating compartments, there were a lounge and a dining
salon. As the three Rosies moved up the aisle toward their own compartment, they passed by other passengers who were already settling
into their seats. Overhead, Emily could hear several loud thumps and

bumps, and seeing her react in some alarm, one of the stewards smiled at her.

"Nothing to be worried about, miss," he said. "That's just the luggage being loaded."

"Oh, yes, I wondered where that would go."

"We've got a place up top that's just like the trunk on your car," the steward explained. "Only it's a lot bigger."

When they reached their compartment, another steward was waiting to help them be seated. He explained the seat belts, the overhead lamps, the operation of the shades on the windows, the vent adjustments for fresh air, and the way to call the steward.

"We'll start serving dinner at six o'clock New York time. You will be in the second seating. Shortly after dinner we'll land in Bermuda, where we will spend no more than an hour. After we refuel, we'll take off from Bermuda and fly all night, reaching the Azores tomorrow, just before noon. You'll have lunch on the Azores, and dinner in Lisbon tomorrow night," he said, laying out their itinerary.

"Across the ocean in one day," Norma Jean said. "Amazing."

"How many passengers on this flight?" Betty asked.

"Thirty-six," the steward replied. "There are twenty-two in the USO troupe, and fourteen others."

"You mean this airplane is big enough to carry thirty-six people?"

"It can carry sixty passengers," the steward said, "plus a crew of ten. Right now we have forty-six souls on board, thirty-six passengers plus two pilots and two copilots, a navigator and flight engineer up on the flight deck, and four stewards working down here."

The phone on the forward bulkhead buzzed, and the steward picked it up. "Yes, sir," he said into the phone. Then, hanging it up, he looked over at Emily and the others. "That was the captain. You ladies better get yourselves strapped in. We're about to take off."

At that moment Donnie Fritz joined the Rosies, strapping himself into one of the seats in their compartment.

"I hope you ladies don't mind sharing your compartment with me," he said.

"Not at all," Emily said.

The three girls and Donnie were sitting on the left side of the plane in the forward-most compartment. Just ahead of the compartment was a small ladder that led up to the flight deck. Emily looked up toward the top of the ladder, but the door was closed so there was nothing to see.

Emily's seat was by the window. From her position she had a good view of the bottom of the wing as well the lower bulge of two of the four engines. She heard a humming sound that started low, then started building up like a siren until it reached a feverish pitch. She was just about to ask what it was when the wail was interrupted by a chirping sound, followed by the cough of a starting engine. The propeller on the outboard engine jerked a few times, then with a belch of exhaust smoke, the engine started, and the propeller spun quickly into a blur. The same thing happened to the subsequent engines until all four engines were turning and Emily could feel a slight vibration in the plane.

The big flying boat began to move, and Emily and the other two girls smiled at each other in eager excitement. The plane pulled away from its boarding pier and proceeded far out into the harbor before it stopped and turned. It stayed there for a few seconds in relative quiet and calm, then suddenly all four engines began to roar very loud and the plane started out across the harbor, much faster than before. When it first started across the water, it was a bumpy ride, but soon the step-plane wing lifted the craft to the surface of the water, and for forty seconds it skimmed along much more smoothly. It was sending out a huge spray of water, splashing so much on the windows that Emily couldn't even see through them. Although she had never been in a tropical downpour, she imagined it must be something like this. Then some of the noise and all the vibration ceased as the plane lifted free and began climbing.

"Oh, look! The Statue of Liberty!" Norma Jean said excitedly, pointing through the window. Emily looked as well and saw, with some surprise, that they were already high enough to be looking down on the famous statue. Behind and below them, a long white streak was painted across the surface of the water, breaking off sharply at the point where the huge flying boat had lifted off.

The plane made one more turn, and for a moment, the towering skyscrapers of New York came into view. As the plane continued its turn, however, the New York skyline fell behind them. Looking straight down, she could see several boats and ships on the water. They continued to climb for several more minutes, then the roar of the engines subsided somewhat and the airplane leveled off. That was when Donnie Fritz released his seat belt.

"What are you doing?" Emily asked.

"We're at cruising altitude," Fritz explained. Fritz was a seasoned traveler, having flown many times before. "Once you reach cruising altitude, you can take off your seat belt and move around if you want."

"You mean, while the airplane is flying, we can just go anywhere we want?" Norma Jean asked, amazed by the concept.

Fritz chuckled. "Well, they might not welcome you up on the flight deck," he teased.

"Oh, I wouldn't go up there and bother them," Norma Jean replied, taking seriously what had been intended as a joke.

"I think I'll go sit in the lounge until time for dinner. Anyone care to join me?" Donnie asked.

"I would be happy to join you," Betty said, taking off her own belt.

"Good girl. Norma Jean, Emily, how about you two?"

"I need to get used to this business of flying first," Norma Jean said. "I think I'll just sit here for a while."

"I'll stay with Norma Jean," Emily said.

"Okay. Come on back if and when you feel like it."

The USO troupe had a grueling tour worked out. Starting in Africa, they were going to perform at as many bases and in as many hospitals as the army could schedule for them. Sometimes they would be doing three shows a day.

At least Emily felt more confident about her own role in the show now than she had when the subject of her performing was first presented to her. According to Donnie, who should know, the three Rosies had overcome their lack of experience by their weeks of excellent rehearsal. In addition to the three weeks of rehearsal, they did six live performances before they left the States, three at Fort Devins, Massachusetts, and three at Fort Dix, New Jersey.

The skits that had been written for them were simple to learn and easy to do. They were also quite humorous and elicited a lot of laughs from the GIs, but the three girls didn't particularly like them. They were designed to poke fun at women who were doing jobs that were hereto-fore the exclusive domain of men. In one skit, for example, "Lipstick for Hitler," the production line came to a complete halt while all the girls searched for a lost tube of lipstick.

"You've got to look at this from the man's point of view," Donnie explained. "Our brave boys overseas don't want to think that they aren't needed. They appreciate you ladies pitching in and helping out like this, but they also want it understood that this is a temporary thing. When the war is over, they expect everything to go back to normal."

"By normal, you mean ironing clothes and raising babies?" Emily asked.

"Yeah, pretty much like that," Donnie agreed, not catching the sar-casm in Emily's voice.

Looking at their act as objectively as she could, Emily decided that while her performance was acceptable, Betty, with her brief experience, was clearly the most talented. Despite Betty's talent, though, Norma Jean stole the show. Norma Jean had something else, something much more valuable than talent as far as the men were concerned. No one had noticed it when they were just rehearsing, but once they actually started doing the shows before live GI audiences, it became very apparent that the blonde, buxom Norma Jean had an earthy appeal that brought the men out of their seats. Part of Norma Jean's appeal, Emily decided, was the fact that she had been totally unaware of the effect she had on men, and once she realized she did have it, she was baffled as to why.

Dinner that evening was a jelled cherry salad, curried shrimp over rice, green beans, rolls, and a choice of coffee, tea, or water. Emily chose water. The meal was delicious, all the more so because of the excitement of eating one's dinner two miles above the ocean. They were barely fin-ished with their meal and had just returned to their seats when the stew-ard told them they would be landing in Bermuda.

They were allowed to get off the plane in Bermuda while it was being refueled, but though Emily would have enjoyed looking around the island, they were kept in a ready room so they could be quickly reloaded.

They listened to the radio and read magazines until it was time to reboard.

"Now boarding, Pan Am's Atlantic Clipper for Lisbon. All passengers holding confirmed reservations, please report to the boarding pier."

"That's us," Betty said, standing up and reaching for her purse. "Has either of you ever done anything this exciting?"

"I saw Vice President Nance Garner once," Norma Jean said. "That was pretty exciting."

Emily and Betty looked at each other, then laughed as they headed for the plane.

They took off just as the sun was setting in the west, and by the time they were once again at cruising altitude, it was dark. Shortly after that, the steward came by to make up their beds, which were very similar to berths in a Pullman car.

Emily's bunk was positioned in such a way as to allow her to look through the window. She watched the moon glow on the water, far below, then finally drifted off to sleep.

She slept the night through, awakening the next morning to a beautiful sunrise. The disk of the sun was just poised on the horizon, sending a blazing orange-gold runner shooting across the surface of the sea. Looking up toward the bottom of the wing, she saw that it, too, had been fired gold in the reflection of the sun's early morning light.

Sitting up in her bed, Emily parted her curtains and looked out. The curtains that covered Norma Jean's and Betty's beds were still tightly closed, but Donnie Fritz's bed had already been made up, and he was nowhere to be seen. Pulling her own curtain closed again, Emily got dressed, then stepped out of her bed and onto the carpeted floor. Seeing her, the steward came over.

"Shall I make your bed, miss?"

"Yes. Uh, would there be coffee somewhere?"

"Absolutely, miss. Coffee and breakfast are being served in the dining salon."

Donnie Fritz was having his breakfast when Emily went into the dining salon. Except for one other man on the opposite side of the plane, no one else was present.

"Well," Fritz said, smiling at Emily. "Aren't you the early riser?"

"I guess I am," she said. "What time is it?"

"It's eight o'clock, Lisbon time."

"Oh. Well, I'm nearly always up by eight. I don't know why I still feel so tired."

Donnie laughed. "It's eight o'clock Lisbon time, but it's only three A.M. in New York."

"Ohh," Emily groaned, rubbing her temples. "No wonder." The steward poured coffee for her. "Thanks."

"Would you care to order breakfast now, miss?"

"Just toast, please."

Fritz watched as Emily poured cream in her coffee, then spooned in sugar.

"What's he like?" he asked.

"I beg your pardon?"

"I'm told you have some guy who is a flier in the army. I just want to know what kind of guy it is who could win you over."

"He's a nice guy," Emily said, taking a swallow.

Fritz chuckled. "Nice guy, huh? Well, I sort of figured that was a given," he said. He stared at her for a long moment, so intensely that Emily became uncomfortable with it.

"What are you doing?" she asked, holding her hand up to block her face.

"I'm staring at a beautiful woman," Donnie said. "If there wasn't a war on, and if you weren't hooked on some guy who is risking his life for our country . . ." He let the sentence hang.

"Donnie," Emily started to say, but Donnie interrupted her.

"You don't have to put me in my place," he said. "I know he's a hero, and I would be a heel if I tried anything. I may be a lot of things, but nobody has ever accused me of being a heel."

"You are also married to Linda May," Emily said. "I think Linda May is such a pretty woman. I just loved her in *My Heart's Content*."

Donnie chuckled. "Disabuse yourself of the idea that Linda May is anything like the roles she plays."

"But she is your wife. That's not a role."

"Our marriage is a temporary condition, I assure you. We would already be divorced if I weren't doing this USO thing. Of course, far be it from Linda to let anything like a divorce stand in her way. From what I hear, she's all but moved in with her next conquest. Believe me, if I had met you before I met her, and of course, before you met your young man . . ." Again, he let the sentence hang uncompleted.

Emily smiled at him. "I'm flattered, Donnie, truly I am," she said. "The more so because I figured you would be more attracted to Betty or Norma Jean."

"Why would you think that?"

"For one thing, because Betty is so obviously attracted to you," Emily replied. "And Norma Jean is . . . well, you know how she is. You've seen the way all the men react to her."

"Norma Jean is every man's fantasy. She's not real," Fritz said. "And Betty? You say she's attracted to me?"

"Don't tell me you've never noticed that."

"No," Donnie said. "No, I haven't."

"Men are so obtuse," Emily said with a little laugh.

The steward brought Emily her toast then, and as she was buttering it, Betty came into the salon. Seeing Donnie and Emily sitting together, she came to the table.

"May I join you?"

"Betty, good morning!" Donnie said, hopping up from the table to greet her. "Of course, please do join us," Donnie invited. Emily couldn't help smiling when she noticed that by the motion of his arm, he was inviting Betty to sit beside him.

Shortly after that, some of the other members of the troupe came into breakfast, and eventually the dining salon was filled. Emily visited with a few of them, then she excused herself to return to her seat. When she looked across the table at Betty and Fritz, though, she realized they scarcely knew she was still there. Betty was positively glowing over the sudden attention she was getting from Donnie Fritz.

It was as if she was certain that her campaign of flirting was at last paying off.

Emily buried her laugh as she left the salon.

The berths were all made up, and Norma Jean was sitting in her seat, staring out the window with a pensive look on her face.

"Good morning," Emily said brightly. "You aren't going to breakfast?"

"I'm not hungry," Norma Jean said. There was something about the tone of her voice that caught Emily's attention.

"Norma Jean, what is it? Is something wrong?"

Norma Jean pointed to the magazine that was lying on the seat beside her. "Have you seen this?"

"*Home Front?* No, where did it come from?"

"I don't know. Someone brought it on the plane before we left, I guess. We're in this issue, Emily."

"Really? They finally got around to doing the story, huh? What's it like?" Emily asked, picking it up and thumbing through it.

"I don't think you're going to like it."

"Oh?" Emily looked up at Norma Jean, then back down to the magazine, just as she opened it to the story. There, leading into the article, was a half-page photograph of Emily and Major Mitchell, their arms intertwined at the elbow as they were drinking champagne.

"Young lovers toast their engagement," the caption beneath the photo read.

Davencourt

"Colonel Grant?" Major Ragsdale's voice called over the intercom.

Mike reached up and hit the switch. "Yes, John."

"Colonel Todaro is here to see you, sir."

"Send him in."

Lieutenant Colonel Todaro was from Chicago's South Side, and his four years in West Point, followed by fifteen years in the army, had not softened that brittle edge. He was a short, stocky man with a pug nose and a scarred chin. He once confessed to Mike that it had been very difficult for him to choose between the army and the family business.

"What is your family's business?" Mike asked.

Todaro flashed a crooked grin. "Well, I could tell you that," he said. "But then I would have to kill you."

Mike hadn't been entirely certain that Todaro was teasing. He was glad, however, that Colonel Todaro had chosen the military. He didn't believe there was a finer air exec in the Eighth Air Force.

When Todaro came in, he crossed the distance between the door and Mike's desk with a few purposeful strides. He neither saluted nor said good morning. Instead, he put a small piece of wire on Mike's desk.

"Do you know what this is?" he asked.

"Good morning to you, too, Vinnie."

"I'm sorry, Colonel," Todaro said. "Good morning, sir. Do you know what this is?"

"It looks like a piece of wire."

"Yes, sir, it is. Safety wire. To be specific, it is A-N zero-point-three-two safety wire."

"All right, it is three-two safety wire. Now, tell me why we are having this discussion."

"I'm sure I don't have to explain to you that anytime a nut or bolt is used in a critical area, it must be secured with safety wire."

"I've jabbed my fingers often enough on the ends of the wire while doing preflights to be well aware of that."

"Yes, sir. Well, keeping that in mind, last week we were given orders for a maximum effort. We put up forty-one planes. On Monday we put up thirty-seven. I just checked the readiness report. If we are given another maximum effort mission, the most we can hope to get in the air is thirty-five." He picked up the piece of wire. "All because we don't have enough of this."

"Thirteen airplanes Red-X'd over safety wire?"

"Yes, sir. To be honest, three of them would be grounded anyway," Todaro admitted. "But even if they were ready in all other respects to go, they would still be grounded, along with the other ten, because we are out of safety wire."

"Why are we just now being made aware of this problem?"

Todaro looked a little sheepish. "I have to admit, Colonel, I've known about it for a few days, but I thought I could handle it without having to get you involved. I've been on the phone with A-4 several times trying to get the situation resolved, but I've had no luck. I'm afraid you're going to have to go directly to General Westland. And I don't believe a phone call is going to do it. You're going to have to see him, eyeball to eyeball."

"I'll see what I can do," Mike said. "In the meantime, is there anything else we can try? Maybe a different size safety wire?"

"We've got plenty of twenty-seven and forty-one," Todaro said. "But twenty-seven isn't strong enough and forty-one is too large for the holes. We have to have thirty-two. Some of the maintenance officers have been reusing old wire, but of course, that is strictly against the regs."

"Of course it is. That's why no one has done it," Mike said, meaning that while he would wink at the practice, he didn't want it known that he knew it was being done.

Realizing what Mike meant, Todaro nodded. "Of course, we'd never do such a thing."

"Of course, we wouldn't. And thanks for filling me in," Mike said as Todaro picked up his piece of wire to leave.

"Yes, sir. I just hope you can wake somebody up somewhere."

As Todaro left, Major Ragsdale stuck his head through the doorway. "General, the chaplain is here."

"Yes, yes, send him in. And, John, see if you can set up an appointment for me to see General Westland sometime today."

"Subject, sir?"

"Safety wire."

"Yes, sir."

Lee came in as Todaro left. Although it was his father and they were alone, Lee saluted him as he would any other commanding officer.

"At ease," Mike said.

Lee relaxed.

"I'm told you have been sweating out the missions over in the operations Nissen."

"Yes, sir, I have," Lee answered.

"I don't want you bothering those men, Lee. They have important work to do in there."

"So do I," Lee said. "I am doing my Father's work."

For a moment Mike looked up in sharp surprise, then realizing that Lee was quoting a passage from the Bible to him, he shook his head. "Don't pull that stuff on me, Lee. You know what I'm talking about. I don't want you in their way, that's all."

"I don't think I've been in the way," Lee said. "From time to time I've even tried to make myself helpful, running errands for them when everyone is busy. Has someone complained?"

"No, no one has complained."

"I'm glad."

"It appears as if you also have a lot of visitors. I'm told that your office and counseling room have as much traffic as the day rooms."

"These are young men under a great deal of stress," Lee replied. "I do what I can for them."

"Yes, they are, but I don't know that all this intense counseling helps the situation," Mike answered. "I would like for you to be less . . . shall we say receptive . . . to their expressions of fear and doubt."

"Dad, how can you say that? How could you possibly be against these men trying to sort through their fears? You've gone on several missions. You of all people know what they must face. Or are you completely without fear?"

"Of course, I'm not without fear," Mike replied. "No sane man could do what we do without being afraid. But fear is something you must conquer from within. I've seen men go off the deep end when they lose a lucky charm, or they don't follow some superstitious ritual. I don't hold with superstitions, and I don't want religion to become their crutch."

"Whoa, Dad, wait a minute. You aren't equating faith in God with superstition, are you? I know you aren't an atheist. After all, attending church with you and Mom helped me form my own religious foundation."

"No, I'm not an atheist, and I didn't mean to imply that religion was a superstition," Mike said. He stroked his chin. "The truth is, I think you do serve some purpose by being here, maybe even more than I was initially willing to admit. But no government anywhere has ever asked more of the military than we are asking of these young men. Daylight precision bombing? It's a noble concept, this idea of destroying the factories and war-making potential while limiting the number of civilians we kill. The only problem is that the geniuses who came up with the idea aren't flying the missions. We are flying them. And I don't want men up there with me who have weakened spirits because of misdirected faith, whether it be in a lucky charm or in you."

"I can't speak for lucky charms, but I can say that the ones who come to see me aren't putting their faith in me. They are putting their faith in God, and they are the stronger because of it."

"What about the ice cream and Coca-Cola?" Mike asked.

Lee smiled sheepishly. "You know about that, do you?"

"Everyone in the Wing knows about it. I've already been asked by other group commanders how we can do this. I assumed you were conning extra rations from the mess officer, but he tells me that he's never given you anything."

"No, sir, he hasn't."

"Then where does it come from?"

"I don't know," Lee admitted. "Corporal Gates gets it somewhere. He seems to have an amazing ability to come up with things when we need them."

"Like your car?"

"You know about that, too, do you?"

"I've been told there is a betting pool in effect to choose the day the MPs are going to come haul your corporal away for stealing that car."

"It isn't stolen."

"You're sure about that?"

"That was the first thing I asked him, and he assured me that he didn't steal it."

"Then where did it come from?"

"Kenny . . . that is, Corporal Gates . . . has it on permanent dispatch from the navy."

For a moment, Mike looked shocked, then he laughed out loud. "From the navy?"

"Yes, sir."

"What do you know? From the navy. Hah! I hope there's some Annapolis grad, class of 'sixteen, who's going crazy about now, trying to find it. I don't suppose you have any idea how he did that, do you?"

"No, sir. I just know that he is a very clever young man."

"I've run across clever and opportunistic people before, and it generally always catches up with them. As long as his extra channel acquisitions are used for the good of the group, I'll let it go. But you keep an eye on him, Lee. People like that, who find it easy to beat the system, nearly always wind up skimming a little off for themselves."

"I don't think Kenny is like that," Lee said.

"Uh-huh, so you say."

"No, I'm serious. I think Kenny's heart is in the right place."

"Yes, well, I'll be honest with you, I wish my maintenance officers had some people who were as enterprising as your corporal. If they did, maybe we wouldn't always be short of parts and matériel. Like thirty-two hundredths safety wire," he said pointedly.

"Safety wire?"

"Thirty-two. Do you get my meaning, Lee?"

Lee smiled. "Yes, sir, I think I do."

15

Tunis
June 1, 1943

T here was a very real possibility that Emily would not get to see either George in North Africa or Mark in England. The reason she might be denied the opportunity was that she had been prohibited from writing them and telling them where the USO troupe would be going and when they would get there.

"I'm sure all of you can understand," Captain Felder, the army liaison officer who was assigned to the troupe, explained. "The enemy would like nothing better than to capture one of our USO troupes. It would devastate the morale of our fighting men."

"To say nothing of our morale," Donnie Fritz said, eliciting a laugh from the comment.

Emily wasn't the only one who had someone overseas that she wanted to see. Nearly everyone was in the same boat, and all were as disappointed as she was that they would be unable to announce their arrival.

How disappointing and frustrating it would be, she thought, *to do a show within a short distance of George and he not know I was here.* To her relief, once they arrived in the theater of operations, Captain Felder made it his sole duty to locate close relatives of the performers and, if possible, get them to the show.

Maurice Felder was very good at his job. Before the war he had been a public relations man in Hollywood and was accustomed to working with performers and their requests.

As soon as the two C-47s, which had been pressed into service to haul the USO troupe around, landed, Felder went to work. He contacted every performer in the troupe, soliciting names and units of the men they wanted to attend the show.

When Captain Felder located George, he was in the middle of a softball game. George's team was trailing by one run, but Larry was at bat and there were two runners on base. There was one out, and Larry had one strike. George was in the on-deck circle.

"Come on, Larry, don't try and kill the ball. Just meet it," George was saying.

"No batter, no batter, no batter," came from the infield.

Larry swung at and missed a second pitch.

"There's a hole in the bat," the chatter continued.

"Come on, Larry, what are you doing? Just get on base."

"Sergeant Hagan?" Captain Felder called.

"Not now," George said, waving at whoever called him.

"Are you Sergeant Hagan?"

Larry swung and hit the ball on one bounce, straight to the second baseman. The second baseman stepped on second, then threw to first, doubling Larry up. That ended the threat and the game, with George's team losing.

"No!" George shouted in frustration.

"Yea!" several of the players on the winning team shouted.

"Sergeant Hagan?" Felder called again.

"What do you want?" George shouted in anger. Then turning to see that he was being called by a captain, he added, "Sir?"

Felder laughed. "Sorry about the double play."

"Yes, sir, well, that's what happens," he turned toward Larry and spoke loudly enough to make certain Larry could hear him, "when you try to kill the ball instead of just meeting it."

"Come on, Sarge, if I would've made a home run, I would've been a hero."

"And if frogs had wings, they wouldn't bump their butt every time they jump," George replied, though the flash of anger was now gone and he was laughing. He turned back to Captain Felder. "What can I do for you, Captain?"

Felder held up his finger. "Ah, Sergeant, it's what I am doing for you," he said. "I have a message from your sister."

"My sister? Emily? What's the matter? Is everything okay? Has something happened to one of my parents?"

"No, no, everything is fine," Felder said quickly. "In fact, I think you will find that things are very fine indeed. Especially as you will get to see your sister tomorrow."

"What? What are you talking about?"

"Tomorrow there will be a USO performance for the troops. Your sister is a member of that show."

George laughed. "Good one, Captain. For a minute there, you had me going."

Now it was Felder's time to look confused, and he checked the name on his form again. "You are Sergeant George Adam Hagan, from Newport News, Virginia, are you not?"

"Yes."

"And you have a sister, Emily Hagan?"

"Yes."

Felder smiled and breathed a sigh of relief. "Then you are the man I'm looking for." Felder gave George a yellow card. "Here, show this pass when you get there. It will get you right up front."

"All right," George said, though the tone of his voice indicated that he was still in doubt.

"You still don't believe me, do you?" Captain Felder said. "Wait a minute. I'll give you something that will eliminate all doubt."

Felder walked back over to his jeep, poked around for a second, then came back, carrying a magazine. "Recognize this magazine?"

149

"Sure, it's *Home Front*," George said.

"There's an article inside that you might find interesting," he said. "It's on page seventy-seven. See you tomorrow."

"What is it, Sarge? What did that captain want?" Larry asked, coming over to George as he was opening the magazine.

"It *is* her!" George said in shock. He shook his head. "But how can this be? I haven't heard anything about this."

"Who? What?"

George showed the picture to Larry and also to Don and Mel, who had come over to see what was going on.

"This is Emily," he said. "My sister."

"Wow! I know now why you're so ugly. She got all the looks," Mel said.

"Who's this guy?" Don asked, pointing to the smiling officer whose arm was intertwined with Emily's.

"Yeah. It says here they're toasting their engagement," Mel said.

"Engagement? I don't know anything about an engagement," George said. "'Course, I didn't know anything about her coming over here either. I hope we have time to talk tomorrow. I've got a lot of questions to ask."

George wasn't good at guessing crowd size, but he figured there had to be four or five thousand people gathered in a large field just outside Tunis. The men were sitting on backpacks, helmets, or the ground, though up front there were a few rows of wounded who were sitting on benches and, in some cases, in wheelchairs. MPs were directing the arriving soldiers to areas where they could be seated. "Sit, don't stand," they were told.

"I, uh, have this card," George said, showing the yellow pass Felder had given him.

"Yeah, Sarge, that means you can go on down front," the MP said. "There will be someone to help you down there."

"Hey, good deal! Come on, guys, we're down front!" Larry said to Don and Mel.

"No, you ain't," the MP said, sticking out his hand to stop them.

"Come on. We're with him," Larry said, pointing to George. "We're in the same tank crew."

"You got a yellow pass?"

"No."

"Then you ain't with him."

"They can't go with me?" George asked.

"Sorry, Sarge. If we let the buddies of everyone who has a yellow pass up front, there wouldn't be no up front, if you get what I mean."

"Yeah, I guess so," George said. He turned to Larry and the others. "Look, if I get a chance, I'll introduce you fellas to her."

"Wow!" Larry said. "Think about it! Our sergeant has a sister in the USO show."

George walked down the center clearing, all the way toward the stage. The stage had been built by the engineers just for this show. It stood about four feet off the ground and was flanked on either side by large GP, or general purpose tents, which were clearly marked as men's and women's dressing rooms. Canvas screens stretched from each dressing room to the stage, allowing the performers to make their entrances and exits unobserved except for the time they were actually on the stage. A large white canvas formed the stage backdrop. On the canvas were the words UNITED SERVICE ORGANIZATIONS SHOWS PROUDLY PRESENTS DONNIE FRITZ'S HOME FRONT REVIEW.

Near the back of the stage was a band, and it was playing "Long Ago and Far Away." There were a couple of microphones standing at the front of the stage, but as yet, only the band was onstage.

Captain Felder met George when he reached the front of the crowd, then escorted him over to an area to one side. There were at least two dozen other soldiers in the same area.

"Have a seat right in there, Sergeant," Felder said. "You'll have a really good view of the show from here."

"Will I get to talk to my sister?"

"Yes, of course. As soon as the show is over," Felder promised.

The band finished its number, but before it could start another one, there was the sound of sirens. A nervous ripple passed through the crowd as everyone wondered what it meant. Then George heard the name Patton being mentioned, and everyone twisted around to get a look.

At that moment, a half-track came roaring up the center aisle. General George Patton was standing up in the back of the half-track, holding on to a highly polished brass rail as if he were a Roman conqueror, riding in a chariot. He was wearing a pair of ivory-handled pistols, and he stared straight ahead, his square jaw straining against the helmet chin-strap. The half-track stopped in front of the stage and Patton got out, then moved quickly up the steps and strode to the center to stand in front of the microphone.

General Patton had replaced General Fredendall shortly after the fiasco of Sidi Bou Zid. From the very moment Patton arrived, he instituted an immediate makeover of the Second Corps. He was a martinet who insisted upon spit and polish. He was especially hard on those who were caught without a steel helmet, levying a fifty-dollar fine against officers and a twenty-five-dollar fine against enlisted men. There were even stories of the general jerking open doors to latrines to see if the men inside were wearing their steel pots.

The men didn't like him at first, but he had won their respect and begrudging admiration by leading them to a series of victories, something the U.S. Army had been in short supply of since their initial landing in North Africa.

Now, as Patton stood at the microphone, the men stood, and a spontaneous cheer erupted through the crowd. George, remembering his own bitterness over the defeat at Sidi Bou Zid, and the sweetness of the victories thereafter, joined in the cheering and applause.

Patton held his arms up, at first to quiet the crowd, then he clasped his hands over his head, and that just incited them to more cheers. He let them cheer for a moment longer, obviously basking in it, then he held out his hands to call for silence. Gradually the cheering stopped, and at a signal from Patton, the men sat back down. The general began to speak.

"When General Eisenhower asked me what I thought would improve the morale of the Second Corps, I told him that the best thing we could to do is, kick the Germans out, and bring a few pretty American girls in."

The crowd laughed.

"So, I'm happy to tell you, that is exactly what we have done. We've kicked the Germans out, and now we've brought some pretty American girls in."

More cheering and laughter.

"I know it has been a long time since you men looked at anything but the ugly faces of your sergeants, and the even uglier tails of the Germans who are retreating from you . . ."

Again, the crowd laughed.

"But that's all changing today because today we are proud to bring you some of the most beautiful young women in America. So sit back and enjoy the show, men, because when it's over, we're going to go to Italy to kick some more German butt!"

Patton left the stage to thundering applause and was replaced by a man wearing slacks and a sport shirt, swinging a golf club. He stepped up to the microphone.

"I'm Donnie Fritz. Who did you expect, Bob Hope?"

The audience laughed, then Fritz introduced the first act.

There were whistles and catcalls when Emily came out front, after the show, to embrace George.

"Come on, guys. She's his sister," someone said.

"I had no idea you were doing anything like this," George said. "You never mentioned in any of your letters that you were in a USO show. And neither did Mom or Dad."

"I told them not to," Emily replied. "I didn't want to get everyone's hopes up in case it didn't work out."

"My sister in show business," George said, laughing. "How in the world did that ever come about?"

Emily told him about the photos *Home Front* magazine took of women in the war industry. "For some reason they selected me as one of the girls to come over here."

"Well, all I can say is, I'm glad they did," George said, embracing her again. "My little sister. I tell you the truth, if a little green man from Mars walked up to speak to me, I wouldn't be more surprised."

"Ahem," Larry coughed, clearing his throat.

Turning, George saw his tank crew standing there, all three of them holding their hats in their hands. "What?" he asked.

"Ahem," Larry said again, nodding just slightly toward Emily.

George laughed. "All right, I guess there's no getting around this, is there?"

"You promised, Sarge," Mel said.

"Emily, allow me to introduce my tank crew," George said, calling their names out to her.

"I know you boys probably have girlfriends back home," Emily said. "So this is from them." She kissed each one on the cheek.

"Larry doesn't have a girlfriend," Mel said.

"Oh? Well, then maybe I'd better take that kiss back," Emily teased, smiling and kissing him again.

Larry grinned broadly while everyone around him whistled and gave catcalls.

"You boys take care of each other, will you?" she asked. Suddenly tears came to her eyes. "And take care of my brother for me."

"Yes, ma'am, we promise you we'll do that," Don said.

"Five minutes, Emily," someone from the show called.

"Five minutes?" George said. "That's all the time we've got?"

Emily nodded. "We have to get back to the airplanes. We have two more shows to do today."

"Five minutes. I have so many questions to ask, I can't get them all asked in five minutes."

"Carol is doing fine and, of course, sends her love," Emily said. She smiled. "Oh, and Crystal is talking up a storm now. She says, 'Good night, Daddy,' every night."

"Who is she saying it to?" George asked.

Emily laughed. "You, silly. Or at least to your picture."

George felt a lump come to his throat, and he blinked several times to hold back the tears. "I can't believe that my baby is beginning to talk and I'm not there to hear her. She won't even know who I am when I get back."

"She'll know. Everyone talks about you to her all the time. Oh, and Mom and Dad are doing well and send their love."

"What about you?" George asked.

Emily smiled. "I don't have to send my love; I brought it. And I'm doing fine, as you can see."

"I don't mean that. I mean, what's this I see in the magazine about you being engaged? I hadn't heard anything about that. And what happened to Mark White, your bomber pilot?"

"Oh," she said in a small voice. "You saw that?"

"How could I not see it? The picture takes up half a page."

"It isn't true, George, none of it. I never even met Major Mitchell until that night. And I haven't seen him since. The whole thing was a publicity stunt. We went to dinner and a show together, not just us, but Norma Jean and her escort and Betty and her escort. I knew there would be pictures, but I had no idea they would say something like that."

"Have you told Mark about it?"

"No."

"You should. It will go down a lot easier if he hears the story from you before he sees the article."

"I know, but it's too late now. Even if I wrote him today, I would beat the letter there."

"Why didn't you write him before you left the States?"

"I didn't know about the article. I didn't find out about it until someone showed it to me on the flight over. And the reason I didn't tell him about being in the USO before is the same reason I didn't tell you. I wasn't sure it would work out, and I didn't want him to be disappointed if he was looking for me, and I didn't show up."

"Emily, it's time to go!" someone called.

"Oh, George, if he sees it before I see him, what am I going to do?" Emily asked.

The trucks that brought the troupe from the airport started their engines.

"Come on, Emily!" Betty shouted from the back of one of the trucks. "They won't wait!"

"It's likely to come hard if he sees the article before you can explain it to him. You don't know what it's like over here, Sis. We live life with exposed nerve endings. Something like this can really knock a guy for a loop."

"I know. I'll just have to make him understand, that's all."

The truck started to drive away.

"Oh, they're leaving me!" Emily said.

Suddenly there was a squeal of brakes as the truck came to an abrupt halt. Looking around, George saw the reason for the sudden stop. The truck's departure was blocked by a tank . . . his tank. Larry's head was sticking through the turret, while Don's and Mel's heads could be seen in the driver's and gunner's slots.

George laughed out loud.

"What is it? What's going on?"

"It would appear that my crew has flagged down your ride," he said. He gave his sister a final hug. "When you get back home, give Mom and Dad a big hug for me."

"I will," Emily called, running toward the truck where hands were reaching down to help her. "Take care, George!"

June 3, 1943

Mission number twelve. Took off on instruments because the fog was so bad that we couldn't see fifty feet in front of us. Broke out of fog at about five hundred feet and had four-tenths cover by the time we bombed the target, Bremen. Flak and enemy fighter resistance were very stiff. We had number two engine shot out, then had to rip the guts out of remaining three in order to maintain formation integrity and return to base safely.

Gideon's Sword required four new engines and extensive sheet-metal repair before it was certified flyable.

16

Davencourt
June 3, 1943

As *Gideon's Sword* trundled out toward the end of the runway, the fog was so thick that Mark could barely see the tail of the airplane in front of him. That concerned him because with five thousand pounds of fused bombs, a collision, even on the ground, could be disastrous. Finally they reached the end of the active, and the airplane ahead of him turned onto the runway. Above the idle of his own engines, he could hear the roar of the B-17 before him as it started its takeoff run, disappearing quickly into the fog bank.

With no visual confirmation, the flight plan called for a thirty-second spacing between takeoffs. Trusting that the aircraft in front of him had taken off as it was supposed to, and wasn't sitting on the runway hidden in the fog, Mark watched the eight-day clock on his panel. When the sweep hand reached thirty seconds, he pushed the throttle and propeller levers forward, brought up the tail almost immediately thereafter, and rushed into the opaque space before him. He was on instruments even before he left the ground, and it wasn't until he heard a cheer from Adrian Rogers, his bombardier, that he realized they had broken clear of the fog.

Once they were above the low-lying bank of fog they had a beautiful climb up through canyons of huge, billowing, sun-brightened clouds. At ten thousand feet they joined the other bombers in formation and went on oxygen. A little later, they tested their guns. They passed over the coast of France at twenty-three thousand feet, their path clearly marked by the long vapor trails that spewed out from every engine of every airplane in the formation.

Over the intercom, Paul, who was from Plano, Texas, began singing "Deep in the Heart of Texas," and at the appropriate time, everyone on board stamped his feet in rhythm so that Mark could actually feel it throughout the plane. Mark should have silenced them, but he didn't. Instead, he grinned and sang along with them, and when everyone else was stamping his feet, he wiggled the rudder, causing the entire plane to shimmy.

The crew got serious as they approached the target, searching the sky for enemy fighters. Charley Phillips in the ball turret saw them first.

"FWs coming up fast."

"How many?"

"At least nine of them."

"Okay, gunners, stay on 'em," Mark called.

Charley opened up first, hosing a long string of glowing shells toward the fighters as they climbed up. He stayed on one of them as it passed by and actually saw the inside of the FW cockpit fill with a red mist as his bullets hit the pilot. The plane fell off to one side, then started spinning down.

For the next few minutes they were kept busy as the fighters approached, made their firing run, then broke away. There was the usual game of chicken as the fighters swung around in front, then bored head-on toward the bombers, pulling up at the last moment.

But in one case the fighter didn't pull up. Mark was looking right at it when it plowed into the nose of a nearby B-17. The bomber swallowed the fighter like a big fish swallowing a smaller one. The fighter's wings were sheared off as its fuselage disappeared into the maw. Pieces tumbled from the nose of the bomber, then the B-17 bucked as it took in the German plane in one large gulp.

The fuselage of the Focke-Wulf stopped somewhere inside the cavity of the bomber, but its engine plunged all the way through, popping out of the bomber's tail. The Fortress, with everything gone forward of the windscreen, nosed over and started down, even as all four engines continued to turn. The carnage inside the ship had to be total, for nothing could have survived the telescoping effect of a six-hundred-mile-per-hour closing rate.

"Navigator to pilot, we're at the IP," Art Bollinger said.

"What?" Mark said, almost distractedly. He had been mesmerized by the horror of what he had just seen.

"We're at the IP," Art said again.

Mark shook off the horror and refocused on the business at hand. "Right. Okay, Adrian, it's all yours," he said, taking his hands off the control yoke so the bombardier could fly the plane from his bombsight.

The next 180 seconds were always the worst. For three minutes the bomber would have to fly absolutely straight and level until they reached the release point. Adrian Rogers glued his eye to the sight. The target passed under the crosshairs, and he hit the bomb release. The plane jerked up slightly as the electromagnetic restraints released their grip to let the bombs fall from the racks.

"Bombs away!" Adrian shouted.

Mark jerked the wheel over hard and kicked the rudder, yanking the airplane around so as not to be an easy target for the gunners below. Already the sky was filled with the dirty puff-balls of exploding anti-aircraft shells.

A shell burst just beneath them, sending fragments up through the wing. At first Mark thought they had sustained no significant damage, but number two engine started shaking so severely that there was a very real danger it could rip off the wing. A thin stream of black began pouring out of the nacelle.

"Fire on number one!" Paul called in alarm, reaching for the fire extinguisher.

"No, wait!" Mark said. He pulled the mixture back to idle cutoff, then feathered the propeller. The prop turned knife-edge into the wind, then stopped.

"It's oil," Mark said. He watched the engine for a moment, then he saw a tiny flicker of flame. "Now hit the fire bottle!" he called.

Paul hit the button, and white foam began oozing out from beneath the cowling. The fire went out.

"Good move," Paul said. "If we had hit it too soon, we wouldn't have had it when the fire really did start."

"We're going to have to go to full power on the other three engines in order to stay with everyone for the trip home," Mark said, moving the throttles and prop levers forward on the remaining three. The roar increased.

"They won't hold together," Paul warned.

"We've got no choice," Mark said. "If we fall out of formation, we'll be sitting ducks."

After the run through the flak, the fighters came back again, and again the gunners managed to hold them off.

"Crane," Mark called on the intercom. "How's our new boy doing?"

The new boy was Staff Sergeant Kerry Lindell from Utica, New York. He had replaced Eddie Gordon on the left waist gun, and this was only his second mission.

"Ah, he's doin' great, Lieutenant," Crane said. "He's already claimed three."

Mark laughed, remembering how when his crew was new, there were often multiple claims made on the same kill. "Tell him to leave some for the other guys."

"Cylinder head temp is going up on number four," Paul said. "Mark, we're pulling forty-two inches and turning twenty-four hundred RPM on all three engines. Maybe we had better ease back a bit on the power."

"It's all we can do to stay with them now," Mark said. "But look at it this way. If we make it back, we'll gut the engines for sure, which all but guarantees some stand-down time. It's going to take them a week to get this bird up again."

"Yeah," Paul said. "Yeah, hey, that's not a bad thought. Maybe we can go to London."

"Hear that, guys? We're goin' to London!" Ross Bird told the rest of the crew.

Lee was at his usual position in the operations shack when he saw Corporal Gates stick his head through the doorway. He stood up and walked over to him.

"How are things going?" Gates asked.

"They've hit the target and they're on the way back," Lee said. "No word on our losses, of course."

"You'll pray most of 'em in, Chaplain," Kenny said. "You've got the best 'prayin' 'em in' record in the entire Wing."

"I appreciate your confidence," Lee said. "Did you get the item you went after?"

"You mean the safety wire? Yes, sir. Piece of cake."

Over in the group's field maintenance hangar, Master Sergeant Logan McMurtry saw a box sitting on one of the worktables. Its presence there irritated him because he had told his mechanics time and time again that a tidy maintenance hangar is a safe maintenance hangar. He walked over to the box in order to get a closer look and also perhaps to get a clue as to the man who might have left it there. Whoever it was, he would see to it that it cost him a stripe.

"What the . . . ?" he said aloud when he looked into the box. Then he hurried into Captain Rodney Gibson's office. Gibson was the group maintenance officer.

"I don't know how you did it, sir, but you sure are going to make a lot of my guys happy. To say nothing of the old man."

"Sergeant, what are you talking about?" Captain Gibson asked.

"Why, the safety wire, sir."

"Safety wire?"

"There's an entire case of thirty-two safety wire sitting on one of the tables out there. Enough to clear every ship we've got on Red-X. Are you telling me you don't know anything about it?"

"That's exactly what I'm telling you, Sergeant," Captain Gibson said, getting up from his desk. "Suppose you take me out there and show me."

They walked through the hangar, passing by the half-dozen B-17s that were in various stages of repair. McMurtry took Gibson over to the table. "There it is," McMurtry said, pointing to the large cardboard box.

Gibson reached down into the box and picked up a spool of the shining silver-colored wire. He hefted it in his hand for a minute, then reached down into the box and pulled out several more. Finally he looked at McMurtry with a huge smile spread across his face.

"Do you believe in the tooth fairy, Sergeant?"

"The tooth fairy?"

"You know, the little girl with wings who leaves a dime under your pillow when you lose a tooth?"

"I never give it no thought, sir," McMurtry said.

"I never did either. But evidently she exists. Only she's grown up now, and instead of bringing us dimes, she's bringing us safety wire. Get it distributed, Sergeant. Get it distributed before she changes her mind and comes back for it."

"Yes, sir," McMurtry said.

As was his custom, Lee was standing out on the tarmac as the bombers landed, those with wounded having first priority, then the others in their proper sequence. One of the landing B-17s was unable to get his gear down. Lee prayed for them as the pilot lined the airplane up just as he would for a normal landing and eased it down onto the grass alongside the runway. The propellers stopped turning the instant they dug into the ground, but the plane continued its long slide forward, kicking up dirt and dust as it did so.

The crash trucks and ambulances rushed out to tend to the bomber, sirens blaring and engines roaring as they sped to the site.

The rest of the airplanes came in, taxiing by Lee. In the ones that were unscathed, some of the crew had already climbed from the plane and were actually sitting on top, while others were leaning out through the waist gun opening. One of the waist gunners pointed to his gun, made a motion with his hand to indicate a plane going down, then held up one finger, using sign language to brag of his victory. Many of the pilots waved through their open windows.

As *Gideon's Sword* taxied by, Lee saw that one of the engines was scarred and blackened, and though it was an inboard engine that was normally off during taxi anyway, he knew it had been lost during the mission. He looked anxiously toward the front and was rewarded with a small nod from Mark. That told him the plane was scarred, but all his people were safe. Lee breathed a quick prayer of thanks.

17

Davencort
June 5, 1943

Paul Mobley got a new airplane. That was a mixed blessing for him because getting a new plane meant that he wouldn't be on stand-down while *Gideon's Sword* was in maintenance. However, it also meant that he was being promoted to pilot and aircraft commander, and he was looking forward to that.

"What are you going to name it?" Mark asked. Mark was lying on his bunk with his hands laced behind his head. Paul was sitting on the edge of his bunk. From the several hardstands outside, they could hear the almost ceaseless roar of engines as the maintenance crews worked on the bombers, getting them ready for the next mission, whatever and whenever that would be.

"I don't know what I'm going to name it. I hadn't thought about it," Paul replied. "I was happy with the name *Gideon's Sword*, didn't figure I'd ever have to come up with a name of my own." He was looking through his pile of records. "Want to hear some Glenn Miller?" he asked, holding up one of the disks.

"That's *Captain* Glenn Miller to you, Soldier," Mark teased, referring to the fact that the popular orchestra leader was now a captain in the army special services.

"Yeah, sure, I mean Captain Miller." Paul put the record in place, then turned on the player. The mellow strains of "Moonlight Serenade" filled the room.

"Airplanes take on their own personality, and I think the name has a lot to do with it," Mark said.

"Say, what about *Moonlight Serenade?*" Paul asked, smiling broadly.

"Yeah," Mark agreed. "Yeah, that would be a great name."

There was a knock on the door.

"The party you are looking for is three buildings down!" Mark called.

Another knock.

"They moved away, no forwarding address!" Paul shouted.

A third knock.

"Persistent, isn't he?" Mark said.

Paul opened the door. "What do you want? Didn't you hear us say nobody lived here?"

"Sorry, sir," the soldier said. "Colonel Grant wants to see Lieutenant White."

"White, White, didn't he go home last week?" Mark asked, not getting up from his bed. "Yes, I'm sure he went home. There was something about them wanting to use him in a bond drive."

"No, that wasn't it," Paul said. "I heard Dorothy Lamour wanted to use him as her pool boy."

"He said right away, sir."

Sighing, White got up from his bed, put on his hat, and started toward the door. "All right, lead on, McDuff."

"It's Lemon, sir. PFC Carl Lemon."

"Lead on, Lemon."

"The CO wanted to see me?" Mark asked the adjutant, trying to read some indication in Major Ragsdale's face as to why he was summoned.

Ragsdale, who was working on some reports, kept his face expressionless. "Yes, go on in, he's expecting you."

Mark knocked on the door.

"Come in."

Mark stepped up to Colonel Grant's desk, stopped, and saluted. "Lieutenant White reporting to the CO as directed, sir."

Grant returned the salute. "You're out of uniform, Mr. White," he said.

Mark looked down at himself, wondering if he had forgotten his belt. No, his belt was in place.

"Sir, I don't understand," he said in confusion.

"You're wearing lieutenant's bars," he said. "Why are you wearing lieutenant's bars when you are a captain?" Suddenly Grant smiled, pulled open his desk drawer, then took out a pair of captain's bars. "Major Ragsdale!" he called.

"Yes, sir," Ragsdale replied, hurrying into the office.

Grant handed Ragsdale the bars. "See if you can get our group's newest captain into the proper uniform."

"Yes, sir," Ragsdale said, and he began taking the lieutenant's bar off Mark's right collar in order to replace it with the set of captain's bars. "You'd think these guys would have enough pride in themselves to at least be in proper uniform."

Mark smiled and accepted the ribbing good-naturedly. It was a game that was played often, this teasing of the newly promoted, and General George Washington had probably played the same game with his officers. No doubt some colonel, as yet unborn, would be playing the same game with his junior officers in the next century.

"What did you think about Paul Mobley getting his own aircraft?" Colonel Grant asked. "Do you think he was the right man for it?"

"Yes, sir. He's a good man. He will make a fine aircraft commander," Mark said.

"Yes, that's what I think as well. But that leaves you short a copilot."

"Yes, sir."

"I've got a man for you. John, is that new officer here?"

"He was putting his gear away," Ragsdale said, finishing with his task. "He should be back . . ." At that moment they heard the door in the outer office open and close, and Ragsdale looked through Colonel Grant's door. "Yes, here he is now, sir."

"Bring him in here."

"Lieutenant Duncan," Ragsdale called through the open door. "You want to come in here?"

"Yes, sir," a muffled voice replied from outside.

A tall, good-looking man stepped into the room then and, seeing that everyone in the room outranked him, saluted. All three officers returned his salute, but it was only Colonel Grant's prerogative to tell him, "At ease."

"Lieutenant Duncan, this is Captain Mark White. He'll be your pilot and aircraft commander. Mark, this is Lieutenant Lyndon Duncan."

"Pleasure to meet you, sir," Duncan said, reaching out to shake Mark's hand.

"Lyndon Duncan?" Mark said. "There was a pretty good ballplayer for the Cardinals named Lyndon Duncan."

"Just pretty good, sir?" Duncan asked.

"I don't think he ever hit three hundred," Mark replied.

"Yes, sir, three-oh-three in 1941. Or at least, it would have been three-oh-three if I had gotten one more time at bat to make it legal."

"You mean you really are that Lyndon Duncan? You are a major-league baseball player?"

Duncan chuckled. "I *was* a major-league ballplayer. Now I'm a co-pilot on a B-17."

"All right!" Mark said. "Now we'll see which squadron has the best softball team!"

The other officers laughed.

"Are you all squared away?" Mark asked.

"Yes, sir, just got moved in. So, when do we get started?"

"We're on stand-down for several days," Mark said. "*Gideon's Sword* is on Red-X for maintenance. As a matter of fact, I'm going into London this afternoon. Care to come along?"

"I just came from London. If you don't mind, I think I'll stay here and get acquainted with the base."

"No, of course I don't mind. Hey, what's Stan Musial really like?"

"Musial? Oh, well, he's a nice guy," Duncan said, a little surprised by the question. "A really nice guy."

Mark laughed. "I'm just teasing you, Duncan. It's as big a treat meeting you as it would be Musial or Slaughter or anyone else. As far as I'm concerned, anyone who can make it to the majors is all right in my book. This is quite a comedown, but welcome to the Six-oh-fifth."

Duncan smiled. "What? You mean I'm welcome even though I've never batted three hundred?"

"Even if you haven't hit three hundred. And wait until I tell my sister you are on my crew. She's an even bigger baseball fan than I am."

Fort Smith, Arkansas

Susan and Mrs. Meyer were sitting on the porch swing drinking iced tea and listening to the radio. It had become a daily ritual for them. Mrs. Meyer initiated the practice because she felt sorry for Susan having to stay all alone back in that little cabin behind the house, five days a week.

For her part, Susan enjoyed her time with Mrs. Meyer, even if the tea was so sweet that she feared insulin shock from drinking it. Right now, an advertising jingle was being sung on the radio. "Super Suds, Super Suds, lots of suds with Super Su . . . uh . . . uds."

"Are you all getting along all right back there, Honey?" Mrs. Meyer asked.

"Yes, we're doing fine."

"I worry about you, bein' all by yourself so much of the time."

"I do get a little lonely during the week, but the weekends are wonderful," Susan said.

Mrs. Meyer chuckled. "Oh, my, I 'spect they are, havin' that fine-lookin' young man come home to you every weekend. I told Mary Margaret that he's so good lookin' he pure gives an old lady the vapors." She fanned herself as Susan laughed.

"It's too bad the soldier boys' wives don't get together more often," Mrs. Meyer continued. "I 'spect y'all'd get along just fine, bein' as you got so much in common. Have you met any of the wives of any of your husband's friends?"

"Not really," Susan said. "But I have been thinking about something. I've been thinking I might tell Bob to invite one of his married friends over for dinner this weekend. That way I could meet someone. And it might be fun to entertain someone."

"Oh, my, I think that would be a wonderful idea!" Mrs. Meyer said, gushing with enthusiasm. "You could decorate with flowers from the garden. And if you want to bake anything, why you're welcome to use my oven."

"Thank you."

"And, listen, I have a perfectly marvelous suggestion. Why don't you use Willie Mae?"

"I beg your pardon?"

"Miz Willie Mae Jenkins. You met her, remember? She's the colored lady that used to live where you live now. She's got a grandson who's a pilot in the army."

"Yes, I remember her, but I don't understand what you are saying. Use her in what way?"

"Why, to do for you. For the party."

"Oh, I don't think that would be . . ."

"Nonsense, Willie Mae would love to do it. She's retired now, but she still does for people from time to time. And just working for one meal like that, she probably wouldn't charge you more'n a dollar."

"I don't know, Mrs. Meyer. I've never had a maid or anything. I just wouldn't feel right about it."

"That's 'cause you're a Yankee girl, and you aren't used to it," Mrs. Meyer said. "Down here nearly ever'one has a maid. If we didn't use them, the poor colored folks would starve for lack of work. Look at it as if you're helpin' out."

"All right, I guess it wouldn't hurt this once."

"Oh, you're going to have a wonderful party, you'll see," Mrs. Meyer said, reaching over to pat Susan's hand.

Fort Smith, Arkansas

Once a week, Bob would go to the telephone center and make a tele-phone call to Mrs. Meyer. Mrs. Meyer would then get Susan, and Bob and Susan would have as intimate a conversation as they could under the circumstances. The opportunity for personal conversation was lim-ited because Bob was surrounded by soldiers waiting their turn for a phone. At the other end of the line, Susan had to deal with the fact that she was standing in the Meyer living room, talking quietly and try-ing to hear over the radio that was always going. Both of them had to consider the fact that Mrs. Meyer's phone was a party line with the dis-tinct possibility that some nosy busybody would be listening in.

When Bob called this week, Susan told him that she wanted him to invite someone over for dinner this Saturday night. "Someone who is married and who has his wife here with him," she said.

Arrangements having been made, Susan then went to the store, ration book in hand, to see what she could come up with for their guests. Her two-and-a-half-pound roast beef cost her one dollar and thirty-two cents, plus thirty red-ration points. The ration points came most dear because that represented a substantial part of her month's meat ration. Since Bob ate most of his meals out at the base, she only got a partial ration allowance for him, while she got sixty-four meat ration points for herself. But she didn't eat that much meat while Bob was gone anyway, so it didn't bother her that much. And since she bought her vegetables—fresh potatoes, string beans, lettuce, and tomatoes—from a home-grown vegetable stand, they required no ration coupons. The result was, she came home from her shopping trip with enough food to make it a real dinner.

"You did tell him this was dress up?" Susan asked. She looked at herself in the mirror and patted her hair to make certain it was exactly the way she wanted it to be.

"I told him," Bob said. "Of course, dress up for him will be just like it is for me. Class A khaki uniform, complete with tie."

"Tell me about the people you invited."

"Well, his name is Roy Carter, and he is from Hastings, Nebraska. Before the war he was a truck driver. The only thing I know about his wife is what he tells me. Her name is Edith, and she is the most beautiful and the most wonderful woman ever to walk the face of the earth."

"He says that about her?"

"Yep."

"How sweet. And do you tell him that about me?"

"How can I? There can only be one most wonderful of anything. I just tell him you're second best," Bob teased.

"Oh, you . . ." Susan hit him on the shoulder.

"Miz Susan," Willie Mae said. "I got the table all set. I'm goin' go up to the big house now and get the roast beef out of the oven."

"Okay, Willie Mae, thank you."

Bob waited until he heard the front door close, then he reached for Susan.

"Boy, am I glad she's gone," he said. "Now we can do some serious smooching!" He put his arms around her and pulled her toward him.

"Bob!" Susan said. "Behave yourself. You'll get me all mussed before our company comes. Besides, Willie Mae will be right back."

"I don't understand what we are doing with a maid in the first place," Bob said. "Think about it, a maid in a house this size. And Willie Mae is no small woman. When she's in here, she takes up half the room that's available."

Susan laughed. "You're awful," she said.

"Besides, it was no fun trying to get dressed in that tiny bathroom," he added.

"You didn't have to go in there. She wouldn't have come in here."

"Come in here? What are you talking about? She's half in here anytime she's in the house."

"Quit complaining. Let's go into the living room and wait for our guests."

"You really think we should wait in the living room? How about we go downstairs to wait in the parlor? Or maybe into the library. Wait, I know, we could wait for them out in our large marble-floored foyer."

Susan laughed again, then they stepped around the little wall that made up the bedroom.

"Look at that," Susan said, indicating the table. "Did you ever think, in your wildest dreams, that table could be so beautiful?"

"I have to admit, the table does look nice."

"Willie Mae did it."

The table was covered with a white tablecloth and a royal blue runner. Mrs. Meyer had loaned Susan four settings of china along with some crystal goblets and silver-plated flatware. Fresh flowers from the garden made an attractive centerpiece. The only problem with the table was that it took up the entire living room. There were no chairs around the table. The end of the table sat flush against the side wall of the house. On one side was the sofa, which was itself against the front wall. On the other side of the table was a bench. With the bench pulled out to allow seating, the table took up the entire living room so that in order to wait there, as Susan had suggested, they would have to be seated at the table.

"So, which side will we sit on?" Bob asked. "The sofa or the bench?"

"The sofa is more comfortable if you are just sitting, but if you are at the table, it's sort of awkward because you have to sit up toward the front of the seat. I think we should give them the bench, don't you?"

"By all means, we should be the gracious hosts," Bob teased. He sat on the sofa, then slid over to the inside corner.

Susan sat beside him, then reached over to take his hand. "Isn't this exciting?" she asked. "Our very first dinner guests."

Willie Mae came back into the house then, carrying the roast beef. "Umm, umm, this does smell good," she said. "It's going to be a fine dinner."

Lights flashed through the window, and when Bob turned to look outside, he saw a 1937 Plymouth pulling into the yard. "That's Roy," he said. He started to get up, but Susan put her hand out to stop him.

"Willie Mae will let them in," she said.

There was the sound of footsteps on the front porch, then a knock at the door.

"Willie Mae?" Susan asked.

Willie Mae opened the front door.

"Oh, I'm sorry," Roy said. "We must have the wrong . . ."

Bob leaned forward in order to look across the table toward the door. "Roy?" he called.

"Bob, is that you?"

"Your name please, sir?" Willie Mae asked.

"What?" Roy replied.

"May I have your name, sir?"

"Uh, Carter. Private Carter."

Willie Mae turned away from the door, then announced, as if announcing guests at a party in some grand mansion, "Private and Mrs. Carter."

"You may show them in, Willie Mae," Susan said.

Bob laughed. "What is this?" he asked. "What's all this about?"

"Shh," Susan replied. "This was Willie Mae's idea. She said that's the way it's done down here."

"Oh, Susan, the table is lovely," Edith Carter said as Willie Mae escorted them the two and one-half feet from the front door to the table.

Bob drove Willie Mae home that evening. He opened the front door for her, but she thanked him, then crawled into the backseat, saying, "I 'spec's it would be better if I rode back here."

"It was a nice dinner, wasn't it?" Bob asked as he drove her through the streets of Fort Smith.

"Yes, sir, it was a lovely dinner," Willie Mae said.

"That's thanks to you. You cooked a marvelous meal, and you made that table look beautiful."

"Thank you. It's kind of you to say so."

"Susan tells me you have a son in the army?"

"My grandson," Willie Mae said. "Though it's like he's my son. I've raised him from when he was a chile."

"He's an aviator?"

"Yes, sir."

"Good for him. I wish him all the best."

"Thank you, sir. That's mighty decent of you."

When Bob let her out in front of her small house, she thanked him again, then, taking her purse and a small brown paper bag, walked up toward the front of the house. Bob waited until he saw her unlock the door, then with a final wave, he drove off.

There was a letter in the mailbox. The return address was Tuskegee, but Willie Mae didn't have to see that to know that it was from her grandson. She would have recognized his neat penmanship anywhere.

Once inside the dark house, she reached up to pull on a string that turned on the single bare lightbulb hanging down from the ceiling. Settling into a comfortable overstuffed chair that had been a present to her from the Meyer family, she opened the letter and began to read.

Dear Grams,

The day we've all been waiting for has finally arrived. We'll be leaving sometime within the next week. Exactly when we are leaving and where we are going, I can't say, but I can say that the men here are very excited about it.

Believe me when I tell you that all of us are very much aware of the load we carry on our shoulders. We know that we will have to do even better than the white pilots in order to be considered as good. If we fail, the Negro may never get another chance like this. We have all taken an oath . . . any differences between us . . . any petty arguments or personality conflicts . . . are to be put aside until all this is over. For the duration of this war, we are truly all for one, and one for all.

Grams, I know you worried about me from the time I started flight school until the day I pinned on my wings. But you also know that this is something I have wanted to do for my entire life. Growing up, I thought it was an impossible dream. Colored men just didn't become aviators. I'm sorry that it took a war for that barrier to come down, but I thank God every night that I was at the right place, at the right time, to take advantage of this opportunity.

Just remember, Grams, your prayers kept me safe during flight school, and I know God will continue to listen to them while I'm overseas.

Your loving,

Lorenzo

Willie Mae wiped the tears from her eyes, then reached over to the table to pick up the picture Lorenzo had recently sent her. He was a fine-looking boy in his uniform, with his wings shining over his left pocket and his lieutenant's bars glistening from his shoulders.

"Oh, wouldn't my papa be proud of you now, chile?" Willie Mae said to the picture. Willie Mae's father had been a Buffalo Soldier, a sergeant in the Tenth Cavalry, who had fought against the Indians, and in the Spanish-American War. "It wouldn't surprise me none if he wasn't up there somewhere, just lookin' down on you now and bustin' out with pride that his great-grandson be an officer and an aviator."

Though Willie Mae was Lorenzo's grandmother, she had raised him as her own, almost from the day he was born. Lorenzo's mother had died of puerperal fever within three days of his birth. Lorenzo's father, Willie Mae's son, brought his infant son home so his mother could help with the raising. Then Lorenzo's father was killed in a ginning accident when Lorenzo was four, and Willie Mae had sole responsibility for him from then on. When one of her friends from church commented about the burden that had been placed on her by having to raise the child, she responded that she considered it a blessing, not a burden.

Willie Mae closed her eyes and bowed her head. "Dear Lord," she prayed. "I thank You again for givin' me that wonderful boy to raise and to love. And I thank You, Lord, for keepin' him safe in Your lovin' hands while he was learnin' to fly those airplanes. Now, Lord, I come to You in prayer, askin' that You protect him when he goes overseas to fight in this terrible war. Keep him and all the boys who trained with him safe."

Willie Mae started to end her prayer, but she paused for a moment, then went on.

"And, dear Lord, I met some nice folks tonight that I want You to look after too. Look after Mist' Bob when he go overseas, and look after Miz Susan's brother who, like my Lorenzo, be a flier. I pray this in the name of Your sweet Son, blessed Jesus. Amen."

Feeling better now, Willie Mae put Lorenzo's letter in a drawer where she kept all the other letters he had sent her. Then she kissed his picture and put it back on the table. After that, she removed a roast beef sandwich she had made for herself from the dinner she prepared tonight and, sitting there in the dim light in her comfortable chair, had her supper.

18

Davencourt
June 7, 1943

"Y ou wanted to see me, Chaplain?" Charley Phillips said, stepping not into Lee's office, but into the chapel itself.

"Yes, Sergeant Phillips," Lee replied. "I understand you were a farmer before you came into the army."

"Yes, sir, I come from Wilson, Arkansas. That's black dirt Mississippi River Delta land, the best farmin' land in the country."

"I have someone I'd like you to meet," Lee said. "His name is Henry Throgmorton, and he farms some of the Davencourt land on a crop percentage basis with the landowner."

Charley smiled broadly. "A crop percentage? You mean he's sharecroppin'? Why, that's what my pa and me was doin'. We was sharecroppin' for Mr. Wilson."

"Then you two should have a lot in common," Lee said. "He's inside."

In the chapel, sitting in the front pew, was a middle-aged man in civilian work clothes.

"Mr. Throgmorton, this is Sergeant Charley Phillips," Lee said. Then to Charley, Lee said, "Mr. Throgmorton came to me with a problem, but I told him I don't know the first thing about farming. I did remember, however, that you were interested in farming."

"Interested in farming?" Charley replied. "Pardon me, Chaplain, but that's a little like sayin' that President Roosevelt is interested in politics."

"Ah, good, then you may be just the man for him," Lee said. "Why don't I step outside and let the two of you just talk for a while? That is, if you don't mind."

"Mind? No, sir, I don't mind at all," Charley said.

"Did you get 'em together?" Kenny asked when Lee returned to his office.

"Yes, they're over in the chapel right now, having a wonderful discussion."

"That ought to cheer Charley up," Kenny said. "The other men in the crew said he's been mighty down lately. You know, he and Eddie Gordon were really close, and when Eddie was killed, it probably hurt Charley more'n it did anybody else. The boys thought that maybe talking farming with a real farmer would cheer him up."

"Well, I must say, he did appear more animated than I've seen him in a while," Lee said.

"Maybe this will work then," Kenny replied. "Oh, by the way, you got a letter today."

"I thought I already picked up the mail."

"This one came to me. Well, it's for you, and I haven't opened it or anything, but it was sent to me."

"Why would it be sent to you?"

"Because it's from my sister," Kenny said. "She didn't want to write you directly, I mean, not unless you invited her to. So she sent it to you in care of me."

"Kenny, what have you gotten your sister into now?" Lee asked.

"Listen, it wasn't my idea, I promise," Kenny said, holding up his hand. "If you don't want to read it, I'll just write her and tell her that . . ."

"No, no, there's no need for that now. Let me see the letter."

Miss Millicent Gates
811 Greer Street
Sikeston, Missouri

Chaplain (Lt) Lee Grant
605th Heavy Bombardment Group
APO 8605, New York, NY

May 31, 1943

Dear Chaplain Grant:

First, let me apologize for writing you this unsolicited letter, but I am moved to do so because I wanted to thank you, on behalf of myself and my family, for being so good to Kenny. I don't think anyone has ever made a bigger impression on him than you have, and certainly no one has ever had a more positive influence on him.

I'm sure you have discovered by now that Kenny is what might be generously referred to as a "free spirit." When he was in school, he played hooky so many times that my father once advertised in the Standard, our local, weekly newspaper, that he would give one hundred pounds of sugar to anyone who could keep Kenny in school long enough to graduate. Our father, as Kenny may have told you, owns a wholesale grocery warehouse. Of course, with sugar rationing as it is, should that offer be made today, the entire population of Sikeston, all seven thousand people, would turn out to see to Kenny's education.

Kenny gives you credit for, and I quote, "bringing some sanity to the insane business of war." He has told me what the boys must go through, and how you counsel and console them. I know that all the newspaper headlines, all the medals, and all the glory go to the aircrews, the men who come face-to-face with death every day. And they deserve all the accolades that come to them. But surely the time will come for recognizing and honoring people like you, people who provide the emotional and moral courage that allows those brave men to go on.

Oh, how I am rambling on. Please forgive me. Forgive me also the boldness of my next question. Kenny tells me that you are not married, and as far as he knows, you are not receiving mail on a regular basis from any woman. If you do not think it too forward of me, I would like to write to you from time to time.

Sincerely,
Millie Gates

Charley Phillips came quickly to the conclusion that Mr. Throgmorton's only real problem was that he didn't have enough labor to get his fields plowed, and that was a problem Charley could easily solve. Since he was in the middle of a maintenance stand-down, he would have plenty of time to do it.

A very grateful Throgmorton offered to pay Charley for his work, but Charley refused.

"You don't understand," he said. "Just being able to work on a farm again is pay enough."

Charley could also have told him that there was something in him that needed renewed, not just the happy remembrance of farming, but the fact that he could do something constructive instead of destructive. What a salve it was to be able to have a hand in raising crops rather than killing people. That was what he wanted to say to Throgmorton, but he didn't think he could put it in words. What he didn't realize was that while he may have lacked the ability to give articulate voice to his feelings, his soul communicated most eloquently, and Mr. Throgmorton understood far better than Charley realized.

Reaching the other end of the field, Staff Sergeant Charley Phillips clucked to the horses, turning them to come back down and plow a new row. Looking over the back of the team and concentrating only on the field in front of him, he was able to transport himself from this time and place to another setting.

In the vividness of his imagination, he was not opening the ground for wheat, but getting acreage ready for cotton, and the long furrow of dirt he saw before him wasn't English gray, but Mississippi Delta black, glistening darkly in the Arkansas sun. His pa was on the other side working back toward him, and his ma had just driven the pickup truck out to the field, bringing a Mason jar full of cold water.

At that moment the Fortresses that had gone out on today's mission were just coming back and as each bomber turned onto its final approach leg in the landing pattern, it would pass right over Charley's head. Charley wondered what so many planes were doing over Wilson, Arkansas.

The Train to London

Mark had no idea how tired he was until he boarded the train. There were only three people in the passenger compartment, a bearded older man who sat with his arms folded across his chest and sucked on an unlit curved pipe that rested on his chin, a young woman who was reading a book, and her daughter, a little girl who was holding a cloth doll that had seen better days. When he sat down by the window, he saw the little girl looking at him through wide, round eyes. He smiled at her, but shyly she turned away, burying her head in her mother's side.

The train gave a high-pitched toot, then pulled away from Davencourt Station. Moments after it left, Mark was asleep. When he opened his eyes sometime later, another older man had joined them. The woman was still reading, and the little girl was still looking at him. He didn't return her gaze this time, but looked out the window as the green fields of England slid by. Again he fell asleep, and when he woke up, the compartment was nearly full of people, but the young woman and the little girl were gone. So was the older man with the pipe.

He got off the train at King's Cross Station in London and, carrying his little AWOL bag, started walking. He passed a vending stand where he saw several stacked cases of Pepsi-Cola. Looking closer, he saw no way of keeping them cool.

"Do you have any cold?" Mark asked.

"Just got them out of the fridge, guv'nor," the vendor replied.

"All right, I'll have one." Mark paid for the drink, then watched as the vendor popped the top off. The cola foamed up the neck of the bottle, then began spewing over, evidence that it had not just been removed from the refrigerator. With a sigh, Mark took the soda, then drank it down, warm though it was. Any American cola, be it Coke, Pepsi, Royal Crown, or whatever, even if warm, was a welcome respite from the equally warm British ale that was the staple of the O Club back at Davencourt.

Having no idea where to go first, Mark saw a USO club, so he went there. He was greeted just inside the door by a pretty young woman whose attractiveness was somewhat diminished by the fact that she was wearing a uniform. A name tag on the uniform read, "Hello, my name is Janet."

"Hello, Captain, first time here?" Janet asked. Mark was a little disappointed to hear the English accent in her voice. He had expected her to be American, and he really wanted to hear a female American voice.

"It's not a hard question, love," the girl said with a chuckle when Mark didn't answer right away.

Mark laughed as well. "I'm sorry. Yes, I've been in England for a while, but this is my first time in London."

"Oh, well, you'll have a lovely time, I'm sure. You're a flier, aren't you?" she asked, seeing his wings.

"Yes. B-17s."

For a moment he thought he saw an expression of intense sorrow in her eyes, but it went away quickly, and the smile came back. "You'll find cookies, cake, punch, and lemonade back there," she said, pointing. "The lemonade is quite cold. I know how you Yanks like your drinks cold. And there's all sorts of things for you to do, games to play, American magazines to read. You can also listen to the radio or play records."

"You knew someone, didn't you?" Mark asked.

"I beg your pardon?"

"You knew someone on a B-17?"

This time there was no mistaking the sadness in her eyes because they brimmed over with tears. Reaching under the table, she opened her purse, then pulled out a handkerchief.

"You're a most perceptive man," Janet said as she wiped her eyes.

"I'm sorry. I had no right . . ."

"No, it's quite all right," she said. "His name was Leftenant . . ." She stopped and smiled through her tears. "He used to get on to me about that. I know you Americans say lieutenant. His name was Lieutenant Barry Sadler. He, uh, went down over Wilhelmshaven. There were no chutes."

"I'm sorry," Mark said.

"Yes, well, that's the way of war, isn't it? I lost my brother in Burma, and my cousin was killed in the blitz. Please do be careful, Captain."

Mark smiled at her. "I'll be as careful as I can be, I promise you."

Mark walked back into the club area. Several men were there, soldiers and sailors, officers and enlisted alike, though many more enlisted than commissioned. There were also a few women, but not nearly as many women as men, and Mark figured it was less than their busiest time.

A navy lieutenant was throwing darts and, seeing Mark, walked over to him. "How about it, Captain? Shall we replay the army-navy game? It'll give you a chance to make up for the fact that we have beaten you four years in a row."

There was a dart board in the O Club back at Davencourt, and Mark had gotten pretty good at it, good enough to accept the lieutenant's challenge.

"You're on," he said. "The name's Mark White." He offered his hand.

"Robbie Robison," the lieutenant said. "You a West Point graduate, Mark?"

Mark shook his head. "Nope. Litchfield College, then a commission by way of Army Aviation Cadet training."

"Too bad," Rob said. He threw his first dart, which was a bull's-eye. "I'm Annapolis, class of forty-one, and it's always good to beat anyone in the army, but I must say, I do take more pleasure in beating West Pointers."

They played three games, and Robison won all three. Then admitting that he was overmatched, Mark excused himself and went over to the snack bar. They were just popping corn, and it smelled so good that Mark got a sack, along with a glass of cold lemonade. He picked up the latest edition of *Home Front* magazine and found a place to sit down. His plan was to just look at the magazine while he ate his popcorn, then figure out the best way to spend his time while in London.

The first article he read was titled "Aviation Has Shrunk the World." It was illustrated with a map of the United States. A compass rose was drawn around Chicago, then dotted lines stretched out from Chicago to various points on the map. The map illustrator had put Singapore where Seattle should be, Moscow in San Antonio's position, and London had replaced Atlanta. The purpose of the illustration was to show that those cities could be reached by air from Chicago in the same length of time it would take a train to travel from Chicago to the U.S. cities at those locations. It was a method of demonstrating how much the world had shrunk.

That meant he was only about twenty-four hours from home. Mark found that a comforting thought.

Thumbing farther through the magazine, he stopped to look at an ad for soup. "How to pull a hot dinner out of a jeep," the ad said, and it showed a group of soldiers who were standing around a jeep and eating C rations they had heated by warming them on the exhaust manifold. The purpose of the ad was to demonstrate that, in addition to soup, this particular company was helping the war effort by canning C rations.

Then he came to the theater section, featuring an article about a new USO show called Donnie Fritz's Home Front Review.

For our fighting men overseas, this terrible war has at least had some gay moments. Never before have so great a number of show business personalities given so much to so many. So far our boys have been entertained by the likes of Bob Hope, Jack Benny, Larry Adler, Al Jolson, Ray Bolger, Judith Anderson, and Martha Raye. Now you can add to that list, comedian Donnie Fritz.

Included in comedian Fritz's USO show is a must-see skit performed by three, non-show-business women: Betty Brubaker, Emily Hagan, and Norma Jean Thompson.

Emily Hagan? Mark thought. *There's a coincidence.*

In real life, these three women are employed in war-related industries. Miss Brubaker turns out antitank shells, Miss Hagan builds ships, while Miss Thompson works on airplanes.

Wait a minute, Miss Hagan builds ships? Is it possible that this really is Emily?

Miss Brubaker, Miss Hagan, and Miss Thompson were selected as the three most beautiful Rosie the Riveters in the country, and according to Fritz, "Our boys need to see just what it is they are fighting for." See page 77, "Rosie in New York," for a photo layout of the three young ladies on the town.

Without finishing the article, Mark turned quickly to page seventy-seven. There, he saw a half-page photo of Emily and some smiling army major. Their arms were linked together as they were drinking.

"Young lovers toast their engagement," the caption beneath the photo read.

Emily Hagan and her fiancé, Major Phil Mitchell, "did the town" of New York recently. Major Mitchell, who was recently awarded the Bronze Star and Purple Heart for wounds received in action on Guadalcanal, came home on convalescent leave just in time to provide escort service for his fiancée before Miss Hagan departed with Donnie Fritz's Home Front Review USO Show.

With a sick feeling in the pit of his stomach, Mark let the magazine drop down in his lap. At that moment Rob Robison came over to him and, looking down, saw the picture.

"Look at that," he said. "There's some army guy with that good-looking girl. And I went to Annapolis because they told us that women were suckers for the navy's white-dress uniform."

Mark didn't answer.

"You finished with her?" Bob asked, pointing toward the picture in the magazine.

"Yeah," Mark said. "I'm finished with her."

Mark got up to leave the USO club. As he passed by the welcoming table, Janet called out to him.

"The Donnie Fritz USO show is playing the Palladium. It's free, but you have to have a ticket to get in. Would you like one?"

"No, I don't think so," Mark said.

"Very well. Do enjoy our town while you're here. I think you'll find London is really quite a lovely city."

"Thanks," Mark said. "I'll try."

It was dark by the time he left the club. His initial plan had been to find a nice civilian restaurant for dinner, but he discovered that he had no appetite.

He walked down the street with his hands thrust in his pockets. Suddenly a young woman stepped out of a shadowy doorway right in front of him.

"Hello," the woman said.

Mark looked at her. Her hair hung dark and loose, and her eyes were clear and deep. She was heavily made up, which in the harsh light of day would have given her a garish appearance, but in the moonlight was actually quite attractive. She thrust one hip out in provocative invitation.

"Would you care for a bit of love, Yank?" she asked.

"A bit of love?" Mark shook his head. "No thank you," he replied. "If I can't have all of it, I don't want any of it."

The American Hospital in London

Emily had to hand it to Fritz. He was good onstage in front of thousands, but she believed he was even better here, "working the wounded."

"Bob Hope warned me before I came over here to entertain the troops that I might give a performance somewhere, then have to flee for my life," Donnie Fritz said. "But I asked him, what's new about that? The way my act bombs, I've had to do that many times."

The audience laughed.

The show was being done in one of the larger wards, and extra beds had been moved in to accommodate those who couldn't get out of bed, while the ambulatory ones were seated in chairs. The more severely wounded soldiers had a nurse right beside them while the act was going on.

"We just came from entertaining our boys down in North Africa," Fritz continued. "They're doing a good job there, and oh, how happy they were to see me. They were on their knees when I got there—what adulation, what respect, what a crap game."

The audience laughed.

Donnie cracked several more jokes, then he introduced the women.

"I know some of you fellas gave up good-paying factory jobs when you came into the service," he said. "You worked while the ladies stayed home, drank tea, played bridge, and made themselves pretty for you. Well, guess what? That's all changed. The ladies have learned how to work in the factories, so now when you go home, they'll go to work while all the fellas stay home, drink beer, play poker, and make your-selves look pret—well, two out of three ain't bad."

Again the men laughed.

"Here are three women that any man would want to stay home for. They've been working in factories for you guys, making antitank shells, airplanes, and ships. They were selected as the three most beautiful Rosie the Riveters in America, and once you see them, I think you will readily agree with that selection. Gentlemen, I give you Betty Brubaker, Emily Hagan, and Norma Jean Thompson!"

The three girls had been waiting just outside in the hall, and at their cue they came into the ward to as much cheering, whistling, and applause as the wounded men could muster. By now, Norma Jean had become aware of the reaction she stirred in the men, and she hammed it up for them, putting a little more sway in her walk, smiling and flirting outrageously. Betty and Emily had long since accustomed themselves to being the supporting cast, and it was a role they took on willingly, for neither of them could do or wanted to do what Norma Jean did.

The writers had also taken note of Norma Jean's effect on the men, and had written the little one-on-one skits that each girl had with Donnie in a way that reflected each girl's personality. Norma Jean was the easiest to write for.

"Norma Jean, we just came back from visiting our boys in Africa. Did you have a good time while you were there?"

"Oh, yes, Donnie. Who couldn't have a good time around all those wonderful boys? Especially all those wonderful privates. They were such nice, friendly young men. And I've never met anyone who enjoyed a job more than the privates did. They all tell me they would rather be a private than a general."

"Wait a minute. You're telling me that the men you talked to would rather be a private than a general?"

"That's right, Donnie."

"Why would anyone rather be a private than a general?"

"Well, as they explained to me, a private means that they are supposed to guard your privacy. So, every time I took a shower, those nice boys kept an eye on me, just to make certain nobody invaded my privacy."

This time the men's laughter had a bit of a ribald edge to it.

There were a few other suggestive jokes with Norma Jean, then it was time for Donnie's routine with Emily and Betty. Their routines were considerably less suggestive. After that, the girls were released, then they separated in order to go around to the various wards and visit each man individually.

Emily was assigned to a doctor named Urban. She followed him down a narrow, dimly lit corridor, then through a pair of swinging doors that led into a ward for the severely wounded. The beds were stretched out in long rows down each side of the cavernous room, some of which were separated by screens. On each bed lay a terribly disfigured or maimed piece of humanity—a man without legs or arms, or a man with terrible burns and scars. Emily felt an uneasy sensation as she walked along with the doctor. The eyes of all the men followed her quietly and, it seemed to her, sullenly.

"Doctor Urban, I don't know. Perhaps this isn't such a good idea."

"Why do you say that?"

"Look at them. They look as if they resent me."

"This isn't part of the show, Miss Hagan. Don't look for cheers and applause in here. They are resentful because you are whole and beautiful, while they are broken and mutilated."

"Then wouldn't it be better if . . . ," Emily started.

"It'll be all right, Miss Hagan," Dr. Urban said. "They are resentful of the situation; they are not resentful of you. Trust me." His voice was calm and reassuring at a time when she needed reassurance.

The physician stopped at the foot of one of the beds, occupied by a man who was wrapped in bandages from his chest up. Both arms were bandaged and suspended from an overhead pulley. His face was also wrapped, with only small holes for his mouth and eyes and nose.

"This is one of our special patients," Dr. Urban explained. "So, Sergeant Billings, how are we feeling today?"

"We are feeling fine," Billings muttered.

"That's wonderful," Dr. Urban said, then to Emily, "He's special, Miss Hagan, because you are standing next to a genuine hero. Although Sergeant Billings survived the crash unhurt, he went back into a burning bomber to pull out three of his fellow crewmen. He received the Silver Star for that, plus, as I'm sure you can imagine, terrible third-degree burns. But he's going to be just fine, aren't you, Sergeant Billings?"

"I'm getting a new face," Billings said. His words were mumbled from behind the thick wrappings, and Emily had to lean forward to hear what he was saying.

"I beg your pardon?"

"I'm going to get a new face," Billings said again. "I'm going to pick me out one, like pickin' out a suit. Only it's going to be good-looking this time, not like the ugly mug I came to England with."

Emily looked at Dr. Urban in surprise.

"It's called reconstructive surgery," Dr. Urban explained. "As you may know, we can do wonders with such things nowadays, skin grafts and such. It's not exactly like picking out a new suit," he added with a chuckle. "Still, I think Sergeant Billings will be pleasantly surprised."

"Oh, how wonderful," Emily said.

"Have you ever seen any of the new faces the doctors have made, miss?" Billings asked in an innocent voice.

"No, I haven't," Emily said. "But I'm sure they must be quite nice," she added, not knowing what else to say.

"They look like the south end of a northbound mule," Billings snarled, his tone suddenly and unexpectedly changing from deceptive innocence to angry derision.

"Sergeant Billings!" Dr. Urban said sharply. "I think you owe Miss Hagan an apology."

"Do I?" Billings replied.

"No!" Emily said, quickly reaching her hand out to the doctor. "No, that's quite all right." She looked directly at Sergeant Billings and smiled. "Sergeant Billings, I've known a lot of men. And believe me, with some of them, having a face like the south end of a northbound mule would be quite an improvement."

Billings's eyes behind the bandages grew wide in surprise. Then suddenly he began laughing, as did the patients who were close enough to have overheard the conversation. The doctor also joined in the laughter.

"You're all right, ma'am," the sergeant said a moment later. "I'm sorry about what I said. I had no right."

"On the contrary, Sergeant," Emily replied. "I've never known anyone who had more right."

19

London
June 9, 1943

M ark lay in bed in his room at the hotel as the morning sun splashed in through the window. He was awake all night long, unable to sleep because his mind was filled with images of the magazine pictures he had seen of Emily and the army major. Where did she meet this man the article identified as her fiancé? Perhaps a better question would be, When did she meet him? How could she have so quickly fallen out of love with him and in love with that major?

Groggy from lack of sleep, Mark got out of bed, took a shower, then went down to the hotel restaurant for breakfast. Breakfast came with the price of the room, but he had to take what was served, which in this case was bacon, beans, toast, margarine, orange marmalade, sliced tomatoes, and hot tea.

After breakfast he wandered around London for a while, then without consciously planning it, he wound up at the USO club again. Going inside, he looked around for the magazine. He wanted to read it once more just to make certain it said what he thought it said, hoping that somehow he may have misread it yesterday. But the magazine was gone, so he returned to the front table where, once again Janet was on duty.

"Good morning, Captain. You are still enjoying London, I see."

"Yes," Mark said. "Listen, Miss . . ."

The young woman pointed to her name tag. "Not miss," she said. "We go by our name tags in here."

"Hello, my name is Janet," Mark read, saying it all together as if it were one name.

For just a second, Janet was confused, then she laughed.

"I asked for that," she said. "What can I do for you, Captain?"

"When I was in here yesterday, I was looking at a recent issue of *Home Front* magazine. You wouldn't happen to know where it is, would you?"

"Goodness, love, those magazines never stay around. We have signs posted everywhere, asking the boys to leave them so that others can enjoy them, but they just disappear. Ah, but a new *Time* magazine just arrived. Perhaps you would like to look at it."

"No, thank you," Mark said. "This one had an article about the Donnie Fritz USO show that I wanted to read."

"Oh, well, I can help you there, love. I have a schedule of where the show is to be. It was here yesterday, you know. In fact, I believe I tried to give you a ticket."

"Yes, I remember."

"Well, I think they are still here. Let me check." She shuffled through several papers on the clipboard. "Yes, here it is. Oh, no, sorry, yesterday was the last day for London. Today they are playing at Alconbury, Davencourt, and Polebrook."

"Davencourt?"

"Yes."

"What time will they be playing Davencourt?"

"Let's see, Alconbury at oh-nine hundred, Davencourt at thirteen hundred, and Polebrook at sixteen hundred hours."

"Thank you."

Mark went back into the club and sat down. It was almost unbelievable to think of Emily at Davencourt. If he left now, he could make it to Davenport by one o'clock. But did he really want to? Did he owe her the chance to explain the magazine article? Or did he owe her the right to be left alone? All he knew for sure was that he didn't want to listen to her explanation. No matter how genuine or heartfelt her words might be, he did not want to hear his Emily talking about being in love with someone else.

He sighed. Well, it was probably an unrealistic notion anyway. After all, how long had they actually known each other? Maybe this was nothing but a war romance from the beginning, and if it was, then it was probably doomed to end this way. And if so, better that it end before they were married than after.

Mark sat in the chair without moving or talking to anyone. The only way he could negate the pain was to keep his mind as blank as he could.

Time passed.

"Captain, are you all right?"

"What?" Mark asked. He had been in such a self-induced trance that he hadn't even noticed when Janet walked over to talk to him.

"You've been sitting right here in this chair, without moving, for nearly two hours," Janet said. "I just asked if you were all right."

"Oh," Mark said. "I've been here that long?"

"Yes."

"I'm sorry. I guess I am a little morose. Maybe I should go. Having someone sitting here with a long face can't be all that good for your business."

"Nonsense, this is England. Being morose is practically our national pastime," Janet teased, and despite himself, Mark laughed.

"What time is it?" Mark asked.

"It's nearly eleven," Janet said. "My relief has come. I'm off for the rest of the day."

Mark was certain that Janet's remark about being off for the rest of the day was a hint that he should ask her out. And why not? With Emily being engaged to someone else, he was no longer under any obligation to her.

"Would you care to have lunch with me?" Mark asked. "I mean, if you don't have other plans."

Janet smiled. "I have no other plans, and I would love to have lunch with you," she said.

Davencourt

The USO troupe did their morning show at Alconbury, then because it was so close to Davencourt, they drove over to have lunch with the officers and men of the 605th before doing their one o'clock show. From Davencourt, they would fly to Polebrook where they would do their last show at four. From Polebrook, they would fly to Lisbon to catch the Pan Am Clipper back home.

"Did you find him?" Emily asked Captain Felder when he came back into the mess hall where the troupe was having lunch.

"You won't believe this, Emily," Felder replied, "but *Captain* White . . . he's just been promoted, by the way . . . is in London."

"Oh, no, this is awful! Mark is in London?" Emily wailed. "But what is he doing there?"

"Evidently he and his entire crew were given a seven-day stand-down."

"Stand-down?"

"That means they are off duty. Mark took advantage of his stand-down to go into London."

"Oh, I can't believe this," Emily said in a frustrated voice. "He might very well have been in London while we were there. And now, he is still there, but we are here. Is there any way we can find him?"

"We can put the word out at all the USO clubs in London. They can post a note on the bulletin board, but if he doesn't happen to go to any of the USO clubs, or if he doesn't check the bulletin board, I don't know of anything else we could do about it."

"I want you to find the chaplain for me," Emily said.

"A chaplain?"

"The chaplain. He is the only one here. His name is Lee Grant, and he is one of Mark's closest friends."

"All right, I'll see what I can do," Felder promised.

Suddenly from the other end of the table, Donnie Fritz clapped his hands. "Boys and girls," he said. "Don't linger over this delicious"—he looked at the meal they were being served—"uh, stewlike substance, too long." His own people laughed. "Remember, show time is at one o'clock."

"That's only twenty minutes," Felder said. "Still want me to find the chaplain?"

"Yes, please, and never mind, there he is!" she said excitedly.

"Mark?"

"No, I wish. But there's Lee, and that's the next best thing," Emily said, pointing out the chaplain.

"I'll bring him over to the table," Felder said, going after him.

"If he sees that magazine article before I have the chance to explain it, I don't know what he will think," Emily told Lee after explaining her dilemma and fear to him.

"You say it is the latest issue of *Home Front?*" Lee asked.

"I don't know if it's the latest," Emily said. "But it is a late issue, certainly the latest I've seen. It's probably a week or so old by now, though."

Lee chuckled. "Well, then I wouldn't worry about it that much. Stateside magazines are always anywhere from four to six weeks old by the time they make it out here to Davencourt."

Emily let out a long, relieved sigh. "Oh, I hope you are right. You have no idea how this has been bothering me. The whole thing is so silly. I have no idea where the writer came up with such a story. I mean, nobody even interviewed me. I didn't think they could write a story about someone unless they talked to her first."

"Oh, I'm sure things like that happen all the time."

"There ought to be a law against it."

"There probably is a law against it. Libel or slander or something like that," Lee said. "Don't worry. I'm sure Mark will understand."

"I'm sure he will, too, if I am able to explain it to him. But I'm afraid now that I won't even have the chance to see him. What is it they always say on *The Life of Riley* radio program? Oh, yes. 'What a revolting development this turned out to be.'" Emily laughed. "It would be funny if it weren't so frustrating. Imagine him being in London while I am here at Davencourt. If only he knew."

London

At Janet's suggestion, she and Mark took a thirty-minute train ride away from the city, winding up in the little village of Edgware. There, they rented bicycles at a shop across the street from the train station, then they bought fish and chips from a vendor who wrapped their purchase in newspaper. With their lunch and a bottle of wine poked down into one of the bicycle baskets, they pedaled out into the country. Finding a nice, shady spot under a single tree in an otherwise open field, they had their lunch.

"What a pleasant area," Mark said. "It reminds me a little of Illinois."

"Illinois? I know Illinois is a state, but I'm not sure where it is."

"It's right in the middle of the country," Mark explained. "Bordered on the west by the Mississippi River."

"Oh, I know the Mississippi River. There are so many romantic stories about it—Tom Sawyer, riverboat gamblers, and such."

"England has its own share of romantic stories," Mark said. "Robin Hood. King Arthur and the Round Table. I read them all."

"I grew up in that house," Janet said, pointing to a small fieldstone lodge about a quarter of a mile away.

"Does your family still live there?"

"My dad is dead and my mum remarried. She lives in Birmingham now."

"What made you choose the teeming city of London?"

"Curiosity, excitement, opportunity. You name it," Janet said.

Suddenly an avalanche of sound beat down on them, and they looked up quickly to see a lone B-17, flying low, with two of the four propellers standing still. The engines were roaring, and one of them was making loud banging noises. The airplane was so low, they could see all the battle damage, every hole in the wings and fuselage.

"Oh, Mark!" Janet gasped, putting her hand to her mouth. "Will they make it?"

"He has no fires," Mark said. "The controls seem to be working. If either one of the pilots is flying, they should make it."

"I don't understand," Janet said. "If a pilot isn't flying, who would be?"

"If both pilots are dead, one of the crew will have to take over."

Janet shivered. "I pray that they make it," she said.

They watched the plane until it disappeared over the western horizon. And while still low, it was at least maintaining altitude. When Mark looked back at Janet, he saw that tears were rolling down her cheeks.

"You're thinking about your friend?" Mark said.

"Yes. Oh, this beastly war."

"How long has it been?"

"Three weeks," Janet said.

"I'm sorry," Mark said. Almost automatically, he put his arms around her, then pulled her to him, embracing her. She let him hold her for a moment, then they separated and sat back down to finish their lunch.

"So, what is your story?" she asked.

"I beg your pardon?"

"Watching you in the USO club this morning, I almost wanted to cry. You were obviously hurting over something."

Mark told her about Emily and about the story he read in the magazine, telling of Emily's engagement.

"She is with the Donnie Fritz USO show," he concluded. "The one that is playing here in England right now. That's why I didn't want to go see it last night and why I am avoiding returning to my base today.

According to the schedule you showed me, she would be at Davencourt right now."

"Is Davencourt your base?"

"Yes."

"What does Emily say of all this?"

"I don't know. I haven't talked to her since I read the article."

"Does she write you?"

"Yes. She's been very good about writing me."

"Have her letters changed any? I don't mean to pry, but what I mean is, have they gotten less personal?"

"No, that's why I'm having such a hard time with this. In her last letter we were talking about marriage."

"Do you love her?"

"I thought I did . . . until this happened."

Janet waved her hand and shook her head. "Forget about this. Assume that it didn't happen or that there is some mistake. Do you love her?"

"Yes."

"Enough to fight for her?"

Mark paused for a minute. "I would fight for her if I thought there was a chance," he said. "But I don't want to make a fool of myself."

Janet laughed.

"What is it?"

"Mark, from my point of view, you'll be making a fool of yourself if you *don't* fight for her. At least go to her while you have the chance to hear the story from her own lips."

Mark pinched the bridge of his nose. "It's too late now. I've really messed things up."

Janet stood up and walked over to the bicycle. "Maybe not. You can get a train from here, direct to Davencourt. You don't even have to go back to London."

"I left my bag in my room at the hotel in London."

"What's in it?"

"My shaving kit and a change of uniform."

"You've got more uniforms, and you can buy another shaving kit. Go," Janet ordered.

Davencourt

The USO show had been held in one of the large hangars, and the stage the performers used was still up when Mark made it back to the base. The stage was there, but the show wasn't.

"Have they left?" he asked one of the men who was sweeping out the hangar.

"Yes, sir. It was a good show, wasn't it?"

"I don't know," Mark said. "I missed it."

"Oh, that's too bad, sir. The show was great. That Donnie Fritz is really something. I laughed so hard, I thought I was going to split a gut."

"Were there girls with the show?"

"Are you kidding? Just the most beautiful girls you ever saw in your life is all," the soldier said. "And they were American girls, too, from good old American places, like Brooklyn and Baltimore and Philly."

Disgusted with himself for having been so stubborn for the last two days, Mark started back toward his BOQ. Halfway there, he saw Lee.

"Oh, Mark, I almost hate to tell you what you've missed," Lee said.

"I know. I missed Emily."

"I was so sorry for her. I've never seen anyone so disappointed. She was crushed that you weren't here. I tell you the truth, it was all she could do to go onstage."

"I'm sure she'll get over it," Mark said. "After all, she's got her fiancé."

"What?" Lee replied, surprised by Mark's response. "Oh, good heavens, Mark, don't tell me you saw that article in *Home Front* magazine? What's worse, don't tell me you believed it?"

"You know about the article?" Mark asked.

"Yes, I know about it. Emily told me all about it. She and two other girls were provided with military escorts for dinner one night. She never met that man before that night, and she hasn't seen him since. It was all a publicity stunt to promote the show."

"A publicity stunt?"

"Yes."

"She could've told me something about it."

"No, she couldn't. She had no idea they were going to write anything like that. And she didn't even learn about the article until she was on the plane on the way over here. She was trying desperately to get to you before you saw the article so she could warn you about it. It was just bad luck that you missed connections."

"It wasn't bad luck," Mark said quietly.

"What do you mean?"

"Lee, you are looking at a certifiable idiot. I knew about the show, and I knew she was a part of it. I could have seen her yesterday in London. And I could have seen her today here. But I purposely did not."

"Oh, Mark, you didn't believe that nonsense?"

Mark nodded. "I'm afraid I did. Now, it's too late."

"Maybe not," Lee said, glancing at his watch. "They are doing a show at Polebrook at sixteen hundred hours. That means it's just started. You won't catch much of the show, but if you hurry, you might be able get there before it's over."

"How long is the show?"

"It's about two hours long," Lee said.

Mark shook his head. "Impossible. It's seventy-five miles to Polebrook. If I had a plane at my disposal, perhaps I could make it, but . . ."

Lee smiled. "Well, I don't have a plane, but I have the next best thing. I have Kenny and a fast car."

"Your car, yes! I forgot about that. You think Kenny would mind driving me over?"

"Are you kidding? He looks for opportunities to drive that car."

"I don't know," Mark said. "It's half past four now. That means we'd have to make seventy-five miles in an hour and a half."

"At least try," Lee said.

"All right. I'll try."

"This little baby may be just the thing we need to get you there in time," Kenny said, showing Mark a red light.

"A police-car light?" Mark asked. "Where on earth did you get that?"

"What police-car light?" Kenny said. "Don't you recognize it, sir? This is a Grimes light, right off the tail of a B-17. I had a mechanic friend rig it up for me. All I have to do is plug it into the cigarette lighter, and *voilà*, our elegant Buick becomes an emergency vehicle."

"Does it work?"

Kenny plugged it in, and the bulb inside the red lens began to rotate, creating a flashing effect.

"No, I mean will it clear traffic and let you speed?"

Kenny laughed as he turned the light off. "Well, I don't know about that. The truth is, I haven't tried it yet. It's your call, sir. Shall we use it?"

Mark thought about half a minute, then nodded. "Do it," he said.

"You've got it!"

Kenny put the light on the floor until they passed through the gate. At the gate, Kenny showed his trip ticket, authorized by Lee, and Mark showed his ID card, which, as an officer, was all he needed for authority to be off base. The MP at the gate saluted, then waved them through. Not until he was a couple of miles up the road from the gate did Kenny pick up the light from the floor, place it on the dashboard, and plug it in.

"Hold on, sir," Kenny said, pressing down on the accelerator. Within seconds, the Buick was traveling at almost eighty miles per hour.

The flashing red light did a wonderful job of clearing all traffic in front of them. Civilian and military, both British and American, moved aside to let them pass. At one police-controlled intersection, Kenny slowed down as they approached, but the policeman, seeing the flashing light, stopped all the other traffic to wave Kenny through. Kenny nodded in somber appreciation as they passed, then laughed out loud once they were clear.

"What about this, Captain?" Kenny shouted. "Is this a hoot or what?"

"I would answer you," Mark said. "But I'm too busy holding on for dear life. This is almost as bad as flak."

Kenny laughed. "You want me to slow down?"

"No," Mark said. "We've come this far. Keep going as fast as you can. I don't want to miss her. I can't miss her."

"How much time do we have left?"

Mark glanced at his watch. "It's seventeen-forty. If the show runs two hours like Lee said, we've got about twenty minutes left."

"Twenty minutes, and twenty miles to go. We'll make it, sir."

Sixteen minutes later, they were approaching the front gate at Polebrook. Leaving the light flashing just long enough for the gate MPs to see it, Kenny turned it off, then stopped as the MP came out to the car.

"Where's the USO show?" he asked the MP.

"It's down at the flight line," the MP said. "What's the hurry?"

"The captain here is one of the pilots," Kenny said.

Looking past Kenny, the MP saw Mark, then saluted. "What do you mean, one of the pilots?"

"The USO troupe flew in here, didn't they? They have to fly out, don't they? Look, Mac, I'll come back and explain it all to you in a little while," Kenny said. "But you've got to figure, if a captain is riding around in a sedan that only generals have, it's got to be important. Now are you going to let us through, or do you want to explain it to General Eaker?"

"No, no, go on through," the MP said. "Do you want an escort?"

"We don't have time," Kenny said, turning the flashing light on again.

The MP waved them through, then saluted again as Kenny drove onto the base.

"That wasn't exactly a lie, sir," Kenny explained. "The USO troupe did fly in, and they are going to fly out. And you are a pilot. I didn't specifically say you were the pilot that was going to fly them."

"If it was a lie, you're forgiven," Mark said, laughing at Kenny's inventiveness.

"Look at all the people there," he said. "The show must still be going on."

"If not, at least they haven't left," Mark replied. He pointed to two C-47s. "There are a couple of Gooney Birds sitting on the runway. I'm sure that's their aircraft."

Mark and Kenny reached the area where the show was being given, just as they were making their final bows. Every member of the cast was onstage, most of them spread across the back of the stage, while Donnie was out front. The GIs were all on their feet, cheering.

Taking the light off the dashboard, Kenny put it on top of the car, then began honking the horn as he drove slowly, but inexorably toward the stage. Seeing a staff sedan with a flashing red light, the men gave way quickly, opening up a path for them. Kenny was able to drive all the way down to the front of the stage that way.

Seeing the limo approach, Donnie Fritz walked down to the front of the stage, then leaned down to see what and who it was.

"You must have someone pretty important in there," he said. "I'm sorry you were too late."

"We're not too late," Kenny said as Mark hopped out of the car from his side.

Mark searched the stage, then he felt a charge of joy as he saw the person he was looking for.

"Emily!" he shouted.

She had already started off the stage, but hearing her name called and recognizing the voice, she stopped and looked back.

"Emily!" Mark shouted again.

"Don't tell me," Donnie said. "You are Emily's B-17 pilot."

"You know about me?"

"Are you kidding? Everyone in the show knows about you. You're about the only thing Emily ever talks about."

"Mark!" Emily cried. Seeing him, she ran toward the front of the stage.

Donnie stuck his hand down toward Mark. "Come on, I'll give you a hand up," he said, pulling Mark onto the stage.

"Thanks," Mark said, opening his arms just as Emily reached him. They embraced, then kissed. Several of the men, who were still in the area, saw what was going on, and they whistled, then cheered and applauded.

Donnie Fritz stepped up to the microphone and, tapping it, saw that it was still live.

"I forgot to tell you boys," he quipped, his amplified voice rolling across the remaining crowd. "We select one lucky soldier at each show and let him kiss any of our girls he chooses. That was why you were all asked to put your name in a hat when you arrived today."

"What? Nobody said anything to me about putting my name in a hat!" one of the GIs shouted, then when they saw Donnie laughing, they knew it was a joke, and they laughed too.

"Emily, I'll hold them off as long as I can so you can talk to your friend," Donnie said. "But I don't think you'd better count on any tanks coming to your rescue this time."

Emily laughed.

"What's he talking about, a tank coming to your rescue?" Mark asked.

Emily told him about the incident with her brother down in Africa. They both laughed, then Emily got serious.

"Oh, Mark, I have to tell you. There is a magazine . . ."

"Article about you and your fiancé in *Home Front* magazine?"

"Yes. You know about it? You read it?"

"I read it."

"There's not a word of truth to it. It was all a publicity stunt. A stunt that I didn't know anything about, by the way."

Mark chuckled. "You don't have to tell me that. Did you really think I would believe that?"

"You mean, it didn't bother you?"

"Not for a minute," Mark said.

"Thank God. You have no idea how much I worried about that. And if I had left England before getting a chance to see you, I don't know what I would've done."

"Well, you would have had to answer my proposal by letter rather than in person," Mark said.

"Your proposal?"

"Will you marry me, Emily?"

"Yes!" Emily said, happily kissing him again. "Yes, I'll marry you!"

"I'm sorry I don't have a ring or anything to give you now, but I'll get one for you as soon as I can."

"I don't need a ring. All I need is to know that you love me. Come on, walk me toward the plane," Emily said. "It'll give us a few more minutes together."

Arm in arm, they walked out toward the flight line where the two olive-drab C-47s sat parked. Already, members of the troupe were loading onto the planes.

"You're flying to Lisbon tonight?" Mark asked.

"Yes," Emily said. "Tomorrow we go back to the States. I'll be at work in Newport News by the end of the week."

"There will be a long letter there for you, nearly as soon as you get there," Mark said.

An engine on one of the C-47s whined, then barked into life, and both of them looked toward the plane.

"My goodness," Emily said, smiling through her tears. "Would you look at this? This is just like the closing scene from *Casablanca*."

"Except Humphrey Bogart was telling Ingrid Bergman good-bye forever. I'm just telling you good-bye until I get home."

The other engine started then, and Donnie came to get Emily. "We've got to go," he said.

Mark and Emily kissed one more time, then reluctantly parted. Donnie hurried Emily out to the airplane, then up the little boarding ladder. Just inside, Emily turned to wave good-bye one final time before the crew chief closed the door. A moment later, Mark saw Emily's face at one of the windows.

The pilot revved the engines, then pivoted the airplane around. A blast of prop wash whipped dust and fine-grained sand against Mark, and he had to reach up to keep his hat from blowing away. Mark stood on the flight line and watched as the two Gooney Birds taxied out to the end of the runway, then, getting the green light from the tower, took off, one after the other. He watched until both planes were unidentifiable dots in the gathering twilight.

"Sir?" Kenny said.

Mark swallowed several times, not wanting the lump in his throat when he spoke.

"Let's go back, Corporal. And thanks for getting me here on time. Thanks more than I can say."

"I was proud to do it, sir," Kenny said.

June 11, 1943

Mission number thirteen, target Nuremberg. A few in the crew were particularly nervous about this mission because it was number thirteen. I told them it was number thirteen for us, but it was number one for our new copilot, Lieutenant Duncan, and only the third one for Sergeant Lindell.

Lyndon did very well. He has almost as good a touch as Paul, even though he has far fewer hours. You could sort of expect that, though, him being a professional athlete and all. I think he's going to work out very well.

During briefing we were given specific instructions about the cathedral in Nuremberg. If the cathedral is damaged, every officer in the formation will be fined two hundred dollars, and every enlisted crewman will be fined one hundred dollars. I guess they really didn't want the cathedral hit.

Flak and fighter opposition were very heavy, but we managed to deliver our bombs on target, destroying the marshaling yards and industrial area. And as we left the burning city, Tim O'Leary, our tail gunner, reported that the cathedral was still standing and undamaged. I'm glad it is still undamaged. It is a beautiful old cathedral. It's just too bad that more Nazis didn't take to heart the lessons that have been there for the last four hundred years.

June 19, 1943

Mission number fourteen. We hit the oil refinery at Merseburg again. There was a foul-up and we overshot the IP, then flew up through the flak over Zeitz. Intense accurate flak with more than a thousand guns shooting at us. Lost several B-17s. In our squadron Payne and Wicker went down. There is hope for Payne but none for Wicker. Gideon's Sword received more than 150 hits. Mission was eight hours long. I hope we don't have to go back to Merseburg; it's one beast of a mission.

June 27, 1943

Mission number fifteen. Target was marshaling yards at Stuttgart. No flak, but weather was awful. We broke up formation in France on the way back to avoid collision because we couldn't see each other. Flew on instruments all the way back. Ceiling was only two hundred feet, and when we returned, it took me three passes at the field before I could land. Art Bollinger did a good job navigating. Mission was seven hours and thirty minutes long.

July 7, 1943

Mission number sixteen. We hit Cherbourg today. The flak was heavy and the formation scattered. We didn't lose any Forts to the enemy, but we did lose two by midair collision.

To people on the ground, a formation of Fortresses looks very precise and beautiful, with all the aircraft in their assigned positions as if connected to each other by rods. But if the people on the ground could hear the element leaders, squadron leaders, and pilots yelling at each other, they would know things aren't always as they look.

"We're being tossed around like a cork in a storm back here."

"Slow down. We can't keep up."

"Pick it up a little, will you, guys? We're practically stalling out back here."

Nobody on the ground would ever notice a low squadron overrunning a lead squadron or see the high squadron leader suddenly chop his throttles and pile his wingmen into his trailing edges.

I've learned that the easiest way to maintain position is to set the two inboard engines at a constant speed and use only the outboard engines for maneuvering.

July 15, 1943

Our seventeenth mission was supposed to have been the marshaling yards at Ludwigshafen. We were flying low squadron. Major Dixon aborted with mechanical problems so we tacked on to the high squadron. The lead navigator of the high squadron couldn't find his dinner plate with a fork, and we got completely lost. We wound up bombing some little town that had a double-track railroad. The whole thing was disgusting.

July 18, 1943

Mission number eighteen. The target was the marshaling yards at Koblenz. We bombed with ten/tenths cloud cover. The only definite thing we can say about our bombs is that they hit earth somewhere. Flak was low and inaccurate.

July 21, 1943

Mission number nineteen. Another easy mission against German troop concentrations. But when we returned from the mission, we got the bad news. For those crews who have already flown twenty or more missions, twenty-five missions is still the magic number. For those who have flown nineteen or fewer missions, the number we must now reach before going home is thirty-five. This was our nineteenth mission, so we missed it by one. We must do thirty-five now before we can go home. Needless to say, this information was not very well received by the 605th, for practically every crew in the group comes under this umbrella.

20

A rticle in *Event Week* magazine, dated July 17, 1943:

The Negro at War

Negroes have served in every American war, including the Civil War and the Spanish-American War. Though they did not perform as well as white troops, most historians agree that neither did they bring disgrace upon their race.

They did very little fighting in the First World War but served in supporting roles, such as longshoremen and laborers. This released white soldiers for combat. In that capacity, nearly everyone agrees, they were a valuable asset to the U.S. war effort. In this war, too, Negroes are serving admirably in those supporting roles. But for some, that isn't enough.

A few colored soldiers, led by Lieutenant Colonel Benjamin O. Davis Jr., son of the army's first and only Negro general, wanted Negroes to be allowed to fly. They petitioned Congress and the War Department, and threatened a divisive lawsuit in this time when all

Americans, regardless of color, should stick together, until finally their agitation paid off. A flying school was started for them at Tuskegee University (a Negro college) in Tuskegee, Alabama.

Congress and the army have watched this project with great interest, for money, airplanes, and instructors that could have been used to train proven white pilots were diverted for use in this experiment. Now the colored aviators are in Africa, getting their first taste of air combat. The results so far have been lackluster. To some, their poor performance has been disappointing. However, to those high-ranking officers and members of government who opposed training Negroes in the first place, the experiment is turning out just as they expected.

Battlefield commanders on the scene complain that the Negro pilot is less disciplined than his white counterpart, is much more likely to leave the formation and go out on his own. It may be time to declare this experiment a failure. In order that the government may salvage something from the money invested in training Negroes to fly, these men should be taken out of badly needed fighters and given transport planes to fly, bringing in equipment and matériel for the frontline soldiers. This would be no disgrace, for like their longshoremen brothers, the Negro aviators would be performing a valuable service.

El Haouaria, French Morocco, North Africa
July 22, 1943

A half-dozen pilots were waiting in the ready room of the Ninety-ninth Fighter Squadron. Six Curtiss P-40 Tomahawk fighters were parked just outside, fueled, armed, and ready to go. Each airplane had its own auxiliary power unit and a fire extinguisher in position alongside to allow for an immediate start, for this was the on-call scramble team.

Four of the officers were playing penny-ante poker, and there was a great deal of laughter and good-natured jiving going on between them. Captain Donaldson, the flight leader, was reading a magazine, while Lieutenant Lorenzo Jenkins was writing a letter home to his grandmother.

"What a bunch of garbage!" Captain Donaldson suddenly said, slamming the magazine down angrily on the table alongside his chair. "I don't know how they can even print such hogwash."

The card players were so caught up in their game that Captain Donaldson's outburst went completely unnoticed by anyone at the gaming table. Lorenzo heard it, though, and he looked up from his letter.

"What is it?" Lorenzo asked.

"You don't want to know," Donaldson said. He picked the magazine up from the table, then tossed it into a nearby wastebasket.

"It's about us, isn't it?" Lorenzo asked.

Donaldson looked up at him in surprise. "Yes, how did you know?"

"I saw the article, but I didn't read it. Thought I would get around to it later."

"Don't bother. It will only . . ." Donaldson paused in midsentence, then looked over at the wastebasket as if just getting a thought. "No, wait a minute. Maybe you should read it. In fact, everyone should read it."

Captain Donaldson fished the magazine out of the wastebasket, tore out the facing pages containing the story about the Ninety-ninth, then walked over and pinned them to the bulletin board.

"You fellas give me your attention for a minute," he called.

"Uh-uh, LeRoy, don't you touch that card," Deon Ware said, and the others laughed. "Cap'n, you goin' to talk to us, you make LeRoy stand at attention. That boy got the fastest hands I've ever seen."

Again, the others laughed, including Captain Donaldson. Then Donaldson got down to business.

"I've pinned a story up here on the bulletin board that I want all of you to read."

"What's it about?" LeRoy asked.

"It's about us."

"Hey, really? Let me see that!" Deon said, starting toward the board.

"Wait a minute," Donaldson said, stopping him. "Before you read it, before any of you read it, you need to know that it isn't very flattering.

As a matter of fact, it's anything but that. The article says the Ninety-ninth should close up shop."

"What?" Deon said. "Cap'n, they can't really do that, can they?"

"They can, and they may," Captain Donaldson said, "if they can find the slightest reason. I'm sure you all know that Tuskegee wasn't the most popular idea to come out of this war. The same people who tried to prevent it, then tried to close it down, are now trying in every way they know to undo the whole thing."

"That's not right. Not after all we've been through," Deon said angrily.

"Look, men, we've known from the very beginning this wasn't going to be a picnic," Captain Donaldson said. "We've said all along we were going to have to be better than the white pilots just to stay even with them. Well, now we are going to have to be twice as good."

"We are twice as good," Deon said.

"Yeah," LeRoy agreed.

Donaldson held up his finger. "The burden has fallen on our shoulders. We're flying not just for ourselves, but for all of our people. If we succeed, there will be more to come after us, and our people will live in the sunlight. If we fail, our race will linger in the darkness for another one hundred years."

"That's quite a load you're laying on us, Captain," Lorenzo said.

In the background, a telephone rang, and they could hear the operations sergeant answer it.

"I'll grant you it's a load. But it's not more than you can carry. You've proved that already. You men graduated from a flight school that was oriented not toward getting you through, but busting you out. And that was the easy part. From now on it gets much harder. We are being watched on every mission. If just one of us breaks formation, if one of you violates radio-telephone procedure, if you miss an assignment, it's going to reflect on all of us."

The men nodded.

"I hope you understand that—"

"Captain Donaldson, we have a mission, sir," the operations sergeant said, interrupting Donaldson's talk.

"Pilots, man your planes!" Donaldson shouted.

With a shout of excitement, all six men ran from the ready room, leaving it so quickly that the screen door didn't have a chance to close until the last man was out.

Lorenzo ran to his airplane where the parachute was waiting on the wing for him. He put it on, then climbed up to the cockpit. The crew chief climbed up with him, then helped him get inside and buckled up.

"Gust locks removed?" Lorenzo asked.

"Gust locks removed, sir," the crew chief replied, referring to the little blocks of wood that held the ailerons and elevator stable so gusts of wind wouldn't cause them to bang up and down.

"All right, stand fireguard."

"Good luck, sir," the crew chief called back to him as he jumped back down to the ground. The crew chief stepped out in front of the fighter, then picked up the fire extinguisher to be ready to douse any fires that might occur during start. Lorenzo held up his two hands and slid the fingers of his right hand into the curve formed by his left. This was a signal to connect the auxiliary power unit. The crew chief returned the signal, indicating that electrical power was connected.

Priming the engine and pumping the booster pump a few times, Lorenzo moved the mixture lever to full rich, prop lever to full increase RPM, then cracked the throttle. Turning on the master switch and magneto switch, he put his finger over the starter.

"Clear!" he called.

"Clear!" the crew chief responded.

The big Packard V-1650 engine turned over a few times, then caught, and the throaty roar of the engine joined that of the others.

"This is Red Tail Leader," Captain Donaldson's voice cracked over Lorenzo's headset. "Our target is a German truck convoy."

"What? More trucks? When are they going to turn us loose on some Focke-Wulfs?" Deon asked.

"Lieutenant Ware, you *will* follow radio discipline!" Captain Donaldson said sharply.

"Yes, sir," Ware replied contritely.

"If we're going to bust up some trucks today, we're going to be the best truck busters in the Army Air Force. Does everyone have that? Respond with your call sign."

"Red Tail Two, roger."

"Red Tail Three, roger," Lorenzo said.

The other three aircraft responded as well.

"We'll take off in groups of two. Once we're airborne, assemble on me," Donaldson ordered.

As Red Tail Three, Lorenzo was flying lead for the second element. He waited until Captain Donaldson and Red Tail Two were halfway down the runway before he started his own takeoff run. Glancing to his right, he saw that Deon, his wingman, was right beside him.

Half an hour later they reached their target, a long convoy of German trucks.

"All right, men, let's go to work," Donaldson said, peeling off to begin his attack.

By the time Lorenzo went in for his run, one of the German trucks was burning from the first two planes that attacked. The burning truck was halfway back in the convoy and was effectively blocking all the trucks behind it. But the front half of the convoy had no such restriction, and it was pulling away quickly. Lorenzo went after the first truck.

Many of the trucks in the convoy were equipped with machine guns, and as the planes swooped down on them, the German gunners were firing up at them. Lorenzo could see the glowing tracer rounds flashing by his cockpit. He pulled the trigger and the guns roared. His own tracers zipped down toward the lead vehicle, punching into the canvas that was covering the back of the truck.

Suddenly and unexpectedly the entire truck exploded.

"I've got secondaries!" Lorenzo shouted, meaning that his bullets had caused an explosion, probably from stored ammunition.

Lorenzo barely got the words out before he flew through the residue of the explosion and bits of shrapnel hit his plane, punching holes through the wings. In addition, the heavy shock wave brought on by the explosion tossed his plane about like a leaf in a hurricane. Lorenzo nearly lost control as his airplane was thrown into a ninety-degree bank. Standing on one wing, he lost all lift, and the plane started down.

At the last minute he was able to level the wings, though with no more than fifty feet of air beneath him. He shoved the throttle to the fire wall and pulled the stick over to level the wings, then back in his stomach to climb. The G force pulled his cheeks back, and by the time he reached the top of his climb, he had nearly blacked out, but his airplane was still flying and he had managed to block the convoy.

"Good shooting, Lo!" Captain Donaldson said. "All right, men, looks like they're not going anywhere now. They are ducks in a barrel. Have fun."

Lorenzo swung the plane around and got back in line for another pass. By now, with the trucks unable to move, the Germans had abandoned their vehicles, even the gunners, so the trucks were literally just sitting there. Every pass took out another one until finally running low on fuel and ammunition, Donaldson called them off. When they started back to their base, twenty-three trucks were burning behind them.

"Captain, request permission to do a low-field pass," Deon asked as they approached the field.

"Denied," Donaldson said.

"Come on, Captain, we had a clean sweep here today. We earned a low pass."

"Remember the article, Lieutenant Ware," Donaldson said.

There was a moment of silence, then Deon replied, "Roger that."

Returning, the six fighters made a standard entry into the landing pattern, an easy landing, and an unremarkable return to the hardstand. Not until they were out of the airplanes was there any expression of excitement, then all six pilots, including Captain Donaldson, whooped and yelled and shook each other's hands in celebration.

There was an even greater cause for celebration later that afternoon when the white commander of the fighter wing to which the Ninety-ninth was assigned sent down three words.

"Well done, Ninety-ninth."

Those same three words, "Well done, Ninety-ninth," decorated the top of a cake baked that night by the chief baker in the officers' mess. The six pilots who had flown the mission were congratulated by every other pilot in the squadron.

"You know, Captain, the congratulations seem genuine," Lorenzo said. "I mean, you'd think there'd be a little jealousy, wouldn't you? But I really do think they mean it when they congratulate us."

"They *do* mean it," Donaldson replied. He smiled. "And that's the first sign that we're going to make it. For just as they understand that one foul-up is a foul-up for the entire squadron, they also realize that a victory is a victory for the entire squadron. Do you know anything about bees?"

"Bees, sir?" Lorenzo replied, confused by the sudden shift in subject. "No, sir," he said. "Well, I know that they make honey, and I know enough not to get stung."

"Bees aren't individuals in the way people are individuals," Captain Donaldson explained. "The beehive is everything. The individual bee to the hive is like your big toe is to you. Do you understand what I'm saying here?"

"Yes, sir, I think I do. You're saying that the Ninety-ninth is our beehive."

"Exactly," Donaldson said. "From now on, until the end of the war, we are all a part of the whole."

"I'll try to remember that, sir."

"At ease!" someone shouted, and all conversation in the mess hall ceased as everyone looked around to see who had come in. It was their commander, Lieutenant Colonel Davis.

"Officers of the Ninety-ninth," Davis said, "I am pleased to tell you that, effective tomorrow, the Ninety-ninth will be flying bomber escort."

"Yahoo!" someone shouted, and his cheer was joined by that of every other pilot in the mess.

Palermo
July 22, 1943

"Olives?" Mel Weiser asked.

"Yes, olives," George said.

"No, these can't be olives. They don't look anything like olives."

"What do you mean they don't look like olives?"

"Well, where's the red thing that hangs out of them?"

Larry laughed. "Are you talking about pimientos?"

"Yeah, every olive I've ever seen has pimientos."

"That's added to them, dummy. After they take the seed out."

"Anyway, these olives aren't even the same color."

George Hagan, who was now a staff sergeant, and every other member of the tank company to which he was assigned were standing in the courtyard of a bombed-out opera house in Palermo. First Tank Company was not the only unit here; there were representative units from all over the army. They had been gathered by orders from headquarters, though they had no idea why.

It was Larry who noticed the olive trees. He picked several olives, then brought them back to share with the others.

"I really should know more about these things," Mel said. "I mean, they raise olives around Jerusalem, you know, and that's my hometown."

"Wait a minute," Don said. "I thought New York was your hometown."

"Jerusalem is every Jew's hometown. Didn't you know that? Or maybe it's dates."

"What?"

"Maybe it's dates they grow there. Or figs. Who knows? Who cares? What are we doing at this opera house anyway? Are we about to get a concert?"

"I don't know," George said. "How am I supposed to know? I didn't get the word any sooner than you did."

"Yeah, but you are a sergeant. I'm just a corporal. I figure all you high-ranking muck-a-mucks get the poop, straight from group."

"Sergeant Hagan," a captain called. "Can I see you for a minute?"

"See, what did I say? You're about to be briefed."

George walked easily over to the captain and handed him an olive. The captain took a bite, then screwed his face up in displeasure and spit it out.

"What is that thing?"

"An olive."

"An olive? Huh. Don't think I've ever seen one without the red thing. Anyway, listen, I just got word that only one platoon from each company has to stay, so when you see the others start moving out, don't get antsy. You're the one selected to stay."

"Selected for what?" George asked.

"That I can't tell you because I don't know," the captain replied. "But you take charge of the platoon, find out what's going on here, then bring the men back down to our bivouac. Word is, we'll be moving out in a few days."

"Any idea where we're going, sir?"

"They say the mainland," the captain replied. He reached down and took two more olives from George's helmet. "Maybe these things just need getting used to."

George watched the captain walk over to speak to the first sergeant. Then First Tank Company, except for the first platoon, marched away, joining the others who were also leaving the grounds. He looked around to his own platoon and saw the men in various stages of rest, some sitting, some lying down, a few even sleeping. They had fought through one hundred miles in only three days during the rush to capture Palermo, and though enemy resistance had been light, the fact that they had moved so quickly over mountainous terrain, blown bridges, and destroyed roads spoke well for them.

Someone started blowing a whistle, then the orders were shouted to form by companies.

"First Tank Company, right here," George called out, holding up his hand as a rallying point.

"There ain't no First Tank Company left, Sarge," one of the soldiers said, looking around and noticing for the first time that everyone else seemed to be gone.

"We're it," George said. "Fall in."

When his platoon was formed, George did a sharp about-face, then waited to render the report. The reports rippled along the formation, each report exactly the same with the exception of the identification of the unit. Finally it came George's time, and he brought his hand up in a sharp salute, sounding off as loud as he could.

"First Tank Company, all present and accounted for, *sir!*"

The reporting continued until the last unit, then there was silence. Ahead of them they could see a balcony hanging out from the remains of the opera house, and from it, an American flag rippled in the breeze. It wasn't until then that George noticed a microphone on the balcony. A full colonel stepped up to the microphone and stood there for a moment, looking out over the troops.

"Officers and men of the American forces, our commanding general," the colonel said.

"It's General Patton," someone whispered, and his words were picked up by others until a buzz of excitement permeated the entire courtyard. Finally everyone grew silent as the group waited expectantly.

General Patton strolled up to the microphone. He was wearing a uniform that seemed to be of his own design, khaki riding breeches tucked into highly polished boots, an olive-drab tunic ablaze with medals and sashes, and a glossy, buffed helmet liner. He was carrying a riding crop and wearing a pair of ivory-handled pistols. He stood there in silence for several seconds, for so long that a buzz of curiosity began to move through the ranks.

Then Patton stated, "I thought I'd stand up here and let you fellows get a good, long look at me, to see if I am as big an SOB as you think I am."

The soldiers were shocked by his remark, and there was a beat of silence, then one man could no longer hold in his laughter, and his laughter was a signal to the others so that the entire formation of several hundred men broke out into uproarious laughter.

"I have been ordered to apologize to all of you," Patton said after the laughter subsided. "It is an odious thing for me to do, but I am a soldier, and I will obey my orders.

"As you may have heard by now, I recently struck two soldiers, men who had cowered from battle and were disgracing the brave wounded, and you brave men, by their very existence. I felt that in striking them I was doing them a favor. I tried to rouse them and restore to them their self-respect. After each incident, I confided to those officers who were with me that I believed I had probably saved an immortal soul."

Patton turned abruptly then and left the balcony to the thunderous cheers and applause of the assembled soldiers. After the cheering died, the colonel gave the order that the formation was dismissed, and the individual units could return to their bivouacs.

"Sarge, answer something for me," Larry said a few moments later.

"What?"

"Was that an apology?"

George laughed. "That's probably the closest thing to an apology old Blood and Guts has ever done or will ever do."

With the Ninety-ninth, in Southern Italy
July 23, 1943

Lorenzo Jenkins was part of a mixed element of fighter squadrons, white and black, who were escorting a formation of medium bombers dispatched to bomb a network of Luftwaffe airstrips. The sky was without a cloud, and visibility was clear as the bomber stream crossed the IP at eight thousand feet.

During their bombing run, the fighters pulled back to make a wide orbit around the target, thus avoiding unnecessary exposure to enemy flak. Lorenzo watched the bombing operation from his cockpit as he brought his P-40 Tomahawk around.

"Whoowee!" Deon said. "Look at that. By the time those babies are through, there's not going to be anything left down there."

"Keep your eyes open for bandits," Captain Donaldson ordered.

"Roger."

The B-25s completed their bombing run, then gathered for the flight back. So far, not one enemy plane had been sighted, and Lorenzo thought it would be another uneventful flight. Then he heard someone call out.

"Bandits at our six!"

Jamming the throttle full forward, Lorenzo pushed right rudder, then moved the stick to the right and back, breaking into a steep, tight climbing turn to face the ME-109s that were coming toward them. It was a good thing he did so, for two Messerschmitts were boring in on him.

Red streaks zipped past his cockpit as tracers from the German fighters peppered his plane. He squeezed the trigger on his control stick and felt the aircraft shudder as the fifty-caliber machine guns began firing. Almost instantly one of the German planes exploded as his incendiary rounds ignited the fuel tank.

The remaining Messerschmitt pulled up into a climb, and Lorenzo shot beneath him.

Frightened that the German would get on his tail, Lorenzo put the plane into another hard right turn.

"Aha!" he said when he saw the Messerschmitt coming out of his climb. The German was trying to get on his tail, but Lorenzo beat him to the punch. Pulling the trigger, he saw his bullets slam into the ME-109's engine. Great chunks of metal began flying away from the plane, and Lorenzo watched as the pilot bailed out.

Now, with no bandit in his immediate vicinity, Lorenzo looked around until he saw a lone American fighter about one thousand feet below him. There were two German fighters on the American's tail, and Lorenzo started toward them, opening up from a long range. At that range he missed, as he thought he would, but it did have the effect of causing the two attackers to break off.

Suddenly a stream of red tracers snapped by Lorenzo's canopy, coming from the rear. Twisting around in his seat, he saw what looked like a huge corkscrew, spinning and coming fast, no more than a hundred yards away from him. At first he was almost mesmerized by the sight, then he realized that the propeller spinner was painted in a yellow-and-black spiral design.

Instantly Lorenzo jerked his airplane into a tight turn, trying to break away. Looking back at his attacker, he saw huge puffs of fire coming toward him as the German fired his cannon. One of the cannon shells slammed through his wing, making a loud clunking sound. Had that shell been over a few more inches, it would have hit and probably exploded his fuel tank.

Lorenzo jerked his plane in every direction, trying to escape, but the

German was staying on him. Then all of a sudden his attacker nosed over and went down in flames. For a moment Lorenzo was baffled until he saw a P-40 slide up. It was the same American he had rescued a short time earlier, coming back to repay his debt. The fighter pulled up alongside him, and the pilot smiled and saluted. Lorenzo smiled and returned the salute. The other pilot was a white man, but at the precise moment, there didn't seem to be any difference in their race. They were both American aviators, sharing the same danger, and the same joy of still being alive.

When Lorenzo returned to the base, he did a low pass, then a victory roll. Such maneuvers were authorized when one had an air-to-air victory, and when he landed and taxied up to the revetments, he was met by more than a dozen other pilots who had seen his victories and come to congratulate him.

"Where's Deon?" Lorenzo asked, laughing with excitement as he stood alongside his plane, taking off his parachute and opening the flight suit, which was practically drenched in sweat.

Nobody answered.

"I know where he is. We bet ten dollars on who would get the first kill, and he's afraid to show up."

He stopped laughing when he saw the expression on everyone else's face.

"Lo, you mean you don't know?" LeRoy asked.

"No," he said, shaking his head. "No, not Deon."

"Sorry, Lo," Captain Donaldson said, putting his hand on Lorenzo's shoulder. "He went down."

"But he got out, right? I mean, he was able to bail out?" Lorenzo asked hopefully.

Donaldson shook his head. "Nobody saw a chute," he said.

21

Somewhere in Indiana
July 22–23, 1943

T he highway, pale under a moonless sky, wound through Indiana cornfields and passed by darkened farmhouses. Before leaving Fort Smith, Bob and Susan Gary had debated whether to find a motor lodge en route, but decided they would rather drive all the way through to New York. This way, they could spend a couple of days together before Bob had to report to his point of debarkation.

"Bob, stop the car," Susan said in a strained voice, and responding quickly, Bob pulled to the side of the road. Getting out of the car, he hurried around to open the passenger-side door and help Susan out. She moved a few steps over to the roadside ditch, then threw up.

It was about two-thirty in the morning, and as they stood alongside the car, their skin was caressed by a gentle breeze. In the woods beyond the cornfield, some sort of night creature was making a sound, but Bob was unable to identify it. The car was dark and silent because when they stopped, Bob had killed the engine in order to save gasoline, and he had turned off the lights to preserve the battery.

In the distance they heard a truck, its tires singing on the pavement. Susan retched again.

"Are you all right?" Bob asked.

"I'll be fine," Susan said. "I don't know why I suddenly got carsick like that. I'm normally a very good traveler."

"Yes, well, normally you don't have to stay cooped up in a car this long without a break."

"You're the one I'm worried about," Susan said. "You haven't gotten much sleep; I've only driven a couple of hours."

The lights of the truck came up then, and Bob watched it approach, then speed by, the wind of its passing shaking the car. He watched the taillights recede as the truck continued down the highway, its tires still singing.

Susan threw up again.

"I wish I had something to give you, a Coke or a 7-Up or something," Bob said.

Susan wiped her lips with a handkerchief, then she looked up at Bob and smiled wanly. "I feel a lot better now," she said. "I think throwing up is just what I needed."

"You're sure."

"I'm positive. I feel much better now. Maybe it was just something I ate."

"Or didn't eat," Bob said. "You hardly touched your hamburger at supper."

"I didn't feel well then either, but really, I'm fine now. In fact, I think I'll be able to grab a couple of hours' sleep, then I can relieve you so you can get some rest."

"All right," Bob said. He opened the door to the '39 Chevrolet, and Susan got in. Then he walked around to the driver's side.

Starting the car, he pulled back out onto the highway. "Do you mind if I play the radio?" he asked.

"No, go ahead."

"That is, if I can find an all-night station out here in the middle of nowhere."

Bob turned on the radio. The light on the dial came on, but it was a moment before the tubes warmed up and the radio began working. Across much of the dial there was nothing but dead air, not even a carrier wave. From some distant station he got a weak signal, but it was overcome by static. Then he found a station that was coming in very clearly.

"Lucky Strike Greens have gone to war! Lucky Strike Greens have gone to war! Yes, ladies and gentlemen, the familiar green package that has for so long identified Luckies is no more. Why? Because the American Tobacco Company recognizes that Uncle Sam needs green dye in its war effort.

"However, though the package has changed, the cigarette has not. Luckies are still easy on your throat because the toasting process takes out certain harsh throat irritants.

"Remember, L.S.M.F.T. Lucky Strike means fine tobacco."

The commercial was followed by the mellow voice of an all-night DJ.

"And now, for all you night owls out there, those of you who are working the graveyard shift in our war effort, those of you who are traveling our nation's highways, and especially to our men in uniform, here comes 'Sentimental Journey.'"

The music began playing, and Bob looked over at Susan to see how she was doing. Her head was leaning against a pillow that was propped up against the window. In the dim glow of the dashboard lights, he could see that she was sound asleep.

He checked his speed, fifty-two miles per hour; his fuel, just over half a tank; and his oil pressure and temperature gauge, both of which were normal. On the last weekend before they left Camp Chaffee, Bob and a mechanic friend had put the car up on one of the lifts out at the base and gone over it thoroughly. Because there were no cars being manufactured for the duration of the war, he wanted to make certain that Susan would have no trouble with this one until he got back.

If he got back.

He looked over at Susan again. How beautiful she was. How he hated to leave her. Of course, he wasn't the only soldier leaving a wife behind. But most of the other wives at least had a family for support. Susan had still not reconciled with her parents, and Bob's own parents, longtime family friends of the Whites, didn't want to get involved in the mess, so they were out of the picture as well. If it hadn't been for Bob's sister, he didn't know what they would do.

Bob's sister, Alice, was married to Clint Taylor, a sailor on duty with the Atlantic fleet. The home port for Clint's ship was Norfolk, Virginia, and he actually got to come home from time to time when his ship was in port. Because of that, Alice lived in Norfolk so she would be there for his rare visits. For the rest of the time she lived alone and had already told Bob that she would welcome the company. The plan was for Susan to stay in New York until Bob shipped out, then she would drive to Norfolk.

The headlights from Bob's car illuminated a series of Burma-Shave signs.

WE'VE MADE GRANDPA
LOOK SO TRIM
THE LOCAL DRAFT BOARD'S
AFTER HIM
BURMA-SHAVE

The sun was a full disk above the eastern horizon when Bob pulled into the parking lot of a roadside restaurant named, appropriately enough, the Coffee Cup.

"Wake up, sleepyhead," Bob said.

Opening her eyes, Susan yawned and stretched. "Where are we?" she asked sleepily.

"Somewhere in Ohio, but I don't know where exactly. Are you hungry?"

"I don't know." Susan laughed. "I just woke up."

"Well, I'm starved. What do you say we have breakfast?"

"All right."

Bob stretched when he got out of the car. It felt good to be able to move around.

There were two other cars in the parking lot, and one trailer-truck.

"Well, if a trucker is eating here, then the food has to be good," Bob said. "At least, that's what they say."

"Uh-huh," Susan replied. "Or it may just be that this is the only place with a lot big enough to park his truck."

"O ye of little faith," Bob retorted.

They went inside and found a table. The jukebox was playing "You Are My Sunshine." A sign on the table read, "Our sugar is rationed, just as yours is. Please make do with as little sugar as possible. Thank you."

A waitress came over to the table to wait on them. She was a big, raw-boned woman, wearing a spattered apron and a pink dress. She pulled a pencil from her hair, then held it poised over a little order book.

"What can I get for you nice folks this morning?"

"I'll have bacon and eggs, eggs over easy," Bob said. "And a side of fried potatoes."

"White bread or whole wheat toast?"

"White."

"And I'll have . . . ," Susan started, then she felt a little dizziness swirling around her head. She put the menu down. "I'll have a bowl of cereal."

"Wheaties, cornflakes, or Cheerioats?"

"Cheerioats," Susan said. "And a 7-Up."

The waitress looked up in surprise. "I beg your pardon, Honey, did you say a 7-Up?"

"Yes."

"You all right?" Bob asked.

"Yes, I'm fine. I just think a 7-Up might be good for my stomach."

Susan thought she was going to be okay until the waitress returned with Bob's bacon and eggs. The sight and smell of them nauseated her, and she shook her head and pushed her cereal away.

"Is it all right if I just take my 7-Up out to the car?" she asked the waitress. "The smell of his bacon and eggs . . ." She let the sentence hang.

"Of course, it is, Darlin'," the waitress said. "I've got six kids of my own. I know what it's like to be suffering from morning sickness. If you need anything, just holler."

The waitress left then, and Bob and Susan looked at each other in shock.

"Morning sickness?" Bob asked quietly. "Is that possible?"

Susan counted back the weeks in her head, then smiling, she nodded. "Yes, it is very possible," she said.

"No, this is not a good time!" Bob said.

Susan chuckled. "Too late now," she said.

Bob got up from the table, and they embraced. "I'm sorry, Sweetheart. I'm sorry I did this to you."

"Darling, you didn't do this *to* me. You did it *for* me," Susan said. "I think it's wonderful. Now, even while you are gone, I'll have a part of you with me."

"I love you, Susan."

"I love you, Bob," Susan replied. "But I don't love your bacon and eggs," she added with a distressed voice. She reached for her drink. "I'll be in the car."

Sikeston, Missouri
July 23, 1943

Millie Gates punched the clock at the Brown Shoe Factory, then walked out to the bicycle rack to get her bike. The shoe factory was on Greer Street, just three blocks from where she lived, and that made it very convenient for her to get to and from work.

Most of the shoe factory employees were women, a condition brought about by the fact that so many of Sikeston's men were off fighting the war. Not too long ago, an official from Brown Shoe Company's headquarters up in St. Louis had come down to Sikeston to give a pep talk to the female employees.

"Like the women who are building the bombers and the ships and the tanks and the ammunition, you are in a war-related industry," he told them. "And if you think making shoes is not as important as making tanks, I would suggest that you ask the soldier standing in the mud on Guadalcanal if he would like to give up his boots."

The official's speech was greeted with cheers. No one bothered to tell him that the current contract for this shoe factory was to make dress shoes for the navy, and while that did qualify as a war-related product, it hardly related to a combat soldier giving up his boots and walking barefoot in the mud.

Down in Legion Park there was a huge sign, shaped like an open book, in which the names of all of Sikeston's servicemen were listed. Most of the women who worked at the factory had someone's name there—husband, brother, or boyfriend. Many had two of the three, and a few wags even suggested that some had all three. Millie's brother, Kenny, was overseas with the Eighth Air Force. And through Kenny, Millie was now carrying on an active correspondence with someone. That person's name wasn't on the big board in the park because he wasn't from Sikeston. In fact, Millie had never seen him.

It seemed odd, writing letters to someone she had never even met. But it was also a freeing experience, for she found that she could tell him things that she wouldn't tell anyone else. It was almost as if he had become her personal diary. She was quite certain that if she had met him, she would be much more reticent about what she wrote.

Millie was just getting her bike from the rack when Lucy Fox called to her.

"Millie, wait a minute."

Millie stood by the rack while Lucy came over. Lucy worked in the same shift and on the same floor as Millie and, like all the other women, had to keep her hair restricted in a net. However, there was no sign of the net now because Lucy, who had a beautiful head of fire-red hair, had removed it the moment she stepped through the door.

"I need a favor," Lucy said.

"How much do you need to borrow?" Whereas Millie was careful with her money, Lucy spent hers nearly as fast as she earned it and was always borrowing. Millie didn't really mind. She and Lucy were close friends and had been from the time they were young girls. And Lucy had always paid her back.

"No, I don't need any money."

"What? Lucy Fox has no need for money? Call the newspaper. This should be front-page news," Millie teased.

"Well, if you put it like that, ten dollars until payday *would* be nice. But that's not the favor I'm asking for."

"What's the favor?"

"As you know, the country club is giving a dance for the aviation cadets out at the airfield tomorrow night."

"No, I didn't know that. Why should I know that?"

"Because they are," Lucy replied as if that answered the question. "And I need you to go with me."

"Wait a minute. Lucy Fox, the most popular girl in our high school class, is now reduced to having to go to a dance with her friend because she can't get a date?"

"No, of course not," Lucy replied. "That's not it at all. I've got a date."

Now Millie was confused. "Then what do you mean, you want me to go to the dance with you?"

"Well, you see, the fella I have a date with is a gorgeous air cadet who has a friend who doesn't have a date."

"I see."

"I told Frankie I could get a date for his friend."

"Lucy, you know I don't like that sort of thing. In the first place, I don't like blind dates. And in the second place, I don't really want to get involved with any of the boys out at the air base; they are here for such a short time, it hardly seems worth it."

"Oh, Honey, there's no involvement to it," Lucy interrupted. "That's the best part of it, don't you see? It's just a way of having fun. Those boys work so hard out there, and they are under the worst pressure you can imagine. Besides, they're all learning to be pilots, which means most of them will probably be killed anyway."

"Lucy! What a terrible thing to say!"

"Well, I'm just being realistic, that's all. And I think it does them good to be able to get out from time to time. In fact, I feel like it is almost our patriotic duty to show them a good time."

"There's another reason I don't want to go. I am involved, sort of."

"Are you talking about that friend of your brother's?" Lucy asked.

"Yes."

"But you've never even met him. You don't owe him anything."

"Maybe not, but . . ."

"But what? Do you think for one minute that he expects your life to just come to an end because you two are writing a few letters to each other?"

"No," Millie admitted.

"Of course not," Lucy reiterated. "Look, just come to the dance with me. They aren't supposed to pick us up or anything anyway. I mean, we'll meet them out at the club. Trust me. It's all perfectly innocent."

Millie was standing out on the porch of the Sikeston Country Club, looking out over the golf course. It was dark, and the night breeze felt good. It smelled good, also, carrying on its breath the perfume emanating from several nearby rosebushes. From inside the club, she could hear the band and its female vocalist doing a pretty good job with "I'm Getting Sentimental Over You."

"Here's your punch," a voice said, coming up behind her. The voice belonged to Pete Gillespie, her date for the night.

"Thanks."

"I tasted it. I don't think it's too badly spiked, though some of the senior cadets in there are getting pretty rambunctious. They're moving on next week. They've only got four more weeks until they are commissioned and receive their wings."

"That means a lot to you boys, doesn't it? Getting a commission and winning your wings?"

"Yes, ma'am, it does," Pete said. "Maybe more to me than to most of the others. My pa was killed the morning the Japs attacked Pearl Harbor. He was on board the *Arizona*."

"I'm sorry to hear that," Millie said. "So you're after what . . . revenge?"

Pete laughed. "No, ma'am, nothing like that," he said. "Those Jap boys who bombed Pearl Harbor were just soldiers and sailors like the rest of us, doing their duty. You don't look for revenge when something like that happens. The reason getting a commission and my wings means so much to me is that it allows me to serve my country, same as my pa and his pa and his pa before him."

"That's quite a record of service."

"Yes, ma'am. Have you got anybody in the service?"

"Yes," Millie replied. "My brother is with the Eighth Air Force in England."

"Any beaus?"

"Yes," Millie said, speaking before she could even stop to analyze it. "Yes, my beau is also with the Eighth Air Force."

Pete held his cup up, inviting a toast. "Here's to both of them then," he said. "May the Lord keep them safe."

Millie held her cup up as well. "I think the Lord is working on that very thing," she said with a bemused smile.

Millie had a better time at the dance than she thought she would. In fact, she had enjoyed herself so much that she almost felt a little guilty. It wasn't that she and Lee had come to any sort of understanding. In fact, she was certain that he wouldn't give a second thought to her having gone to the dance tonight. But the guilty feeling was there, nevertheless, intensified by the fact that there was a letter waiting for her when she got back home.

Dear Millie,

No, I don't think it at all improper for you to share things with me, to use me as your sounding board, so to speak. I think we all need such outlets, and indeed I have made it my life's avocation to provide a means for men and women to unload their troubles. I like to think that I am helping them, and I believe I am, except for the two men I would most like to reach.

One is my friend Mark White. Remember, I told you about him. He is as fine a man as anyone I have ever met, but he is absolutely unable, or unwilling, to let me minister to him. Just to see him, or to hear him talk, one would think he has no place for God, yet he is the author of one of the most brilliant books on theology I have ever read.

The other person I can't reach is my father. Unlike Mark, who hides his need for God behind an agnostic facade, my father is, and always has been, a practicing Christian. But I'm afraid he believes that going to God in prayer is a sign of weakness. He is determined not to show that perceived weakness to the men he commands, and especially not to me.

And now you see, Millie, my dear, that my need to share with you is just as great, if not greater, than your need to share with me. I am surprised at how important these letters have become to me, and I cannot tell you how much joy each one brings. Thank you for coming into my life at this point, albeit by means of long-distance correspondence.

With great affection,

Lee

It wasn't exactly a love letter, Millie thought as she read, then reread it. On the other hand, it wasn't a weather report either. It was a letter that bared his soul and, in so doing, touched hers.

July 25, 1943

Mission number twenty. We bombed Hamburg today, after the Brits had already bombed it for four straight nights. The fires were still burning when we got there, and we dumped more incendiaries on them. No flak, no fighter resistance. The poor slobs down there are too busy trying to duck to be able to fight back.

July 26, 1943

Mission number twenty-one. We returned to Hamburg. Evidently we have created something called a firestorm. This phenomenon occurs when the fires in the center of the city are so hot that they create a partial vacuum. As a result, winds rush in from around the city, and as they do so, they create a blast furnace effect with temperatures over one thousand degrees. They tell us that under such conditions all the oxygen is sucked out of the air, and even those who have taken refuge in bomb shelters aren't spared. Hamburg is Germany's second largest city, but it is a city no more and may never be again. Nothing in history can compare with what has happened here, not Pompeii, not the San Francisco earthquake. Compared to the conflagration we have caused here, the great Chicago fire was no more than something you would roast hot dogs over.

The Germans started this war, and they have much to answer for. But my part in this murder of a city will leave a scar on my soul that may never be erased.

August 4, 1943

Mission number twenty-two. Our target was Würzburg. Flak was intense and accurate. The German fighters were many and determined, so determined that they pressed their attacks through their own flak! Perhaps they are incensed by what happened at Hamburg. I know I would be.

22

On Board the Truculent Turtle
August 4, 1943

C olonel Iron Mike Grant was flying his eighth mission. As group
commander, he didn't make as many missions as his other pilots
or even his squadron commanders. He made as many as he could,
though, and in the number of missions flown, he was one of the most
active among the group commanders.

"Left waist gunner to pilot. Here come our Little Friends."

"Roger," Mike replied.

Little Friends referred to friendly fighters, the P-47s that would be
providing them with escort for as long as possible.

Mike could taste the rubber as he breathed the raw oxygen through
his mask. The formation was at twenty-eight thousand feet. Up here
the sky was a bright, crystal blue, cloudless except for the vapor trails
that extended for miles behind the bomber formation. The planes were
enveloped in an avalanche of sound, emanating from the pounding
engines and beating propellers. Far below them, the green and brown

fields of rural France stretched from horizon to horizon. From here the scene was so pastoral that it was hard to believe there was a war on.

Mike turned his head to look back at the leading edge of the left wing. Behind the blur of the spinning propellers he could see the luster-less glare-reducing paint on the inside of the engine nacelles, the black of the wing deicing boot, and the orange unit ID stripe at the wingtip.

"Colonel, I have a fix," the navigator said, cutting through the static of Mike's earphones to interrupt his thoughts.

"Go ahead," Mike said into his microphone.

"We are one hundred eighty miles from the IP on a radial of zero-eight-zero. Our ground speed is two hundred twenty-five miles per hour."

"Roger."

Two hundred twenty-five miles per hour, he thought. Anytime the public saw a picture of the B-17 in a magazine or in a newsreel, they were assured that the speed was "over three hundred miles per hour." Three hundred miles per hour might be possible in a very clean B-17 with no crew except perhaps pilot, copilot, and flight engineer, and no bombs, no machine guns with ammo, no patched-over bullet holes, and fuel tanks that were only one-quarter full. But in a fully fueled, gun-bristling, antenna-sprouting, bomb-carrying, ten-man-crewed B-17, two hundred twenty-five miles per hour wasn't all that bad.

The P-47s stayed with them as long as they could, then when their fuel ran low, they came zipping back through the formation from front to rear, wagging their wings in good-bye.

"Is that it?" the copilot, Lieutenant Billy Butler, asked. "They're leav-ing now?" This was Butler's first mission; the *Truculent Turtle*'s original copilot was now in command of a plane of his own.

"They have to," Mike replied. "That was all the on-station time they had. As it is, their engines will be sucking air by the time they land."

"They sure didn't do anything, did they? I mean, they just sort of hung around for a while."

"When they don't do anything is when they do the most," Mike said.

"I don't get it."

"I used to know a man in Manila who sold tiger powder to the local citizens. He promised them that if they would just spread tiger powder around their houses, no tigers would ever come to bother them. He sold a lot of powder. None of the citizens were ever bothered by tigers."

"There aren't any tigers in Manila, are there?" Butler asked.

"Pretty effective powder, huh?" Mike quipped.

"But the powder didn't have anything to do with it," Butler insisted in an exasperated tone of voice.

"How do you know? The powder is there; the tigers aren't."

"What does that have to do with the P-47s?"

"Think about it, Lieutenant. As long as they were here, the Germans weren't."

"Oh," the copilot said, not certain if he was being kidded or not.

They flew on in relative silence for another forty-five minutes, then Mike heard his navigator's voice in his headset. "Coming up on IP, Colonel."

"Give me the tick," Mike replied.

"Roger, count to follow. Five, four, three, two, one, now."

"Okay, Bombardier, it's all yours."

Now came three minutes of walking the tightwire, steady, unwavering flight while Mike sat in his seat with his hands in his lap.

For the first minute and a half, nothing happened, then it began.

"We've got flak," the ball turret gunner called.

It was as if every gun below had opened up at the same time. Like an artillery time-on-target coordinated barrage, several hundred shells burst around them as one big blast. Many of them were so close that the shock waves from the explosions rocked the bomber.

"Colonel, fighters are coming up!" the tail gunner called in an excited voice.

"You sure? Through their own flak?" Mike replied.

"Yes, sir!"

"We must be hurting them pretty bad for them to do something as desperate as fly through their own flak."

The plane bounced hard, and the tail gunner called to the pilot. "We just got us a hole in the horizontal stabilizer back here, the size of a full-grown pig."

"Bombardier, how are we doing?"

"Almost there!" the bombardier replied. "Okay, bombs away!"

Mike yanked the yoke over hard and stamped on the rudder.

"Get us out of—" the bombardier shouted, but at that exact moment there was a loud bang in the front of the airplane and the bombardier's words were cut off in midsentence. Mike saw the flash of light and heard the explosion, then felt a sudden blast of frigid air. An 88mm shell had burst in the nose compartment. When he looked down between his legs into what was supposed to be the navigator and bombardier's area, he saw nothing but open sky. Neither the bombardier nor the navigator was there. In fact, nothing was there, for he had lost the first six feet of his airplane.

Flak was going off all around them, a terrifying cannonade beneath, above, and to either side. Another shell burst just below the belly, ripping open the bomb bay doors.

The Focke-Wulfs, braving their own flak, saw the *Truculent Turtle* in trouble and began to take advantage of it. Instead of coming in one at a time as they usually did, the fighters were approaching in echelons of four, all of them opening fire at the same time. The shells of sixteen cannon and eight machine guns hammered at the bomber. Cannon shells exploded against the wings and fuselage; others burst with ear-shattering roars inside. Bullets ripped through the plane, punching scores of holes and causing beams of sunlight to crisscross in crazy angles.

A German fighter pilot came up from below. His machine guns raked the bomber for the entire length of its belly, while his cannon fire slammed into the ball turret. Miraculously the ball turret gunner wasn't hit, but there was a huge hole blasted in the side of his turret. He was sprayed by deicing fluid, blinded by smoke, and numbed by the minus-forty-degree wind that screamed in through the hole in the turret at better than two hundred miles per hour.

Number one engine was hit, the shell smashing the drive shaft. The engine began to vibrate so badly that there was a very real possibility it would tear off the wing. Mike shut the engine down, but not before pieces of it slammed into number two engine, causing it to gush oil back across the engine nacelle. Afraid that it might catch fire, Mike shut that engine down and feathered it as well. Now he had no power on the left wing.

No sooner was that accomplished than number three engine started vibrating. The source of the vibration was the propeller, which had been hit by flak. The vibration caused it to slam against the cowling, tearing off chunks of aluminum and creating a spray of sparks.

"Colonel Todaro, take over the lead!" Mike called through his radio. When he didn't get an answer, he called again. "Todaro, are you there?"

"Colonel, we aren't transmitting," the radio operator said.

"It doesn't matter. He'll know what to do," Mike said.

Flying on only two engines, the *Truculent Turtle* began falling back. Suddenly Mike rolled the aircraft upside down, then let the nose fall through so that he was in a screaming dive. Nearly twenty thousand feet below them was a deck of clouds. Glancing over at his copilot, he saw panic, for Lieutenant Butler thought that Mike had just lost control of the bomber. Mike heard screams through the intercom, but he held the plane in the dive, unable to tell them this was a planned maneuver, designed to make the German fighters think they had gotten them.

And in truth, the Germans may have gotten them, for he didn't know if he would be able to pull out at the bottom of this dive. If he could pull out, would the wings stay on?

On Board Gideon's Sword

"There goes the colonel's plane," Lyndon Duncan said.

"Pilot to ball turret, let me know if you see any chutes," Mark called.

"It just went into the cloud bank below. No chutes," Charley reported.

"They really came after him, didn't they?" Duncan asked. "It's almost like they knew he was the group leader."

There was a loud clank from underneath somewhere, and Mark knew they had been hit.

Immediately he looked over toward engines one and two. They looked okay. "Do a visual on three and four," Mark ordered.

Duncan did so.

"See anything?"

"They look fine."

Mark checked the instruments. Everything was in the green.

"I know we were hit somewhere."

"Ball turret to pilot," Charley called up. "We've got a couple of holes in the gut."

"We trailing anything?" Mark asked. "Fluids, wires, cables, smoke?"

"Negative."

"Flak's way behind us now, Captain," Tim O'Leary called from the tail.

"Yeah," Mark said. "Yeah, looks like we're out of the worst of it now. All right, stay alert, guys. We're going home."

On Board the Truculent Turtle

Plunging down into the cloud bank, Mike pulled the throttles back on the two engines that were still working. "Flaps!" he shouted.

To his copilot's credit, Billy reacted quickly, dropping the flaps at the same time Mike started hauling back on the yoke. Though he had no visual confirmation, he could feel the G forces increasing on his body, which told him that the airplane was coming out of its dive. By the time they punched through the bottom of the cloud bank the aircraft was nearly level again, and he pushed the throttles forward on three and four, taking the engines back up to full power. He was rewarded with a throaty roar in response, but they were now less than one thousand feet high, having dropped more than four miles in their wild descent.

"You did it!" Butler shouted. "You pulled us out!"

"You have any idea where we are?" Mike asked.

"Uh, no, sir," Butler replied. "This is my first time here, remember?"

Mike looked at his instrument panel. The gyros had all tumbled, thus he had no artificial horizon and, more important, no gyro compass. The magnetic compass was still working, though, and using it, he took up a heading of two-seven-zero, or due west. That way he was bound to hit the Channel eventually.

"We've got to lose more weight," Mike said. Keying the intercom, he called to his crew. "Report in."

"Top turret, okay, sir."

"Radio, okay, sir."

"Colonel, this is Miller in the left waist. Right waist gunner is dead. Tail gunner is bad hit."

"Ball turret?" Mike called. When he didn't get an answer, he called again. "Ball turret?"

"Yes, sir, I'm alive and I ain't hurt too bad. Only thing is, I can't see," the ball turret gunner replied.

"Can you get out of the ball?"

"Yes, sir, I think I can."

"Miller, help him out of his ball. Then jettison his guns."

"Yes, sir."

"And get rid of all the oxygen bottles. We won't be needing them again."

"Radio to pilot. I've managed to get the receiver working, and I have a fix on our position. Check your ADF."

"Good man, Greg!" Mike said, checking his azimuth direction finder. According to the needle, he was going to have to make about a twenty-degree correction to the right. Normally that would be a simple thing. But he had only two engines, both on the right wing, and on number three the propeller was vibrating so badly that it was chewing up the cowling and Mike estimated it to be only about 40 percent effective. That meant that any bank, regardless of how shallow, might cause them to lose precious altitude. He didn't want to do that because with his power restricted to this degree, even a single foot lost could not be easily regained.

Using the rudder only, which was also dangerous because at this altitude if he slipped off into a spin he would never recover, he managed to catch up with the ADF needle.

243

"Are you a praying man, Lieutenant?" Mike asked.

"Yes, sir, I am," Butler answered.

"Never thought I'd hear myself say this," Mike replied. "But I'd give anything to have my son along. I could sure use his prayers about now."

Davencourt

Lee Grant was standing, along with several others of the base, on the concrete apron in front of the tower. Like them, he was watching the returning bombers of the 605th. Gradually the distant dots grew larger, and larger still, until they became Flying Fortresses. He could hear the reverberation of many engines as their song rolled down from the approaching airplanes and moved quickly across the English countryside. If Lee lived for seventy more years, it was a sound he would never forget.

Entering the landing pattern, three planes broke away from the main group and, sending out flares to indicate wounded on board, started down. The bomber in the lead was trailing smoke. On the apron behind him, Lee heard the ambulances and fire trucks start their engines, then one of the ambulances and one of the trucks sped toward the end of the runway.

The first Fort made a bumpy landing, rolled all the way to the end of the strip, then taxied off a few yards along the perimeter track to clear the way for the aircraft behind it. Before the props had even stopped turning over, the ambulance was alongside it.

The second Fort to land had no flaps or brakes, and it touched down hot, then sped along the runway with no decrease in speed. At the last, possible moment, the pilot gunned his two starboard engines and stood on the left rudder. The result was a left-turning ground loop. The bomber made a 360-degree turn before coming to a stop.

The third plane, also with wounded aboard, was under somewhat more control than the first two, and it taxied all the way up to the apron where it was met by an ambulance. The back door opened, and as the ambulance team tended to the wounded on board, the crew members who could exited the aircraft. One of the crewmen was carrying something wrapped in canvas, and he walked right by Lee, with his eyes glazed.

"What have you got there, Mac?" someone asked.

"This here is Pee Wee Gilder's leg," the aircrewman said, holding the bundle out toward the questioner.

The questioner recoiled. "What am I supposed to do with that?"

"I don't know," the crewman said. "I just . . . I just . . ." He couldn't finish the sentence.

"Where is Pee Wee?" Lee asked gently.

"We put a tourniquet on his leg, then bailed him out over Germany," the crewman said. "I hope they . . . I mean, they'll take care of him, won't they, sir?"

"I'm sure they will," Lee replied.

By now the other B-17s were coming in, touching down one after another, then taxiing by to their respective hardstands. Looking up, Lee saw that *Gideon's Sword*, instead of taxiing around to its own hardstand, had stopped right in front of the tower. Someone got out of the bomber, then the plane resumed taxiing.

Lee was still trying to figure out what that was all about when he saw Mark walking directly toward him. He felt his stomach drop. This couldn't be good.

"Is it Dad?" he asked quietly as Mark approached.

Mark nodded. "I'm sorry."

"What happened?"

"The last we saw of him, he was headed straight down."

"Any chance he might have . . . ?"

Mark shook his head. "None. The nose of the ship was completely shot away. He was inverted for most of the descent, and we saw no chutes. He disappeared into the clouds, far below."

"But you didn't actually see him hit the ground?"

"No."

"Then I shall pray for a miracle."

"Lee, I don't want you to get your hopes up. That cloud cover couldn't

245

have been much higher than a thousand feet. There's no way he pulled out of that fall."

"Thanks for telling me," Lee said. He sighed. "I'd better go to the chapel. People will be needing me."

"I'll come with you."

Despite his sorrow, Lee allowed a small smile to play across his face. "You are coming to the chapel? Well, that's a small miracle in itself."

Mark followed his friend over to the little church, then he sat in the back pew and watched as Lee went up to the altar, knelt, prayed, crossed himself, then stood up and turned around just as the first aircrewman came in.

"Chaplain," the crewman said in a pained voice. "Chaplain, they killed Darrell."

Mark watched Lee console that young man, then counsel and console nearly two dozen others. It was the first time he had ever actually witnessed these sessions, but he could see the results. As they entered, the faces of the young men were contorted with grief, pain, and fear. But to a man, they were much more composed when they left. And Lee was doing all of this, Mark knew, while bearing the heartbreaking loss of his own father. *Who is there*, Mark wondered, *to comfort the comforter?*

On Board the Truculent Turtle

For two hours the badly crippled B-17 limped along, its desperate crew searching the skies for any enemy aircraft. Finally Simmons, in the top turret, called out, "I see water, sir! The Channel!"

"I see it!" Mike said.

"I can't believe we made it," Butler said.

"We've made the Channel," Mike replied. "But we haven't made it home. We're right down on the deck, we've got more than a hundred miles to go, and we have just one and a half engines to get us there."

"What about the guns? We're over the Channel now."

"Good idea. Ditch 'em and all the ammo."

"Colonel, I think I can drop the ball if you want me to try," Simmons said. In addition to being the top turret gunner, Simmons was the flight engineer and chief maintenance specialist aboard the aircraft.

"Yes, try it."

"Yes, sir," Simmons replied, heading toward the middle of the ship.

Once again the crew began throwing equipment overboard, this time the guns and ammo, and after working on it for a while, Simmons was able to jettison the ball turret itself. Gradually the B-17 climbed back up to a thousand feet.

"Colonel, England!" Billy shouted. "I can see the coastline!"

They cleared the coastline cliffs by a couple hundred feet, then were over the welcome fields of England. Just in front of them they saw a British airdrome.

"Radio, can you raise them?"

"No good, sir! We can receive, but we still can't transmit!"

"What's the smoke color of the day?" Mike asked.

"Uh, green. No, no, orange!" Butler answered.

"You certain?"

"Yes, sir. I think so."

"You think? Or you are certain? If we pop the wrong smoke, they'll shoot us down."

"I . . . I don't know."

"We'll go with orange," Mike said. "Pop it!"

The copilot reached under his seat and pulled out a canvas bag. Looking through it, he found an orange smoke grenade, then pulling the pin, he tossed it out his window. Halfway down, it streamed orange smoke, and instantly a green light came on in the tower.

"Colonel, fire on number three!" Butler shouted.

"We'll keep it turning as long as we can," Mike replied.

Those on the ground at the British airfield looked up at the approaching bomber with disbelief. Two engines were dead, and smoke was streaming back from one of the two remaining. Much of the sheet metal covering the rudder was gone as well as the left horizontal stabilizer. There, metal ribs could be seen where the skin should be. There were also several holes in the belly, including one gaping hole instead of a ball turret. The plane had no nose.

"Gear down," Mike called.

"It won't go down!" Billy replied.

"Pilot to crew, prepare for belly landing," Mike said, touching the rudder and banking slightly to move over to the grass alongside the runway. He chopped the power, then eased the ship down, slowly, slowly, until finally it kissed the grass and slid for several feet before coming to a halt. As it came to a stop, number three engine burst into flames.

A British crash truck was on the scene almost immediately, and they began smothering the burning engine with foam. An ambulance arrived to take care of the wounded.

Davencourt

Major Ragsdale stepped in through the door of the chapel just as Lee had finished with another crewman.

"Lee?" Ragsdale called from the back of the chapel.

Lee and Mark looked toward him. Ragsdale was smiling broadly. "It's the old man, Lee," he said. "Colonel Iron Mike Grant! He's safe!"

"He's safe?" Mark said. "But how can that be? I saw him . . ." Mark paused. He hadn't actually seen him crash; he had only seen him in an inverted dive going into the top of a low-lying cloud bank.

"He landed at Wimbleshoe," Ragsdale said.

"Is he all right?" Lee asked.

"He's fine. In fact, I spoke with him on the phone." Ragsdale laughed. "He wants to know if you will come and get him in your car. He said he's not quite up to a long jeep ride just now."

"I'll get Kenny to . . ."

"No, Lee," Ragsdale said quickly. "He wants you to come get him. Just you. He said he wants some time alone with his son."

"I'll . . . I'll go right away," Lee said.

Major Ragsdale left, and Mark went toward the front of the chapel. "That's wonderful news, Lee. Absolutely wonderful," he said.

"Yes," Lee replied. "Uh, Mark, would you excuse me for a few minutes?"

It wasn't until then that Mark saw the tears that were sliding down Lee's face.

August 12, 1943

Mission number twenty-three. We bombed Munich. There was a ten-tenths overcast so we saw nothing of the country below, not the grape arbors of the wine country, not the Rhine or anything else. We saw only the sun on the cloud cover, and we dropped our bombs through the clouds. Somehow it's better this way. You have the illusion you are just bombing clouds, not people, and you don't see the flash of the explosions so you don't think about the arms and legs and torsos that are being blown away down there. The trip to Munich and back took eight hours.

August 17, 1943

Mission number twenty-four: Target was Bromberg. We were to bomb at 16,000 feet but ran into bad weather and had to bomb from 23,000 feet. Had a very close shave in a squadron collision course. I was really scared. No flak at target, but had very intense flak on the way back. We were fired on by a submarine at the coast, coming out. It didn't hit us. I can't imagine what it would be like, having to confess that you were shot down by a submarine.

August 26, 1943

This was our twenty-fifth mission. It didn't mean that much to Duncan or Lindell; they weren't part of the original crew. But for my navigator, Lieutenant Art Bollinger; my bombardier, Lieutenant Adrian Rogers; Sergeant Stewart

Richardson, our top turret gunner; Ross Bird, the radio operator; Charley Phillips in the ball turret; Gil Crane, our right waist gunner; and Tim O'Leary in the tail, all of whom were part of the crew that brought Gideon's Sword to England, this was supposed to be our ticket back home.

Nobody talked much about it, but Ross said, "Boys, this is number twenty-five," in a way that all of us understood what he meant. I'm sure we all thought about it for the entire mission. And we had a lot of time to do that because the mission was very uneventful. We flew diversion, encountered no flak, and drew no enemy aircraft. I don't know why we waste time and fuel with the diversionary missions. To my way of thinking, they accomplish nothing. But they do give a combat crew an easy way to log another mission, so there is that to be said for them. Dry cheese sandwiches in our lunch kit. Six hours, fifty-five minutes.

September 9, 1943

Mission number twenty-six was to Augsburg. We took off at 0520, then climbed up through broken clouds. The ship wasn't responding very well, and the cylinder head temperature on number four was forty degrees above normal. It was difficult forming up, and when we did get formed, we were at the tail end.

The tail end of the formation is not a good place to be. Not only are you constantly fighting the air churned up by the aircraft in front of you, but by the time you pass over the target the gunners below have your speed, altitude, and heading all worked out.

At 0742 we crossed the Belgian coast. At 0815 we picked up our first flak. We were out of it by 0825. At 0900 we crossed the Rhine. At 0930, we hit the IP.

Then I heard someone call, "Bandits."

"Three o'clock level, coming toward us," Stewart Richardson said from the top turret. He squeezed off one burst. "Charley, they're going under," he said.

"I've got 'im," Charley answered.

We started our bomb run. Bollinger called doors coming open, and Bird in the radio room confirmed that they were.

Suddenly in the top element, Major Dixon's Fortress was hit, and it turned over on its back and started screaming down straight at us.

"It's going to hit us!" Duncan shouted.

I pulled the yoke all the way back in my stomach, standing Gideon's Sword on its tail at a ninety-degree angle. The plane from the top group fell past us, missing us by no more than ten feet. It went about another hundred feet or so, then blew up, filling the sky with fire, chunks of metal, and pieces of people.

"Oh, man, what was that?" O'Leary screamed from the tail. I believe this was the first time I've ever heard O'Leary react to anything.

Major Dixon was a good man, probably the best-liked squadron leader in the entire group.

23

Davencourt
September 10, 1943

Putting on his class A khakis, Charley Phillips checked himself out in the full-length mirror by the door in the squadron orderly room.

A SOLDIER LOOKS THE PART, a sign said above the mirror. Also alongside the mirror, in the appropriate positions, were more signs such as:

HAT CORRECT?

BRASS POLISHED?

TIE STRAIGHT?

SHIRT IRONED?

BELT BUCKLE POLISHED?

GIG LINE STRAIGHT?

PANTS CREASED?

SHOES SHINED?

The signs were placed to be in the correct position for a six-foot soldier. The problem was, most of the aircrew were smaller than that, and the tail gunners and ball turret gunners were much smaller. Charley Phillips was only five feet three inches tall.

He squared his hat on his head, adjusted his gig line, which was the line between the shirt closing and the edge of the belt buckle, then walked over to the pass sign-out book and entered his name and destination.

Leaving the orderly room, Charley walked down to the special services hut and checked out a bicycle. A few minutes later he was riding down the road toward the Throgmorton house, where he had been invited for dinner.

Charley had been back to Henry Throgmorton's house many times since that day last June when he plowed the field for him. He had become friends with the Thorgmorton family, and he helped with chores around the farm, never accepting any pay, doing it for the love of being on a farm once more.

Unlike the huge, palatial home of Lord and Lady Davencourt, the Throgmorton house was a modest four-room house consisting of two bedrooms, a parlor, and an eat-in kitchen. It had neither electricity nor running water. The Throgmorton house was located on Davencourt land; thus, the house actually belonged to the Davencourts, and it was identical in size and design to the half-dozen other tenant farmers' houses that were also on Davencourt property.

It reminded Charley of home in more ways than one. Charley's father worked for a man named Wilson, who owned several thousand acres of land around the town that was named after him, Wilson, Arkansas. The house Charley grew up in was a four-room house, with two bedrooms, a living room, and an eat-in kitchen. It did have electricity, but no running water. There was a pump on the back porch and a privy in the backyard. The house was painted green, with a red roof, one of more than one hundred identical houses—all green, all with a red roof—that were owned by Mr. Wilson and lived in by his sharecroppers, black and white.

But there had been another incentive that kept drawing Charley back.

The added incentive was Henry Throgmorton's daughter, eighteen-year-old Roselyn.

Roselyn would never be mistaken for a pinup girl. She was a skinny little thing with light brown hair, gray-green eyes, several freckles, and a rather significant gap between her two front teeth. Charley had seen English girls, especially the ones who came out to the base to dispense coffee and doughnuts, and he had even talked to them. But in truth, he was rather intimidated by them, by the sophistication of their language and their rather courtly air.

Roselyn's language was not as sophisticated, nor were her ways as courtly as those of the Doughnut Dollies. Except for the way she sounded when she talked, Roselyn could have been a girl he met in the skating rink in Blytheville or at a football game in Jonesboro. She had an innocence about her that he found very appealing.

Smiling, Roselyn met Charley on the sidewalk in front of the house. He set the kickstand on his bike, then took the little package from the basket.

"Oh, you brought something," Roselyn said. "Let me see!"

Roselyn reached for the package, but Charley pulled it away from her. "It's not just for you," he said. "It's for the whole family."

"What could you bring in a box that small that's for the whole family?"

"You'll just have to wait and see, won't you?" Charley teased as he went inside.

"Hello, Charley," Henry greeted him. Mrs. Throgmorton came in from the kitchen to greet him as well.

"Umm, umm, Mrs. Throgmorton. I don't know what you are cooking in there, but it smells mighty good."

"It's steak and kidney pie," Mrs. Throgmorton replied.

"I brought this," Charley said, handing the little package to Mrs. Throgmorton.

"Why, thank you, Charley. That's very nice of you."

"Open it, Mum," Roselyn said.

Mrs. Throgmorton looked at Charley. "Is it all right if we open it now?"

"Yes, but you might want to save it until later. I wouldn't want to spoil anyone's appetite, what with that good meal you're fixing and all."

"Ah, something to eat then, I see," Mrs. Throgmorton said. She unwrapped the package, then opened the box. "My word," she said. "Are these chocolate bars?"

"Yes, ma'am. Two dozen Hershey bars," Charley said. "I bought them at the PX."

"Well, then we shall all have one after our dinner. Henry, if you, Roselyn, and our guest will come to the table, we can eat now."

Charley followed them into the kitchen, then he held the chair, first for Mrs. Throgmorton, and then for Roselyn, before he sat down.

"Well, doesn't our young gentleman have good manners, though?" Mrs. Throgmorton said. "Henry, you used to help me into my chair when we were courting. Why do you not do it now?"

"I didn't know you that well then," Henry replied. "I wasn't sure you could get into a chair by yourself. Now I know you can."

Henry laughed, and Charley laughed with him.

"Yes, well, if we'll all hold hands, Henry can ask the blessings of our Lord."

Roselyn was sitting to Charley's left, and when he reached out, her hand was already there. He took her hand in his, feeling a little thrill at the physical contact. With the others, he bowed his head as Henry began to return the blessing.

"Bless this food to our use and ourselves to Thy service. In Christ's name we pray. Amen."

"Heavens, Henry, you would think you were starving to death, you make such quick work of the blessing," Mrs. Throgmorton said.

"It's a blessing that is found in the Book of Common Prayer," Henry defended. "It wouldn't be there if it didn't please the Lord."

"It's an Anglican prayer," Mrs. Throgmorton replied. "I'm quite sure Charley isn't Anglican or even Episcopalian."

"No, ma'am," Charley said. "I'm Southern Baptist. But our chaplain, Lieutenant Grant, is Episcopalian. He's a very good man, so I reckon if all Episcopalians and Anglicans are like him, why, there's not that much difference."

"All who come to the Lord are welcomed by Him," Henry said as he helped himself to a generous serving of mashed potatoes.

They ate heartily, talking about farming as they did so. Charley pointed out the many things that were similar between farming here and farming back in Arkansas. He also pointed out some of the things that were different, managing to find humor in them, often at his own expense.

"Why is it, lad, that you never talk of your flying experiences?" Henry asked.

Charley was quiet for a moment. Then he said, "There's not much to talk about. We fly out, drop our bombs, and fly back."

"But surely there's more to it than that. I mean, I know it's very dangerous. Do you find excitement in the danger?"

"I guess I don't think about it that much."

"Are you ever afraid?" Roselyn asked.

"Constantly."

"Then, no wonder you don't want to talk about it," Henry said. "I'm sorry I brought it up."

"No, don't be sorry," Charley said. He sighed. "Maybe we should talk about it. I'd like for someone to know what I think and feel, just in case something happens."

"Oh, Charley, say a prayer quickly!" Roselyn said. "You mustn't jinx yourself."

Charley smiled. "I don't have to say a prayer quickly," he said. "Ever since I arrived in England, my life has been one long prayer."

"How can you do it?" Mrs. Throgmorton asked. "How can any of you do it? Go out, day after day like you do, knowing that at any moment you could be killed?"

"We can do it because we are already dead."

"Already dead? What do you mean by that?"

"I don't know that it is anything I can explain," Charley answered honestly. "But fear comes when you are afraid you are going to be killed. Pretty soon that fear takes over your mind, body, and spirit, so that you can no longer function. You are just a zombie, totally consumed and paralyzed by fear.

"But"—Charley held up his finger—"if you assume that you are going to die, that there is nothing you can do to stop it, it has the wonderful effect of freeing you. You can watch the German tracer rounds zipping toward you, and you don't give them a second thought. You don't think about them because you are already dead, you see. And if you are already dead, nobody can hurt you."

Mrs. Throgmorton shivered involuntarily.

"Charley, that's terrible," Roselyn said. "Why, someone like that has no dreams of a future."

Charley nodded. "That's my point, Roselyn. I *have* no future."

Suddenly tears sprang to Roselyn's eyes, and she got up and hurried away from the table.

"Roselyn, wait!" Charley called toward her as she went into her own room and closed the door behind her.

"I'll go to her," Mrs. Throgmorton said, getting up from the table as well.

Charley shook his head slowly. "Mr. Throgmorton, if I said something to offend someone, I'm terribly sorry."

"You didn't offend anyone, lad," Henry replied. "And 'tis a wise decision you're making not to concern yourself with a future, for if you did, and if you brought someone else in with you and the worst did happen, you'd be spreading the grief even more."

"I'm glad you can see and understand that," Charley said.

"You're a fine lad, Charley, and I've no doubt but that my daughter's dreams of her own future are built around you."

Charley gasped. "Mr. Throgmorton, I assure you, I've made no mention of the subject with her."

"I know you haven't, but love is a funny thing. When it comes, it comes, and there's no holdin' it back. Sure'n you're not so blind as not to see how Roselyn feels about you?"

Charley was quiet for a long moment, then he nodded. "Yes, sir, I know how she feels about me," he finally said. "And truth to tell, much as I don't want it to be under these circumstances, I'm afraid I feel the same way about her. I just don't think it's fair to involve her in my own uncertain future."

"I agree with you, m'lad," Henry said. "What do you say that you and I do what we can to keep things under control until we know what the good Lord has in store for you?"

"Yes, sir," Charley said. "I'd appreciate that."

Norfolk
September 10, 1943

Shortly after Susan moved in with Bob's sister, she got a job with the Red Cross and family services. Because of that, she didn't have much of a problem getting gasoline, since her job gave her an extra ration. Not only did she have to drive to work every day, she also had to make frequent visits to the homes of the wives and families of servicemen.

Today had been a difficult day for her. It had been necessary for her to arrange a Red Cross loan to the widow of a soldier who was killed in Italy. The loan was to allow her to go back to Texas to be with her family. What made it particularly difficult for Susan was the fact that the woman's husband had been part of the Forty-fifth Infantry Division in Italy. Bob was part of the Forty-fifth Infantry Division in Italy.

Gasoline wasn't a problem, but tires were, and when she stopped the car in front of the apartment she shared with her sister-in-law, Alice Taylor, she looked with dismay at the right front tire. It had a large oval-shaped spot exactly in the middle. There was not the slightest hint of tread.

Some of her coworkers at the Red Cross office had been cautioning her about continuing to drive on that tire.

"You have to go all over the place," they said. "What if you are out somewhere . . . stranded on the highway or in a bad neighborhood and the tire blows? You are pregnant. You've got no business driving on that tire."

Susan couldn't agree with them more, but neither did she have any idea as to what she could do about it. She had applied for another tire, new or retread, and her name was on the list. But when she tried to get her name moved up because of her job, the clerk at the tire store pointed out that those ahead of her—doctors, nurses, and volunteer firemen—had even more valid reasons to be on the list, and they, like Susan, were having to wait.

Of course, if she had to wait much longer, it would all be moot anyway. She was five months pregnant now, and she had promised Bob that she wouldn't work beyond her sixth month.

Susan leaned over to put her finger on the oval. She pressed in on it to see if she could gauge its strength.

"Don't fret about the tire, Honey. I brought one with me," a familiar voice said from behind her.

Turning quickly, Susan saw her father standing on the bottom step of the apartment building.

"Dad?" she said in a small voice. "Daddy!" she squealed, using the diminutive as she rushed toward him.

"Hello, Sweetheart," Professor Harold White said, opening his arms to his daughter. He embraced her and kissed her as she clung to him.

"Mama?" Susan said, suddenly frightened that his appearance might portend something more.

"She's inside, visiting with Alice, waiting for you," Harold said with a broad smile.

Susan hurried up the steps, then down the hall to the apartment she had been sharing with Bob's sister ever since Bob's deployment. Edna White jerked the door open even before Susan got there, and mother and daughter stood in the hallway in a tearful, but joyful embrace.

"Will you two please go inside?" Harold asked, coming up the hall behind them. "No sense in putting on a show for all of Norfolk."

"Oh, hush, Harold," Edna scolded. "I'm so happy, I would be willing to kiss my daughter in the middle of Main Street if Norfolk has a Main Street."

When they went inside, Alice greeted them with a smile.

"Can you believe it, Alice?" Susan asked happily. "I haven't seen my parents in . . ."

"Six months and ten days. I know," Alice said, laughing.

"Oh, I can't tell you how happy I am to see both of you," Susan said.

Then, realizing that their presence here was rather unusual, she asked, "But what are you doing here?"

"Isn't it obvious? We've come to see you."

"Yes, but why? I mean, after all this time."

"We came here to take you home with us," Edna said.

"This is my home for now. This is where Bob expects me to be and . . ."

Harold held up his hand to stop her. "Honey, I was wrong. I should not have objected to your marrying Bob. It's quite obvious to me now that you two should be together, and I'll not do anything to get in the way of that."

"I appreciate that, Dad, but much as I love you and Mom, and as happy as I am to see you, I can't come back and live in the same house with you again. Not now. It would be like . . . like I ran away from home and . . ."

"Was welcomed back like the prodigal son? Or in this case, the prodigal daughter?" Harold asked.

Susan chortled. "Something like that," she admitted.

"Well, here's the thing," Harold said. "We're not asking you to come back to live with us. I've found a small house that will be perfect for you and the baby when it comes."

"How much?"

"You don't have to worry about that, Honey," Edna said. "Mark has already paid a year's rent in advance."

"Mark?"

"He says it is his wedding present to you and Bob."

"But I don't understand. How did Mark know I would even come back?"

Harold snorted. "He threatened to disown me if I didn't admit what a big fool I've been over this whole thing."

Susan laughed.

"What do you say, Honey? Can we start again?" Harold asked.

"It sounds good. It sounds great, in fact, since I didn't want to be any trouble to Alice when the baby came."

"Nonsense, you wouldn't be any trouble."

"And I don't like intruding on their privacy when Clint is here."

"We didn't mind at all," Alice said.

"Well, I did feel like an interloper when he was here last. And you can't tell me you wouldn't have enjoyed a little more privacy."

Alice laughed. "Having my husband without privacy is better than not having him at all."

"Will you come?" Edna asked.

"I'd like to. I really would. The only thing I'm concerned about now is Bob. What would he say?"

Harold and Edna laughed.

"What is it? What's so funny?"

"Don't worry about Bob. He and Mark have been writing to each other, and they are the ones who set this up. Bob not only wants you to return to Litchfield; he expects you to," Harold said.

"Whoa, wait a minute. He *expects* me to?" Susan replied.

"Harold, will you for heaven's sake shut up?" Edna ordered. "You are going to queer this whole thing with that big mouth of yours." She looked at Susan. "Of course, he doesn't expect you to in that way. What your father meant was, Bob believed you would want to do this, and he wanted you to know that he was all for it."

"How come he hasn't written to me about this?"

"Maybe this letter will explain," Edna said, pulling a familiar-looking little yellow envelope from her purse. She handed it to her daughter.

Dearest Susan,

If you are reading this letter, then your parents are in Norfolk, asking you to move back to Litchfield. I am taking the unusual step of writing to you through your parents because I wanted everything to be taken care of before you had to worry about it.

I am leaving to you the final decision as to whether or not you want to go back to Litchfield. If you choose to stay in Norfolk, even after the baby is born, I'm sure everything will work out well. I know Alice will be there for you whenever you need her. But I must tell you in all candor that I would feel better if you were back in Litchfield, around familiar surroundings and with our friends and families.

By now you know, also, that Mark has given us a very generous wedding present, in that he has paid the rent for a year in advance on a small house on Monroe Street. After what you did with our little place in Fort Smith, I'll be anxious to see what you can do with a real house.

Please write to me right away and let me know if I need to change the address on all future mail.

Your loving husband,
Bob

24

East Termini, Sicily
September 11, 1943

Major Spanky Roberts was now in command of the Ninety-ninth Fighter Squadron, Colonel Benjamin O. Davis having been called back to the States to testify before Congress. With the Ninety-ninth now located at a new airfield on the north coast of Sicily, they were able to range farther in their missions and could escort the heavy B-24 Liberators out of North Africa, as well as the medium bombers that had moved to Sicily.

Lorenzo Jenkins, with two kills to his credit, was tied with two other officers for the most number of enemy planes shot down. When he received word to report to Major Roberts, he was sure it was to be a briefing for an upcoming mission.

"Sit down, Lo. Take a load off your feet," Major Roberts said after returning Lorenzo's salute.

"Thank you, sir."

"Lieutenant, we are selecting six men to return to the States to instruct other Negro aviators in combat flying. Since you have proved yourself in combat, you are one of the names being considered."

Lorenzo didn't reply.

"What do think about that?" Major Roberts asked.

"Major, I'll do anything the army asks of me," he said. "I'm an army officer, sworn to obey the orders I receive."

"That doesn't answer my question," Major Roberts said. "What do you think about going back to the States to be an instructor?"

"It's an important job, sir, I'm sure."

Roberts slammed the palm of his hand down on the desk so hard it made a loud pop.

"Blast it, man! What do I need to do to get a straight answer from you?" Roberts demanded. "My question is this, Lieutenant. Given your choice to go home and instruct others, or stay here with the squadron, which would you rather do?"

Lorenzo smiled broadly. "Well, sir, I didn't understand I was being given a choice. If I have a choice, I would rather stay here."

Now it was Roberts's time to smile, and he nodded his head. "I told them you would choose to stay here," he said.

"Them, sir?"

"The higher-ups," Roberts said with a dismissive wave of his hand. He leaned forward across his desk. "But now that you have made your decision, I have another offer to make to you. One that I think you will appreciate."

"What is that, sir?"

"What do you know about the P-51 Mustang?"

"Other than the fact that it is without doubt the hottest and best airplane in this war . . . not much, sir."

"Rumor has it that the Three-thirty-second will be given Mustangs early next year."

"Rumor?"

"Well, at this point, I'm not at liberty to confirm or deny the rumor," Roberts said. Again a big smile spread across his face. "But I can say that one pilot from the Ninety-ninth is being selected to transition into the Mustang immediately and conduct an in-depth evaluation of the airplane, to include flying it in combat. I've chosen you, Lo. That is, if you want the job."

The grin that split Lorenzo's face lit up the room. "Do I want the job? Major, I would give my firstborn son for that opportunity."

Roberts waved his hand dismissively. "Keep the kid," he said. "I wouldn't want to have to change diapers."

"Yes, sir!"

Salerno Beachhead, Italy
September 12, 1943

After two days of hard fighting, the Second Battalion of the 143rd Infantry regiment of the Forty-fifth Infantry Division held a hill near Eboli. The hill was important because it controlled the corridor between Eboli and Altavilla. And because of exceptionally heavy casualties during the fighting, Corporal Bob Gary of A Company was now a squad leader and the second-highest-ranking soldier in his platoon.

"Get your men dug in!" the first sergeant shouted, moving up and down the line. "Then all noncoms report to the CP for briefing."

Bob checked the position of each of his men, making certain that they had overlapping fields of fire, then he ran crouched over to the foxhole that was serving as company command post.

"You got your squad dug in, Corporal Gary?" Lieutenant Kilgore asked. As the only remaining officer in the company, Second Lieutenant Kilgore was now the company commander. Two days ago he had been a platoon leader. Just slightly more than three months ago he had been sitting in an auditorium at Texas A&M, listening to the commencement address before receiving his bachelor's degree and a commission in the U.S. Army.

"Yes, sir," Bob answered. "And I've got our field of fire laid down."

"Good man. Where are the other squad leaders from your platoon?"

"Sergeant Patterson and I are the only NCOs left in the Second. We have PFCs acting as squad leaders."

"All right, you'll just have to brief them when you return," Kilgore said. "You're taking over second platoon. I'm moving Sergeant Patterson to third platoon. They don't have any NCOs left at all."

"Yes, sir."

The lieutenant is young, Bob thought. *He's young and he's scared.*

Kilgore's face was ashen and covered with sweat. When he spoke, it was with a high, thin voice. But Bob gave him an A for grit. The kid didn't flinch when he was faced with the awesome responsibility of taking over a decimated company in the midst of a firefight.

"What do you want us to do, Lieutenant?" one of the sergeants asked.

"Let half your men rest if they can," Kilgore said. "Keep the other half awake and alert." He looked at the first sergeant. "We have land line strung to every platoon CP?"

"Yes, sir, all the phones are wired back to here," the first sergeant replied.

"Good. You platoon sergeants, if you see anything, if you hear anything, get on the phone and let me know. Now, get back to your platoons, and set up your final defensive fire perimeter."

Bob knew what a final defensive fire perimeter was; he had learned about it and practiced it during his training. It was literally a last-ditch desperation ploy whereby all remaining weapons fired not at individual targets, but at a preselected zone. It is implemented only when a position is about to be overrun. Not at any time during his advanced infantry training back at Camp Chaffee did Bob ever think he would hear the words, "Final defensive fire perimeter," used for real. And yet he had just heard them.

"Final defensive fire, Lieutenant?" Sergeant Patterson asked in an awe-tinged voice. It was obvious that he was having the same thoughts as Bob.

"Yes," Kilgore said. "Then dig in and pray that we don't have to use it."

"Sir, any word on a relief column?" one of the other NCOs asked.

"No."

"What about some of the other companies in the battalion? Maybe they could move some of their men over here."

Kilgore shook his head. "I don't know how to break this news to you, Corporal, but personnel wise, we are as strong as any other company in the battalion. Okay, get back to your men and get ready. It'll be dark soon, and my bet is that before morning, we'll have some unwanted company."

"Yes, sir," the NCOs replied as one.

Holding his rifle at knee level and bending forward at the waist, Bob hurried back to his platoon's position. He darted back and forth as he ran in order to make himself a somewhat more difficult target to any sniper who might be watching them.

The normal complement for a platoon was thirty-eight men, including the platoon leader, the platoon sergeant, and the squad leaders. As the only NCO remaining in the second platoon, Bob Gary was now in command of eighteen men.

Roy Carter was a PFC in this same platoon. He was also one of the acting squad leaders. This was the same Roy Carter who had been a guest for dinner at Bob's house back in Fort Smith. *"You may show them in, Willie Mae,"* Susan had said that night, four months ago. *Only four months? It seemed a lifetime ago.*

"What's up?" Roy asked when Bob returned.

"I've got the platoon now," Bob said. "Patterson has gone over to the third. You're second in command. If anything happens to me, it's up to you to take over."

"Have I ever told you that I have absolutely no ambition as far as this man's army is concerned?" Roy asked. "If it's all the same to you, I'd just as soon you not let anything happen to you."

"Yes, well, I'll try to keep it that way." Bob was silent for a second, then he took a deep breath. "We've been ordered to establish a final defensive fire perimeter."

Roy's eyes grew wide. "Are you serious?" he asked in a somber tone.

Bob nodded.

"That doesn't sound good, does it? Final defensive fire. It sounds so . . . so . . ."

"Final?" Bob asked with a chuckle.

"Yeah," Roy said, laughing with him. It was good to laugh, even over something so macabre.

"We'll probably be hit tonight, so keep one man awake in each hole."

"Where's your hole going to be?" Roy asked.

"I expect I'd better move to the middle."

"All right, just so that I know where you are." Roy smiled. "Us high-ranking military tacticians have to be able to communicate, you know."

"If I need you, I'll have my staff get in touch with your staff," Bob said.

They began laughing then. And it wasn't just a little laugh. It was a deep, belly-wrenching, side-splitting laugh that grew more intense until both of them were wiping tears from their eyes. Soldiers in nearby holes looked over toward them, wondering what was going on.

Finally the laughter stopped, and Bob and Roy looked at each other.

"We've both gone crazy. You know that, don't you?" Roy asked.

"Yeah, I know it."

Roy started back to his hole, then he stopped and turned toward Bob. "Oh, by the way, I just checked my Cs. I have a can of ham and lima beans. You want to trade? I know that's your favorite."

"I don't know what I have. I haven't looked yet."

"Doesn't matter. Far as I'm concerned, *anything* is better than ham and lima beans."

Bob was unable to sleep during the night. He tried, but his new, unaccustomed responsibility got in the way. Afraid that he might be needed for something, he was still awake at 0430 the next morning, and by then he was so groggy that he was seeing things. Every shadow in front of him looked like a German soldier.

He thought about Susan and wondered how she was doing tonight. It was the middle of the night in Norfolk, so she would be asleep right now. If he thought about her hard enough, if he concentrated with enough intensity, maybe he could be there with her.

Susan had a way of burying her head in the pillow, then pulling the sheet all the way up to her ears. Sometimes back at Fort Smith when he couldn't sleep, he would look at Susan—she wouldn't know he was looking at her—and marvel at how lucky he was to have her. Because of those moments, it was very easy now to reconstruct little imaginary events with her.

In this reconstruction her hair is spread out on the pillow, shimmering in a beam of moonlight that has slipped in through the window.

Her breathing is a soft whisper, and when he reaches to touch her with his finger, she wraps her hand around it and pulls it to her cheek. A small, contented smile passes across her lips, but she doesn't wake up. And now she is a part of the miracle of creation, for she is carrying God's greatest gift. She is pregnant with their child. What will it be, a son or a daughter? And what kind of world will it grow up in?

"I'm picturing you as a son, but you might well be a daughter. It doesn't matter. Son, daughter, I love you all the same."

"I know," his child replies.

"I want to apologize for not being physically present while you were growing up. I hope you understand that I was always there in spirit . . . with you in school . . . at play . . . when you were sick . . . when you celebrated Christmas and your birthdays. I was always there."

"I was aware of your presence."

There are the rumble of engines and the clanking, squeaking sound of tank tracks in motion.

"You had better go now," Bob's adult child says to him. "Your men need you."

"Yes, I must go. But remember that I will always love you."

"You must hurry, Dad. The Germans are coming."

Suddenly Bob snapped out of his sleep, not even aware he had been asleep, his heart pounding, his breath coming in ragged gasps, his face drenched with sweat. Somewhere in the middle of his musing he had fallen asleep and dreamed the conversation. What did he mean when he apologized for not having been there while his child was growing up?

But even as he was contemplating the strange dream, he realized that he really was hearing the things he had heard in his dream: engine noise and the clanking, squeaking sound of tank tracks drifting through the darkness. Fully alert now, he cranked the handle on the field phone.

"Mad Dog," Lieutenant Kilgore answered at the other end of the land line.

"This is Mad Dog Two. There is something out there."

"All right, I'll call in some illumination," Kilgore replied.

A few moments later Bob heard a half-dozen pops high in the air, and flares, launched by American artillery, floated down on parachutes. The flares painted the entire valley in a harsh white light. And in that wavering light, Bob could see hundreds of German soldiers moving toward them, interspersed with dozens of tanks.

"Platoon, here they come!" he shouted. "Get everyone awake!"

Within a few seconds after that, the whole corridor exploded with gunfire as the Germans attacked en masse, firing machine guns, rifles, mortars, and recoilless rifles. The Americans answered with rifles, machine-gun fire, and an artillery barrage. One by one the flares went out, but the valley continued to be lit by white phosphorous explosions and the fiery crisscross of tracer ammunition.

The whole scene had an incredible, rather bizarre beauty to it, and one could almost get caught up in the mesmerizing effect of the graceful flight of the tracer rounds. Often they would hit the ground or rocks, then ricochet, creating erratic patterns of fire. Sometimes the tracers would burn out en route, becoming blackened missiles of death, racing dangerously through the sky under the cloak of darkness.

"Pull back! Pull back!" someone shouted, and several in the company jumped up and started running to the rear.

"Wait! Wait! We haven't gotten any official word to pull back!" Bob called. He picked up the phone and turned the crank. When nothing happened, he turned the crank again. Suddenly Roy Carter appeared at the top of his foxhole.

"Bob, the lieutenant's dead! So's the first sergeant! There's nobody left alive back at the CP," he said.

By now German artillery was exploding all around them, and many more tracers were coming toward them than going away.

"Who called pull back?" Bob asked.

"I don't know. But under the circumstances, it seems prudent, don't you think?"

"Yes, but I'm not going to pull back until I'm certain everyone in the platoon has gotten the word. I don't intend to leave anyone stranded here. Roy, stay here as long as you can. If any of our people show up, tell them to pull back. I'm going to check the other holes. If I'm not back soon, get out of here yourself."

Bob rolled out of his hole and lay on the ground. Almost immediately there was the whizzing, popping sound of machine bullets snapping by overhead, and Bob buried his head under his arms. When the bullets had passed, he raised his head again.

"Bob?" Roy said.

"Yes?"

"Come back soon, okay? Don't get into any long conversations!" Roy said, rolling over the lip and down into the hole Bob had just vacated.

Bob nodded, then slithered off into the darkness.

Salerno Beachhead
September 13, 1943

They were bringing the dead men down the side of the mountain, lashed onto the backs of mules. The bodies were belly down across the wooden pack saddles, their heads on one side, their rigor-mortis-stiffened legs sticking out on the other. At the foot of the trail a graves-registration team sat at a field table, filling out papers on the KIAs who were being laid on the ground alongside a low stone wall.

Sitting on that same stone wall, Sergeant Patterson lit a cigarette with a hand that was still shaking, though the battle had been over for almost eight hours. He had been called into service to help identify the bodies from A Company. He wasn't needed for the company commander,

Captain Tongate, or the XO Lieutenant Shell, or the platoon leaders, Lieutenants Fillion, Ward, and Kilgore. They were officers, known to the battalion adjutant, so he was able to identify them. But Patterson's help was needed for the enlisted men of Company A.

"Here's two more from A Company's sector," one of the men leading the pack mules said as two bodies were pulled down from a couple of mules, then dragged over to be put with the others. The mules, free of their loathsome burden, moved off to graze serenely amid the dandelion weeds that grew alongside the trail.

Patterson got up from the stone wall and walked over to check out the two new additions to the long row of dead. He looked down at faces that were totally drained of color but still recognizable. Staring at them for a long, silent moment, he took a deep puff from his cigarette.

"You know them?" the lieutenant from Graves asked.

"Yes, sir," Patterson said. With a hand that was trembling so badly that it was shaking ashes from the end of the cigarette, he pointed to one of them.

"That one is PFC Roy Carter. The other one is Bob Gary. Uh, I guess that would be Corporal Robert Gary."

The lieutenant knelt down and examined the dog tags, taking information from them as he did so.

"He was going to have a kid," Patterson said.

"Beg your pardon?" the lieutenant replied distractedly, concentrating on his job.

"His wife, that is," Patterson said. "She's going to have a kid."

"Too bad," the lieutenant said.

"He was really excited about . . ."

"What the . . . ?" the lieutenant suddenly said, interrupting Sergeant Patterson. The lieutenant's attention had been arrested by an army deuce-and-a-half truck that was about to drive away. "Hey, wait a minute! Hold up over there!" he shouted, pointing to the truck driver. "You don't leave here until I tell you to leave here!" The lieutenant started over to straighten out the matter.

". . . his wife havin' the baby," Patterson finished, though by now he was talking to himself.

Patterson stood there for a moment longer, looking down at Bob and Roy. An ant crawled across Bob's unflinching face, and Patterson bent down to brush it off. Then he walked back to the end of the stone wall and sat there all alone. With a shaking hand, he lit a new cigarette from the old.

25

Davencourt
October 14, 1943

T he morning was cold and rainy, and Mark and Paul had run out of
coal two days earlier. Although Paul now had his own airplane, he
and Mark continued to share the same room because they had become
close friends over the last year. Now, grumbling about the lack of heat,
they dressed hurriedly, appreciating the high-altitude gear.

Mark glanced through the window at the fog and rain. "Wow, it looks
really bad out there," he said.

"Maybe they'll call it off," Paul suggested as he pulled on his sheep-
skin-lined boots.

"Maybe," Mark agreed, buttoning up his wool shirt.

"Who are we kidding? The way they're putting out the missions now,
we'd fly today if we were in the middle of a blizzard."

"Let's get some eggs," Mark said, heading for the door.

"How's your sister doing?" Paul asked. "I've been thinking about her
a lot lately, about what a rough break she got."

"Well, losing Bob was hard on her," Mark said. "Especially with the baby coming and all. But an awful lot of babies are being born these days who will never know their fathers, and Susan's made of good stuff. I expect she'll get through this all right."

"Listen, the next you time you write, tell her I'm thinking about her, will you?"

"Yeah, I will. And I'm sure she'll appreciate that."

They ran through the cold, wet rain to the mess hall, joining several others who were also hurrying through the dark and the rain.

During breakfast several of the officers at Mark's table began a discussion about movies they had seen. As often happened, the discussion deteriorated into an argument over the best movie ever made. Lyndon said it was *Citizen Kane*. Mark, perhaps remembering his and Emily's good-bye at the airfield at Polebrook, insisted it was *Casablanca*. Paul, on the other hand, argued vociferously for Abbott and Costello's *Keep 'Em Flying*. There was no disagreement on the best Western movie. All thought it was *Stagecoach*.

After breakfast the crews gathered in the Nissen hut for their briefing. It was still cold and raining outside, but the furnace orderlies had the two coal stoves blazing, and that, plus the body heat of the assembled men, caused the temperature inside to rise to a comfortable level.

The men were sitting on wooden benches or in chairs. They were talking with their neighbors or dozing or staring straight ahead with the glazed look of individuals who were trying hard to put all feeling—fear, hope, thoughts of home, and plans for a future—out of mind.

Colonel Grant stepped onto the platform in front, and all conversation came to a halt. The men were proud of Iron Mike, not only because he had flown more missions than any other group commander, but also because of the fantastic feat of flying he had exhibited last month when he had brought his shot-up bomber back. Even the new crews knew the story now, for it had been told and retold a dozen times since then.

Grant jerked aside the black curtain that covered the map. Those in the back couldn't see the target, but those in front could and someone said aloud, "Schweinfurt."

"Schweinfurt!" another said, and the word was repeated several times until even those in the very back row knew the grim truth.

"Schweinfurt."

"Schweinfurt."

"That's right, Schweinfurt," Colonel Grant said.

There were several groans. Although it would be the first time for the 605th, Schweinfurt had been bombed before, and everyone knew that the losses had been very heavy. It was deep inside Germany, and the strike route would take them within attacking range of more than eleven hundred German fighters.

Grant was silent for a moment, allowing it soak in, letting the men prepare themselves mentally and emotionally for the ordeal ahead of them.

"Schweinfurt is the city where the Germans make all their ball bearings, and everything they use in the war against us depends on those ball bearings, from their fighter planes to their tanks, all the way down to the Führer's desk chair."

"Well, by all means, let's take out Hitler's chair," someone shouted, and the others laughed nervously.

The lights went out then, and slides were projected on a screen.

"This is our primary target for today. It is the Kugelfischer Werks ball-bearing plant, and we will find it in a large triangular configuration, located about one mile south of the sports stadium. The plant will be well camouflaged and screened with smoke. There are more than three hundred known flak batteries, all eighty-eight millimeter guns, in the target area."

Colonel Grant paused for a moment, then scratched his chin.

"Well now, since we know there are at least three times that many flak batteries there, what our intelligence people must mean is, they know only three hundred of them by name . . . Lieutenant Oscar Nagel, Sergeant Heinrich Rodl, Corporal Rudi Maas," he said as an aside. His audience laughed.

"However," he continued, still tongue-in-cheek, "I'm sure you share my unbridled joy in knowing that we have been routed through the best possible channel so that only a minimum of their guns can come to bear on us at any given time."

Again the aircrews laughed. Nearly all their briefings told them that they were being routed away from all but a few of the flak batteries.

"We'll pick up FW-190s and ME-109s on the way in and on the way out. They stay on station and are radar-vectored to us. We may also get some of the twin-engine ME-210s as well. They like to sneak up from a long way off, hide in the vapor trails, and fire rockets, so you tail gunners must be on the lookout for them."

"What about fighter escort?" someone asked.

"We're supposed to have P-47s take us halfway in, then they'll meet us again, about halfway back. But right now, they're socked in worse than we are, and there is a very good chance they won't even get off the ground. It doesn't matter. With or without them, we're going to have to do most of it by ourselves."

Colonel Grant was followed by a meteorology briefing, given by a bespectacled captain who told them that, though the weather was bad over England, it would be clear over the Continent. An intelligence officer then cautioned them not to have anything of a personal nature with them other than dog tags and ID cards.

"Today's authentication code is Buster," he said. "I say again, Buster. And if you are diverted and have to use smoke to signal the tower, the color of the day is green." He went on to assure them that a ship would be on station in the Channel to rescue anyone who had to ditch.

Out on the flight line the airplanes loomed like ghostly shadows as the trucks delivered the crews. The maintenance people had been working on them since long before the aircrews were even awake, and now all of the bombers were full of fuel, bombs, machine-gun ammunition, coffee, sandwiches, and everything else it would take to make them ready to go.

Mark and his crew stayed outside the airplane while Adrian fused the bombs, then they climbed in and took their stations. After a wait of thirty minutes, the operations order was activated, and the silence of the early morning English countryside was broken up by the whine and cough of engines as the airplanes were brought to life.

In the Throgmorton House

Roselyn was still in bed when the sound of the starting aircraft engines awakened her. She lay there under the comforter, aware of the cold, drizzling rain outside, and thought of Charley Phillips, all cramped up in the little ball beneath one of the bombers.

"Oh, Lord in heaven, please protect Charley and the others in his airplane, and bring him back to me," she prayed.

She listened as, one by one, the bombers took off and roared directly over her house. She didn't know which one Charley would be in, but she knew he would be looking down on the house as he passed over, so with each passing bomber, she repeated her prayer.

Three and One-half Hours Later

"How much fuel left?" Mark asked the flight engineer.

"Eleven thousand pounds," Richardson replied.

"Wow, we're burning it pretty fast," Duncan said. "Think maybe we should ease back on the power?"

"And wave bye-bye to the rest of the formation?" Mark replied. "We don't want to do that. Anyway, don't worry about it. We always burn a lot more fuel going to the target than we do coming back. It's all been computed for us by the boys with the slip-sticks."

"That's good," Duncan said. "Because I was beginning to sweat it."

"Don't even think about it," Mark said.

Despite his admonition not to think about it, Mark did just that. He knew that the four big R-1820 engines were drinking fuel at the rate of 1,600 pounds per hour; however, as the weight decreased, so would fuel consumption. Minus bombs and minus fuel they would use only 960 pounds in the final hour, providing, of course, that they weren't bucking unusually strong head winds for their return flight.

"It's funny how peaceful Germany looks down there, isn't it?" Duncan asked.

"You ever had bratwurst, Lyndon?" Mark asked.

"Sir?" Duncan answered, surprised by the question.

"Bratwurst. You ever had it?"

"Yes, well, I play baseball in St. Louis, and as I'm sure you know, there are a lot of Germans in St. Louis."

"A lot of them in my part of Illinois too," Mark said. "They are an industrious people, and I've always rather liked them. I'd like to come back to Germany someday when I'm not trying to kill them and they aren't trying to kill me."

"That would be nice, wouldn't it?"

"Fighters at ten o'clock," Richardson suddenly called from up top.

The entire airplane began to shake with the recoil of its guns being fired. Tracer rounds flew through the sky in flashing blurs. An FW came toward them, wings and nose winking brilliantly as it fired its two machine guns and four cannon. Mark heard a loud bang, louder than the engines, louder than the hammering guns.

"Where were we hit?" Mark asked.

"Now, don't get nervous, Captain," Richardson said in a voice that was amazingly calm under the circumstances. "I mean, our fuel tank wasn't hit or anything. But we've got a hole in our wing, just outside number one, that's as big as a bathtub."

"You think the wing spar was hit?"

"No, sir."

"More bogies at six o'clock and climbing!" Charley called from the ball.

"How many?" Mark asked.

"I don't know, sir."

"Come on, Charley, you know better than that. Give a complete report."

"There's too many to count," Charley said in exasperation. "I'd say sixty or seventy at least."

"What?" Mark called.

"Looks like they've got the whole German Luftwaffe up here!" Charley said.

Suddenly every gun station began reporting German fighters, coming in from all directions. The intercom was filled with excited babble.

"Hold it! Hold it!" Mark shouted. "Only call out the ones that are actually coming toward us! And whatever you do, don't waste your ammunition shooting at planes that are out of your range."

For the next several minutes the German fighters pressed their attacks, and *Gideon's Sword* shuddered and shook as its gunners returned fire.

"ME-210s, firing rockets!" Tim O'Leary called from the tail.

Looking out the left window, Mark saw two fast-moving rockets streaming past them, trailing long tails of smoke. The rockets detonated about one hundred feet in front of them, huge blobs of fire and energy, their burst-radius about four times greater than ordinary flak. Whereas flak was often silent puffs of black, these rocket explosions could be heard, sounding as if someone had thrown a handful of rocks onto a tin roof.

"Oh, no, Mark, it's Paul!" Duncan said then, putting his hand on Mark's arm to get his attention.

Looking toward *Moonlight Serenade*, which was slightly above and to his right, Mark saw that Paul's airplane had just been hit by a rocket. The left wing folded upward, breaking off and opening up the side of the fuselage as if it were a lid being rolled back on a tin of sardines. Mark saw a body flung into space. Amazingly Paul was still sitting almost calmly at the controls, even though the side of his plane was completely open. Paul looked around. He was wearing his oxygen mask and goggles, but Mark could picture exactly what his friend's face would look like now, for he knew that the expression would be closer to bemused surprise than to panic.

The severed wing, with its two engines still turning, drifted to the rear with fire shooting from its jagged edge. The B-17 fell off to its left and started spinning down. Within two turns, the entire bomber exploded in one huge fireball, then began fluttering down in small, unidentifiable pieces.

The whole thing was over in a few seconds, though to Mark, it was like watching the slow-motion film of a football game. He saw every frame of it with crystal clarity.

Southern France

Lorenzo was out of his usual territory, but that was by design. As a test of the long-range capability of the P-51, his Mustang, painted with the bright red tail of the Ninety-ninth Fighter Squadron, was fitted with a drop tank to give him extreme range. His mission was to rendezvous in southern Germany with a flight of Eighth Air Force B-24s that were attacking Cologne.

This would be the first time he had ever had any connection with the Eighth Air Force, which was stationed in England. All his previous experience was with the Fifteenth Air Force, flying out of Libya and Sicily. However, if today's operation was any indication of how the Eighth made their station time, he decided he would just as soon stay with the Fifteenth.

According to the mission operational orders Lorenzo had received, the B-24s should be right here, right now. He made a very wide 360-degree turn looking for them, but saw nothing.

Initial Point, 20 Miles West of Schweinfurt

As the aircraft from the 605th swung around on the IP for their bombing run, Colonel Todaro's airplane, just in front and to the left of Mark's, was hit by one of the rockets. The rocket slammed into the bomber just aft of the waist gun ports, then exploded, cutting the bomber in two. The tail tumbled one way, while the front half of the bomber went the other. According to the mission orders, Mark was now lead pilot for this element.

"This is Goodnature Three," Mark broadcast to the other aircraft in the flight element. "Authentication Buster. I say again, authentication Buster. Close in on me and drop on my command."

None of the other pilots replied, but Richardson informed Mark that they were responding.

"All right, Art, Adrian, you Double-A boys in the nose have it all on your shoulders now. We're leading the squadron."

"Roger that," Adrian replied.

No longer was the sky a crystalline, cloudless blue. Now it was filled with smoke and jagged flashes of light in red, orange, yellow, and white. Having crossed the IP, the bombers continued through the aerial minefield of exploding cannon shells and rockets, jagged chunks of disintegrating airplanes, out-of-control propellers, and red-hot splinters of steel. They were also sharing the sky with falling bodies, some still alive, waiting for the opportunity to open their parachutes, others already dead.

The sounds were as terrifying as the sights—a crashing cacophony of wrenching metal, hammering machine guns, bullets ripping through aluminum, and the high, thin, nerve-jarring banshee wail of German fighters, their engines overrevved as they screamed by within a few feet of the bomber.

There was another loud clang from inside the plane itself, and Mark felt the aircraft jerk hard, as if he had driven a car very fast over railroad tracks.

"Fire! We got a fire back here!" Lindell shouted.

"Art, get back there and help with the fire," Mark ordered. "Bird, do what you can!"

"I'm on it, sir!" Bird replied.

Art Bollinger, the navigator, crawled out of his spot in the nose, then wriggled through the narrow catwalk over the bomb bay to get amidships to help fight the fire. Still in the nose, Adrian Rogers was in the kneeling position, peering down through the optical lens of the Norton bombsight.

"Doors coming open," Adrian called.

Normally Bird would confirm that the doors were open because from his position in the radio room, he could look right down through the bomb bay; in fact, he could follow the bomb path all the way down if he wanted to. But Bird was busy fighting the fire right now so they would just have to trust that the enunciator light was correct when it indicated that the bomb bay doors were open.

"Bombs away!" Adrian said.

Mark felt the sudden lightening of the plane as the six one-thousand-pound bombs tumbled from the racks.

"All right, boys!" Mark shouted through the intercom. "We're working for ourselves now. Let's go home."

As he made the wide 180-degree turn, coming off the bombing run and starting back, Mark got his first look at the sky behind him. Not only were airplanes—both bombers and German fighters—going down, but the sky was filled with blossoming parachutes. He didn't have time to count them, but he was sure there were more than a hundred of them: the white canopies of the Americans, and the brown canopies of the Germans.

"Top turret, can you get a count how many B-17s there are in our group?" Mark asked.

"Eight in our squadron, sir, counting us. Ten in the top squadron."

"Nine in the low squadron," Charley called up.

"That's twenty-seven," Mark said. "Twenty-seven remaining out of thirty-six."

With the radio operator, one of the waist gunners, and the navigator all fighting the fire in the back, the amount of machine-gun fire coming from Gideon's Sword was greatly decreased. The German fighters noticed it and began concentrating on them. Three ME-109s bore down on them. By the time the attack was finished, number four and number two engines had been knocked out. In addition, number four was burning.

"Hit the fire bottle on four!" Mark shouted, shutting off the fuel and feathering the props on both.

The other Fortresses began pulling ahead, and as Gideon's Sword was falling back, the fighters, like sharks at a feeding frenzy, jumped on it. They made another pass, filling the Fort with holes as their bullets punctured the skin in scores of places.

"How are you boys doing with the fire?" Mark called.

"I think we've pretty much got it out," Art said.

"All right, get back where you belong. We need you at your gun stations."

A few minutes later Duncan noticed the oxygen level was dropping rapidly.

"Mark, you better get us down pretty quick," he said. "We're losing oxygen fast. We must've taken a round in our main oh-two tank."

In addition to the central O_2 bottle that supplied, through a network of tubing, oxygen to every crew station, there were a few self-contained oxygen bottles—one in the nose, one in the cockpit, and one amidships.

Mark jerked his mask off and grabbed the portable. He took a few deep breaths, then handed it to his copilot.

"We'll share this," he said. "You control it."

Duncan took his own mask off, took a breath, then held it back up to Mark's face.

Mark set up a two-thousand-feet-per-minute rate of descent, which was a steep descent but would still take from five to ten minutes to get them low enough to be able to breathe. Without oxygen, the crew would pass out in two minutes.

His ears popped as the plane plummeted.

Charley Phillips had passed out from lack of oxygen. When he regained consciousness in the ball turret, the B-17 was once again flying straight and level, but at a much lower altitude. It took him a second to get his bearings, and when he did, he saw that a Focke-Wulf was sneaking up on them from underneath. The German fighter was so close that Charley could actually see the pilot's eyes, looking up, studying the bomber he was about to shoot down.

Reacting quickly, Charley opened fire with the twin fifty-caliber guns, and he saw the German throw up his hands, just before his airplane started down.

"Pilot to crew, report in!" he heard Mark calling over the intercom.

"Ball turret, okay, sir," Charley said. The other stations reported in, also, and Charley was amazed to hear that, despite the pounding they had taken, so far not one crewman was wounded.

Charley examined the bottom of the plane. Looking aft, he could see several holes in the bottom of the fuselage as well as gaping holes in the horizontal stabilizer. Turning his ball, he checked out the wings, and what he saw made him gasp.

"Ball turret to pilot."

"Go ahead, Charley."

"Captain, it looks like somebody took an ax to the wings down here. There are holes everywhere, big jagged ones. And I see fluid leaking out."

"What color is the fluid?" Richardson asked quickly.

"Red."

"That would be hydraulic fluid, Captain," Richardson said.

"Flaps, brakes, landing gear."

"We'll have to worry about that later," Mark said. "On your toes, boys. Here come some more fighters."

The German fighters were determined that this B-17 wasn't going to get away from them, and they made repeated attacks, firing at nearly point-blank range and tearing off more chunks of metal with each pass.

"If they keep this up, we'll be leaving more of the airplane here than we're taking back," Mark said.

"That's fine with me, just as long as we take something back," Duncan said, his voice edged with fear. Mark wondered if his own voice sounded like that, and decided that it must, for he could not remember ever having been more terrified.

Mark watched the Germans coming toward them. If it weren't for the horror of it, he could almost appreciate the gracefulness of its *tanz des todes*—the half roll, then the winks of light, and the glowing balls of fire that beat a tattoo against his plane.

Then, almost unbidden, Mark found himself praying.

Dear Lord, I need help. I know I haven't come to You before because I thought I could do it alone. But I know now that I can't, and I ask that You not let my crew suffer because of my arrogance. Please, dear Lord, help me get them through this safely. And if I am to die, then, Lord, have mercy on my soul. In Jesus' name I pray. Amen.

A strange thing began to happen to Mark. He knew a calmness, "a peace that passeth all understanding." He could almost feel his heart-beat slowing, his blood pressure lowering, and his fear and confusion drop away. He didn't have to wonder about it. He knew he was experiencing the presence of God.

Mark's headset crackled with an excited call from his tail gunner.

"I'm out of ammo, and there's one coming up on our six!" Tim O'Leary called.

The fighter that was coming up behind them raked the belly of the bomber with machine-gun fire. Tim couldn't shoot back, but Charley could and he exchanged fire with the German. The fighter plane's bullets slammed into the ball turret, and though Charley wasn't hit, sparks flew everywhere. Charley tried to turn his turret to track on his attacker. It made a ninety-degree turn to the left, then stopped.

"My turret's jammed!" he said. "I can't track on them!"

"I'm out of ammo!" Crane said.

"So am I," Richardson said from the top.

"That makes four gun stations out of commission," Duncan said.

"They're forming up back here!" Tim said. "They're getting ready to come in for the kill, and the only thing I can do is spit at them!"

Mark had never been in a more critical position in his life, and yet he had never been more at peace.

"Take it easy, boys," he said over the intercom. "We're going to be all right."

"I wish I had your confidence, Captain," Lyndon said.

The B-24s never showed, and Lorenzo was about to start back when below him he saw a solitary B-17. At first he was puzzled by it. *What is a B-17 doing here all by itself? And why is it flying so low?* His questions were answered when he saw that two of the bomber's propellers were feathered, and even from here, he could tell that it had been pretty badly shot up. Then looking a thousand yards behind the bomber, he saw three Focke-Wulfs queuing up for their final attack. He dropped his belly tank and shoved the throttle into overboost.

"Oh, great, here comes a Messerschmitt at twelve o'clock high," Adrian said from the nose.

"Why not?" Art asked. "No sense in letting the Focke-Wulfs have all the fun."

"Wait a minute, guys!" Mark said. "That's not a Messerschmitt! That's a Mustang. It's a P-51, one of our guys." Mark laughed. "What in the world is a P-51 doing out here all by itself?"

"We're not out of the woods yet. There's only one of him. There are three Germans," Richardson said.

"Maybe the Germans don't see him," Mark suggested. "He's high and pretty far out."

Mark was right. The German fighter pilots, not expecting any company, were coordinating what they figured would be the coup de grâce against the lumbering bomber that had fallen into their laps.

The P-51 came down toward the German fighters, his speed approaching five hundred miles per hour in the dive.

"He's going after them!" Richardson said.

Mark saw the sun flash on the Mustang's propeller and followed him as well as he could, until the Mustang flashed by, going out of his sight behind him.

"Richardson, Tim, keep an eye open, let us know what's happening!"

The P-51 shot down one of the German fighters before they even knew he was there. Then the pilot pulled up through the debris of the exploding Messerschmitt and hurled the plane around in a turn that was so tight that he was lined up on a second one. One short burst, and it went down as well.

"Dang!" Richardson said. "Captain, I wish you coulda seen that!"

"What happened!"

"Two of them!" Tim shouted. "He's shot down two of them already, and the third is running!"

The remaining German forgot all about the B-17. Looking to his left, Mark saw the Focke-Wulf trying to outrun the Mustang, but the P-51 was too fast and the American pilot was too good. Mark saw a stream of tracers rip into the German, then he saw the German climb out onto the wing and jump from his plane. The Mustang made a wide turn, came back by the B-17 so fast that he was there for just a blink, then he was gone.

"Where did he go? Are there others back there?"

"No, he's coming back up alongside us now," Richardson said.

The red-tailed Mustang slid up beside the bomber and slowed to the bomber's speed. Then the pilot took off his oxygen mask, pushed up his goggles, smiled, and waved.

Startled to see a black face in the airplane that rescued him, Mark waved back.

"You wouldn't be in the Ninety-ninth, would you?" Mark asked.

"Yes, you know of us?"

"I've heard of you. And my sister knows the grandmother of one of your pilots."

"Really? Who would that be?"

"I don't remember the pilot's name, but I remember his grandmother's name. It is Willie Mae . . . can't remember the last name."

"Does your sister live in Fort Smith, Arkansas?" Lorenzo asked.

"Yes!" Mark said excitedly. "Well, not anymore, but she did, and that's the Willie Mae I'm talking about."

"Her name is Willie Mae Jenkins," Lorenzo said.

"Yes, that's it. Willie Mae Jenkins. So you do know her."

Lorenzo laughed. "You're not going to believe this, but Willie Mae is my grandmother. I'm Lorenzo Jenkins."

"Wow! What an amazing and happy coincidence!"

"Well, they say the Lord works in mysterious ways," Lorenzo said.

"Nothing mysterious about it," Mark replied. "I was praying for a miracle, and He sent you."

Lorenzo laughed again. "I've been called lots of things, but I don't think I've ever been called a miracle. Wish I could stay, but I don't have enough fuel. Good luck."

"God bless you, Lorenzo Jenkins. I'm going to remember you," Mark said.

Lorenzo waved one more time, then, wagging his wings, flew off, heading south. Mark continued west.

The crew let out a cheer when they saw the coast of England, then they cheered again when Davencourt Airfield came into view. That was when Richardson came up front and knelt on the floor between Mark and Lyndon.

"Captain, I don't want to rain on everyone's parade," Richardson said, "but we've got us a problem. A big problem."

"What is that?"

"Charley's ball is jammed tighter than a rusted bolt, and the openings aren't lined up. We've been trying to get him out for the last half hour, but we can't do it. We have to get him out or the gear down. Otherwise . . ." Richardson let the sentence hang. He didn't need to finish it.

"We don't have hydraulics. Can you crank the gear down manually?"

"No, sir, I've tried that. The backup mechanism was shot away. But there is one more thing we can try."

"Then by all means, try it," Mark said quickly.

"It's something you'll have to do just before we touch down."

"What's that?"

"Do you remember, back at Langley, when we hit that real sharp updraft on final? You had just started to lower the gear and . . ."

"Yes, they popped down, I remember."

"We can't pump the gear down manually, but we can disengage the locks. So maybe if you could duplicate what happened at Langley, you know, give us a real sharp bounce on final . . ."

"As I recall, that was one heck of a bounce. I don't know if I can re-create that intentionally. And even if I can, what's to say our wings will stay on? I could be putting the entire crew in jeopardy for one man . . . and it might not even work. I've got a feeling our wing spars are like Swiss cheese about now."

"That's true, Captain. But it's Charley's only chance," Richardson said. "I reckon you're just going to have to make that decision yourself."

"All right," Mark said. "Let me think about it."

On the ground at Davencourt, Lee Grant was in his normal position on the apron in front of the tower. Most of the planes were back by now, but there were still several missing, so everyone was looking east anxiously, trying by willpower alone to bring more of them home.

Everyone knew that Mark's plane was close. Mark had already called the tower, apprising them of the situation on board *Gideon's Sword*. They knew that he could not put his gear down, and they knew, also, that the crew couldn't get Charley Phillips out of the ball.

"Everyone's praying with you, Son. You're not alone in this." Turning, Lee saw his father standing beside him, still in the flight suit he had worn on the mission just completed.

"Good. The more prayers, the better."

"Well, I know the Lord will listen," Iron Mike said as he put his hand on his son's shoulder. "I'm living proof of that."

"There he is, on final," someone said, pointing.

"Is his gear down?" another asked.

"No. No gear!" The report came from someone who was standing out on the deck of the tower, watching the bomber's approach through binoculars.

Lee mouthed a continuous prayer as he saw the bomber approaching the end of the runway, getting lower and lower.

"Gear yet?"

"No! No gear."

"Pilot to crew," Mark said. "All of you know our situation. Charley is stuck in the ball, we have no hydraulics, and we can't get the gear down manually. There is one thing I can try, but if I try it, there is about a fifty-fifty chance our wings will come off. So I'm going to call the roll right now. 'Yes' means try it. 'No' means don't."

"You can start with me, Captain. I say yes," Adrian said.

"Navigator?"

"Yes."

"Copilot?"

"Do it," Lyndon said.

"Top turret?"

"Yes."

"Radio?"

"Yes."

"Captain, this is Crane. Me 'n' Lindell both say yes. Right, Lindell?"

"Right," Lindell agreed.

"I say yes," Tim said from the tail.

"All right, find someplace to hold on because . . ."

"Wait, you didn't ask me!" Charley said. "I say no. I don't want to take a chance on everyone getting killed because of me."

"You've got no vote in this, Charley," Richardson said. "Do it, Captain."

"It's too late for debate now, boys," Mark said. "Here goes."

He jerked the wheel back into his lap, then slammed it forward again.

From the ground, everyone saw the plane make a very noticeable bounce, almost like a basketball . . . up . . . then sharply back down onto the glide path.

"He's lost control of it!" someone shouted.

"No, wait, he . . . yes! He did it!" the man with the binoculars shouted. "He popped the gear down!"

The cheers were as loud as the cheers at any ball game Lee had ever attended.

"That was one nifty piece of flying," Colonel Grant said.

"Gear down and in the green!" Duncan shouted excitedly.

"Over the fence!" Mark said, coming back on the throttles. *Gideon's*

Sword kissed the runway as lightly as if it were the most routine of land-ings. "Hold on, guys, remember, no brakes!" Using the rudder pedals only, Mark kept the airplane right in the center of the runway until it reached the far end. Then he made a squealing turn on to the perime-ter track. By then they were at normal taxi speed.

The plane stopped in front of the tower, and Mark shut down the engines. Immediately the crash crew ran to the bomber to begin the job of extracting Charley Phillips. The crew climbed out with not one wounded among them, and the crowd cheered again. Several rushed out to shake hands with Mark and the others, and while Mark was as congenial as he could be, he broke away from the oth-ers as soon as he could and asked Lee if he would come with him to the chapel.

Lee was pleasantly surprised by the request, and he accompanied Mark to the little church where he was equally surprised to see Mark kneel at the altar rail. Lee knelt beside him, giving thanks for the safe delivery of Mark and his crew, and praying for those who had not returned. He prayed also for direction. He recognized that Mark was at a critical crossroads in his spiritual life, and he asked for guidance in help-ing Mark with this journey.

After a time, both men rose, then moved back to sit on the front pew.

"I had an epiphany today," Mark said.

"You found Jesus?"

"Yes, though I think it would be more appropriate to say that He found me."

"Mark, I don't know what to say except welcome home."

"I've been a fool, Lee. I'm like Thomas. I'm like Paul. I'm like Constantine. I'm like every doubter and every sinner who has ever been blind, but now can see. And I know what you are thinking."

"Oh? And just what am I thinking?"

"You are thinking that I'm intoxicated by the adrenaline rush, that I am so thankful to still be alive that everything is oriented around that. But that's not it, Lee. That's not it at all. When I was up there, when I thought I was going to die, I was praying to be spared, yes . . . but more than that, I was praying for the salvation of my soul. And I don't know if I can explain this, but when I knew that my soul was no longer in jeopardy, then I was no longer afraid."

"Captain White?" someone called from the door of the church.

Looking toward the door, he saw Captain Gibson, the group maintenance officer, and Sergeant McMurtry, the line chief.

"Don't tell me you're going to make me fill out a report of survey for damaging your airplane," Mark teased. "You maintenance guys are always . . ."

"How were you flying that airplane, Captain?" Gibson asked.

"What do you mean, how was I flying it?"

"Tell him, McMurtry."

Sergeant McMurtry cleared his throat, then ran his hand through his short hair.

"There's no way on earth you could have been in control of that plane, Captain," McMurtry said. "All the cables to the ailerons, to the elevator, and to the rudder have been shot away. When you move the yoke or the rudder pedals, nothing happens."

"What? That's impossible."

"That's what I told him," Gibson said. "I even suggested that you may have had a few strands still connecting them, and they didn't separate until the shock of the landing."

"No way," McMurtry said. "First of all, your cables weren't just broke. They were gone, whole pieces of them shot away. And even if there had been a few strands holding them, it wouldn't have mattered. Your bell-cranks were shot away too. I don't know who was flying that airplane, Captain. But you weren't."

Gibson and McMurtry left the chapel then, and Mark and Lee were alone. They were silent for a long moment, then Mark took the wings off his chest, got up, and walked up to the triptych.

"What are you doing?" Lee asked.

Mark looked around the triptych until he found a small opening between the triptych and its base. He slipped the wings into the opening, then let them fall down inside.

"Sergeant McMurtry said he didn't know who was flying that plane. Well, there is no question in my mind who it was. By rights, these wings belong to Him."

Epilogue

London, England
Today

The twenty-four members of the English Heritage tour group were having dinner in a private room of the Fox and Hound Restaurant. When the retired bishop returned from his visit to the little church at Davencourt, several greeted him, and Emily walked over to kiss him.

"How did it go today, Darling?" she asked.

"It was very moving," Mark replied. He looked over at Lee and Millie. They were sitting at the table with Emily, keeping a seat open for him. "I wish you had come with me, Lee."

Lee Arlington Grant, who had retired as the dean of Litchfield College, shook his head.

"No, Mark, this was your pilgrimage in more ways than one. You needed the time alone. Did you get a chance to visit Charley's grave?"

"Yes. And I saw his wife, son, and grandson also. Charley left a wonderful family over here."

"Is it true?" one of the other travelers asked. "You were a bomber pilot during the war?"

"Yes, it's true."

"That seems strange, doesn't it? I mean, here you are a bishop, a man of God, but you flew a bomber during the war."

"Are you suggesting that being a man of God and defending your country are incompatible concepts?" Lee asked.

"No, I didn't mean that, I just meant . . ." Unable to explain exactly what he meant, he stopped in midsentence.

"That's all right, Lee," Mark said. "Mr. Warren, if you talk to ten men who have gone through the horrors of war, I believe eight of them can tell you the story of a personal experience that they have had with God. I am one who had such an experience."

"How many of your crew are still alive?" one of the other travelers asked.

"Five, counting me," Mark answered. "The man who was my second copilot, Lyndon Duncan, married my sister after her husband was killed. He was a wonderful father to Susan's son."

"Lyndon Duncan? Wait a minute, you don't mean the Lyndon Duncan who used to be a sportscaster on TV, do you?"

"That's the one. Of course, before he was a sportscaster, he was a baseball player." Mark chuckled. "He never did hit over three hundred, but he's quick to tell you he missed it in 1941 by just one at bat.

"I had what I called my Double-A team in the nose, my bombardier, Adrian Rogers, and my navigator, Art Bollinger. Art died a few years ago, but Adrian is still alive. He got into the stock market and made a fortune. My top turret gunner, Stewart Richardson, is still alive too. He wound up managing country and western artists. And finally there was our tail gunner, Tim O'Leary. Tim retired from the Phoenix Fire Department and still lives in Phoenix. I had the pleasure of being the commencement speaker at Tim's grandson's graduation from Arizona State University."

"I think it's really great that you men keep up with each other," one of the others said.

"Dear, there's one more they might be interested in hearing about,"

Emily said. "He wasn't a member of your crew, but he certainly played a significant role."

"Yes, indeed, you are talking about Lorenzo Jenkins," Mark said.

"Lorenzo Jenkins? Wasn't he a general?"

"Yes, he was air force chief of staff during the Johnson administration. General Jenkins is a great man. The only problem with him was, he was just a little ahead of his time. If he had come along ten or fifteen years later, we might be calling *him* Mr. Secretary instead of Colin Powell."

"Not quite," Emily said. "If he had come along ten or fifteen years later, we wouldn't even be having this conversation because he wouldn't have been there to save your life."

Mark nodded. "True enough," he admitted.

"Ah, here comes our dinner," Lee said. "Bishop White, would you do us the honor of returning thanks?"

"I would be happy to," Mark said.

The members of the tour group, young and old, stood at their tables to hold hands. There, in a circle of friends in a London restaurant, Mark W. White, retired bishop of the Missouri Dioceses of the Episcopal Church, gave thanks. And the thanks he gave went far beyond the food they were about to receive.

Acknowledgments

R obert Vaughan would like to acknowledge the following individuals:

Bob Robison
Brian Hampton
Kyle Olund
Hiram Griffin

About the Author

R obert Vaughan is a retired Chief Warrant Officer–3. He entered military service in 1953 as a member of the Missouri National Guard. Transferring to active duty, he attended the Aviation Maintenance Course in Fort Rucker, Alabama. After serving a tour of duty in Korea as crew chief on an H-19 helicopter, he returned to the Army Aviation flight school at Ft. Rucker where he became a warrant officer.

After receiving his appointment to warrant officer, Robert was posted to the 101st Airborne Division at Ft. Campbell, Kentucky. His next assignment was the Seventh Cavalry in Germany, "Custer's Own." While in Germany he was historical officer for the Seventh Cavalry, and in that capacity was custodian of the Custer memorabilia (such things as Custer's field diaries, saber, hat, etc.). That assignment created a fascination with Custer, which eventually led to four published books.

From Germany, Robert went to Ft. Riley, Kansas, where he accompanied the 605th Transportation Company to Vietnam for the first of what would be three tours in Vietnam.

In Vietnam he was a recovery officer (when an aircraft would go down, Robert would take a rigging crew to the site and rig it so it could be sling-loaded by helicopter, back to base; on several of these missions the crew would encounter intense and accurate enemy fire). Later, he would serve in the same job for the Fifty-sixth Transportation Company. His last assignment in Vietnam was with the 110th Transportation Company, where he was chief of the Open Storage Depot. During his three years in Vietnam he was awarded the Distinguished Flying Cross, the Air Medal with "V" device and 35 oak-leaf clusters, the Purple Heart, the Bronze Star, the Meritorious Service Medal, the Army Commendation Medal, and the Vietnamese Cross of Gallantry.

During his military service Robert Vaughan was selected by *Army Aviation Digest* as having written the "Best Article of the Year" for six consecutive years. He also wrote and produced several training films for use in the Aviation Maintenance Officers' Course. His last assignment was as Chief of the Aviation Maintenance Officers' Course.

As an author, Vaughan sold his first book when he was nineteen. That was forty-two years, two hundred titles, and twenty million books ago. Writing under thirty-five pseudonyms, he has hit the *New York Times* and *Publishers Weekly* bestseller lists twice: In 1981, his pseudonymous novels *Love's Bold Journey* and *Love's Sweet Agony* each reached number one on both mass market lists, with sales of 2.2 million each. His novel *Survival* won the 1994 Spur Award for best western novel, *The Power and the Pride* won the 1976 Porgie award for best paperback original, and *Brandywine's War* was named by the Canadian University Symposium of Literature as the best iconoclastic novel to come from the Vietnam War. In the 1970s Vaughan was an on-air television personality with "Eyewitness Magazine" for WAVY-TV in Portsmouth, Virginia, and later, doing a cooking show for "Phoenix At Mid-Day" on KPHO-TV in Phoenix, Arizona. He is also a popular speaker who has spoken at several colleges and appeared at numerous writers' conferences throughout the country. Each winter he runs the "Write on the Beach" writers' retreat in Gulf Shores, Alabama.

Robert Vaughan lives on the beach in Gulf Shores, Alabama, with his wife, Ruth, and his dog, Charley. A lay eucharistic minister, Robert is a past warden and vestry member in the Episcopal Church. He is currently very active in the Holy Spirit Episcopal Church in Gulf Shores.

Boyd County Public Library